John Harman was ⟨…⟩ London. He has worked in newspapers, publishing and the conference industry in most parts of Britain and America. In the early '80s he formed his own film production company which he sold a few years later in order to write full time. He now lives in a pretty village close to Cambridge with his wife Abigail, a professional photographer. They have five children.

Called to Account

John Harman

First published in 1994
by HEADLINE BOOK PUBLISHING

First published in paperback in 1995
by HEADLINE BOOK PUBLISHING

A HEADLINE FEATURE paperback

10 9 8 7 6 5 4 3 2 1

ISBN 0 7472 4442 1

Typeset by
Letterpart Limited, Reigate, Surrey

Printed and bound in Great Britain by
Cox & Wyman Ltd, Reading, Berks

HEADLINE BOOK PUBLISHING
A division of Hodder Headline PLC
338 Euston Road
London NW1 3BH

For
David and Sheila

My grateful thanks to Michel Chasseur St Etienne for revealing some of the intricacies of accounting and the international movement of money.

Chapter One

They were eleven minutes from the drop when the voice came through.

Night made the transmission sharp, with no more than an edge of static.

'Speedbird four five nine, report your position.'

The voice filled the flight deck. It was laced with concern. The co-pilot looked to his left. In the muted lighting of the cabin's computer screens he could see the pilot's face. He was frowning.

'*¿Qué decimos?*' the co-pilot asked. 'What do we say?' He was Mexican and had once flown with the Mexican air force.

The pilot, an Hispanic-American, gave him an angry look. '*¡Habla Inglés!* Speak English,' he ordered.

The voice of the air traffic controller, tracking the numbers on his glowing radar screen 900 miles to the south east, came through again. More urgently. 'Speedbird four five nine, report your position.'

The pilot pressed the small white transmission button on his control column. 'Madrid Area Control, this is Speedbird four five nine. We are 120 miles southwest of Cape Finistère. Course bearing two five zero.'

The air traffic controller's voice came back almost immediately. The co-pilot noticed that his English had a strong

1

Spanish inflection. Like his own. 'Speedbird four five nine, your flight level reads two zero zero. Repeat, two zero zero. Please confirm.'

The previous day the pilot had filed a flight plan for the night flight from Charleston to Milan. The Aerospace Gulfstream IV had been assigned an altitude of 41,000 feet.

Now the small passenger jet was down to 20,000 feet and losing altitude.

The air traffic controller's concerned tones continued. 'Speedbird four five nine, your airspeed reads mach zero five. Please confirm.'

The pilot had filed in the flight plan that the Gulfstream would be flying at its operational cruising speed of mach zero eight. Now, on approach, the pilot was easing back. The plane's speed was less than 220 knots.

They were ten minutes from the drop.

'Madrid Area Control this is Speedbird four five nine,' the pilot began, 'we confirm our flight level is two zero zero and our speed is mach zero five. We have a systems malfunction. Our air pressurization system has a failure and our altimeter is malfunctioning. We are working on the problem.'

For a moment the cabin was quiet, the only noise the subdued roar of the Rolls Royce twin turbofans back down the fuselage, behind the wings.

'Speedbird four five nine.' The suddenness of the air traffic controller's voice over the cockpit audio made the co-pilot start in his seat. 'Do you have an emergency?'

'Negative, Madrid Area Control. Repeat negative. We are okay. I repeat, our status is okay. We are working on the problem.'

There was another, longer silence. The pilot, his face furrowed by anxiety, glanced at his co-pilot.

This was the moment of maximum danger.

The pilot knew that on a plane like the Aerospace Gulfstream IV, a systems failure such as he had described was extremely rare. The Gulfstream was equipped with leading-edge avionics; with satellite communications, computerized control and laser flight-guidance systems. It was a state-of-the-art executive jet . . . which was why his bosses, the men in Miami, had willingly shelled out several million dollars to buy it. It was not an aircraft that often went wrong.

What, thought the pilot, if air traffic control in Madrid didn't believe his story? What if the men in the large air-conditioned room, with its subtle lighting and its amber radar orbs flecked with a myriad moving yellow dots, guessed what was really happening aboard the Gulfstream?

He already knew the answer; knew that the area centre controller would lift a bright red, high security telephone sited above his command console and scramble a couple of Spanish air force Mirages out of Valladolid. The Spanish fighters would be under orders to investigate his plane and, if they didn't like what they saw, to shepherd it down onto the nearest airfield. Probably Santiago. And if the Gulfstream tried to make a run for it, the Mirage pilots would have orders to blast it out of the sky.

The pilot guessed that the Madrid area controller, if he was going to scramble the fighters, would be doing it about now.

They were nine minutes from the drop.

'Speedbird four five nine,' came the voice from Madrid, 'cancel mode Charlie.'

The two men on the Gulfstream's flight deck grinned simultaneously. Madrid Area Control had bought their story.

The co-pilot turned around in his seat and flicked a switch on the avionics control panel which turned off the aircraft's secondary radar. Now, with only mode alpha or primary radar operational, all that air traffic control in Madrid knew about the Gulfstream IV was its location. Mode Charlie, which through the aircraft's dual transponders had been transmitting the Gulfstream's call sign conversion and flying height, was terminated. For a crucial few minutes, Speedbird four five nine would be out of close scrutiny by big brother Madrid.

'They may still send the fighters,' the co-pilot said darkly.

The pilot had been thinking the same thing. Maybe, by allowing the Gulfstream to cancel mode Charlie, Madrid was lulling them into a false sense of security. Maybe the Mirages were already rolling down the runway at Valladolid.

They were eight minutes from the drop.

The pilot tried to work out how long it would take the Mirages to scream westwards over the dark Sierra Cabrera. Four minutes? Maybe five?

He knew that night would not hide them, for by the time the Mirages had crossed the coastline south of the Olieros lighthouse their radar would have locked onto the Gulf-stream and the computers in their air-to-air missile systems would be calibrating its height, distance and the planes' closing speed. Three minutes out over the Atlantic, the pilot reckoned, would bring the air force jets to within a few miles of his plane.

The Mirages would be arriving at the drop zone at the same time as the Gulfstream.

The pilot ran his tongue over his top lip. It was salty with sweat. If Madrid Area Control had scrambled the Mirages then in less than eight minutes he might be dead.

'It's almost time,' he said, reaching up for his oxygen mask. His voice was cracked with strain. He wondered if the co-pilot noticed. 'Seven minutes.' He leaned forward and switched off the plane's navigation and anti-collision lights. There was, he thought, no point in helping the Mirages to kill him.

The co-pilot unbuckled his belt, moved out of his seat and opened the door of the flight deck. Inside the passenger cabin three men dressed in white windproof jumpsuits were sitting in easy chairs.

The passenger cabin, which on a standard Gulfstream could accommodate up to nineteen passengers, seated eight. It was laid out like a luxurious sitting room with soft, spacious seats and bench sofas on a grey, thick-pile carpet. At its rear was a lavatory and small galley. The galley had a bar, though no one on the plane was drinking.

'It's time,' said the co-pilot. 'Go to oxygen.'

The men looked relieved. At 20,000 feet, with reducing air pressure in the passenger cabin, their heads were starting to ache and their breath came in short, hard gasps.

They got to their feet and from within the lavish sofas pulled out oxygen sets, military pilots' helmets and broad leather belts. One of the men handed the co-pilot his equipment. Quickly the men buckled on their belts and air cylinders and fitted their full-face oxygen masks and helmets with special protection for the ears. On a signal from the co-pilot they filed through the galley to the rear of the cabin.

One of the non-standard modifications aboard Speedbird four five nine was its luggage compartment. The bulkhead had been moved forward, doubling the size of the conventional Gulfstream's walk-through, air-pressurized luggage compartment to over twelve feet. The lead man opened the door in the bulkhead and the four moved through into the dimly lit hold.

Lying on the deck was a dark, bulky, cylindrical object, measuring almost the length of the compartment floor. It was what the senior army officer from whom the men in Miami had illegally obtained it called a Canadian Tube. Stripped to its essentials it resembled an expanded, ten-foot oil drum, but with the attachments the men in the plane had added, it looked more like a fat torpedo. Or a shark.

One of the men bent to check the instruments fitted to the body of the Tube. After a few moments he nodded to his colleagues. Everything was set.

Each man moved to a pre-set place on the wall of the hold. They attached nylon safety belts, winding off inertia reels fitted to the bulkhead onto solid brass hooks set into the back of their leather belts. Immediately they were secured the men peered towards a forward corner of the hold, to where two unlit lightbulbs were fixed high on the bulkhead.

Located between the twin Tay engines, the luggage compartment was the noisiest area in the plane. Even without the ear protectors inside their helmets, the men could not have relied on hearing the pilot's voice accurately over the intercom. They resorted to the tried and tested methods of the military and waited patiently for the lights.

Suddenly, the red bulb was flickering; a steady on-off pulse which every other second infused the hold with a garish crimson glow.

They were two minutes to the drop.

The men moved to the Canadian Tube, their safety straps trailing behind them in the pulsing light. Together they pushed its great black bulk across the deck of the starboard side of the plane. The Tube weighed more than 300 kilos and the effort took all their combined strength. On the flight deck the pilot adjusted the controls, compensating for the shift in the weight.

Two of the men moved to the luggage-hold door on the port side of the aircraft and waited.

The air-pressurized door was the most innovative alteration on Speedbird four five nine. Not even the Aerospace SRA-4, the military version of the plane, had such a modification. The size of the door had been doubled to almost five feet square; when opened, it hydraulically moved back into the compartment and up the curving surface of the bulkhead. The modification had been made by people who knew about military supply from aeroplanes. It had cost the men in Miami a lot of money.

The men in the hold anxiously adjusted their face masks as they watched the flickering red light. They knew what was coming.

As soon as he had started the descent from 40,000 feet, the pilot had been de-pressurizing the plane. Now the interior air pressure of the Gulfstream was close to that of the air outside. They were at 17,000 feet, flying at an air speed of 140 knots, just eighteen knots over the aircraft's stalling speed.

Twenty miles an hour less and the aircraft would fall out of the sky.

As suddenly as a heart attack the red light stopped flickering and went to full on.

They were one minute to the drop.

The two men at the hold door heaved on the levered locking wheel which kept it sealed. A thin line, marked by the screaming whistle of air entering the hold under pressure, appeared at the door's outer edges. Then with one smooth, hydraulic movement the door swung in and up and a five-foot hole emerged, running from waist height on the bulkhead down through the curve of the airframe to a ghastly black void beneath the men's feet.

It was like being hit by an iceberg. A screaming, howling wall of ice. The men clung to the bulkheads as the plane, reacting to the equalization of air pressure and the sudden great hole in its fuselage, dropped hundreds of feet. At the controls the pilot fought frantically to stabilize his aircraft whilst in the hold his crew were pounded by the storming force of freezing air rocketing into their confined space at 160 miles an hour.

The noise was incredible. Feet away from the men's heads was the roaring vent of the port-side Tay turbofan, developing 14,000 pounds of thrust. Without the protectors in their helmets their eardrums would have split like ice on a puddle.

Like old men they shuffled forward, stooping against the battering airstream. Crouching over the Tube they manoeuvred it until its nose was hanging out over the opened door. Desperately they watched the lights on the bulkhead, praying for the endless red glow to turn green. Inside their oxygen masks their teeth chattered with the cold. They had thirty seconds to wait. It was the longest half-minute in the history of the world.

Then, without warning, the red changed to green and the crimson, hellish glow in the freezing compartment turned to a sickly, undersea green. The co-pilot felt as if he was being dragged beneath a tidal wave.

The men heaved on the Canadian Tube. It didn't budge.

Immediately they realized that manoeuvring a 300-kilo cylinder sideways was relatively easy. Trying to push it forward was something else. They heaved again and it moved. About an inch. Despite the intense cold the co-pilot felt the sweat prickling on his neck. Frenziedly the men heaved again and the Tube moved forward another inch. They heaved once more, a gut-wrenching, hernia-erupting effort, and suddenly the Tube was gone. One moment it was there, a solid implacable shape, like a fallen obelisk, and the next it had disappeared. Literally swallowed up by the night and the howling wind.

The pilot, sitting alone on the flight deck, knew at once that the plane's precious cargo had been jettisoned. Feeling the lift with the loss of more than a quarter of a ton, he trimmed the controls, compensating for the change in the plane's centre of gravity.

The men in the hold moved to the door and with two on each side heaved it downwards against the iron wind. Slowly they inched it into place. One of them turned the locking wheel and sealed it airtight. They shuffled out of the hold, grateful that for the first time in what seemed an eternity they were not being pummelled by the freezing wind.

Already the pilot had switched on the navigation lights and was re-pressurizing the aircraft's cabins as he scanned his radar for Spanish air force jets. Not that it mattered now if they came. As far as they were concerned his was a civil aircraft that had experienced problems, had put them right, and was returning to its flight plan. The Gulfstream IV was already climbing steeply; in six minutes it would be back at 40,000 feet.

Gratefully, the co-pilot pulled off his equipment and returned to the flight deck as his colleagues changed in the passenger cabin, substituting their jumpsuits for business suits. By the time they landed at Milan the men would appear to be exactly what the flight manifest said they were; senior executives of an American food distributor come to visit their Italian suppliers.

Within seconds of leaving the aircraft the Canadian Tube had reached its terminal velocity of 120 miles an hour. It fell for sixty-eight seconds; silently hurtling down into the night, free-falling through two and a half miles of billowing alto-cumulus faintly dappled by the light of a ghostly moon.

The first of the barometers kicked in at 3,000 feet.

Suddenly, a twenty-eight-foot SC15 parachute blossomed out into the night, wrenching the container back from its headlong drop and slowing its velocity to less than twenty miles an hour.

Immediately, four small radio-controlled servo motors, attached to the parachute's guide lines, switched into action, tugging and slackening the lines and vectoring the chute and its cargo in the direction of the man operating the Parapoint system. He was inside the deckhouse of a Spanish fishing vessel seven miles to the south east.

A minute later, at 200 feet, the flotation tanks were barometrically deployed and two large self-inflating rubber airbeds sprouted like wings on either side of the ten-foot container.

Thirty miles off the coast of Galicia it was blowing a force six and the sea was dark and tumultuous. The Tube, like an immense black insect, settled onto the heaving Atlantic. The slight impact activated the auto-disconnect system on the SC15; the parachute released itself from the floating container and within a minute had sunk.

Deep inside the Tube the impact also triggered a sophisticated electronic locator beacon. Its signal, undetectable to any possible eavesdroppers and good for twenty miles, was picked up by the Spanish fishing boat which was already making twelve knots north west towards the floating cylinder.

The boat was a modern, sixty-foot stern trawler out of Villagacía. Furnished with all the apparatus of modern fishing, the trawler's bridge was also equipped with the kind of highly sophisticated tracking technology reserved only for naval vessels.

The radio transceiver for the Parapoint system, the servo motors and the control display unit which the man on the trawler's bridge was using to guide the parachute, were in service with the British armed forces. The equipment was not available to civilians. It had been stolen to order by a flight-lieutenant in the Royal Air Force, who had been paid a large sum of money for it by a man who worked for the men in Miami.

The electronic locator beacon, steadily signalling its presence from the belly of the Tube, along with its tracking unit aboard the trawler, was also top secret. It had gone into service with ships of the Nato navies only months earlier. One of the men in Miami had bribed a senior executive of the manufacturing company to smuggle out a unit.

Unerringly the trawler steered the course indicated on the CDU by the beacon's signal and in under half an hour was within yards of the source of the quiet insistent pinging inside the darkened deckhouse. Checking that the horizon was clear of navigation lights, the captain ordered a powerful spotlight above the deckhouse to be switched on. The harsh light swept the black, rolling waters.

It was on the starboard bow, less than fifty yards away. Pinned in the spotlight it looked like a sinister, primeval monster from the deep, surging effortlessly in the heaving sea.

Carefully the helmsman brought the trawler alongside.

The crew swung out a derrick with a net attached which they attempted to get underneath the Tube and its flotation tanks. They tried more than a dozen times, each time cursing louder as the net snagged or failed to cradle the Tube. Twice they came close, but the rolling waves and the awkward flotation tanks defeated them. The captain ordered three men into the trawler's dinghy. With its outboard roaring, it powered in close to the Tube. The men, caught in the brightness of the spotlight, struggled frantically in the pitching sea to attach a line to steel rings set in the Tube's body.

The dinghy was smacking hard into the flotation tanks. The captain, watching anxiously from the bridge, screamed above the wind: 'For Christ's sake don't lose it.'

He knew that if the flotation tanks detached or burst and the Tube sank then he and the rest of the crew might just as well throw themselves over the side and follow it down to the bottom of the ocean. The men in Miami did not forgive failure.

At last the men in the dinghy managed to make fast a rope. The rest of the trawler's crew hauled it in. They winched the Tube on board as if it were a baby.

In the cold brilliance of the deck lights one man detached the flotation tanks. Another stripped the Tube of its waterproof covering before a third, crouching on his haunches, unscrewed a plate in the centre of the canister. Inside were exactly 100 tightly packed black bundles, each one wrapped in 400-gauge polythene and bound by industrial tape. Each package weighed fractionally more than two kilos. With the deck lights gleaming on the polythene, the fat black bundles looked like malignant embryos in the womb of a mother of monsters.

Like a surgeon at a Caesarian section, the crouching man reached into the belly of the Tube and began pulling out the slightly malleable packets. A crew mate carefully placed them inside fish canisters, four to a canister, which he passed down the fish hatch to two men in the hold.

The trawler had been at sea for twenty-four hours and the hold was half full of anchovies and hake. Slipping and sliding on the glistening fish and crushed ice, the men shovelled fish into the canisters until the packages were completely buried.

The captain turned his craft due east and set course for home, as the empty Canadian Tube, along with the deflated flotation tanks, was taken below deck. Both the Tube and the tanks would, ultimately, find their way back across the Atlantic to be used again.

Three hours later, with the dawn silhouetting the dark, pine-covered hills of the Pontevedra, the trawler sailed into the calm, protected waters of the fjord-like Ría de Arosa. Soon afterwards it came in sight of the glimmering harbour lights of Villagacía.

The captain berthed his vessel at the far end of the small harbour and the crew immediately began landing the catch onto the dock with a deck hoist. Unlike the hauls from the other boats, which were taken straight to the gutting sheds close by, the trawler's haul was loaded onto a refrigerated truck. None of the other skippers and crews working in the chilly dawn took much notice of this exception; the man who owned the trawler also owned a fish processing plant a couple of miles out of town. He was a big businessman in Galicia – a *capo* – and sane people didn't poke their noses into his affairs. In Galicia, people minded their own business.

The truck set off, closely followed by a dusty Mercedes containing four tough-looking men. At the processing plant the truck and its escort stopped at a solid, single-storey building set some way from the main plant, where the men unloaded twenty-five fish containers. As the truck moved on to discharge its load at the plant, two of the men from the Mercedes carried the containers into the building. The other two stayed outside. They were holding short-wave radios and, beneath the coats they wore against the chill October dawn, were carrying Star Z70 short-barrelled machine pistols.

The owner of the processing plant was waiting inside the building. He was a large, middle-aged man with a heavy belly, dark hair and hard eyes. It was rumoured by some of the local people that the man was a *traficante*. The rumour was whispered with a mixture of awe and envy, for in that part of Galicia many people admired *contrabandistas*.

There were other men in the building. Men in suits from the big cities. They watched as the fish canisters were emptied into stainless steel sinks, wrinkling their noses at the sharp, briny smell. When all the black packages had been recovered and counted the men collected their orders. Five bags for the man from Madrid, seven for the man from Barcelona and three for the man from Lisbon.

No money changed hands and no one in the room, with the exception of the guards, was carrying a gun. In this transaction, money and guns were unnecessary. All the men worked for the same multinational organization. They were colleagues working in what, to them, was a civilized and congenial business. And a profitable one.

The men in Miami had bought the 200 kilos of white powder inside the black packages from producers in Colombia. It had cost them a million dollars. Now, on the European mainland, it was worth, wholesale, twenty million dollars. Yet what made it such an attractive business for the men was its retail value, the price on the street. On the street their million-dollar investment was worth two hundred million dollars.

As with most businesses, distribution, getting the product onto the street, to the point of sale, was one of their biggest difficulties.

The men in suits shook hands with the hard-eyed *capo* and left. They had a long drive back with their new supply of product.

Of the eighty-five kilos left, the *capo* ordered forty-five to be set aside. Half the amount was due for delivery within forty-eight hours to Paris, the other half to Frankfurt. To get the white powder safely to its destinations, the packages had to be opened and the powder carefully spooned into the false bottoms of thousands of tins of Spanish anchovies. The tinned anchovies would be taken across the French and German borders in sealed container trucks, to be delivered to associates of the hard-eyed man, small food wholesalers, in both cities.

The remaining forty kilos was destined elsewhere. Theirs would be the most risky delivery.

At a word from the man, the two guards fitted the remaining two-kilo bundles inside strong, plastic, airtight cartons, four to a carton. Each carton was placed in the bottom of a fish canister. Then the man ordered the guards to bring in the offal.

If the men in suits had stayed around they would have fainted at the stench. It was breathtaking. Even the *capo* and his henchmen, men who had worked with fish all their lives, gagged at the disgusting odour of rotten fish. It clawed in their throats and heaved in their guts. The stinking offal was piled into the canisters which were sealed with lightweight polythene sheeting. The covering did nothing to lessen the awful odour. It wasn't meant to. The offal was noisome but necessary. There wasn't a police dog in the world whose nose could detect beyond the smell of the stinking fish what was inside the polythene bundles.

The guards took the canisters outside and loaded them onto a beaten-up Seat fish truck. The truck set off, followed by the Mercedes with the four men. It headed east, to Puenta Cesures, where the driver turned north onto autoruta A9. It was still early and Santiago, its streets peaceful and its buildings washed pale by the new day's sun, was barely coming to life as the truck chugged innocently through the city.

The truck reached La Coruna fifty minutes later, weaving its way through the awakening streets to the Darsena de la Marina, the busy fishing port, where it stopped close to a French inshore trawler. No one took any notice of the men unloading ten fish canisters and putting them aboard the trawler.

The French vessel, a seventy-foot stern trawler similar to her Spanish counterpart, sailed an hour later and set course north east into the Bay of Biscay. Out at sea the crew threw the offal overboard and extracted the plastic cartons from the bottom of the canisters. The black bundles inside the containers had scarcely been touched by the odour of the stinking fish. The canisters and plastic containers were thrown into the sea.

The forty black bundles were transferred to what looked like an enormous suitcase. The case was a sea container, a top secret device which an associate of the men in Miami had bribed off a captain in the Russian Pacific fleet. The Russians had stolen the plans for the device from the Americans. The container could withstand water pressure of up to 5000 feet and had built into it a sonar transponder which transmitted ultra-high-frequency signals. It had been an expensive capital purchase but necessary. Like all the others. The men in Miami had to protect their investment.

The sea container was sealed and secured to the trawler's deck with quick-release straps. The captain's orders were simple; if he thought he was likely to be boarded by French naval or customs vessels, he was to jettison the container. Lying on the ocean floor, its location would be pinpointed later by a vessel fitted with the special type of naval receiver designed to pick up the transponder's signals. Once located it would be raised from the seabed by a robot submersible operated by the vessel. It would be an expensive operation but worth it for the value of the container's contents.

The fishing boat trawled for three days in moderate weather and netted a plentiful haul of cod, even managing to catch a few tuna in the Gulf of Gascony. It sailed north, keeping always within a few miles of the coast and over the continental shelf where the depth was rarely more than 200 fathoms. On the first night another vessel came dangerously close and a couple of nervous crewmen made ready to release the container and slide it into the sea. At the last moment the vessel sheered off. It was another trawler. Early in the evening of the third day the French vessel sailed into the harbour at Brest.

Later that night the sea container was transferred to a French dayboat; a small, thirty-five-foot fishing smack with a hold full of mackerel. The boat set sail immediately, without unloading its catch.

Once it had rounded St Matthew's point and headed out into the English Channel, the dayboat's crew transferred the contents of the sea container into two canvas sailbags. A crewman covered the polythene packets with some wet-weather gear which he stuffed into the sailbags as the sea container was stored below.

It took the small fishing boat eleven hours to reach the Channel Islands, chugging into the port of St Helier on Jersey not long after the break of another day. The port's fish dock was crowded with French and English craft and the crew were kept busy unloading their catch.

At precisely ten o'clock two members of the crew casually lifted the sailbags onto the quay just as a couple of well dressed yachtsmen in their early thirties approached. The men were carrying similar sailbags. They were clearly on their way to find a ship's chandler. The men stopped to ask the crewmen the way. It was a brief encounter. The French crew knew no English and the men's French was terrible. After a few 'adieux' the yachtsmen walked away. It was a smooth, well-practised switch, though it wouldn't have fooled a trained observer. But there were no trained observers. In the autumn sunshine of the busy port no one had paid the men any attention.

The men returned to their yacht in the Marina. It was a Nauticat 521, a sleek, powerful, ketch-rigged motorsailer, made in Finland and registered in Poole. It was moored to a short pontoon. They went aboard, stowed the sailbags in a forward sail locker and made ready to cast off. The yacht moved out under power. Once clear of the harbour the men shut down the engine and raised the main and jib sheets. The weather had moderated, a gentle breeze was blowing from the south west and the yacht made good time to Alderney, where the men anchored off the lee of the island. They ate a meal and drank half a bottle of wine before each took turns at keeping watch. They set sail early the next morning, steering due north.

At just after three that same afternoon the Nauticat glided past South Haven Point and entered the vast harbour at Poole.

Just beyond Brownsea Road, with the island on the port beam, one of the men on the yacht spied a man and a woman gently cruising the harbour in a seventeen-foot Lysander. The couple were middle-aged, short and portly, their heaviness emphasized by their life-jackets. They looked like a retired bank manager and his wife.

The man hailed the couple, who waved in return. The four appeared to be friends. The Nauticat's helmsman put the boat over as the Lysander came alongside on its port beam, out of sight of any casual observer who might be watching from the ferry building at Sandbanks. The two men on the yacht chatted happily with the man and his wife for about half a minute; more than enough time for one of them to drop the two sailbags into the cockpit of the Lysander.

With shouted farewells the boats turned away, the Nauticat gracefully heading up the harbour's main channel towards the yacht marina, the Lysander setting course through the narrow channel between Brownsea and Furzey Islands.

With her husband keeping a watchful eye on the mudbanks on either side of the channel, the plump woman heaved the heavy sailbags into the Lysander's cabin where she set to work transferring the black packages into four wickerwork picnic baskets.

The outboard chugged contentedly, propelling the Lysander at a steady four knots westwards out of the harbour and into the broad Wareham Channel. After the woman had finished transferring the bundles she joined her husband at the tiller. A little more than an hour later the Wareham Channel had funnelled itself into the river Frome, which, beyond Swinham Point, narrowed to less than forty yards wide.

The woman kept a watchful eye over the Lysander's stern, looking out for floating clumps of weeds that could clog the outboard's water intake. Although it was late in the season, there were a number of pleasure craft cruising the Frome and the last thing she and her husband wanted was to lose power in the middle of the twisting river.

At Redcliffe Farm the river turned sharply north and soon after the Lysander had gently rounded the bend, Wareham came into sight across the fields. The Lysander's usual mooring was on the river bank, close to the town, but as they drew near the man saw that there was space at the town quay. Gently he brought the small yacht alongside the quay's stone wall.

The top of the wall was a couple of feet above the Lysander's gunwale. The woman stepped up onto the quay and made fast fore and aft before helping her husband unload the boat.

They looked exactly like any other couple innocently unloading their gear after a day's sailing, though they had more picnic hampers than a casual observer might have expected. Heavy picnic hampers.

Four times the portly man puffed his way to a silver-grey Volvo 800 estate parked on the quayside, each time carrying a square, wickerwork basket. But none of the scattering of people on the quay took much notice. They were late season tourists who had come to bask in the sleepy prettiness of the small Georgian town and if they noticed the man and his wife at all, it was because by unloading their boat on the quaint little quay they added something to the atmosphere of the place.

Except for one man. He was taking a lot of notice of the couple unloading their boat.

The man, dressed like a tourist in a dark pair of slacks and a lightweight polo-neck jumper was sitting casually on a wrought-iron bench outside the Old Granary restaurant, which bordered the east side of the quay. Like everyone else on the quay he had watched the couple disinterestedly for a couple of moments before returning to his copy of the *Daily Telegraph*. But from behind his newspaper and his sunglasses the man carefully watched every move the couple made.

He watched as they finished loading the Volvo and the woman drove it across South Bridge and along the south bank of the river. He watched as her husband adroitly manoeuvred the Lysander around in the river and steered it to its permanent mooring. Unhurriedly, he stood up and walked to a spot on the quay where he could see down river to where the couple were making the yacht fast. He watched as they finished securing the vessel and drove back along the south bank, recrossed the bridge, and sedately motored past the entrance to the quay, heading northwards through the town towards the bypass.

The man walked to a telephone kiosk on a corner of the quay and called London.

Another man, a man with sharp, narrowed eyes, a man they called the Profit, watched him make the call.

He had been sitting in a quiet corner of the Quay Inn, the pub bordering the far side of the quay. He had been there for more than an hour in a seat next to the window, slowly sipping a pint of bitter. The man had seen the other watcher take his seat on the iron bench . . . had observed the Lysander tie up at the quay and the couple unload the picnic baskets.

Now, as the man finished his call and hurried away from the telephone box, the silent watcher in the pub stood up, strolled to the bar and ordered another drink.

The middle-aged couple lived in an affluent suburb of Bournemouth. They arrived home in under twenty minutes. Hurriedly, they carried the picnic hampers into the house where they extracted the black bundles and placed them carefully inside the seat of a late Georgian settle they had bought the previous week.

The doorbell rang two hours later. At the door was a London antique dealer. With scarcely a word he and an assistant picked up the settle and loaded it into a white Ford Transit. No money changed hands; the antique dealer was in and out in less than three minutes. The couple were relieved to see him go.

The dealer drove to London, to an antique shop just off Kensington Church Street where he and his assistant unloaded the settle and took it into a small, secure back room. After locking the doors of the shop they emptied the settle's contents and put them in a safe.

The following day the dealer was visited by a number of antique buyers. By appointment they arrived from Glasgow, Leeds, Manchester and the other big cities. Each of them stayed in the shop for a few minutes before emerging with a fine piece of antique furniture which they loaded into a vehicle. They drove away, back to where they had come from.

It was seven days since the Gulfstream IV had taken off from Charleston. Forty million pounds' worth of Colombian cocaine was on the streets of Britain.

It was one of the largest consignments ever to have been smuggled into the country.

Everything had gone smoothly and exactly to plan. Like a military operation.

Which was the way the men in Miami did things.

Chapter Two

She felt like a cheat. A coward. As if she was running away.

No, she thought, that's bloody ridiculous. She caught the thought and stopped herself. Over the past months her language had grown steadily worse. Now she was even *thinking* in expletives. It wasn't bloody ridiculous, it wasn't even ridiculous. It was just irrational. That's all. It was absurd to feel this way about taking a day off work. But she knew it wasn't taking the day off that made her feel this way. It was the reason behind it.

She had risen early, showered and washed her hair, and was dressed in a navy-blue wool and silk suit by Perry Ellis and an Ecru silk shirt in pale lilac. It was her most elegant business outfit. The one in which she knew she looked absolutely great. Had known. She wasn't sure any more.

By the time she'd finished her makeup in the mirror she looked even better. Or would have done, if there had been anybody else in the house to appreciate her good looks, somebody who didn't know the deep blue of her eyes and the fine structure of her face as well as she did.

Eleanor wasn't fooled. The mirror clearly showed what ravages the last few months had wrought. The blue of her irises was paler now and her eyes looked washed out. There were little lines around them and dark circles beneath. They hadn't been there a year ago, and although the makeup hid them well enough, Eleaner knew they were there. Her cheeks were still pale and there were tight lines at the sides of her mouth. She could swear her lips were getting thinner.

Her hair was cut in a layered bob, which allowed lots of natural movement and was meant to emphasize her lovely eyes and wide, generous mouth. A couple of weeks earlier she had found a grey hair. A grey hair at twenty-nine, for God's sake. Her mother, whom everybody said she took after, was over fifty and still a beautiful woman. She'd scarcely begun to go grey. Eleanor had burst into tears. Now that *was* bloody ridiculous, she thought, crying over your first grey hair. But the smallest thing made her cry these days.

After coffee and half a slice of toast she put on a warm lambswool overcoat, ready to brave the snow showers the weatherman had told her to expect. It was the middle of January and the weather, like everything else, was foul. London was battered by high winds, freezing rain and snow. It seemed to Eleanor as if bad weather, filthy streets, metropolitan gridlock and a disrupted underground had been around for ever.

Of course that wasn't true, she reflected. There would have been good days and there would have been sunshine; it was just that she hadn't noticed. One of the things she'd discovered about personal unhappiness was how starkly it highlighted the worst side of all things; all she could recall of her recent past was the bad weather on the way to work, the bad food in the restaurants, the bad manners of the people.

She shook her head. It was pointless thinking that way. It set up a cycle of depression which made everything appear even worse than it already was. The whole point of today, the day off, was to interrupt that cycle, to break the mould, to start again.

Outside it was sleeting, which reduced the chances of getting a cab to zero. She tried to think positively. 'There will be a cab,' she chanted it under her breath, like a mantra, 'there will be a cab at the corner.' She struggled against the wind to the corner of the street where it intersected West End Lane. A long line of vehicles was moving slowly south towards the city, the pellets of sleet hurtling through the steamy glow of their headlights. Nowhere in the grey light could she see any sign of salvation, the warm, glowing, electrified sign of an empty cab. It was no more than she should have expected.

The tube station was five minutes' walk. She turned to cross the street, looking back the way she'd come. Moving fast towards her was a cab, its yellow sign shining in the dull morning light. She was shocked. An empty cab. It was impossible. Had something, she wondered, actually gone right for her? She was almost too surprised to hail it, only at the last moment managing to step off the curb and frantically wave her umbrella. The cab pulled over. 'Waterloo,' she said.

The station was crowded. Eleanor bought a return ticket before sidestepping the streams of intent, dour-faced commuters scuttling off the concourse. She headed for the bookstall where she bought the *Financial Times*, the *Economist* and the latest copy of *Elle*.

The Weymouth train, a Wessex Electric, was already waiting at the platform. Unlike the packed carriages slowly coming to a halt on the platform opposite, it looked to have no more than a dozen passengers on board. She found a seat in one of the long, deserted carriages. Her ticket was first class, although now she wasn't sure why she'd bothered.

There didn't seem to be any advantage on an empty train. She put it down to Alec's influence. He had always liked to travel first class. And with a lot of baggage. Like a wife, a few mistresses, an increasing dependence on alcohol and a big chip on his shoulder. He travelled lighter now, she thought. He didn't have the wife.

She opened her attaché case. It was very slim and very expensive, a present from Alec after one of his many trips to the States. She guessed that he'd gone over there with one of his women and had bought it for her to ease his conscience. That was in the days when Alec still had a conscience. She took out her newspaper. She didn't want to think about Alec.

The train moved out of the station on time, crawled through Vauxhall and came to a dead stop at Clapham Junction. Eleanor began to fret. It would, she thought, be consistent with everything else currently happening in her life if she arrived late for the interview. After about twenty minutes the train moved off and by the time it was rattling through the New Forest and approaching Bournemouth it had made up some lost time.

Poole, she concluded, was even more miserable than London. The station was cold and draughty and outside the freezing rain was whipping horizontally against the buildings, driven by a fierce wind coming in off the Channel. There were no cabs on the rank and she had to wait some time for one to arrive.

The offices of Hagerty Clark were a small Victorian house in the old part of the town, at the far end of Poole Quay, with a view out over Fisherman's Dock, the breakwater and the angry waters of the vast harbour.

Eleanor entered a square hallway furnished with easy chairs and small tables littered with business magazines. The main administration office and reception area was just off it; a large, light-coloured room dispersed with ferns, broadleafed plants and a few young women working at word-processors. A teenage girl seated close to the door and wearing a lightweight headset, was operating a desktop telephone console. Eleanor was surprised. With this number of clerks and assistants, Hagerty Clark was bigger than she had imagined. A middle-aged woman approached her.

'I'm Eleanor Lambert. I'm here for an appointment to see Mr Passmore. I'm sorry I'm late.'

The woman smiled at her; it was the warmest thing Eleanor had seen all day. 'That's all right, dear. They're eating sandwiches in the office, catching up on their lunch. They're not in any hurry.'

Eleanor returned the smile. It was the second break to have gone her way. 'Do you think I have time to tidy up?' she asked.

'Yes, of course. Take your time. This isn't the big city, you know, there's no need to rush.'

The woman, whose name was Alice, was waiting when Eleanor emerged after doing the best she could with her ruffled hair. She led her upstairs to a large office at the front of the building.

Two men were in the room. The one who moved forward to greet her was well built and in his early forties, with a fleshy face and dark, well-barbered hair brushed straight across, public-school style. He was about medium height, scarcely taller than Eleanor, and was dressed in a dark, well-cut chalkstripe suit.

The other man was taller and older; Eleanor guessed he was in his late fifties. He was thin, with the tough, lean physique often possessed by the blood-sporting aristocracy and a face made leathery by the elements. He had a full head of grey hair and was wearing a medium-brown check tweed; the kind of suit a country gentleman would wear. Eleanor was aware of his eyes, sharp and arctic blue, appraising her as his colleague held out his hand.

'Miss Lambert. I'm Philip Passmore.' His grasp on her hand was firm. 'Thank you for coming. Let me introduce James Hagerty, the founding partner of the firm.'

Hagerty's hand was like teak. 'Please don't mind me being here, Miss Lambert. Philip has asked me to sit in on the day's interviews.'

She said something she hoped was appropriate. She was flustered, both by being late and by her appearance; her cheeks were still flaming after being out in the wind. It was also strange to be addressed by her maiden name; she had reverted to using it only a few weeks previously. Passmore invited her to sit down and offered her coffee.

'We are conducting a full day of interviews,' he told her, 'so this preliminary discussion will be quite short. If we think you might fit in with us, we will ask you back for a second, longer discussion. Is that all right with you?'

She told him that it was and he started straight into her *résumé* which she could see on the desk between them. Quickly he went through her career: university, articles at Karding Hillier Longland in their Bristol office, her move to the London office of the practice and her subsequent progress up the ladder culminating, two years previously, in a junior partnership. The coffee arrived and she sipped it gratefully as Passmore began inquiring about the work she had done at Karding Hillier Longland.

In the early years it had been mainly audit work and tax, she explained. She liked doing both. Now, she concentrated on tax and corporate financing. Yes, she'd done quite a lot of insolvency work, she said, though she didn't like it quite so much. Made her feel like an undertaker. As soon as it was said she regretted it. She wasn't sure if it was the right thing to say and though he grinned a little she wondered if it was out of politeness. Throughout the interview she was conscious of the silent, still figure of James Hagerty seated off to one side of the desk; his eyes, unmoving, fixed on her face. Every now and then she gave him a fragile smile. He didn't respond.

Passmore began digging deeper, checking her experience and probing her competence. Eleanor responded cautiously but confidently; she knew her job well and when it came to talking the technicalities – accounting standards, takeovers, the taxation of trusts, computers, company law and the like – she was on familiar territory. She asked a lot of questions, quizzing him about the firm and its clients, and as the interview drew to a close she sensed that she had handled herself competently. Or at least not badly for her first time out. Then Hagerty intervened.

'It seems to me, Miss Lambert,' his voice, dry, sharp-edged and unexpected, startled her, 'that so far you have managed your career exceptionally well. You are evidently well-qualified and it's obvious that Karding Hillier Longland value you. You look to have a good future there. So why do you want to give all that up?' His eyes were examining her.

She had expected the question and had mentally prepared what she hoped would be a satisfactory answer. 'I'm not giving up my career,' she said lightly, smiling at him, 'I just want to change it slightly, move in another direction.'

What might have been a smile passed across Hagerty's hawkish face. 'You mean that you wish to move your career downwards?'

She frowned. 'I'm sorry?'

'What I mean, Miss Lambert, is that you are not changing

29

your career for the better. Hagerty Clark is a small firm and
we do what we do quite well, but with the best will in the
world we could hardly claim to compete with Karding Hillier
Longland. They get the cream of the crop. With major
offices in practically every country of the globe, they're one
of the world's big five accountancy practices. The position we
are advertizing pays less than you are already earning there,
even as a non-profit partner, and as you know we are not
offering a partnership here for at least six months. Even then
it hardly has the cachet of your present position. So why are
you here? Why are you applying for this job?'

She took a deep breath. Hagerty was too sharp to be
fobbed off by talk of career changes. Which, Eleanor realized, left her with only one option. She would do what she
always did under such circumstances – tell the truth. Or at
least some of it.

'My marriage broke up a few months ago. It was fairly
unpleasant and now I'm divorced I want to leave it all
behind. I know my career has gone well and that I'm leaving
a good job but . . .' Her voice trailed off.

She was acutely aware of how lame her explanation
sounded; what a pathetic lack of ambition it indicated, what
a denial of empowerment and independence and all the other
liberated traits she was supposed to espouse. But she
couldn't help any of that; it was the way she felt.

'It reminds me of a past that turned out to be unhappy.
Everything, the job, my social life, London, has lost its
attraction. It has too many memories. Unhappy ones. So I've
decided to leave it and start somewhere new. Somewhere
where I can begin again.'

She knew it sounded weak. But feeble or not, it was the
best explanation she could give him. The only explanation.
That was how it was and he would have to accept it. She had.

She returned Hagerty's stare unwaveringly and shrugged her shoulders in a small gesture of take it or leave it.

The room was quiet for a few moments. Passmore shot a glance at Hagerty, then said, 'Fair enough. Thank you for being so honest. Well,' his voice changed to a lighter note, 'unless you have any other questions, Miss Lambert, I think that about wraps up our discussion.'

She had no other questions. She shook hands with the two men and Passmore showed her down to the foot of the stairs where he said goodbye and Alice helped her on with her coat. The next applicant was sitting in the hallway. He was about her age and looked as if he was a local. He appeared confident and, Eleanor decided, was probably much more the kind of person Hagerty Clark was looking for. Alice phoned for a taxi to take her to the station.

Outside, the wind had slackened and the rain ceased. Now a wet, grey blanket of sea mist hung over the streets and Eleanor noticed as the taxi moved away from the front of the building that Brownsea Island, a mile away in the middle of the harbour, was almost completely hidden. The mist was even more depressing than the freezing rain and, settled in the warmth of the train as it pulled out of the station, Eleanor felt relieved to be leaving Poole.

She stared at her reflection in the darkened windows of the carriage. She hadn't got the job; she knew she hadn't. She had managed to make a mess of the interview, mainly through the candour of her reply to Hagerty's question.

She guessed he and Passmore had her tagged as a weak-willed wimp. Even though she was a highly-qualified chartered accountant. But she hadn't pushed that enough . . . hadn't emphasized her experience. She had allowed them to focus on her personal life.

It wasn't fair; if she had been a man moving after a broken

marriage, the past wouldn't have made any difference. Especially if the man had her track record. But a woman leaving behind a messy divorce; well, they were bound to think that she was either an emotional time bomb waiting to explode all over them, or some kind of irrational bitch who would be here today and gone tomorrow.

The train arrived at Waterloo thirty minutes late and she was forced to wait in the cold for what seemed forever for a cab. Back in the house she kicked off her shoes and poured herself a large gin. The day had not gone well; it was not an auspicious start to breaking the mould of her current, unhappy life.

Raymond cornered her in the office the following day. She had been working on a printout covered in figures and was wearing her spectacles. There had been a time when she would have hated Raymond to see her wearing glasses . . . but not now. Now, she couldn't care less.

'How did it go?' He tried to feign sincerity but she heard the desperation breaking through his voice. He wanted her gone; wanted to get her out as much as, a year ago, he'd wanted to get himself in. Inside her. She stared at him, scarcely hiding her dislike. He'd succeeded too. The bastard.

At a time when she had been most vulnerable, after the discovery of Alec's infidelities; after it had at last dawned on her that she was married to a resentful, drunken shit, Raymond had been there to turn to.

Raymond, the older man; wise, concerned, understanding. Someone to listen sympathetically as she poured out her heart. Raymond, a senior partner in the practice. Someone to admire, to respect, to have dinner with. Someone to fly to Paris with. 'On business,' he said . . .

Someone to be seduced by. Easily.

Raymond the urbane. Raymond the experienced, the

sophisticated, the man of the world. The *married* man of the world, with his eldest child only five years younger than her. Raymond the manipulator who, she now realized, had seen what a soft quarry she was and had coldly stalked her until she was snared in his bed and tangled in her affections.

For a while she had thought herself in love with him. Then the office rumours had started and suddenly it was Raymond the reasonable.

'Be reasonable.' All of a sudden it was his favourite word. 'Rumours can wreck careers.' And marriages, she thought. 'We must see less of each other. Cool things down. One of us ought to leave the practice.'

Of course it had to be her. She wasn't married, not any more; she didn't have a wife who would fall to pieces if she got wind of what they had been up to. She didn't have a family to support; she hadn't got children at university. She hadn't put twenty-three years into building a career in the practice. She was a junior partner. She was a woman.

At first she had refused to be the one to leave. Why should she? she'd argued. Her career was just as valuable to her as his was to him. They would have to weather the rumours. And then, in November, she'd missed her period and for a sickening time had thought she was carrying his child. She wasn't; it was her hormones which, like her emotions, were in turmoil. But, it had been a gut-wrenching experience; and the shock that she'd needed. It made her realize that she should go. Not to protect Raymond but to preserve herself.

She had resolved to leave the whole boiling. Raymond, embarrassed by her presence; Alec, skulking somewhere in Chiswick; the friends that she didn't see, the house that wouldn't sell, Karding Hillier Longland, London – everything.

She would, she'd decided, start again. Somewhere she

wasn't known. Which excluded the option of returning to the warm, loving bosom of her family in Gloucestershire.

'Well, what happened?' Eleanor was startled by his insistence. Focusing on his face she saw the concern in his doggy brown eyes; the pleading to be relieved of her. She considered him coldly.

'I screwed it up.' Her tone was bitter, almost jubilant. She knew it was not what he wanted to hear. She stayed long enough to register his disappointment before walking away.

She was wrong.

Three days later she received a brief letter from Philip Passmore which, after saying that he and Hagerty had enjoyed their discussion, asked if she would return to Poole for a further meeting. After she had got over her surprise she thought about it. Was it a job she really wanted? she asked herself. The money was less than she was getting at Karding Hillier Longland and since the split-up she had been paying the whole mortgage on the house. The move would cost her.

And did she really want to live in Poole? The town was not what she'd remembered as a child when she had sometimes visited it with her parents and older brother. Then it had seemed a warm, golden, old-fashioned place with a blue sky and a huge, blue-green harbour spotted with yachts. This time what little she had seen from the taxi's windows had been nothing but urban ugliness, the modern jumble of ringroads, filling stations and monstrous office blocks. Everywhere had been grey and cold. The more she thought about it, the less she felt inclined to take the application further.

She finally made up her mind on the day of the interview. She was on her way to the office. She had decided to call Philip Passmore to tell him she wouldn't be seeing him. Walking to the tube station she slowly became aware that the weather had turned milder and that a pale sunlight was bathing the pavements. It was the first sight of sunshine she could remember for weeks. She lifted her face to its feeble warmth and then the impulse seized her. She took the tube to Waterloo.

Strap-hanging as the carriages rattled through the tunnels she found herself as if woken from a dream, to find she was on a train going in the wrong direction. She'd always been impulsive, at least in her personal life. About men. But rarely up to now had she been impetuous in her career. Now she found herself making rash decisions about work and her future. It was almost as if her personality was changing. It worried her. At the station she called her secretary and told her that she was sick. She frowned as she replaced the receiver. She had never done that before; never feigned an ailment to take a day off work. It should have bothered her. But it didn't. Not today.

For some reason she felt mildly euphoric. She couldn't imagine why. Could a glimpse of winter sun make that much difference? What else, she wondered, could it be? It couldn't be the spring, that was weeks away. It certainly wasn't a man; there hadn't been a man in her life for months. Thank God. And it couldn't be the job at Hagerty Clark.

Even if she *had* passed the first interview, she was pretty sure she wouldn't make it through the second. So why, she wondered, was she bothering? Was it because she wanted to find out how far she could get with her application? To discover if she might actually be preferred to a male contender? Why should she care about that? What was she trying to prove? She pulled a wry face and gave up on the self-analysis as she headed for the ticket office. Today she felt happier than she had done for months. And for that she was grateful. The reason why didn't matter.

The sun in Poole was brighter than in London and Eleanor decided to walk from the station. She had an excellent sense of direction and as she drew closer to the harbour and the quayside she noticed that the town, bathed in the winter sunshine, looked more the way she remembered it from her childhood.

She was twenty minutes early, and after she had freshened up Alice again led her up the stairs to the office. Passmore was alone. Her surprise must have shown on her face for he smiled as he shook her hand and gestured to her to take a seat.

'I know we're conducting the interviews the wrong way round,' he said, 'with two of us present at the first and only myself here for the second. Hagerty Clark tends to do things in an unorthodox fashion sometimes.' He laughed and Eleanor warmed to him. 'James is hunting today. In fact, he spends most of his time hunting, fishing or shooting. Either that, or at his club in London. He has a house there, in Dulwich, as well as his flat in Bournemouth. Actually, he's rarely here. You'll notice on our letterheading that his name appears as a consultant to the practice. He doesn't get involved in the day-to-day business.'

Secretly Eleanor was relieved; she had found Hagerty's icy gaze disconcerting. 'So are you the only working partner?' she asked. Passmore nodded. 'But the firm seems much bigger than a single-partner practice.'

'It is. Which is why we want to bring someone in and make them a full partner pretty quickly.'

'What about the people here already? Surely some of them must be in the running for the job?'

Passmore shook his head. 'Apart from the clerks and administration staff we have three recently qualified accountants in the practice. They're all very willing but they're also very young. None of them will be ready for a partnership for at least three years.'

Eleanor frowned. 'How well are they going to take to someone from the outside being promoted over them?'

'They know we're conducting interviews, of course. How well they take to the person we appoint will depend upon the calibre of that person.' He gave her a penetrating look. 'Naturally we shall be expecting the successful applicant to win them over quickly and to get them working happily and productively.' Passmore's voice was precise.

The interview moved on, covering much of the same ground as before, though this time Eleanor was asked to go into more detail about her experience in tax and audit work. She found it easier with Passmore on his own; she could establish a rapport with him.

Soon she had a notion of the kind of person he was looking for; someone competent, who knew what they were doing but who wasn't super-efficient, wasn't big-city slick. It was easy to respond as he wanted; her answers to his questions were factual and intelligent but not overly clever. He didn't want someone too clever, especially not a woman. She guessed he was the kind of man who would feel threatened by a clever female colleague and she was careful not to reveal too clearly how good she was at the job.

After ninety minutes Passmore brought the interview to a close. 'We shall make our final decision within a week,' he told her. 'I will be in touch after that.'

The day was bitter and bracing. Eleanor walked back to the station beneath a brassy sun in an ice-blue sky. It had been a good day out.

She didn't hear from Passmore for almost two weeks, by which time she had made up her mind that she hadn't got the job and had almost forgotten that she'd applied for it. It had been a bad two weeks. Raymond had heard of a good position in another of the big London accountancy practices; one, he said, that would be a good move in her career and which he was sure he could swing for her. He was putting pressure on her to go for it, implying that once she was safely out of Karding Hillier Longland they could re-start their affair. The thought made her nauseous. She would as soon make love with a monkey as start up again with Raymond.

It was a Saturday. The letter, postmarked Poole, had been posted two days earlier. She opened it carelessly, knowing that it would say, in the nicest possible way, that she hadn't got the job. She unfolded the single sheet of expensive letterheading and spread it on the kitchen table.

She was shocked. Passmore was offering her the job. She sat down. She needed to think. She read the short letter again to make sure she had not misunderstood. She hadn't. Passmore even wanted to know when she could start. Her first reaction, after feeling gratified that she had been successful, was to turn it down. She couldn't see herself living and working in Poole, even though London was unbearable. Even though Raymond was breathing down her neck.

It was the next letter in the day's small pile of mail that changed her mind. It was from the estate agents. A couple who had viewed the house had put in an offer. It was for less than she was asking but they were cash buyers and the offer was serious. And for immediate possession. Suddenly she realized that in the space of two minutes, all the doors to her prison had been flung open. She had the chance to pay off the mortgage, clear out of London and start again. Even if it wasn't a perfect start, it was a start.

She leapt up from the kitchen table, hurried into the lounge, found a sheet of writing paper and dashed a letter off to Philip Passmore accepting the job. Scrabbling around in her handbag she found a stamp before flinging out into the street and hurrying to the postbox.

Afterwards she leaned against the pillar box, grateful for the support of its red, circular permanence. She was trembling slightly and found herself seriously speculating whether there was some latent madness in her family that came to the surface in the late twenties. Her impulse to do things without thinking them through was getting hard to handle. Even though it was exciting, her recklessness scared her.

Already she was wondering whether she had done the right thing . . . what, by posting the letter, she might be getting herself into.

Chapter Three

Shephard drove the dirty, rust-pitted Granada into the alley and stopped halfway along. He waited a moment then, with his foot on the brake, slipped the gear lever into reverse. The bright reversing lights lit up the alley behind him as he turned and looked through the rear window. No one was there. He hadn't been followed. He put the headlights on full beam and checked in front. The lights showed nothing but a few heaps of ancient rubble and piles of garbage. Nothing moved.

He flicked off the lights, turned off the engine and got out, closing the door quietly. He waited by the car until his eyes grew accustomed to the blackness then, slowly, began to walk down the alley.

Before he'd killed the beam of the headlights, Shephard had noticed that the alley was long and narrow; only a few feet wider than the car. It was set between a couple of tall, empty buildings, two of the last Victorian warehouses in Deptford. It was, thought Shephard, the kind of alleyway Jack the Ripper had favoured; dark and malevolent. Suddenly, something scuttled away in front of him. A rat. It gave him a start. He hated rats. Somewhere out on Greenwich Reach a tug sounded its horn. The sound, hollow and ghostly in the mist of the river, raised the hairs at the back of his neck.

The further down the alley Shephard moved the darker it became. The place smelled; of damp, of neglect, of things decomposing. His hair and skin were clammy from the mist. The alley was as dark and oppressive as a grave. It chilled his blood. It was the stuff of nightmares and for once the feel of the holstered gun beneath his jacket brought him some comfort. The blackness was awful. Malevolent. As if something horrible was hiding in it. Waiting for him. Some terrible *Thing*.

'Gotcha.'

Shephard leapt sideways, grunting stupidly and scrabbling for his gun. His heart battered against his chest like a trapped animal.

The ghastly voice from somewhere in the blackness chuckled.

'Hello, John.'

Shephard released his grip on the pistol. 'Mickey?'

The quiet chuckles continued in the darkness. 'Who else? Wassa matter John, scared of the bogeyman?'

'You stupid Scouse bastard,' Shephard whispered vehemently, 'you damn near gave me a heart attack. I almost peed my pants.'

The chuckles grew slightly louder. 'That would go down well with the old man. He told me to wait here for you.' A shadow moved in a doorway.

'He didn't tell you to frighten me to death. You're a bloody lunatic.'

'We're all lunatics, doing this job. Come on, the old man told me to show you the way.' The figure stepped out in front of Shephard. 'Were you followed?'

'No.'

'Sure?'

'Yes.'

'Okay. Come on then.' Mickey Cheetham moved rapidly along the dark alley. Shephard, his heart still racing from the fright, followed close behind. A few yards further on, Cheetham suddenly stopped at a door set into a wall. It was so dark Shephard wondered how he could have known it was there. Cheetham fumbled for a key which he inserted by touch into the lock. From the sound of it the lock was new, although the door, made of metal, seemed old. By rights it should have squeaked as Cheetham pushed it open. Somebody, thought Shephard, had thought to oil the hinges.

There was a dim light on the staircase, impossible to see from the outside. The two men bounded up four flights and emerged through a set of double doors into a huge, well-lit, loft-like room with bare floorboards and a ceiling sloping up beneath the warehouse eaves. Thick blackout curtains covered the windows. Close to thirty men were in the room, some working at makeshift desks, others talking quietly and drinking coffee. Everyone was wearing navy trousers and dark blue jumpers with 'Police' emblazoned on the front and back. Three men were seated at a rough trestle table at one end of the room. The wall behind them was covered in charts and maps and black-and-white photographs.

One of the men behind the table stood up. He was in his early fifties, tall and heavy with a mop of unruly grey hair. Shephard crossed the room to him.

'Sergeant Shephard. I'm glad you're here. Were you followed?'

'No sir. No one recognized us in the pub and I followed anti-surveillance procedures on the way here.'

'Good. Well?'

'WPC Marsland got most of it, sir. It's on tape.' Shephard dug into the pocket of his jacket for the Olympus Pearlcorder.

'Never mind the tape right now,' the man said impatiently, 'what does it boil down to? Are they on tomorrow or not?'

'Yes sir, I'd say so. Definitely.'

Chief Superintendent Kellerman smiled wolfishly and glanced at the men sitting at the table beside him. One man stood up.

Shephard and Kellerman were, at around six feet, about the same height. The other man topped them by at least four inches. He had broad shoulders tapering to an athlete's waist and the hollow, well-sculptured face of a man who trains fanatically. He was wearing a police jumper though Shephard knew he was no more of a policeman than the men they were getting set to catch.

'When?' asked the tall man.

Shephard looked inquiringly at the Chief Superintendent, who nodded.

'Billy wanted to do it now. Tonight. But Jack said they'd do it in the morning. Around eight. He said there would be a few people out and about then and they wouldn't look conspicuous.'

Kellerman nodded. 'Jack always was the clever one.'

'Not any more, it seems.' The tall man's voice was scornful.

'We haven't caught him yet,' Kellerman said quietly. 'Right, Sergeant, give me that tape and go and get a cup of coffee. I'll call you when I need you.'

Shephard handed over the small tape recorder and turned to go. The Chief Superintendent called him back.

'Have you checked your firearm with the armourer?'

'No sir.'

'Make sure that you do.'

'Yessir.' Before searching out the firearms officer, Shephard wandered into a small room adjoining the large loft where a

44

woman constable was handing out sandwiches and coffee in polystyrene cups. Mickey Cheetham followed him.

'How come you have all the luck, John?' Cheetham had a broad Merseyside accent. He grinned as Shephard pulled a face at the taste of the coffee. 'There's you, you lucky bastard, in a pub, getting feelies off some luscious young tart, whilst the rest of us are going out of our skulls sitting around in this shithole. Marsland. Isn't she the one with the big tits?'

Shephard smiled. 'She does have a good figure.'

'So what were you doing?'

'Finding out what Tommy Colliston and the Bayer brothers had to say to each other.'

Cheetham was surprised. 'What, with a mike?'

Shephard shook his head. 'We couldn't risk a mike. Anyway it was too noisy; it was the pub's karaoke night. Annie Marsland reads lips. She repeated what she could of their conversation into a tape mike I had up my sleeve.'

'So,' Cheetham gave him a friendly leer, 'you had to get in close, eh? Got to move your hands all over her lovely young body, eh?'

Shephard shrugged. 'We were supposed to look like we were an item. I kept touching her cheek so the mike could pick up what she was saying. She couldn't exactly shout it out.'

Cheetham's grin widened. 'A likely bloody story. Anyway, never mind about touching her cheek, did you get a feel of her tits?'

'No, I didn't.' Shephard's brow furrowed slightly. 'That's not what I was there for.'

Cheetham laughed loudly. 'Sometimes, John, I think you take this job too seriously.'

Shephard took another sip of coffee and put the cup down on a nearby table. 'Annie read Jack Bayer saying that they'll pick up the stuff tomorrow morning.'

'Thank God for that. At least we might see a bit of action and get out of this hole.'

'What's happening now?' asked Shephard.

'Not a lot. A couple of the lads are on the floor above, watching the boat with infra-reds. If we're going to hit them tomorrow morning, the old man will be laying plans now with the ACIO from Customs and Excise. And with Captain Invincible. What I don't understand is why he's here; why do we need the army in on the operation? We can take care of it by ourselves. Why the hell do we need them?'

'I think he's a marine actually,' Shephard said.

'What?'

'Marines. SBS are the marines. And they belong to the navy.'

Cheetham snorted. 'Army, navy, marines, it's all the same. Bunch of bloody cowboys. All boots and black ski-masks.'

'Personally,' Shephard responded, 'I'm glad they're around. If there's any shooting to be done, they can do it. Anyway, the Special Boat Squadron know about boats. They'll shin up the sides of that old bucket on the Thames quicker than we can walk up the gangplank. And if the crew go to ground inside the boat, they can flush 'em out. Rather them than me.'

'So what's left for us to do?' moaned Cheetham. 'The Customs and Excise boys will be making the arrests and the SBS will be doing our job and providing armed back-up. It looks like all we've got to do is stand around and play with ourselves whilst Captain Invincible and his blokes have all the fun.'

Shephard laughed. 'That's okay in my book. Tommy Colliston, the Bayer brothers and the rest, they're lethal.

Crazy and dangerous. They carry guns and they're happy to use them. Billy Bayer is a nutter, a total psychotic. I'll tell you, Mickey, I was sweating buckets in that pub, in case they sussed what I was.'

'Nobody's ever sussed you yet, John.'

'Yeah, well there's always a first time. I was bloody glad I was carrying.'

Cheetham's eyes widened in surprise. 'You were carrying? On surveillance?'

'The old man told me I had to.' Shephard pulled aside his brown leather jacket to reveal the holster nestling below his armpit. 'I had to protect Marsland. She's only a kid. Though that wouldn't have made any difference if Billy had guessed what she was up to.'

Cheetham eyed the 9mm semi-automatic pistol snuggled inside the holster. 'How come you've got the Glock?'

'I've trained on it. It's lighter, easier to conceal than the S and W. Much better for surveillance.'

'You want to hang on to it if you can, John,' Cheetham advised him seriously. 'With one of those in your hand you could take on Colliston, the Bayer boys and the whole mob single-handedly.'

'No thanks, I'd rather leave that to the marines. Anyway the old man said I had to check it in.' Shephard turned as he heard his name being called by the Chief Superintendent. He hurried out into the other room.

Kellerman and the two other men at the trestle table were hunched over the tape recorder, listening hard. The chief looked up as Shephard approached. 'Apart from you and WPC Marsland acting like a couple of lovelorn teenagers and telling each other sweet nothings,' he said irritably, 'much of the rest of this tape is indistinct or irrelevant.'

Shephard felt himself reddening. 'We had to talk like that,

sir. Especially when anyone was passing on the way to the bar. We were supposed to look like boyfriend and girlfriend.' He noticed Allsop, the Customs and Excise man, smiling quietly. The marine officer looked bored. 'It was a helluva noisy pub, sir,' he hurried on, 'there was a lot of singing. Maybe that's why Jack chose it. And they kept their conversation very general. It was about half an hour before closing time before they finally got around to talking about picking up the stuff. They suddenly went into a huddle.'

'Find the place on the tape.'

Shephard wound the tape backwards and forwards until he found the appropriate spot. Annie Marsland's voice was distinct and unhurried as she repeated what she was reading off the lips of the men at the noisy table littered with glasses twenty feet away. Music blared loudly in the background.

On the Chief Superintendent's orders, Shephard rewound the machine twice more and replayed the section of tape. The four listened fixedly to Marsland's voice. Finally Kellerman looked up. He contemplated Shephard for a few moments. 'Yes, I agree,' he said. 'They're going for it. Tomorrow morning.'

The marine officer leaned back in his seat. 'But is this lip-reading woman any good?' His voice was crisp. 'I mean, can we rely on what she says?'

Shephard's eyes hardened as he looked at the officer. 'Annie Marsland was deaf until she was thirteen. She learned to read lips before she learned to talk. If that's what Annie said they said,' he indicated the tape recorder on the trestle table, 'then that's what they said.'

'That's all very well, but is she right? Has she read their lips accurately? Is there a chance she may be mistaken?'

'Deaf doesn't mean stupid,' Shephard told him coldly. Two spots of colour appeared high on the officer's cheeks.

'That's definitely the way Billy and Jack talk.' Kellerman was staring at the tape recorder in front of him. 'Neither of them can string two words together without effing and blinding.' WPC Marsland had punctiliously repeated every expletive and blasphemy she had seen on the lips of the Bayer brothers. 'Yes, I'm convinced. They're going to pick up the stuff tomorrow.' He looked up again. 'Well done, John,' he said warmly.

Shephard frowned. 'Actually, sir, Annie Marsland did it all. I really didn't do anything.'

The Chief nodded. 'Is she here?'

'No sir, she's not authorized for firearms.'

'I'll have a word with her when this is all over.'

The warmth stayed on his face for a moment longer then disappeared like it had never been. He appraised Shephard dispassionately. 'Have you checked that gun yet?'

'No sir.'

'Do it now.'

'Yessir.'

Shephard walked into a small anteroom where a police officer was seated at a table. Behind him was a large, heavy steel cabinet. Shephard shrugged off his jacket and unstrapped the holster. The firearms officer eyed the holstered Glock 17. 'You're a lucky bastard getting one of these. Nice weapon.'

Shephard gave him a grim smile. 'Isn't that a contradiction in terms?'

He handed over the pistol and signed its return in the weapons manifest. Emerging into the large room, he found everyone gathered around the trestle table at its far end.

The Chief was standing by the display of charts and photographs with the anonymous marine officer and Allsop, the assistant chief from Customs and Excise, standing beside him.

'Right, pay attention.' Kellerman's powerful voice was flat and dispassionate. Excitement palpitated among the men in the room like sexual arousal.

Mickey Cheetham sidled up to Shephard. 'Look at them,' he whispered, grinning and nodding at the Chief and the men flanking him by the wall, 'you'd think they were the blessed Trinity.'

'Sergeant Cheetham.' The Chief's eyes were as menacing as gun barrels. 'You got anything to say?'

'No sir.'

'Then shut up and let me do the talking.'

A subdued chuckle ran through the crowd. Mickey Cheetham was always good for a laugh.

'Tomorrow,' the Chief began, dragging his eyes back from Cheetham to survey the crowd, 'will be the climax of an investigation which we, along with Customs and Excise, have been conducting for over four months. As you know, most of the big London gangs have turned to dealing in drugs and the biggest and most violent of them, the one run by the Bayer brothers, has become a major supplier. Recently, Jack and Billy teamed up with Thomas Colliston. Our information is that Colliston has been smuggling class A drugs into this country for years. A few months ago Colliston went to Turkey, to Adana, supposedly for a holiday. He was tracked there by a couple of undercover Customs boys who did some fine surveillance work.'

Shephard smiled to himself. Like all top policemen the Chief was a politician who knew the value of good inter-departmental relations. His deft piece of praise for the Customs people would go down well.

'In Adana, Colliston contracted to buy a hundred kilos of

pure heroin.' There was a brief murmur among the group. Kellerman ignored the low hubbub. 'The stuff was moved overland to Istanbul where it was carried onto a freighter and shipped to Cyprus. From there it was taken by boat to Genoa and then transported across Europe, in a sealed container of tinned fruit, to Antwerp. The heroin left Antwerp three days ago, in a 2000-ton Greek-registered freighter carrying a cargo of rolled steel. That freighter is now moored a few yards away from here on the river.' The man shuffled and there was a low murmur.

'We are certain that Jack and Billy intend to make the pick up tomorrow morning. Soon after first light.' The murmurs increased and the Chief's voice was edgy. 'Settle down.' There was instant silence. 'We intend to arrest them after they have boarded the freighter. It will be a joint operation with Customs and Excise and,' he paused, 'a branch of Her Majesty's forces. The gentleman on my right is Mr Allsop, an assistant chief investigations officer with Customs and Excise. He and two of his men will be boarding the boat to impound the drugs and make the arrests. The police will be there to back them up. The military,' he indicated the tall, unnamed officer standing on his left, 'will approach the freighter in fast inflatables from the Millwall side of the river. They will board the freighter from the river at the same time as we go aboard from the dock. It's their job to secure the boat and its crew. They'll also have the job of flushing out anyone who tries to hide aboard the vessel.'

The Chief paused again. 'I cannot over-emphasize the need for extreme caution in this operation. The Bayer brothers will be mob-handed; including the drivers there will be at least eight of them. And there's no doubt that they will be armed. The freighter has a crew of twelve. As far as we can make out, at least half of them know what the vessel is carrying, and our information is that there may be automatic weapons on board. So although all of you, with the exception of Mr Allsop and his men, will be armed, I think you can understand why we need our friends from the military.'

Shephard shot a meaningful look at Cheetham who shrugged nonchalantly in response. 'For identification purposes everyone, including customs officers and military personnel, will be wearing police jerkins and flak jackets. The military will also be wearing ski-masks. For security reasons.

'Now . . .' Kellerman turned to the black-and-white photographs pinned to the wall behind him and began putting names to the faces that John Shephard knew almost as well as his own. Later he moved to a large-scale plan of a ship which, he explained, was a fairly accurate representation of the freighter moored close by. He began outlining the roles that each of the men under his command would fulfil and pointing to where the men from the SBS would be boarding.

Mickey Cheetham grinned at Shephard when Kellerman announced that they would be among the first to board the vessel. Shephard, concentrating on the Chief's instructions, ignored him.

The Chief looked at his watch. 'Very well. It's now past one am. There are camp beds in the next room. I expect all of you to get as much sleep as you can. There will be final briefing on the operation at six thirty tomorrow morning, at which time firearms will be issued. In the meantime all movement is restricted and no one is to leave the building without my permission. We're pretty sure that the Bayer brothers are having the area round the boat watched, just in case we've got wind of their intentions.'

Shephard had not expected to sleep. The peace of the dark, tension-filled room had been regularly punctuated by the quiet laughter of men making nervous jokes and he was surprised to find himself blinking awake at a little after six the following morning. He rose quickly. The windowless dormitory was rank with the sour, acid smell of sleeping men. Quickly, he pulled on his dark trousers, boots and police jerkin, and folded his police baseball cap under an epaulette of the jerkin. Logistics had provided chemical toilets and a few plastic containers of water to wash in. He splashed his face in the lukewarm water and went in search of coffee. It was the same policewoman who had served him the night before. He wondered where she had slept. She gave him a tired smile. He wondered *if* she had slept.

By six thirty everyone was assembled in the large briefing room. Shephard noticed that the tall marine officer was no longer present. After Kellerman had briefed them once more they were detailed away to draw their firearms. The armourer handed Shephard a Smith and Wesson .38.

'Why can't I have the Glock?' he asked, signing for the weapon. 'I'm authorized.'

'The guvnor says standard issue only,' the armourer replied, passing over a belt holster and flak jacket. Shephard exchanged disappointed looks with Cheetham who was standing in line behind him. Putting on the flak jackets and holster belts, they watched as men from Specialist Operations signed for Heckler and Koch carbines. They returned to the briefing room and found a couple of seats.

'Now all we can do is wait,' said Shephard dismally.

Cheetham was reversing his police baseball cap, creating a half-circle of forehead above the band. His face below the line of the cap was covered in a broad grin. 'Relax, John. The surveillance boys up in the roof will bell us when they show up. They'll come, don't worry.'

'I hope to God they do. If they don't, the old man will have my balls in the shredder.'

'Jesus, John, you're such a worrier,' Cheetham laughed. Pulling the baseball cap out from under Shephard's epaulette, he stuck it sideways on his friend's head. 'Look at you. With that doleful mug of yours, you look like Donald Duck.'

Despite himself, Shephard chuckled loudly, his appealing, slightly serious face crinkling into laughter and his brown eyes gleaming in the dull light. Cheetham appraised him. 'You want to do more of that, John. Laughing suits you.' Still grinning, Shephard pulled off the cap and ran his fingers through his mop of dark hair before replacing the cap on his head. Unlike Cheetham, he put it on the right way round.

They waited for almost an hour. The room was gloomy, with only a few of the dusty, naked lightbulbs hanging from the long rows of dark flex dully glowing. Shephard noticed that the blackout curtains were as good at preventing light getting in as they were at letting it out. Everywhere was quiet, with only an occasional cough or shuffle of black boots on grimy floorboards to break the silence. The air was drawn tight. Like a bow string.

Shephard noticed a young constable talking to Kellerman. The constable was holding a short-wave radio. Without a word he and Cheetham stood up and, with the rest of the men in the room, moved silently towards the Chief. They gathered about him like silent disciples round a shrine.

'Three cars have just arrived on the dock,' Kellerman announced. His tone was hard and precise, like a chisel. 'With nine, maybe ten men. Three men have got out and are taking a good look around. They're carrying short-wave radios.'

'That means they could warn the men on the boat we're coming, sir.' The speaker was Kevin Dunaff, a big, rawboned

DCI with the squad. Dunaff had a hard, scarred face and a reputation for knocking down the doors. Shephard liked him: felt glad that Dunaff was on his side.

The Chief glanced at him. 'We've thought of that, Kevin. The navy has laid on a counter-intelligence unit. They'll be operating radio-jamming equipment. As soon as we go, all short-wave radio transmissions in the area will be jammed.'

'Does that include ours, sir?' Cheetham asked with a grin.

The Super scowled at him. 'Yes it does, Sergeant. So you had better know exactly what you're doing. All of you.'

The constable's radio crackled with static. He held it close to his ear and listened intently as twenty-four pairs of eyes swivelled to his face. 'Gottit,' he said and turned to Kellerman.

'Sir, the boys upstairs say that five men are going aboard the boat. The Bayer brothers, Colliston and a couple of others. Four men are still on the dock, close to the cars. There are no weapons in sight but they're all wearing anoraks so they could be carrying.'

'Very well,' the Chief's voice was composed. 'Final radio briefing will be when you're at the jump-off.' He surveyed the silent, immobile group. 'Well, what are you waiting for? Go.'

The tension sprang apart. The men turned in a running, jumbled bunch, making for the double doors of the loft. Two dozen pairs of boots hammered down the stairs, eager hands crashed open the heavy metal door and the armed body of men burst out into the narrow alley. Five storeys above them was a narrow band of grey sky. They split up, a dozen men running one way down the alley, a dozen down the other. Shephard and Cheetham were numbers two and three in their group, following a constable from SO19 with a Heckler and Koch carbine slung across his chest. The sergeant immediately behind them was carrying a short-wave radio.

They ran to the end of the alley and stopped. It was a short run, less than a hundred yards, yet Shephard noticed they were all breathing hard. He guessed it was the excitement.

The sergeant was talking into his radio. He signed off and looked up at the panting men. 'Everyone's in position,' he told them in an elated whisper. 'Ten seconds to jump off. Then the radios go out.' He kept the radio to his ear as each man in the group began counting under his breath.

'Go,' exploded the radio man. 'Go, go, go.'

They charged out of the alley and pounded along the side of the warehouse. Seventy yards ahead of them was a patch of empty wharf; beyond that, spears of light glinting on the grey river.

The man from SO19 could run. He was about twenty-five and Shephard felt the difference eight extra years made; he had a job keeping up. Above the noise of pounding boots and rasping breath he could hear Mickey Cheetham swearing. 'Jesus, what's the fucking rush?'

Reaching the corner of the warehouse, Shephard caught sight of three Gemini inflatables arrowing across the river, lines of foaming white water spreading out in their wake. Behind the bulbous prows bouncing over the surface of the river were dark groups of crouching, heavily weaponed figures.

The dozen men rounded the corner onto the wharf at a hard run. A couple of hundred yards along the dock, their opposite numbers had emerged from the far side of the warehouse. Charging towards each other the groups began shouting. 'Armed police. Stand still. Armed police. Stand still.' For a moment the men by the cars were startled into paralysis. Then one began gabbling into his useless radio. The others made a dive for the cars.

Shephard ignored them; they were not his responsibility. By now his group was beneath the freighter's rust-streaked side, heading for the gangplank. The freighter's bows were pointing downriver. At the top of the gangplank, set close to the bows, a large man in an anorak was carrying a black plastic sack. With a yell the man dropped the sack and ran back along the ship's deck. They reached the gangplank and the constable from SO19 pounded up it, Shephard, Cheetham and a few others close behind.

They parted at the top; the constable and the others turning in the direction of the ship's prow, Shephard and Cheetham to their left, towards the stern; their job to secure the after part of the freighter's starboard deck.

They drew their handguns. Across the deck, Shephard momentarily caught sight of a score or more black-masked men armed with machine pistols clambering over the ship's rails. Then, as he and Cheetham moved slowly towards the stern, the bulk of the ship's superstructure blotted out the noise of shouting and pounding feet.

The starboard deck astern of the gangplank was deserted.

Cautiously, they edged forward.

Suddenly, about forty feet along the superstructure a door clanged open and a man bounded onto the deck. It was Billy Bayer. He was holding a short-barrelled machine pistol. Like a frightened crab Shephard scuttled sideways, taking what cover he could behind a lifeboat davit. He could hear himself shouting, the noise of his voice coming over the loud pounding in his chest. 'Armed police. Stand still.' His words were echoed by Mickey Cheetham standing behind him and to his right.

Shephard took the best stance he could behind the davit; bringing the pistol up to eye level, locking his elbows and cupping his gun hand in the palm of the other, knowing as he did so that the chances of hitting his target with a handgun at forty feet were small. He shouted again. 'Drop the gun, Billy. Stand still.' For a moment he thought – hoped – that Bayer might comply. But only for a moment. He saw the zero of Billy's podgy face fill with hate and knew, as he watched him raise his weapon, that Billy meant to kill him. Unless he killed Billy first.

He aimed low to allow for the recoil, and steadily squeezed the heavy trigger pull. The pistol cracked and reared. Behind him he heard two sharp reports from Cheetham's Smith and Wesson.

Amazingly, Bayer staggered back. Back but not over. Calmly, almost mesmerized, Shephard watched Billy straighten his gun arm; saw his stumpy finger pull the trigger. It was a quiet weapon; the automatic fire sounded like someone clearing their throat. Bullets screamed off metal as Shephard, like a child burying itself in its mother's skirts, pressed himself desperately into the davit. Something behind him clattered to the deck. Despite his terror Shephard sighted his pistol and fired again, instantly bringing the gun back from recoil to loose off another shot. This time Bayer went over, smacking backwards as if he had taken a punch on the jaw, his gun flying out of his hand and along the deck.

For a few moments Shephard stared like a half-wit at Bayer's inert figure. His eyes felt as if they were about to explode out of their sockets. Very slowly, he moved out from behind the davit. Without taking his gaze off the body he began edging warily forward, his arms outstretched, his gun pointing at Bayer's head. 'Come on, Mickey,' he said. His voice was shaky.

Two black-masked men ran around the stern of the boat, their boots ringing on the metal decking. Suddenly Shephard was aware of noise and activity around him. One of the men bent to Bayer's body as the other covered the fallen man with his machine pistol.

Shephard turned to Cheetham. 'That bastard tried to shoot us, Mickey.' He laughed, a nervous, half-hysterical titter, and then frowned. Cheetham wasn't there. He stared blankly along the boat, to where groups of armed police near the prow were pointing guns at men lying on the deck. Then he looked down.

Mickey Cheetham was lying face down on the grey metal plating, his arms spread wide and his legs twisted and crossed at the ankles as if he had fallen on his face in the middle of some complicated dance routine. His police baseball cap lay a couple of feet away, close to his gun.

John Shephard felt something abhorrent surge in his gut; felt the bile spout in his throat, sick and bitter. There was a spreading puddle around Mickey's head. It was thick and viscous and in the metallic light of the river it could have looked like an oil spill. Except that it was red; the deep, luscious red of arterial blood, spreading like an epidemic over the grey metal deck.

'Mickey.' It was a howl of anguish. Shephard bent to the body of his friend, half hearing the pounding of boots along the deck. He pulled Cheetham onto his back. Some of the bullets from Bayer's gun had caught his flak jacket, tearing away the nylon covering. Others had caught Mickey's head, ripping away part of his face. What was left was a red, nightmarish mess.

Shephard screamed.

A hand grabbed him and pulled him to his feet. A very strong hand. Stupidly, Shephard stared into a pair of relentless blue eyes surrounded by a black mask. The mask looked down at what had been Mickey Cheetham, assessed the situation instantly and looked up again. 'Come on, mate.

There's nothing you can do. We've got to get you out of it.'
The man grabbed his gun from his hand and began pulling
him along the deck. He was shorter than Shephard but
immensely strong.

Shephard tried to resist. 'No, no. I have to help Mickey.'

Another pair of hands grabbed his other arm; another
masked man. He tried to shake them off, to resist them, to
fight, but they were too powerful for him. The men bundled
him towards the gangplank, his feet scarcely touching the
deck, and rushed him down onto the dock.

'Mickey,' he shouted over his shoulder.

'Leave it, mate, leave it,' the powerful, rushing man
muttered at him. 'He's dead. There's nothing you can do.'

The dock was crowded with flak-jacketed policemen. A
number of police vehicles had appeared, their steadily churning lights swiping the grey buildings with blue. The four men
who, seconds before, Shephard had seen standing by the
cars, were lying face down and spreadeagled on the dock,
policemen's guns pointing at their heads.

The SBS men rushed him towards a police van, opened its
rear doors and pushed him onto a benchseat along its side.
One of the men made to close the doors then, as an
afterthought, pulled them open again. 'If it's any help, mate,'
he said, 'you nailed that other bastard.' The mask surrounding his mouth gave his voice a peculiar timbre. 'Punched his
ticket. I'm sorry about your mucker, it's a complete mind-
fuck when you lose one of your own . . . a mate.' For a
moment the hard blue eyes encircled by the mask softened.
Then the doors slammed in Shephard's face. He gazed at
them stupidly, seeing but not registering the grubby paintwork and the dark scuffmarks made by countless kicking
feet.

None of it made any sense. Not Billy Bayer's dead body,

nor Mick Cheetham's shattered face and, now, not words of consolation from a man wearing a black mask and toting a Biretta SMG. It was all a tortured nightmare.

They took him to Southwark police station, to divisional HQ, where a chief inspector relieved him of his flak jacket. They put him in an interview room, gave him lots of hot, sweet tea and left him alone.

He had no notion of passing time; the room was windowless and he could have been there ten minutes or ten hours. He didn't know.

The door opened and Kellerman walked in. He sat down across the scuffed, pock-marked desk from Shephard and stared at him for a while. 'I'm going to need your report, John,' he said gently.

'Yes sir,' Shephard's reply was mechanical.

'You know Billy Bayer is dead?'

Shephard nodded.

The Chief shook his head. 'We lose a good police officer in exchange for a piece of shit like that. It doesn't make any bloody sense.' He stood up. 'I need the report now, John.'

'Sir.'

The Chief stopped at the door.

'What about the rest of it? Did we get the drugs?'

The Chief nodded. 'A hundred kilos. And we found a cache of automatic weapons. Drugs and guns. Even with the best brief in London, Colliston, Bayer and the others aren't going to get out of this. They're not talking of course, but the ship's crew are singing their heads off.'

'That's good.' Shephard's voice was flat.

The Chief frowned. 'It's not all good news, I'm afraid. Some bloody busybody saw what was happening from his highrise near Evelyn Street and has got it all on a camcorder. Everything; the SBS crossing the river, the police boarding the boat,' he paused, 'the shooting. I've just had a call from a television producer. The interfering bastard has sold the video to one of the television companies. I'm on my way to look at it now. We'll try to get an injunction to stop them showing it but . . . you know the media.'

Shephard frowned up at him, trying to make sense of what he was hearing. 'I'm sorry,' he said dully.

After he had finished his report a police car was waiting to take him home. He was surprised to discover that night had fallen.

Shephard saw the video two days later in the Chief's office. It was obviously amateur; the images were shaky and nowhere near up to broadcast quality, yet they were good enough to have been networked by the BBC, ITV and Sky.

Shephard was numbly surprised to see that the exchange of fire between him and Billy Bayer had lasted no more than three seconds. It had seemed much longer at the time.

The camcorder had caught Billy Bayer raising his machine pistol, Shephard firing, Billy staggering back and opening fire before one of the two subsequent shots from Shephard had whacked him to the deck. Mercifully Mickey Cheetham had been partially hidden by the lifeboat behind whose davit Shephard had taken cover. Except for a partial blur, the camera had not caught the moment of Mickey's death. The cameraman had, though, used the full extent of his zoom lens to focus on John Shephard as he had turned towards his friend. Although distant, the magnetic images were distinct enough to register the horror on Shephard's face; to record the moment of his agony for millions to see.

Already Shephard knew that his career as an undercover drugs squad officer was at an end. His photograph, along with those of Bayer and Mickey, had appeared in all the papers the day after the shooting.

The inquests into the deaths of Mickey Cheetham and Billy Bayer were a nightmare. For some reason Shephard, although he was desperately sorry for Cheetham's parents, found it almost impossible to look them in the face. The jury at the coroner's court found that Mickey had been unlawfully killed by Billy Bayer.

Bayer's lawyers and family were screaming police brutality; claiming that Shephard had fired first and in so doing had caused Billy to return fire. The coroner would have none of it – the television pictures showed Bayer raising his gun before Shephard had opened fire. The jury returned a verdict of justifiable homicide. There was a rumour that Jack Bayer, on remand in Brixton and obsessed with revenge for his brother's death, had put out a contract on Shephard's life. Shephard was assigned an armed police escort for a few weeks and moved to a desk job in the Drugs Profit Confiscation Unit. Instead of capturing drug runners he was given the job of capturing their money.

He made a brief appearance at the trial of Bayer, Colliston and the others and stood resolutely in the witness box, indifferent to the screams of hatred from the Bayer family in the public gallery and the pitiless hatred in Jack's narrowed, piercing eyes. Bayer and Colliston got twenty years apiece; the others' sentences ranged from five to fifteen. It was a major victory for the squad and afterwards there was a big party to celebrate.

Two days later John Shephard suffered a nervous collapse. He was on sick leave for two months.

A few weeks after he had returned to his desk in the Confiscation Unit, Chief Superintendent Kellerman sent for him.

Knocking on the door, he walked into Kellerman's large office. Sunshine was streaming through the Venetian blinds, bouncing off a clump of silver cups and medals on top of the filing cabinets.

'Sit down,' Kellerman ordered.

Shephard sat on the far side of the big polished desk.

'Right, John.' Kellerman's tone was brutal. 'I'm going to say something to you that the police psychiatrist has told me I shouldn't say. Not under any circumstances.'

Shephard looked at him in surprise. 'Sir?'

'Pull yourself together.' Kellerman paused. 'That's what I'm *not* supposed to tell you. You've had long enough to mope, John. Now it's time to pull yourself together.' For a while the room was silent as motes of dust danced in the slatted sunlight. Kellerman continued. 'I've been reading the psychiatrists' reports. They say that you've got mixed up with the killings . . . that somehow you think by shooting Billy Bayer you shot Cheetham.'

Shephard said nothing.

'Well, it's a lot of bollocks. And so is believing that you're no good in the job any more. That you should resign.'

Shephard was surprised. 'Did the psychiatrists tell you that?'

'They don't have to, it's bloody obvious. I've had a report from your DCI in the Confiscation Unit. He says you're displaying all the symptoms of someone who's ready to give up. To quit.'

Shephard didn't deny it.

'It's just self-pity, John. Despite what happened it was a successful operation. Bayer and Colliston are inside for a long time. We recovered millions of pounds' worth of heroin as well as the cache of guns. God knows whose hands *they* were meant for. A lot of that success is down to you; to your undercover work.'

'You might think it's a success,' Shephard mumbled, 'but

two men are dead.' The Chief glared at him. 'Sir,' he added.

'I know that,' Kellerman snapped, 'I don't need you to tell me two men are dead. Though, God knows, one of them isn't any loss. Billy Bayer was nothing but scum and the world is a lot better off without him. Billy wasn't worth the blood in his veins and the only people who think differently are his mother and his brother Jack. Even the hardcases out there are bloody pleased you shot him.'

'Maybe, but I let him shoot Mickey Cheetham first. And Mickey wasn't scum. Mickey was a good bloke. And now he's dead.'

'And it's your fault?'

Shephard shrugged. 'I don't know. I feel like it is.'

'Why is it your fault?'

Shephard pulled a face. 'I hit Billy but I didn't put him down with the first shot. I let him shoot Mickey.'

The Chief sighed. 'Bayer was forty-three feet away from you. You know the odds as well as I do against hitting a man at that distance with a handgun. You hit Billy twice. That's close to miraculous.'

'But he didn't go over until the second shot.'

'I know, but you might just as well say that was my fault.'

Shephard screwed his face in confusion. 'Your fault?'

'Sure. I ordered everyone to be issued with Smith and Wessons. Remember? If I'd let you have the Glock you were carrying the night before, you'd have put Billy down with the first shot. The Glock has a better muzzle velocity. So, you could say it's my fault.'

'Well, I wouldn't say that, sir . . .'

'No? Then why should you say it was your fault?'

Shephard stared at the floor and slowly shook his head. 'Because I think someone else, somebody who's a better shot, would have put Billy on his back with the first bullet.'

He heard Kellerman snort in exasperation. 'To tell you the truth,' he looked up, 'I don't like guns all that much.'

'I know that.'

'You do?' Shephard was surprised.

'Of course. It comes out in the personality and aptitude reports for your weapons assessment. Do you think the Metropolitan Police puts guns in the hands of officers who *like* guns? You're exactly the right kind of officer to handle firearms. Get it into your head, John, that shooting Billy Bayer was a job. It had to be done. You did it.'

Shephard was staring at the floor again. His head was beginning to ache. Again. These days his head ached most of the time. 'But why did it have to be me?' His voice was low and hollow. 'If it had been somebody else, somebody better, Mickey might still be alive.'

'You were there, that's why.' The Chief stared at him then stood up, walked around his desk and hitched himself onto a corner close to Shephard. 'Look, John.' His voice was soft, almost fatherly. 'I don't really want to say this, but basically the reason Cheetham's dead is because he got it wrong. *He* got it wrong. It's his own fault that he's dead.'

Shephard looked up, scowling. 'No it isn't. How can you—'

'Yes it is, John.' Kellerman ploughed on, quietly but firmly. 'You followed procedure. You saw an armed man and you took cover. Cheetham didn't. He stood out there in the open, adopted the firing pose and expected to hit his man. Only two bullets were taken from Billy Bayer's body. Did you know that?'

Shephard, staring at the floor once more, shook his head.

'They were both from your gun. Mickey missed. His shots went wild. Bayer was carrying an Ingham MAC 10 and in the second between your first and second shots he got off fourteen rounds. Six of them hit Mickey.' He paused. 'Mickey Cheetham was a good police officer, John. You weren't the only one who liked him. I liked him too, even though he was an insubordinate bastard. But Mickey was like a lot of Scousers. He had too much moxie. He was just a bit too brash, too self-confident. And it killed him. He put himself in the wrong place at the wrong time, John. And that's all there is to it.'

The office was silent.

'Even if that's true,' Shephard looked up at Kellerman, 'what difference does it make? I'm still finished in the job. My face has been all over the television, the newspapers. All I can do now is shuffle paper and try to track down where the likes of Jack Bayer and Tommy Colliston have hidden their money.'

'Don't knock the Confiscation Unit, John. Finding the money and taking it off the dealers is as important as putting them away.'

'I know that, sir. But it isn't what I joined the force for. I'm not really very good at it.'

'Well, that's partly the reason why you're here.' Kellerman stood up. 'I've got something for you. Something much more up your street. Something I think you'll be good at.' He glimpsed a momentary gleam of interest behind Shephard's dull, hurting eyes. It was gone in an instant, but it was all Kellerman needed.

He turned, hiding a faint, satisfied smile, and walked back to his seat with a bounce in his step. He sat down and looked serious. 'But first you've got to drop this notion about being responsible for Cheetham's death.' His voice was stronger, more definite. 'You shot Bayer, Bayer shot Cheetham. That's the end of it. It's over and done with. It's in the past and you've got to let it go, put it behind you.'

He waited for a while, letting his words settle in Shephard's head.

'Now, I agree your face is too well known in London for you to be much use undercover. At least for a while. But it's not so well known outside. A new, special drugs unit has just been set up, covering the south coast. I've pulled a few strings, called in a few favours and got you transferred to it.'

Shephard grimaced. 'So what will I be doing? Stopping kids on the sea front at Brighton for doing speed?'

Kellerman shook his head. 'No. It's big stuff, John. The Drugs Intelligence Unit has got word that large shipments of cocaine are coming in somewhere on the south coast. Somewhere around the Bournemouth, Southampton area. A businessman from there has been spotted a couple of times in Santiago, in the company of a Spanish trafficker. The DIU thinks this bloke may be importing the stuff and shipping it to London for distribution. The new squad needs experienced people. They're desperate for someone with your kind of background and training. You're due your promotion. You can get it in the new unit. It's a good chance for you to get back into the game.'

Shephard said nothing for a while. 'Do I have much choice?' he asked finally.

Kellerman shook his head. 'No. Not unless you want to carry on in the Confiscation Unit.'

Shephard thought of the piles of paper covering his desk. He shrugged. 'All right,' his voice was dull, 'I'll give it a whirl. When do you want me to go?'

Kellerman smiled. 'You'd better pack your snorkel right away. They're expecting you on Monday.'

Chapter Four

For the first time in over a year she was happy. Not deliriously, ecstatically happy, but happy all the same.

Perhaps, Eleanor thought, it was more contentment than happiness; a kind of release. Yes, that was it. It was a sense of deliverance, the feeling that she had been liberated from the stamping tantrums and cloying demands of a couple of overgrown adolescents.

Raymond, the hypocritical bastard, had shaken her hand and said goodbye at the small party to mark her leaving Karding Hillier Longland and then, later that evening, had appeared on the doorstep of the house in West Hampstead, his eyes shining in the hope of being let inside. Back inside her.

She had told him to fuck off. She shook her head when she thought about it; despite her efforts, her language had not improved in her last few weeks in London.

He had tried to laugh off her evident loathing and had suggested that he visit her on the coast. She'd told him that if she ever saw him again she would telephone his wife. That had wiped the wheedling expectancy off his face; his eyes had been filling with self-pity as she had closed the door firmly in his face. No doubt by now, she thought, the self-pity had turned to malice and he was assassinating her character.

The sale of the house had gone smoothly, though Alec had never been off the phone, demanding, in whisky-thickened tones, his share of what was left after the mortgage. It wasn't much. Eleanor thought they were lucky there was anything at all, but half of not much is even less and Alec began accusing her of cheating him. She told him what she'd told Raymond and put the phone down. He phoned once more, a little more sober and a lot more conciliatory, wanting to know where she was going. She told him to mind his own business. He had her solicitor's number and that was all he was going to get.

She found a spacious, first-floor flat in Meyrick Park, a wide-avenued suburb of Bournemouth, lined with pines and rhododendron bushes and got herself an ex-directory telephone number. The flat was one of three apartments in a large, converted Edwardian house set in spacious grounds. It had square, handsome rooms with big windows which let in lots of light. She took out a year's lease. She had in mind that she might, ultimately, buy a small cottage somewhere to the west, out towards Dorchester and Hardy country. The flat was less than half-an-hour's drive to the offices of Hagerty Clark. The people who lived below were a young couple who threw lots of noisy parties.

After London, Eleanor found Bournemouth small and slow and provincial. It was just what she wanted. The town was filled with flowers and green parks and had an unpretentious affluence. Some of the hotels along the sea front were large, white, art deco palaces, with straight outlines, curving, steel-framed windows and splashes of chromium plate. They gave the place a legacy of nineteen-thirties elegance; parts of the town seemed almost in a time-warp. It was a place to which bank managers and brigadiers retired with their wives. Yet it was also filled with young people, many of them foreign English-language students. The streets were cluttered with hotels and boarding houses and, with the International Centre attracting political rallies and trade association junkets, there was plenty of night-life.

Not that Eleanor bothered with the clubs and pubs and the social scene. She wasn't interested in any of that. She joined a health club, working out in the gym three nights a week, and went for brisk walks along the promenades. Apart from that she hardly went out. She saw a few movies and went to the theatre occasionally, but always on her own. She wasn't looking for company; she wasn't looking for a man. Not yet anyway. She was enjoying the luxury of her liberation, and apart from the people at Hagerty Clark she scarcely had contact with anyone.

She settled into her new job as easily as into her new way of life. Philip Passmore gave her a light, airy office overlooking the harbour and introduced her to a few of the firm's more important clients, parading her before them like a minor celebrity. She didn't mind; in fact she was quietly amused. Passmore exhibited a quaint, old-fashioned attitude towards her; he seemed impressed by her abilities, even though she was careful not to reveal them fully, and intimidated by her good looks.

Less than a week after she joined the firm, and evidently under instructions, he invited her to his home for dinner, where she was inspected by his wife, a plump, dark-haired woman with a loud voice and a nervous laugh, and his two teenage daughters. She must have passed muster as, two weeks later, she was invited over to Sunday lunch.

The firm's three young, newly-qualified accountants, David, Steven and Lindsey, had been won over easily. Within days they had discovered that Eleanor was a skilled and accomplished accountant and that they could learn a lot from her. Already they had come to rely on her advice and comply with her gentle directions. They liked her; David perhaps a bit too much.

The clerks and the girls in the office were either friendly or benignly indifferent. Alice, the office manager, was the most welcoming. She became Eleanor's biggest fan. As soon as Eleanor had arrived at the practice she had taken her under her wing, loudly expressing her delight that a woman was to be made a partner. More than once Eleanor had told her that the partnership wasn't a certainty, that she would have to earn the position, but Alice was convinced that Eleanor's name would be on the firm's letterheading in less than six months.

Secretly, so was Eleanor. Some of the work Passmore was handing on to her was interesting and some was mundane . . . but none of it was unduly difficult.

After nine weeks in the job she knew that she had made the right move. She had been lucky. She had found herself an undemanding job in pleasant surroundings with a bunch of nice, easy-going people, though she got a shock when she received her first monthly salary advice. She'd stared at it for a moment, gulping at the drop in her income. Then she'd shrugged. She hadn't left London to join Hagerty Clark for money and position. She had abandoned all that urban ambition . . . said goodbye to yuppie money.

'Can I come in?'

David Rudge was at the door of her office, a quizzical grin stretched across his broad, open face. David was about medium height and slightly heavy, as if he hadn't yet lost his puppy fat. His light brown hair was cut in a French crop, the casual style emphasizing his chunky features.

She smiled at him. 'Yes, of course.'

He had a question about advanced corporation tax; a

problem he was trying to sort out for one of the firm's clients. It wasn't, in Eleanor's view, an especially difficult problem; it was intricate, it had to be thought through carefully, and it was essential to know the relevant sections of the Taxes Acts. But it wasn't really all that hard to find an answer. Privately she thought that David, who had been qualified for almost a year, should have been able to solve it on his own. Sometimes she wondered about him. She couldn't quite work out whether he was a little slow or whether he just liked to spend time with her, poring over complicated questions of tax.

She finished her explanation. He grinned gratefully, his eyes seeming to disappear into his face. 'Thanks a lot. I get it now.' He appeared disinclined to leave. 'How are you settling in?' His voice was polished; Eleanor guessed the product of some minor public school.

'Very well. I like the firm a lot. All the people in the office are very friendly.'

'No, I didn't mean at work. I meant socially. I mean, have you been out much? Met some people?'

Eleanor was evasive. 'A few. But I'm not looking for a momentous social scene, David. Not for a while, anyway. I'm enjoying the quiet life.'

He looked puzzled. 'But there's so many things to do here; a hell of a lot more than in London.'

Eleanor smiled at his vaunting. David was twenty-four, yet he seemed so adolescent. They could have been separated by a generation, not by little more than five years. 'I expect there are,' she said, 'that's one of the reasons why I came. I just haven't got around to doing them yet.'

He was silent for a moment. 'Do you sail?' he asked.

She'd had a boyfriend at university who had sometimes taken her sailing in a small yacht off the south coast of Devon. She recalled how, every couple of hours, they would

73

sail into some small harbour, tie up at a mooring buoy and go below to make noisy, energetic love; bringing a whole new meaning to the nautical term 'mooring up'. 'I've been out in a small boat a few times,' she said, smiling at her memories, 'but I can't say that I did much sailing. Why?'

'A few of us are sailing this Saturday,' he explained. 'From Wareham. Down the Frome and into the harbour. We'll sail about the harbour for a bit, and if the sea's not too fresh, maybe go out as far as the Pinnacles, past Handfast Point. Why don't you come? If the weather holds, it should be a good day.'

The invitation was tempting. It was mid-May and for the past few days the weather had been warm. Eleanor glanced out of the window behind her. The sunlight, sparkling on the great sweep of green water, made the harbour look like an enormous bowl of emeralds. Brownsea Island seemed almost close enough to touch. She grinned. 'Why not? I'd like that.'

David's delight was obvious. 'Great. I'll pick you up about nine.' She wrote down her address and telephone number. 'I'll see you Saturday,' he said, bundling up his papers. She watched him leave.

The talk around the office was that David was spoiled. His father, who was also an accountant, was a successful businessman in Swanage. According to office gossip, David, as the only son, was given everything he wanted.

David spoke of his father often. He told Eleanor that sometimes he discussed his work with him. Eleanor wondered about the ethics of doing that, but as she had come to Dorset for the quiet life she kept her opinions on professional ethics to herself.

Eleanor didn't think that David was especially spoiled, though she could see from his clothes that he wasn't short of money. No, not spoiled, she thought. Just young and eager and full of life. And a little bit dim. Like a young puppy.

The doorbell rang at ten to nine. Eleanor was finishing a cup of coffee. She tripped down the stairs and opened the door. David was dressed in a pair of spotless white cord trousers and a striped Breton pullover; he made Eleanor, who was wearing a pair of navy slacks and a denim shirt beneath an Aran jumper, feel dowdy. Behind him, standing in the sunshine of the sweeping circular drive leading to the big house, was an Isuzu Trooper. Attached to its tow bar was a grey metal trailer on which rested a white-hulled, seventeen-foot dinghy, its polished wooden mast lashed flat to the deck and an outboard motor clamped securely to its transom.

'Ready?' David was grinning from ear to ear.

They took the bypass north of Poole before turning southwest through the flat country round Holton Heath and the mudflats north of Wareham Channel. Crossing the bridge over the River Piddle they drove into Wareham and turned right just before South Bridge onto Abbots Quay. Three other vehicles with trailered dinghies were already on the quay, surrounded by a bunch of noisy men and women of about David's age. A couple were expertly winching one of the dinghies and its trailer down the concrete slipway towards the river.

David leapt out of the Isuzu and introduced Eleanor to the group. They were a loud, laughing, bubbly bunch with names like Jeremy and Henrietta, Quentin and Emily. Eleanor found it difficult remembering who was who. She caught a couple of the girls appraising her. Probably, she thought, trying to decide if she was David's latest girlfriend.

'It's going to be a little while before it's our turn to launch,' David said.

'Our turn?'

'Yes, the others have to get their boats into the water first.'

She nodded. She hadn't realized that they would be by themselves on the boat. Somehow she had thought they would be sailing with other people aboard, though, thinking back, she realized there was no reason why she should have assumed that. She looked at David's eager face. Was he manipulative? She wondered. He didn't seem the type. She doubted he had the guile for it. She frowned, annoyed at herself. She had to stop suspecting every man's motives. She was becoming neurotic. Just because . . .

'What's wrong?' David had seen the frown.

She shook her head vigorously, waving the luxuriant bob of her hair. 'Nothing. Nothing at all.'

'Well, why don't we go and get a quick cup of coffee?'

She gave him a radiant smile. 'Yes, let's.'

They crossed South Street, already busy in the bright sunshine with tourists and Saturday shoppers, and walked onto the quay, into a teashop next door to a pub. David bought a couple of coffees and they sat at a small table where he talked loudly about Wareham and the river.

After a few minutes he glanced at his watch. 'Hell, we'll have to get back. It'll be our turn to launch.'

Hurriedly he led the way out of the teashop – smack into the arms of a heavy-set man dressed in beige slacks and a check shirt. 'Dan,' he cried, recovering.

The man looked surprised. 'Why, hi David. How are you?'

'I'm well. What brings you here?'

'Oh, nothing especially. I often come to Wareham on a Saturday.' The man's eyes switched to Eleanor.

David turned to include Eleanor in the conversation. 'Dan, let me introduce a new colleague of mine, Eleanor Lambert. Eleanor has recently joined the firm.' He announced it proudly, as if her joining had been a great coup for Hagerty Clark. 'Eleanor, this is Dan Lassiter.'

They shook hands. Lassiter, who looked to be in his early fifties, was a little over medium height with short, salt-and-pepper hair and wary, calculating eyes. Businessman's eyes.

'Dan,' David explained, 'is chairman and managing director of Drumanon Consolidated. Our most important client,' he added with a grin. Eleanor nodded. She had seen the name in the office files. 'Dan's the boss,' David went on, his grin broadening. 'He always makes a profit, never makes a loss.' He laughed loudly. 'What do you think of my little poem?'

Eleanor winced inwardly. It was such a gauche thing to say in front of a client. Typical of David. She could tell that Lassiter wasn't impressed.

'Well,' he said with a faint smile, 'I guess that's been right up to now, David. You guys at Hagerty Clark ought to know. You've been looking after Drumanon for a lot of years. Done a pretty good job too.' He had an American accent.

'I hope we'll continue to do so.' Eleanor smiled at him.

The smile he gave her back moved his mouth but didn't reach his eyes. 'I guess that's up to David.'

Eleanor looked inquiringly at David.

'I'm in charge of their audit,' he explained proudly.

She kept the shock off her face. 'Ah, I see.'

David was eager to be off. 'I'm sorry to be rude, Dan, but we have to dash. We're sailing down to Poole harbour today.'

Lassiter nodded. 'I see. Well, have a good time. It was good to see you, David. And nice to meet you too, Miss Lambert.'

'I hope we meet again,' she replied.

He turned away as Eleanor and David dodged the cars and

crossed the road to Abbots Quay. 'He sounds American,' Eleanor said.

David shook his head. 'Canadian. Dan had a company in Toronto. He came over here on a business trip, discovered Drumanon and bought into it when it was on its last legs. That must be about fifteen years ago. Since then he's built it into a big business.'

'How big?'

'Last year's turnover was over forty million.'

'And you're doing the audit.' Her voice was neutral.

'Me and a couple of the clerks.'

Eleanor smiled to herself, touched at the laid-back faith Philip Passmore placed in David. Putting the audit of a forty-million-pound business, not to mention the financial welfare of one of your most important clients, under the care and supervision of a newly qualified and not very talented accountant like David was taking the country practice ethos of easy going to extremes.

Even more interesting was her own reaction to what David had told her. In London, David in charge of the audit would have worried her. Here, she found it slightly amusing. Had she changed so much so soon? she wondered. Or was it merely because the sun was warm on the nape of her neck and it was the weekend?

At Abbots Quay David reversed the trailer to the top of the slipway, winched it a little way out into the river and quickly and expertly began lowering the dinghy into the water. Eleanor helped where she could; untying ropes, jacking things up, letting things down. Within minutes the dinghy, moored to a ring set in the quay, was bobbing about in the easy flow of the river. David helped Eleanor aboard then went off to park the Isuzu and trailer. He was back within minutes. He started the outboard motor and steered the vessel under the low arches of South Bridge. On the other side he moored at the riverbank where, with Eleanor doing what she could to help, he erected the mast and boom. 'There's too many craft on the river for us to sail down,' he told her when he had finished. 'We'll use the outboard until we get into open water.'

Forward of the cockpit the dinghy had a modest cabin with a couple of settee berths and a small calor gas cooker. Eleanor descended the companionway steps into the cabin, found some cups and made tea. She emerged to be confronted by David's fairly ample backside leaning over the stern. He was holding the tiller and trying to steer blind. 'What on earth are you doing?' she asked.

'Grab the tiller will you,' his voice was sharp, 'and steer straight.' She knew enough about being on boats to do as she was told.

'What is it?' she repeated.

'Bloody weeds, they choke up the water intake. It's all right now.' He straightened up and took over the tiller.

She gave him his tea, then gazed at the slowly passing scenery. The river, meandering towards the harbour in wide loops, glittered in the bright mid-morning sun like a silver chain. Most of the land beyond the banks was low and richly green; the nearest fields, lush and spangled with bright flowers, looked like water meadows. Close to the banks were bunches of bright yellow marsh marigolds and deep purple willow herbs. Where the banks were thickly overgrown there were clumps of bulrushes and pollard willows. The river was crowded with vessels sailing in both directions and craft of all sizes and shapes were moored along its banks.

Eleanor sipped her tea, relishing the sensation of the breeze ruffling her hair and caressing her face. She turned her face up to the sun and closed her eyes. The sun's rays made shimmering, purple curtains behind her eyelids. She sighed, opened her eyes and watched the mallards and pintails deftly avoiding the river traffic as they bobbed across the water, up-ending in search of food. Close to the bank she saw a pair of swans. 'How fast are we going?' she asked.

'About four knots.'

The river began to widen, and soon there was water stretching away for hundreds of yards on both sides of the boat. They were in the Wareham Channel, though the traffic kept to the centre of the river, the craft steering between huge square wooden posts as thick as trees standing out of the water. Beyond the posts, David told her, it was all mud with the water only a few inches deep.

Later, as the channel widened and they steered further from the shore, Eleanor watched the harbour-side buildings at Poole slip by on the port beam. There were buildings and concrete landing stages and slipways and, further on, the ugly edifice of the ferry terminal where an enormous, white-painted ferry was berthed. Even at that distance its size made Eleanor realize how vulnerable they were in their small vessel.

She squinted, trying to make out the offices of Hagerty Clark, more than half a mile across the harbour. After a while she picked out her window.

'Right,' announced David, 'we'd better put on our life-vests.' He opened a cockpit locker and lifted out two bright orange buoyancy waistcoats.

As Eleanor was struggling into her waistcoat, something rolled onto the deck. It looked like a fat cardboard tube. 'What's that?' she asked.

'A parachute rocket. It's a distress signal. Every boat has one. Or should have,' David added seriously. 'Look, I'll show you.'

He took off the brightly coloured cap at either end exposing, at the tube's base, a small lever. Close to the lever was a thin cord dangling from a pin inserted into a hole in the base.

'This,' David explained, in his serious voice and pointing to the pin, 'is the safety pin. You pull the cord which ejects the pin, point the rocket at the sky and press the trigger by slapping this lever upwards with the palm of your hand. Like so.' Without taking the safety pin out he demonstrated the action. 'Here.' He handed the tube to Eleanor. It was heavy.

She peered into the exposed top of the tube. 'Jesus, don't do that.' David grabbed the tube off her. 'This thing's like a gun. It's bloody dangerous. Don't ever look down the barrel. Or point it at anyone,' he added, 'not even with the safety pin in. The rocket has a phosphorus flare. It could blow your face off.' He replaced the caps and put the flare back inside the locker.

Out in the middle of the harbour, David cut the outboard motor and showed Eleanor how to hoist the sail. A fresh breeze was running, and once hoisted, the sail cracked and billowed and the boat leapt across the water in the wake of the other dinghies.

The harbour was crowded with all kinds of craft, from spanking two-masted yachts and fabulous ocean-going motor cruisers down to open sailing boats smaller than their own.

David was a good instructor. He gave Eleanor the tiller and showed her how to tack, telling her to watch the wind indicator, teaching her the tricks of sailing close-hauled. She hadn't had so much fun in ages. They headed for the harbour entrance.

Eleanor was alarmed when she saw the Sandbanks ferry coming up on their port beam but David, taking over the tiller, slipped them expertly out of harm's way and out past

Southaven Point into Studland Bay.

Immediately, Eleanor felt the difference in the swell of the bay compared to the gentler waters of the harbour. The boat heaved and pitched and David, opening the locker once more, got out some wet-weather gear which she pulled on over her slacks and jumper. She was a good sailor and the constant rolling had no effect upon her. They sailed in the bay for a couple of hours, tacking as far south as the collection of rocks known as Old Harry and Old Harry's Wife. Then, as the wind began to slacken, they turned tail and sailed close to the shore where they dropped anchor and climbed out of their wet-weather clothing.

One of the other dinghies had a small inflatable lashed to its cabin roof. Its owner, Jeremy, paddled across to their boat and ferried them to the shore where they sat on the warm sand, waiting for the others to be brought to land. Once complete, the party set off up the hill to the hotel.

They had lunch in the hotel's dining room then stayed drinking at the bar for most of the afternoon. It was the first time Eleanor had been out socially with a group of people for months. She enjoyed herself, although she felt vaguely outside much of what went on. It was as if she was somehow distanced.

The others were locals, they'd grown up together, they knew people in common, they'd been sailing as a group for years. Certainly they were good company; bright and cheerful with plenty of witty, bubbling talk and noisy shouts of laughter. But they all seemed so young. Perhaps, she thought, bad marriages, rotten love affairs and life in London had the effect of prematurely ageing a girl. She remembered her grey hair and accepted the offer of another vodka.

Late in the afternoon they set off down the hill to the shore, where Jeremy paddled them back to their boats. The breeze had come up again and they sailed south and east, round the Foreland, and into Swanage Bay. Sailing back they were running before a freshening wind and made close to six knots all the way back to the harbour and the Wareham Channel where David hauled down the sails and started the outboard motor.

They chugged westwards along the winding river. Dusk was falling. The distant trees were misty and low over the darkening meadows beyond the banks of the river and the sky was layered in blurred, fuzzy furrows of magenta and indigo blue. The twilight was alive with buzzing, humming insects, as swallows, like black arrows, darted into the dark trees. Peace had fallen on the shadowy river and what few craft still lapped the water were calm and ethereal. Despite the quietly growling outboard, Eleanor felt a mellow serenity, though, like a tired pilgrim at the end of her journey, she was heartened to see across the fields the dark, crenellated outline of the tower of Lady Mary's church at Wareham.

After taking down the mast, David brought the dinghy close in to Abbots Quay where he and Eleanor winched it back onto the trailer. They said goodbye to the others; Eleanor relieved that David had refused their offer of a farewell drink in the Quay Inn. By then it was dark and during the drive home she almost fell asleep, jerking back to life as David drew up outside her door.

She thanked him warmly. 'David, it's been a lovely day. Thanks so much for inviting me and for driving me home.' Despite her tiredness she decided to be polite. 'Would you like to come in? For a coffee or beer or something?' She hoped he'd say no.

He grinned. 'Love to.'

He asked for a beer and she fixed herself a vodka and tonic before dropping onto a sofa and curling her legs beneath her.

'It was a marvellous day, David,' she repeated. 'I really enjoyed myself. And I've learnt a lot about sailing.'

David got up from his chair, walked across the room and sat down heavily on the sofa next to her. She was surprised. 'It's been great, hasn't it?' His voice was strained. 'Why don't we round it off and go out to dinner?'

'When, now?'

'Sure.'

She laughed. 'I'm sorry, David, I'd be terrible company. I'd fall asleep. I really am very tired.'

'But it would be a good way to finish the day, wouldn't it? It seems a shame to end it now. It would be great if we keep it going. Have a little longer together. I'd like that. What I really mean is that I like you. A lot.'

Without warning he leaned across and tried to kiss her.

Eleanor, with her legs curled beneath her, was unable to move out of the way; all she could do was lean back and turn her head. David's lips smacked into the side of her jaw. She pushed him off, glimpsing as she uncurled her legs and leapt to her feet the startled, flustered expression on his face.

She was angry. 'What the hell do you think you're doing?' she yelled at him. 'Don't ever do that again. Not ever.' She paused, gulping in breath, already realizing, as she looked down at the broad, babyish face filling with sheepish dismay, that anger was an inappropriate emotion. She was dealing with little more than a boy.

'Look, David.' Her voice was stern but emptied of anger. 'I like you. I like everyone at Hagerty Clark. But I don't want you to ever do anything like that again. Do you understand?' He nodded and made to speak but Eleanor pressed on. 'The last thing I want right now is to get involved with someone. I'm not interested in a relationship with a man right now. And even if I was, there's no way I'd get mixed up with someone I work with. No way.'

He frowned. 'But you don't understand. I really like you. I can't see any harm . . .'

'David,' she was intense, 'we have a professional relationship. That's how I want to keep it. I like you too, but I'm not getting into an emotional entanglement with you or anybody else in the business. Now, either you understand that or we're not going to get on.' She paused again. 'And believe me, David, I would like to get on with you. As a colleague and as a friend.'

He stared up at her. Understanding slowly flared in his wide, startled eyes. 'All right.' He sounded hurt and petulant, like a little boy denied a treat. 'I suppose. If that's what you want. We'll just be friends.' He screwed his face in embarrassment. 'Look, I'm sorry for what I—'

'Forget it. We won't talk about it. Ever. Okay?' He smiled wanly. 'Now, it was a marvellous day and I'm really grateful, David, but I am awfully tired and I think it's time for you to go.' He stood up.

She saw him to the door, waved him off, shut the door and leaned on it heavily. She was exhausted. All she wanted was a hot bath and bed.

She had the impression that David was avoiding her.

For about a week after the sailing trip she didn't see anything of him. She wondered if the Drumanon audit was keeping him busy or if he was convalescing from a crushed ego.

After about ten days, he began reappearing in her office with questions about the audit. He acted as if nothing had happened and she was pleased; her nightmare had been that her happiness at Hagerty Clark would be jeopardized by yet another set of problems with a man.

Her relief was short-lived. David's appearances became

increasingly frequent and soon he was turning up in her office every evening, bringing with him what, to her, seemed simple, basic accounting problems. All of them were to do with his work on the Drumanon audit. He appeared pre-occupied with the company's contracts and its distribution arrangements and absorbed in its product marketing. He was having difficulty reconciling items on the sales ledger.

Eleanor grew irritated. She answered David's unusual and naive questions as best she could but began to suspect that either David, despite her rejection, was getting some perverse kick out of being in her company, or he was even more obtuse than she had thought.

Close to the end of a particularly hectic day in which she had been piled with work and pressured by deadlines, he appeared with a question about statutory records, company ownership and the share register. It was an easy matter, one which he should have been able to resolve himself, and she was curt with him.

'Look, David, I'm happy to help you with complicated problems, ones which you really don't know how to handle, but frankly I think this matter is something you could resolve on your own.'

She saw his face crumble. 'I'm sorry,' she went on, 'but I'm very busy and I do think that if you don't know the answers to questions like this, you should at least be capable of looking them up.'

He sat silently opposite her for a few seconds and she had the impression that there was something else on his mind; something he wanted to talk about. She recalled the scene in her flat and prayed that he wasn't going to raise all that.

'David,' her voice was clipped and cold, 'I haven't time right now.'

She watched him walk out of the office like a scolded dog

and immediately felt guilty. She'd been too abrupt. She was sorry and felt like calling him back. Instead she resolved that next time she'd do her best to help.

Next time she was even busier.

A client had phoned to say that the Revenue was about to undertake an investigation of his business. The client was in a terminal state of panic which, in Eleanor's experience, meant that he had something to hide. She was feverishly stuffing files into a large, black flight case, in readiness for a meeting at the client's offices, when David poked his head round her door.

'Hello,' he said tentatively.

'Hello, David.' She scarcely looked up.

'Do you think you can spare me a moment? There's a few things I want to talk to you about. It's Drumanon. I've been working on their audit for a while now and, frankly, there's a lot of things that just don't make any—'

'David, I'm busy right now. I have to go out.'

He seemed not to hear her. 'I've been doing extra work. Trying to sort things out. But I can't make sense of it. It doesn't add up. Yesterday, I went up to—'

Eleanor shut the flight case savagely. 'David, for God's sake. Not now. If you have a problem, if the audit is too much for you, talk about it with Philip. I'm sorry, I haven't got time. I'm sorry.' She brushed past him on the way out.

She was out at the client's offices for the rest of the day, and for most of the weekend was preparing papers, ready for the onslaught of the Revenue.

Monday morning she arrived at the office forty minutes late. There had been roadworks en route and she had tried to find a way around them. It was a mistake; she'd got hopelessly lost.

Hurrying through the reception area she noticed Alice

sitting at her desk in the general office. She stopped. Alice's normally ruddy face was dirty yellow. There were deep, darkly etched lines around her eyes and down her cheeks. Alice saw Eleanor, jumped up from her desk, and scurried towards her.

'What's wrong?' Eleanor's voice was filled with alarm. 'What's happened? God, Alice, you look awful. What the hell's the matter?'

Tears brimmed in Alice's eyes. 'You haven't heard?'

'Heard what?'

'It's David.'

'David? What's the matter with him?'

'He had an accident. On Friday night. Late. In his car.' The tears streaked her cheeks.

Eleanor jerked back as if she had been slapped. 'An accident. But is he all right?'

Alice's voice was thick and croaking. 'No, he's not all right. David's dead.'

Chapter Five

He was called Clapham Fats, on account of the fact that although he stood at just under five ten, he weighed almost twenty stone. He was black, and despite his roly-poly appearance he was hard and nasty and as dangerous as a pack of rabid dogs.

Not many people called him Fats to his face; only his friends and he didn't have many of those. But he did have a lot of respect. He was the undisputed overlord of a territory stretching south of the river as far as Tooting and east all the way to Greenwich. That was his turf and nothing happened on it that he didn't know about, nothing he didn't dictate and rule. It was all his. Everything, the loan-sharking, the pornography, the protection, the prostitution. And the drugs. He controlled it all and grew fat on the profits. Especially the drugs.

Clapham Fats had dealers out on the streets twenty-four hours a day, every day of the year. The dealers, salesmen and women who worked exclusively for Fats on a commission-only basis not only supplied existing customers but hustled to drum up new business, ruthlessly pushing E, acid, skunk, mau mau, crack, blow, China white and anything else addictive into the schools, the nightclubs, the shopping malls and onto the single mothers who did no more than exist in the middle of the ghastly, graffiti-and-dogshit-decorated council estates.

Whatever the trends in the national economy, business for Clapham Fats was always booming. From its original source, the farmers in Pakistan and Colombia, to the point of sale on the street, the merchandize he was marketing attracted a mark-up of 2000 percent. And demand always outstripped supply. Not only that, but the range of his products had, over the years, expanded, so that now he was able to offer his buyers plenty of consumer choice. His customers had complete brand loyalty, and if they did switch to a different product they always traded up, moving to a more potent and therefore more expensive chemical substance. Although the products Fats sold were not price sensitive, the market for the merchandize had grown enormously. Aggressive salesmanship had more than doubled the size of his customer base, his only, minor, problem being the high incidence of early death among his biggest spending clients.

Fats had never read a book on economics in his life but he was enough of a natural entrepreneur to know that the illegal narcotics industry, in which he played a small but important role, was the ultimate in capitalist enterprise; the apogee of the free market system. The only other business that he thought could in any way be compared to his own was the arms industry. And that was controlled by the government.

Like all good chief executives Fats was sharp and artful; astute enough to keep a wary eye on political trends that could affect his industry. Sometimes he worried that the government might try to take over his business; that the politicians might decide to decriminalize drugs. For Fats, that was a bigger worry than the possibility of going to prison. Prison, in the remote chance that the police could persuade or blackmail some terrified squealer into testifying against him, would be, what with parole and all his other civil liberties, a temporary setback.

The nationalization of his business by the government would wipe him out overnight. It was not a joyful prospect, although as far as he could see it was a fairly remote one. So long as the politicians concentrated on drugs and crime at street level, Fats knew that they were like doctors prescribing aspirin to Aids victims. They weren't looking for a solution to the real problem. That made Fats happy. He could carry on trading. Safely.

Another anxiety Fats harboured was the thought that the authorities might find his money and take it away from him. All of it. He knew that they had the power to do that, and the notion that some insignificant civil servant could deprive him of the three-and-a-half-million profit he had worked so hard to accumulate over the past few years worried him sick. Fats spent almost as much time secretly investing his profits as he did making them.

The rest of Fats' strategic concerns were of a more common nature; the usual worries of any chief executive about his business.

Overheads were a problem. They were always going up. Every year Fats spent an enormous amount of money on bribes – just like the arms industry – and every year it was costing him more for people to look the other way. Enforcement, too, had turned into a major expense. The cost of crushing a cheating dealer's legs in an industrial metal press had rocketed. So too had the price of slicing open the face of some double-crossing tom who had been holding back on the take. Fats no longer outsourced such work; no longer put it in the hands of specialist outside contractors. Instead he undertook cases of industrial discipline himself. It was his way of controlling costs. And he liked hurting people; it was an aspect of the business he enjoyed.

Fats lived in a terraced house in Peckham Rye, less than four miles from the slummy tenement in Clapham where, forty-three years earlier, he had been born. In Fats' line of work it was essential to live on the turf.

He had induced his neighbours to sell their homes at knockdown prices by terrorizing them. Now, a Jersey property group, owned by a trust company registered in the Netherlands Antilles and secretly controlled by Fats, had clear and unencumbered title, not only to the house in which he lived, but to the whole terrace. The houses immediately on either side of his own had been integrated, the walls on both floors having been knocked through to allow increased living space. The renovations also permitted Fats and his closest associates the choice of a number of escape routes in the event of an unannounced, pre-dawn social visit by members of the Metropolitan Police.

Fats had turned his extended home into a fortress. The doorways of the properties immediately either side had been bricked up and the front and back doors to the house in the centre were of heavy metal. All the windows had the benefit of steel shutters, the kind advertized by ex-policemen to provide homeowners with a reassuring sense of security. The ex-policemen's assertions were no more than the truth; Fats and his friends felt entirely secure, convinced that by the time any warrant-waving coppers finally broke through the terrace's defences, they would have burned, dissolved or flushed away anything incriminating and disappeared down one of the bolt holes.

The defences were also necessary to deter the opposition. Fats often had on the premises more than a million pounds' worth of illegal narcotics. It was a prize for which gangs from some of the other London territories, as well as any bunch of chancers from the home turf, would go to great lengths to snatch. Fats was prepared to go all the way to defend what was his. Secreted in strategic places inside the house were caches of pistols, sawn-off shotguns and a couple of Uzis.

The house's interior was bizarre. The walls were painted in blaring colours, with reds, yellows and purples fighting each other for attention through the rooms and up the staircases. The carpets were deep and luxurious, the curtains hideous and cheap. The furniture, much of it stolen, was garish. Nothing went with anything else. An excess of occasional tables with gold lacquered legs and glass tops shared space with music centres, television sets, one-arm bandits and arcade video games. The ceilings and walls in the bedrooms were covered in mirrors. The house, flickering with all the tacky glitz of Las Vegas, was bombarded with noise and loud music.

One room was different. It was the boxroom directly above the fortified front door. Sitting on metal shelving attached to the walls was a stack of live television monitors, their shimmering images filling the small shadowy room with frail light. Set outside, high on the building at both ends of the terrace and along its front and rear elevations, were a series of closed-circuit video cameras. The cameras, with infra-red capability, enabled a watchman sitting in the small room to monitor day and night the approach of vehicles and pedestrians to the terrace.

The watchman, a young black man of about twenty, was studying one of the screens, watching through narrow, suspicious eyes as a BMW 750i turned the corner and coasted slowly down the darkened street towards the terrace. The watchman picked up a phone on the desk in front of him. 'He's coming.'

'Who?'

'K. Who do you think? The bleeding tooth fairy?' The watchman chuckled as the man at the other end cursed him and slammed down the phone. Watchman was a boring job and jerking around the doorkeepers downstairs was a way of relieving the monotony. One of the cameras set above the door picked up the BMW as it smoothed to a stop. A man got out of the front passenger seat and opened the rear door.

The man who emerged was tall and well-built with fashionably cropped blond hair. He was about twenty-five and looked like a recent graduate of Hatfield Poly or one of the other polytechnics, now called universities, which had a reputation for good courses in business and finance. In fact the man had left school at sixteen without benefit of any qualifications and had never been near a polytechnic, university or any other institute of higher education. All he had was a first-class street degree.

The man, followed by his minder, strolled the short distance up the path to the solid metal door. The watchman, tracking their progress on screen, noticed that the car driver, a large, swarthy, heavy-set Maltese called Leon, kept his engine running. The man reached the door and waited. He didn't bother to knock but stared up into the video camera with a relaxed, expectant look.

He was wearing an unbuttoned, voluminous, stone-coloured, calf-length raincoat by Jean-Paul Gaultier, cost £1500, over an off-the-peg two-piece pinstripe suit in light worsted by Brioni, cost £2000. His shoes, £950, were hand made by New & Lingwood; his shirt, £180, was made to measure in Jermyn Street. His tie, £130 by Nino Cerruti, was silk, as was his underwear. The man was £5000 of quality gear on the hoof.

His watch, a Rolex Oyster, was worth twice as much as his entire ensemble.

The young man believed, fervently, that a street degree was the best degree. The only qualification worth having.

One of the doorkeepers swung the heavy door open and the man and his minder stepped inside. Close to the door was a walk-through metal detector and on a nearby table a hand-held security scanner. The doorkeeper didn't bother with either. The visitor often carried a weapon . . . but never when he came calling on Fats. He didn't need to. He was a supplier and that gave him all the power he needed.

The doorkeepers, two tall, heavily built black men, didn't check out the minder either, even though he was almost certainly carrying a weapon: an old-fashioned ten-inch bayonet, hidden out of sight up his left sleeve. That was the weapon he was said to favour though neither of the men, despite the loaded sawn-off on a table less than six feet away, felt inclined to prove the rumour. Despite the minder's slight build, five feet six and about ten stone, he was not a man to mess with.

It was rumoured that a few days earlier he had blinded a small-time pusher who'd been cheating on his payments by spearing his eyeballs with a sharpened bicycle spoke. It was said that he had left the pusher holding the spoke – with his eyeballs skewered to it like kebabs.

The minder's name was Donnie Boyle and he was blood crazy. He came from Barrhead, near Glasgow, and unlike his sartorially elegant boss he looked to be coutured by the Salvation Army. He was wearing a grubby, pale grey anorak, a faded denim shirt open at the neck, and dark, badly creased trousers. His boots were heavy and black, with Stanley knife blades nailed into the welts beneath their steel toecaps. Once ordered to make an example of a minor dealer grassing to the law, Boyle had kicked the dealer several times in the crotch. The man had bled to death. Another, treated to the same, had reached the accident and emergency unit of the local hospital in time to save his life – though the doctors had been forced to castrate him surgically.

The doorkeepers glanced uneasily at the little man with the greasy hair and the pallid, ratty face. Boyle stared back, his eyes, the colour of stale urine, filled with generations of Celtic prejudice.

'He's waiting,' one of the keepers said and led the well-dressed man and his minder into an enlarged sitting room, lit up like a lighthouse by a large, mock-crystal chandelier. Fats, sprawling on a deep moquette sofa, attempted to stand up but gave up the struggle when his visitor dropped, uninvited, into an easy chair opposite. Two of Fats' men were standing at the far end of the room. Boyle took up a position close to the door, his face impassive, his mad eyes fixed on Fats.

'Lo, K.' Fats smiled affably. The young man ignored the greeting.

K was a diminution of Mr Kilo. Nobody knew the young man's real name; nobody cared. Mr Kilo summed up exactly who and what he was.

K reached into an inside pocket and pulled out a Psion 3 palmtop organizer. He pressed a couple of keys and the little LCD display came to life. The entries in the organizer were in code, the numbers and notations on the screen meaning nothing to anyone except K. And the people he worked for.

'Your last remittance was short,' K announced. His intonation was southeast London; drawling and with flattened vowels. He sounded what he was; a money man.

'Yeah?' Fats was unperturbed.

'Eleven thousand, four hundred.'

Fats raised his eyebrows. 'That ain't right.' He frowned. 'That's a lotta shit.' He reached for his own organizer and punched it up. His accounts too were in code.

For the next ten minutes the two men argued over the shortfall in payment. At first they discussed it in the manner of financial professionals, intensely but without animosity. Then Fats turned angry. Whatever figure they finally settled on, he would have to stand the loss himself and though he could easily afford it, he hated being screwed. Which, he knew, was what K was doing to him.

Fats was a franchisee. Although the protection, prostitution, moneylending and pornography on the turf was exclusively his, Fats held the drugs concession on a franchise from K and his masters. They knew to the last penny what the prices were on the streets, knew from what he re-ordered how much of each product line had been sold, and knew exactly how much money he should be paying them. They understood stock control and how to move merchandize as well as Tesco.

K's people knew the narcotics business backwards. The reason they didn't trade on the street themselves was that street trading was for blacks. White men didn't do it, not unless they were junkies. In which case they didn't last long; either the heroin got them or a rival trader did.

Fats hated K and his people. Hated them because they were racist, because they despised him, because although he did all the work and took all the risks he only got to keep thirty percent of the drug profits. And even then they tried to screw him for more.

But Fats needed K and his people. The money from the thirty percent amounted to more than all his other enterprises combined.

And, to a certain extent, K's people needed him. So long as he managed the turf well, didn't make waves with the law and sold the product aggressively, he was useful to them.

And as long as he didn't try to cheat them. Not too much anyway.

They settled on a figure of £8,900, to be paid over immediately. Fats signalled to one of his minders, who left the room.

'That's the second time in five months you've been short on the payments.' K's voice was level and unemotional. 'My people don't like it. You'd better get it right from now on.'

'Whaddaya saying? You saying I'm trying to cream you?' Fats was still angry and his voice was emotional. Donnie Boyle shuffled his feet.

K shrugged nonchalantly and flicked a fictional speck off his immaculately tailored trousers. 'No point leaping out of your tree with me. I'm the messenger. The man told me to tell you to watch it. You don't like it, take it up with the Profit.'

Fats glowered as K punched up another programme on his electronic organizer. 'Okay, what do you want to order?'

Fats told him. How much cannabis, how many amphetamines, how much E, how much LSD, morphine and opium. 'I need three kilos of coke,' he added, 'and two of H.'

K shook his head. 'I can do the coke, there's plenty about. A regular supply. Horse is short. I can let you have a k.'

'Fuck. How the hell do you expect me to do business if you don't get me the shit?'

Again the young man shrugged. 'It's a temporary interruption. When the filth hit the boat on the river they intercepted our supply. Bastards got a hundred k.'

'That was months ago,' complained Fats. 'There's plenty come in since then.'

'Yeah, from independent traders. From cowboys, mules, and one-off imports. Enough to keep us going. But no bulk supplies. It takes time to set up a big score like that. When the law stormed that boat they grabbed Tommy Colliston. He was useful. Now he's doing twenty in Parkhurst.'

Fats leered. 'He's still better off than Billy Bayer.'

K was rapidly writing an address on a piece of paper. 'Billy didn't matter. He was no loss. One k is all I can let you have.'

'Shit.'

'Don't worry. There's a big supply on its way. Another couple of weeks, it'll be here.'

'Yeah, but in the meantime, how am I supposed to make money on one lousy kilo?'

'Cut it finer, for Christ's sake.' K knew that immediately Fats took delivery of the heroin, his people would go to work, carefully spooning the thousand grammes into four thousand small heaps. They would mix each quarter of a gramme with powdered milk or sugar to make the weight back up to a gramme, spoon it into a small plastic bag and sell the bag on the street for £75. Fats would gross £300,000.

K wasn't interested in Fats' problems. 'Here's the address. You sending a biker?' Fats nodded. 'Tell him to be there at exactly eleven tomorrow morning. He's to say that he's got a delivery for Red Mary. He'll be given what you've ordered.'

'Red Mary.'

'Yeah.'

Fats shook his head. All this stuff about passwords and collecting the stuff from different addresses each time was a lot of unnecessary crap. K never carried the shit himself; never took the risk of being caught with it. It was Fats and his people who took all the risks. All K ever carried was the money.

Fats' minder came back into the room carrying a black nylon carry-all.

'That the money?'

'Yeah it's the money.' Fats' voice was bitter. He hated

handing over money. 'What do you think? I'm going on my holidays?'

K was rapidly punching the buttons on his organizer. 'Should be £570,000.'

Fats shot an enquiring look at the man holding the bag, who nodded in confirmation. 'That's right.'

'Plus £8,900.'

Again the minder nodded in response to Fats' look. 'It's all there, for Christ's sake,' he snarled.

'It had better be. Give it to him.' K jerked his head in the direction of Donnie Boyle. The minder, a tall, heavy-set man, walked across the room and dropped the bag unceremoniously at Boyle's feet. The little man looked up into the minder's face and shimmered with hate.

K stood up. 'I'll see you in a couple of weeks.' He made for the door, then stopped. 'Oh yeah. You know a dealer in Brockley called Jimmy Pierce?'

Fats looked up at him from the sofa with suspicious eyes. 'I might do. Why?'

'Do you or don't you? He's dealing on your turf. You ought to know him.'

'Yeah I know him. Piece of white shit. Lives in a crappy pad on a council estate near the station. I hear he's mainlining.'

'He deals for you, yes?'

Fats shrugged. 'He uses so he deals. That's the only way he can get the stuff for himself. He does a bit of business and pays the usual percentage. He's only small-time.'

'He still hustling as much as usual?'

'I guess. Why?'

'I hear he may be trying to go direct. Set up his own import deal.'

'What?' Fats' face was savage. 'The whitey bastard. I'll saw his arms off.'

'No. No you won't. We'll wait until he's set the deal up and then we'll grab whatever he's brought in. After that *we'll* handle it.' He glanced at Boyle.

'He's on my turf. It's my business to fix him.' Fats was angry.

'He's on your turf but it's us he's trying to cross up. We control import. We say who's allowed to handle bulk sales. So we'll take care of anybody who tries to go direct. You just keep your eyes on him; let me know if anything unusual goes down. But don't do anything. Right?'

Fats shrugged his heavy shoulders. 'If you say so,' he growled.

'Yeah, well don't forget. We've got people watching him too.'

K turned and left the room. Boyle picked up the holdall and followed his boss along the passage. Fats got to his feet in time to hear the heavy metal front door boom solidly shut behind them.

Fats' face was deformed by fury. 'Fuck,' he bellowed and took a vicious kick at a nearby glass-topped coffee table. The glass shattered with a loud smash. A couple of his men came charging into the room, their eyes wide and startled.

'Shit,' Fats screamed at them. 'Shit, shit, shit.'

K had just given him a whole new set of problems to worry about.

Chapter Six

Now she was glad of the distance.

The bunch of youngsters with whom she had spent the day sailing, Jeremy, Henrietta, Quentin and the rest, were grouped together among the darkly dressed mourners at the funeral. Eleanor nodded to those she recognized as they silently filed into the church. Their faces, the carefree countenances of noisy laughter she had witnessed less than a month before, were pale and strained, their eyes wide in the shocking incomprehension of David's death. Their loss was obvious; the stark, blatant grief of children.

Eleanor, though heavy-hearted at the pointless death of someone so young and carefree, was less smitten. She had known David for no more than three months and mingled with her sadness was a stinging pinch of guilt. She remembered her last encounter with David; her final words to him had not been congenial. She wished now that she had been kinder.

Philip Passmore was taking the death badly. He had given everyone except the new girl on the switchboard the morning off to attend the funeral. Eleanor watched him turning to stare at the coffin on the shoulders of the pall-bearers as they shuffled in ponderous unison down the stone-flagged aisle. His face was twisted in grief; he seemed almost as distraught as David's parents. Standing next to him was the tall, dignified figure of James Hagerty. His hawkish face, in profile to Eleanor, was sombre but impassive. Probably, she reflected, like her own.

Afterwards, after the service and after the crowd of quiet, dignified mourners had filed into the bright sunshine and followed the coffin to the graveside to witness its committal to the dark, constricted pit, Hagerty came up to her. She was dabbing her eyes with a handkerchief.

He looked at her sympathetically. 'It's a bad business.' His voice was flat and unemotional. 'Are you going back to the house?'

She shook her head and managed to control her sniffles. 'Are you?'

'No. Philip is the firm's representative. He'll be going.'

She nodded again. 'He's taking it quite hard, isn't he?'

Hagerty glanced at her sharply. 'Why? Don't you think he's up to it?'

She was shocked at the insistence in his tone. 'What?' she stammered.

'Don't you think he's fit to go back? To the house. Do you think he'll break down?'

'Oh no, I didn't mean that.' She was flustered. 'What I mean is that he's upset. That's all. He must have known David a long time. So must you,' she added weakly.

She felt herself reddening. Hagerty's eyes searched her face for a moment before looking past her to where Passmore, in the middle of a small group of people from the firm, was talking dolefully to Lindsey and Steven. Lindsey was crying. Hagerty stared at the group for a moment, then his eyes softened. 'Yes,' he shifted his gaze back to her face. 'We'd both known David for years. He came to us at seventeen, straight out of school.'

They started walking towards the parked cars, their shoes scrunching on the gravel path of the cemetery. 'Well,' Hagerty's voice softened, 'how are you settling in?'

'Pretty well, I think.'

'Enjoying it?'

'Yes, very much. I like the work and I like the people.'

That wasn't entirely true. She wasn't sure whether she liked James Hagerty. There was something cold and unfeeling about him. He seemed to Eleanor, on the few occasions they had met, to be too commercial, too attuned to business to understand much about the human side of it. Maybe, she thought, it was the hunting. A professional accountant who liked killing animals was, she concluded, a pretty heartless combination.

'You think you made the right move, leaving Karding Hillier Longland?'

'Oh, I think so.'

He nodded. 'That's good. Philip says you've made a big difference to his life, taking so much work off his shoulders.'

'I'm glad.' They arrived at her car, parked on the grass verge of the country lane leading to the church. She fumbled for her keys.

'Well,' Hagerty announced, 'it was nice seeing you again. Even if it was under such unhappy circumstances. I'm sure we'll see each other again soon. Goodbye.'

'Goodbye.' Eleanor flashed him a smile as he turned and walked away, moving with an easy, loping stride to a Range Rover in British racing green parked further along the verge.

She heard a noise behind her and turned. It was Alice. Her broad, normally beaming face was puffy with crying. 'Isn't it terrible,' she croaked. 'Such a shame. Especially for his parents.' Her eyes filled with tears. 'They doted on him.'

Eleanor put her arms around Alice's plump body and held

her tightly. 'Come on,' she said, 'I'll give you a lift back to the office.'

They drove in silence for a while then Eleanor said, 'Philip is taking it badly, isn't he? He must have been fond of David.'

'I suppose he was.' Alice was rummaging in her handbag for a fresh Kleenex. 'Though he never gave much sign of it in the office. I got the impression that he thought David was a bit, well, you know.'

'What?'

'Well, a bit slow. Philip often got irritated with him. Sometimes I wondered why he kept him on.'

Eleanor frowned, remembering her own opinion of David's abilities. 'David could be irritating, Alice. But Philip must have thought he was up to the job, otherwise he wouldn't have employed him. David was young, that's all.'

'That's the tragedy,' Alice blew her nose. 'Still, we mustn't speak ill of the dead.'

Eleanor gave her an encouraging smile. 'We're not speaking ill of him, Alice. We all liked David. Philip more than anyone realized.'

They were silent for a while.

'Tell me about him,' said Eleanor. 'Philip, I mean. Is he local?'

Alice shook her head. 'No. I think he's from London. Like you.'

Eleanor smiled. She'd told Alice that she was a country girl, from a village in the Cotswolds south of Stroud, but Alice had forgotten. Eleanor's voice, which was soft and resonant, had lost almost all trace of her Gloucestershire roots. It was accentless and most people outside London assumed she was from the city.

'He came to the practice in the late seventies, when Edwin

Clark was still around. Of course it was before they took me on.'

'Edwin Clark. James Hagerty's first partner?'

Alice nodded. 'He and Mr Hagerty set up the practice a few years earlier, before Philip joined.' Eleanor noticed that she called him *Mr* Hagerty. No one else in the practice was given a title; even Philip was called Philip by all but the most junior staff. Hagerty had that effect upon people. 'Then, pretty soon after Edwin Clark died, Mr Hagerty made Philip a full partner.'

'Where did Philip come from? I mean, which firm was he with in London? Do you know?'

Alice shook her head. 'No. Why?'

'No reason really. It's just that Philip must have been about thirty when he joined the practice. I was wondering what could have made him give up a career in London to come down to Dorset.'

'You mean like you?'

Eleanor laughed. 'Whatever Philip's reasons were I'll bet they weren't anything like mine. Philip's a man.' She was pleased to see Alice laugh.

Philip Passmore didn't return to the office that afternoon. Nor did he appear the following day. Alice had a message from his wife saying he was sick. 'Some kind of virus,' Alice repeated to Eleanor in her office.

Eleanor raised her eyebrows. 'I think he's really upset over David's death. It's funny, I wouldn't have thought he would have taken it so hard.' Alice shrugged and said nothing and it occurred to Eleanor that she was waiting for instructions. With a shock she realized that, in Philip's absence, she was expected to make the decisions. 'But,' she added quickly, 'I suppose life has to go on and we had better sort out what needs doing.'

She talked with Wendy, the girl who acted as Philip's secretary. Everything seemed under control except that, she was surprised to discover, nothing had been done about David's workload. Followed by Wendy and Alice she marched into the small office that David had shared with Steven and Lindsey.

The place was untidy. There were papers everywhere and on a chair in a corner was a stack of at least a dozen magazines. Eleanor picked one up. It was an up-market home furnishings and interiors journal. 'What are these here for?'

Lindsey shrugged. 'They're David's.' Her face changed. '*Were* David's. Maybe he was thinking of moving into his own place,' she added mournfully.

Eleanor dropped the magazine and moved to David's desk where she examined a pile of files stacked in an untidy heap. 'You mean nothing has been done about any of this since David's accident?' she inquired.

Wendy shrugged and Alice looked sheepish. 'I asked Philip about it a couple of times,' she explained, 'and he told me he would sort it out.'

'Well, we'd better get on with it.' Eleanor was decisive. Most of the simple stuff she assigned to Steven and Lindsey, with instructions to report back to her on progress. The remaining files related to the audit of Drumanon Consolidated. 'I'll take on the supervision of the audit,' she announced, gathering up the files.

'You?' Alice seemed surprised as she followed Eleanor out of the room.

'Who else do you suggest?' Eleanor asked as she slapped the bundle of files onto the desk in her office. 'Drumanon is one of the firm's most important clients. I really don't think it would be a good idea to assign the audit to either of the others.'

Eleanor knew that, if anything, Steven and Lindsey were even less experienced than David. Recalling Alice's objections to speaking ill of the dead, she avoided mentioning that David had been having trouble with the audit.

'Drumanon Consolidated is a large group of companies,' she went on, 'with a pretty impressive turnover. I met Dan Lassiter, the group's chief executive, a few weeks ago. He doesn't strike me as the kind of man who's willing to accept second best. I don't mean to be unkind about Steven and Lindsey, but they're both newly qualified. I think Lassiter is going to want someone with a bit more experience looking after his company.'

'But do you really want to go back to doing audit work?' Alice queried. 'I mean, I thought most accountants, once they got some experience, try to get out of them. It must be dreadfully boring, ploughing through all the company's financial affairs; all the invoices, all the receipts, all the systems and expenses.'

Eleanor laughed. 'It's not quite as bad as that. Sometimes it can be quite interesting, finding out about a company, discovering what makes it tick. But it's true, auditing is almost always for the juniors. Still, I don't mind getting my hands dirty now and again; it's good for me to keep in practice. I'll get the clerks and Steven and Lindsey to do most of the donkey work. But I want to be involved. I want to make sure it's done properly and that Dan Lassiter knows that he's getting good professional service from the firm.'

'He's never complained up to now.'

Eleanor shrugged. 'Accountancy stopped being a nice, gentlemanly profession years ago, Alice. Now it's a dog-eat-dog business, and if we don't look after Drumanon properly there are plenty of competitors who will.'

Alice frowned. 'I wouldn't have thought that would happen.

Philip and Dan Lassiter are good friends. They're often on the phone together. I think they see each other socially.'

Eleanor laughed once more. 'When a business deal goes sour, even the closest bosom friendship won't save it. Usually, in those circumstances, personal relationships go down the toilet.'

Alice wasn't used to big city business-speak. She looked shocked. 'That's a bit cynical.'

Eleanor looked serious. 'I don't mean it to be. That's just the way it is. Anyway, if Philip and Dan Lassiter are friends, then there's all the more reason to do a good job.'

'I suppose so,' Alice conceded. 'Oh, talking of Philip, he has some Drumanon papers in his office.'

'Okay, I'll go along and get them.' Eleanor walked down the short corridor with Alice and turned off at Philip's room. A bulky brown manilla file, labelled Drumanon, sat on top of a pile of papers. Eleanor cast her eyes over the rest of the papers on the desk, making sure she could see nothing else relating to Drumanon. She picked up the file. 'Will you tell Philip I've got this?' Alice, who was standing in the doorway, nodded.

By lunchtime she had made some sense of the figures and notes in David's files. Whatever problems he'd been having with the audit were not shown up by their contents; the audit trails were clear and unambiguous. She picked up the phone and asked the girl on the switchboard to get her Drumanon's finance director, Richard Jamieson. His secretary put her through.

'Hello, this is Eleanor Lambert at Hagerty Clark.' She kept her voice light but precise. 'I'm sure you know about what happened to David Rudge, the accountant who was conducting your audit. I mean, about his tragic accident.'

Jamieson, whose voice was deep and strong, said that he did.

'Well, I'm calling to say that I shall be taking over the supervision of your audit.'

Jamieson sounded surprised. 'Really? Philip Passmore didn't mention anything about that.'

Eleanor took a deep breath. She was learning that there was a kind of masonic brotherhood among businessmen in small towns. It excluded outsiders. Especially if they were women. It wasn't unkind or impolite; in fact it was extremely courteous and tactful. It was just there. A private sanctum of small-town big business; an inside exclusion zone. And Eleanor was outside it.

'Well, Philip is away sick at the moment. He has a virus and I didn't want you to think we were neglecting you. So I thought I'd take over the supervision and get on with it. That shouldn't be a problem, should it?' She said it softly but assertively; she was never going to be *invited* inside the exclusion zone: she was going to have to crowbar her way in.

'I don't know. If Philip says it's okay, then I suppose . . .' Jamieson sounded uncertain.

Eleanor took another deep breath. What, she wondered, did Jamieson think she was? Some wet-behind-the-ears articled clerk? Whatever he thought, she knew she wouldn't win by pointing to her stripes. Telling Jamieson that she was a highly qualified accountancy practitioner, an expert on tax and on the financial structure of corporations, who could conduct the audit of a company like Drumanon Consolidated standing on her head, wouldn't get her anywhere. The trick, she had learned, was to play it cool; not to appear to be a clever, know-it-all female.

She kept her voice sweet, icing over her resentment. 'Actually, as I've been qualified for a little longer than David, he'd already asked me to give him a hand with some of the work.'

'He had? What work?' Jamieson's voice was sharp, protective.

'He'd brought a few queries to me.'

'What queries?'

She flicked through the files on her desk. 'There was a question about the tax treatment of a few asset disposals you made last year and also some queries about some of your off-balance-sheet financing. I was able to give David some help, point him in the right direction.' She waited. The other end of the line was silent. 'So you see, to a certain extent I'm already involved with your audit.' The line remained silent. 'Hello, are you there?'

'Yes, I'm here,' Jamieson snapped. He didn't sound as if he wanted to be there. He was quiet for a while longer. 'All right,' he said finally, 'I suppose it's okay. I just want to get the bloody thing over and done with.'

In Eleanor's experience, finance directors, especially of private limited companies like Drumanon, thought the annual audit was a bloody nuisance. At best, a necessary evil. But few were as ungracious about it as Richard Jamieson. She wondered what he was like.

'Fine,' she said brightly, 'why don't I come over to see you this afternoon? I'll bring a couple of our clerks so they can get on with some work.'

Jamieson said he was free at two thirty and rang off. Forty minutes later Philip Passmore came on the line. Eleanor smiled as the girl on the switchboard put him through. The exclusion zone had a marvellously efficient grapevine.

'Eleanor,' his voice was strained. Whatever virus he had, it sounded as if he was suffering from it. 'I hear you intend taking over the Drumanon audit. Don't you think we ought to discuss that first?'

She was surprised. 'What's to discuss, Philip? It needs

completing and I'm half involved already.'

'So I understand. Richard Jamieson tells me that David had been coming to you for help. He should really have been coming to see me.'

She made an uncertain face. Up to now she hadn't thought Philip cared over much about his position in the practice, or about who reported to whom. He had seemed pleased that she was taking over the direction of the new, young accountants.

'I don't suppose he wanted to bother you, Philip. They were fairly straightforward matters; perhaps he didn't want you to think he couldn't handle them.'

'What were they?' Passmore asked.

'The queries he brought to me?'

'Yes.'

Eleanor repeated what she had told Jamieson. 'They're not the kind of things he would have wanted to trouble you with. So, as I've dealt with them, it makes sense for me to carry on and finish the audit.'

'I don't know, Eleanor. I think Steven could handle the rest of it quite easily.'

'Steven can do what's left of the legwork, Philip, but he needs to be closely supervised. If we leave him all on his own, Drumanon may think we're giving them a second-class service. They could decide not to reappoint us as auditors.'

'They wouldn't do that. If Dan Lassiter wasn't happy he would tell me. I know him quite well.'

Eleanor smiled cynically. Caesar, she thought, had known Brutus quite well. But she wasn't about to argue the strength of the old boy network with Passmore. Maybe it did count for something in a place like Poole, but she doubted it. Business was business everywhere. Plenty of senior partners in country accountancy practices had found themselves dumped by businessmen whom they had thought were good friends.

'Okay, Philip, you know best. But if something went wrong, I think Drumanon might think they had cause to bring an action against us for malpractice.' She heard Passmore let out a derisory snort. 'And supposing the Revenue decides to do the business on Drumanon?'

'What?'

She pulled a face. She had to stop using the business-speak; nobody understood it. 'Supposing the Inland Revenue decides to investigate Drumanon?'

'Why should they want to do that?'

Philip, she thought, had to be really suffering from the virus. He wasn't thinking at all. 'Who knows why the Revenue does anything, Philip? But the fact is that sooner or later they could get round to taking a look at Drumanon. They get around to everyone in the end. And suppose they find something; some technicality, something our audit should have picked up, something we missed? Apart from dropping Drumanon in it, Hagerty Clark will be in deep . . .' she paused . . . 'hot water. With the Revenue.'

He was silent for a while. 'All right. Then I'll supervise the audit.'

She had sensed this was coming. Her first real test. Now she was about to find out if she could ease her way into the exclusion zone; if she could edge herself into what Philip obviously thought was a male preserve. And not make enemies doing it. That was the *real* test. 'Philip, I've done quite a lot of work on Drumanon already, helping David. I think it makes sense for me to continue and see it through.'

'Yes, but Drumanon is more complicated than it looks. I've been involved with the company for years. I know the wrinkles.'

Don't tell him I can handle it *easily*, she thought. That isn't what he wants to hear. 'Of course. I realize that. But why don't I do the work and bring anything I don't understand to you? Anything that's,' she paused, 'really difficult.' He took a breath to speak but she continued, her voice smooth and low and insistent. 'James Hagerty told me at David's funeral that I had already made a difference to the firm; that I had taken a lot of work off your shoulders. So why shouldn't I carry on? Why shouldn't I handle the detail of the Drumanon audit and keep you posted on progress?'

'I don't know.' He was weakening.

'Frankly, I think it will look a bit suspect if I don't handle it.'

'Suspect?' He sounded startled.

'Yes. I've already told Alice I'll take it on, so by now it will be common knowledge in the office. I've also told Richard Jamieson the same thing. I'm supposed to be meeting with him this afternoon. If, now, I'm seen not to be involved people may wonder why. They might believe I'm not competent.'

Passmore guffawed. 'No, nobody could think that, Eleanor.'

'Then they're going to wonder what's so special about Drumanon that I can't handle it.'

Passmore was silent for a moment. 'Yes,' he said grudgingly, 'I suppose you may be right. Okay, you carry on with the audit. But,' his voice was low and intense, 'keep me in touch. Make sure you bring anything to me that you don't understand.' She promised that she would. 'I'll be in tomorrow,' he said and hung up.

She stared out of the window at the glittering harbour and a smile spread over her wide, generous mouth. She had made some space; made the first small break into the inner circle.

After lunch, Eleanor, following two of the firm's clerks, drove over to Drumanon's offices which were on a business park in Ferndown, north of Bournemouth. The offices were a modern, two-storey, brick and prefabricated metal block of about 15,000 square feet. Behind them was a large industrial shed, emblazoned with the Drumanon Consolidated sign. The shed looked to be about 50,000 square feet. Eleanor was surprised.

Richard Jamieson was the next surprise. He was tall and good-looking with hazel eyes and a cowlick of dark hair over his forehead. Eleanor guessed he was in his mid thirties. He stood up and walked around his desk to shake her hand as his secretary showed her into his office. He was in his shirt-sleeves, the jacket of an Armani suit hanging neat and uncreased on a hanger hooked to a stand in a corner of his large office. He was tanned and fit and moved easily. Another outdoor type, she thought.

'Eleanor, it's good to see you,' he said warmly. 'May I call you Eleanor?'

She was faintly puzzled by the question. From their conversation of the morning she hadn't guessed him to be the chivalrous, old-fashioned type. She wondered if it was a subtle put-down. Her face was impassive. 'Yes, of course.'

'Come and sit down.' A trio of expensive-looking sofas squatted in a corner of the well-appointed office, surrounding three sides of a low, glass-topped table. 'I've organized some coffee,' he said. She positioned her brief-case on the other half of the sofa and smoothed her skirt over her knees. She noticed him take a sideways glance at her legs, their length emphasized by the lowness of the deep seat.

'Look,' he went on, 'I'm sorry if I seemed less enthusiastic about you doing the audit this morning. I didn't mean to appear rude. You caught me at a bad moment.' He smiled at her, crinkling the lines around his eyes. She noticed that his teeth were white and even. When he smiled he looked about ten years old.

She smiled in return and told him that she understood. Now that she had convinced Jamieson that she could do the job and had won her small battle with Philip, she could afford to be gracious. The coffee arrived as she opened her briefcase and took out her papers. 'I've left two of our clerks in your boardroom,' she said, 'picking up where they left off before David's accident. Now, I have a few questions.'

Jamieson leaned forward, a serious look on his face.

They spent an hour on the questions. Eleanor took out a pad and made notes of his answers and explanations in her quick, decisive handwriting. Everything he told her was helpful and made sense. He was a good accountant; she had seen from the company's letterheading that he was an honours graduate as well as an FCA. It all seemed perfectly straightforward, though she was learning that Drumanon Consolidated was a more intricate and complex organization than she had imagined.

It was really a mini-conglomerate; an umbrella company for a series of subsidiaries, all called Drumanon something or other, and all operating out of the Ferndown premises. The company's main business was as the European sales agent for a Spanish company making kitchens and conservatories as well as industrial air-conditioning. Drumanon also imported ceramics and floor tiles from Tuscany, light fittings from northern Italy and furniture from Holland and Germany. It appeared to be doing well.

'Let me take you on a tour of the premises,' Jamieson said after she had finished with her questions.

He took her down the carpeted corridor to an office even larger and more opulent than his own. Inside, the air hung heavily with the smell of expensive cigars. Dan Lassiter was talking on the phone, his feet up on the corner of a magnificent polished mahogany desk. He looked up as they walked in. 'I'll call you back,' he said and put the phone down.

'Dan, you remember Eleanor Lambert. I believe you've met.'

'Sure.' Lassiter held out his hand, his hard eyes examining her. 'It was a while back, in Wareham. You were with David. You were going sailing down the Frome.'

'Yes.'

'We were all really sorry to hear about what happened to David. It's a helluva shame. He was a nice guy. But you know, some of these kids, they drive too fast.' He shook his head. 'You know we sent a wreath but well, maybe,' he looked at Jamieson, 'maybe one of us should have gone along to the funeral.' Jamieson nodded and made a contrite face. There was an appropriate pause. 'So,' his voice was brighter, 'you're gonna be looking after the audit.'

Eleanor said she was and they talked for a few minutes before Jamieson made noises that it was time to move on.

'Okay, well listen, Eleanor. Anything you want, any questions or anything, don't hesitate to ask. If Richard isn't around just come right along and ask me. Okay?'

'Yes, of course.'

'And I'll tell all our people here to give you whatever help and co-operation they can.'

'That's very kind.'

'Good.' Lassiter's smile remained a moment longer before it switched off. 'And when do you think you're gonna finish the audit?' His voice was hard and insistent.

She had expected the question. Eleanor had spent enough time with presidents, vice-presidents and senior executives on both sides of the Atlantic to know the technique. It was a trick particularly favoured by businessmen from Lassiter's side of the pond. First be friendly, soften them up with smiles and affability – then make the switch, play it tough, and get the sucker to punch up the deadline.

She held his gaze steadily. 'I can't say,' she said mildly. 'I may know better in a couple of days. But I can assure you, Dan, that it won't take any longer than is necessary to do a good job.' She smiled sweetly at him. 'We don't have to file with Companies House until the end of October. We have plenty of time.'

His sharp stare remained a moment longer before the smile that never reached his eyes returned. 'Okay. Well, let us know as soon as you can.'

They shook hands and Jamieson shepherded her out of the office. Accompanying him along the executive corridor she reflected on the brief meeting. Lassiter's attitude, in contrast to Philip's and Jamieson's cautious postures of the morning, had been to accept her unreservedly – and then to try bullying her into finishing the job quickly. She allowed herself a sly smile. She'd resisted the pressure and won herself yet another modest victory.

She was introduced to the group marketing director, a hearty man by the name of Graveson, and to various other directors, managers and executive officers, noting as she went the size and position of their offices, in Eleanor's experience always the true indicator of status and influence in an organization. By the end of the tour she knew that the real power in Drumanon Consolidated lay with Lassiter and Jamieson and with nobody else.

Jamieson said he would show her the operation, by which he meant the activities inside the large industrial shed at the rear of the offices. He took her along a covered walkway which, at first-floor level, led onto a long glass-covered gallery running along the end wall of the shed. The place was busy. It was sectioned off into operating areas by low partitions in which men and women in overalls and white coats moved purposefully. A small fork-lift was moving crates and flatpacks off a container truck and storing them in one of the bays.

'The ceramics, light fittings and furniture come in by road,' he explained, 'and are stored here before being sent out against orders from domestic distributors and wholesalers. It's a very smooth operation. Over there we've just received a delivery of some more furniture . . .'

Eleanor wasn't listening. Standing high on the windowed gallery she had suddenly become aware that she was being watched.

Most of the nearby workers had glanced up briefly as she and Jamieson had walked onto the gallery and some of the men had allowed their gaze to linger on her for a while. But, standing next to the finance director, she wasn't someone they could conspicuously ogle for long and they had turned back to their work.

Except one man.

He was wearing a pair of faded blue overalls and working in a bay off to Eleanor's left, partially obscured from Jamieson's view. Like the others he had looked up as Eleanor and Jamieson had walked onto the gallery. Unlike the others, he hadn't quickly turned back to his work. He was staring at her, hard, fixedly, studying her as if she was a target. A potential victim.

All the while Jamieson kept up his explanation of the distribution depot, the man persisted with his scrutiny. She looked in his direction. He dropped his eyes and played with a screwdriver for a moment, making believe he was opening a flatpack, but as soon as she half turned to listen to Jamieson, she glimpsed him raising his head. She knew without looking that he was staring at her again.

The hairs at the back of her neck stood up. There was something menacing about the intensity of his gaze. Eleanor felt her throat reddening; her heart began to race.

She thought to complain to Jamieson but dismissed the idea immediately: she had just broken inside the exclusion zone, it was not the time to be screaming sexual harassment. Anyway, what could she complain about? That a man in the depot was staring at her? Big deal. It happened. All the time. She glanced at him again; the fixed, staring eyes switched down to the flatpack.

There was something about the searching, almost malignant gaze that spooked her. She didn't know why. It wasn't as if the man looked frightening; from where she stood he appeared to be about her age, quite tall and with medium brown hair. But she knew that his eyes, whenever she wasn't looking in his direction, were fixed on her.

Men who fixated on women, men who tracked women down, who attacked, raped and killed them, almost never looked out of the ordinary. She knew that. She shivered.

'I'm sorry, you must be getting cold.' Jamieson gave her a concerned look. 'It's draughty up here, even in the middle of summer. It's warmer down on the depot floor. Do you want to go down and have a closer look?' He nodded at a flight of steps at one end of the gallery.

'No,' she snapped. Jamieson gave her a surprised look. 'I mean, no thanks. I'm fairly sure I've got everything you've told me.'

A slow, discerning smile grew over his face. 'I understand. I forgot. All auditors are the same. Not really too interested in what the company does, just in what it does with its money.' He laughed sharply. 'Not bothered about the game, only about the scoreboard, eh?'

That wasn't true of Eleanor, and under normal circumstances she would have protested. But she said nothing, pleased to be escorted by Jamieson away from the glass gallery and the staring man.

She spent the next hour with the clerks working on the figures in the company's boardroom. After they'd gone home she wandered down the corridor to Jamieson's office to say goodbye.

He offered her a drink from a veneered walnut cabinet in a corner of his office. By then the knocking beneath her left breast had gone. To be sociable she accepted a small whisky. Usually she didn't drink when she had the car; it was a white Honda CRX and she had long since discovered that a good-looking woman driving one of those was a prime target for traffic cops. Frequently she was pulled over. After the drink she told Jamieson she would be back in a couple of days and said goodbye.

The offices had closed for business at five thirty, the distribution depot half an hour earlier. The executive car park, bathed in six o'clock sunshine, was half empty.

Eleanor got into the CRX and gunned it towards the car park's exit.

Standing close to a low brick wall at the exit was a man. He was wearing a pale grey blouson and faded blue trousers. Eleanor swept past him and turned into the road before she realized. It was the man from the depot. Startled, she shoved the accelerator to the floor and shot a glance in her rear mirror. The rapidly diminishing figure in the mirror was standing at the edge of the pavement. His head was bent. He was writing something on a scrap of paper. She yanked the gearstick into third and the car surged away. The man looked up. Suddenly, with a cold, jolting shock Eleanor realized what he was doing.

The bastard was taking her car number.

Chapter Seven

She was a smurf.

She was short, blonde and slightly breathless. Dressed like a student, she looked no more than twenty. In fact she was twenty-six. She was next in line and when the cashier's light flicked on she scurried up to the woman behind the grille.

'I've just sold my car.' Her voice was young and panting and anxious. 'He gave me cash. Actually, I didn't want to take a cheque. I didn't know him and, well, you know, I wasn't sure about him. The car's all I've got and I didn't want to take the risk.' The cashier smiled sympathetically. 'Anyway, now I'm walking around with all this money on me. Can I deposit it in my account?'

The cashier smiled again and told her that was what banks were for. The girl dived into the large canvas satchel she was carrying and came up with wads of dirty notes; fives, tens and twenties. The cashier was surprised, they totalled close to £9000. The girl caught her look.

'It was an Escort,' she explained eagerly, 'only a couple of years old. My father bought it for me new. For my birthday. But I can't afford to run it. I've got to get through two more years of my course and I really need the money. I hate to part with it. It's such a shame.'

The cashier thought so too and chatted about how hard it

was to be a student these days. She had a daughter at college and she understood the difficulties. As she talked, she inspected the tens and twenties for forgeries. There were none.

The girl could have told her that.

The day before, her boss had checked the notes for counterfeits, passing all of them under an ultra-violet scanner. It was standard procedure. Good smurfs were hard to come by, and the last thing laundrymen wanted was for any of their little workers to be on the receiving end of a lot of unwanted attention because, unwittingly, they had been passing funny money. The police could be involved, which would mean statements and the taking down of names and addresses. Smurfs were supposed to be pleasant and nondescript; amiable and insignificant and easily forgotten. That was why they were smurfs. The girl filled in a deposit slip, signed it and slipped it beneath the grille. The cashier checked and stamped it before passing her a copy and giving her a final smile. It had been a common enough transaction in a busy bank and if, five minutes later, the cashier had been asked to describe the girl, she would have been unable to say more than that she was nice and that she was a student. But nobody did ask her, and in a few minutes she had forgotten all about the girl. As had the other cashiers with whom that morning, in seven separate transactions, the girl had deposited more than £60,000.

She walked out of the bank and around the corner to where a battered VW delivery van was parked. She climbed in. Her boss was at the wheel. She handed him the deposit slip. The other two had already returned and were sitting on the benchseats in the back, their feet up on a padlocked steel box welded to the floor. The Laundryman was working three of them that day; all girls.

Girls were better than men. Unless the girls were drop-dead good-looking nobody took much notice of them; the student get-up made them almost invisible. There was also less suspicion attached to a girl carrying a large amount of cash than to a man. And the selling-the-car story was perfect. It worked every time. So long as they didn't go over the top and try to pass too much in a single hit. Nine thousand was the highest they ever tumbled at one bank. Usually it was less; normally between six and seven thousand, but the man behind the wheel needed to wash £250,000 that day and the girls were depositing the maximum.

The Laundryman fired up the VW and drove off. They had hit the banks in Mitcham, Merton and Wimbledon, now they were headed for Kingston. Soon it would be lunchtime and they would have to take a break. Banks were busy at lunchtimes and someone depositing a stack of cash when there were long lines of impatient customers might be remembered.

The girl leaned back in her seat and lit a cigarette. She smoked a bit, but apart from a few drinks when she wasn't working it was her only vice. The money men never used addicts to smurf; addicts were too flaky, too unreliable. She drew deeply on the cigarette and closed her eyes. Smurfing could be hard on the nerves. She had only two more banks to hit before she got her pay. Five hundred for the day's work. Cash.

The money men used her a lot; at least ten days a month. She was smart, intelligent, reliable and above all, honest. At least honest in their terms, which meant that she never tried to skim cash off the top or to make a break with the money. She'd never even considered it. She knew that however much she might skip with, it wouldn't be enough to keep them from catching up with her. And what they would do to her when they caught up with her . . . it didn't bear thinking about.

There was something of the actress in her; one day she could look like a impoverished student, the next like a Sloane Ranger. Much of the time they used her for tumbling money at the banks but sometimes she was employed as a courier. Once she had taken £100,000 into a bakery in Eltham. The bakery was part of a chain owned by – she didn't know who it was owned by. Whoever was behind the money men, she supposed. All she knew was that the bloody suitcases she was carrying had been packed with cash and had weighed well over twenty pounds.

The most she had ever moved in one hit was half a million.

Late one evening she and one of the few guys the money men used had swanked, dressed to kill, into a well-known West End casino. The only false note in their modish evening wear had been the cheap tartan soft-top suitcases they had been lugging with them. The cases had been stuffed to bursting with £500,000 of street money. The bundles had been counted by a Greek assistant manager with fast hands and a face as impassive as a stone statue. The Greek had exchanged the cash for its equivalent in chips, whereupon the girl and her escort had gone to the tables and lost £50,000 in record time. Then, as ordered, they had cashed in the rest of their chips. The cash that had come back to them was in new, £1000 notes, which the girl was easily able to fit into her handbag. She'd heard later that the money had been flown out to a *bureau de change* in Toronto. The bureau was part of a chain of currency exchanges across Canada. She didn't know who owned that chain either . . . maybe the same people who owned the bakery in Eltham.

Two hours later she and the other two girls had finished their shift. The driver of the VW paid them off and dropped them at Kingston railway station before starting back for London. Halfway along the A3 he pulled into a layby. He killed the engine, locked the doors, put on the pair of heavy horn-rimmed spectacles he used for close work, and took out from beneath his seat an attaché case. Inside was a Compaq laptop computer.

For its size it was a powerful piece of kit. It needed to be, for the Laundryman was running some very complex programs. Sitting in the passenger seat of the van he started working at the keyboard, inputting in code details of the day's activities; recording which bank branches had been visited and by which girls. It was vital to ensure that the bank wasn't visited again for at least three months and that, when it was, it was by a different smurf.

After he had finished, he switched to a new program and input the details from the deposit slips. The girls had been working on six accounts, each of which was now healthier by over £40,000. The man recorded all the payments.

The bank accounts into which the girls had deposited the money belonged to people who didn't exist.

In the mid-eighties, when credit had been easy and the banks had been desperate for and indiscriminate about new customers, the money men had worked closely with the people organizing the big social security frauds. They had created hundreds of false identities, each with its own social security number and bank account.

Even though now the banks were more cautious about whom they took on, it was still possible to open accounts in false names. The Laundryman knew of two branch bank managers, three assistants and three building society managers who would, for a fee, verify the authenticity of people who didn't exist and recommend that accounts be opened in their names.

The middle-aged, bespectacled man frowning at the screen of the laptop computer personally operated eighty-four bank accounts whose holders were variously registered at half a dozen different addresses in and around London. The addresses were safehouses, where an old-age pensioner, usually an ex-con, would hold all the account statements and new chequebooks posted by the banks ready for monthly collection by the Laundryman. In the unlikely event that the pensioner ever received a visit from the police, the banks' security staff, or any other investigative body, he was to say he was holding the accounts for a friend who was abroad, plead ingorance about anything else and, as soon as possible, make one quick phone call.

For the services they supplied, each of the old lags received a monthly supplement to their pensions of £200. Tax free.

In the ten years that the Laundryman had been doing his job not one of his safehouses had ever been visited, not one of the accounts he operated ever questioned by the banks.

With close to fifty million bank accounts in the country, it was impossible for the banks to check every account and the Laundryman was scrupulous in operating the ones he managed.

He avoided them going into debit, even for a day. Nor did he allow them to exceed £50,000 in credit, the amount which might trigger a bank's interest in the account's activities. The average credit balance in each account was less than £100; the cash deposited by the smurfs one day was cleared out the following day by cheque. The Laundryman worked hard at *reducing* any interest accruing to the accounts for, although tax on interest was paid at source, large amounts of interest could mean enquiries by the Revenue.

And for a bank account holder who didn't exist, a Revenue investigation was bad news.

The man in the van finished inputting the data, stabbed the save key, placed the laptop on the seat next to him and took out of the attaché case half a dozen chequebooks.

Two of the cheques he wrote were in favour of an account in a Channel Islands bank, one in favour of an insurance broker in West London, two were made payable to the bank account of a company specializing in home extensions and the last to a dealer in precious stones near Hatton Garden. The man put the cheques into stamped, pre-addressed envelopes and coded the transactions into the computer.

He was finished. All that remained for him to do was post the envelopes, park the VW in the lock-up he rented in Wandsworth, pick up his Daimler Double Six and drive home to his wife and children in Ascot.

The man's business card stated that he was a financial consultant, which meant that he sold insurance for some of the smaller life companies. He was quite skilled at it, and on the few days he worked at the legitimate job he made a good living.

Though it was nowhere near the quarter of a million a year that he made as a Laundryman. Tax free.

Lionel came around the corner at a fast, rolling lope. He was carrying and when you were carrying you kept moving; you didn't keep still for a moment. You couldn't. Not with that amount of adrenalin racing through the bloodstream.

Everything in Lionel's system was fine-tuned to explode into motion. The arms loose and mobile, moving to an uptight beat inside his head; the legs taut and jittery, the calf muscles and the big femorals at the front of his thighs quivering in anticipation of instant flight. He was like

Linford Christie warming up before the hundred-metres sprint.

Lionel admired Linford Christie. Christie was rich, young, black and beautiful and could run faster than you could piss down a pan. Lionel was also young, black and good-looking and like Christie he could run like hell. Unlike Christie, who prospered by running faster than anybody else towards things, Lionel's athletic ability came from running *away* from things. Mainly the law.

Lionel was a bagman and in his line of work the streets were a jungle. Flight was survival; you were quick or you were dead. Lionel was fast and he had survived. Up to now.

Once around the corner, Lionel's head swivelled like a gun-turret, his eyes darting from side to side. His eyes were the most mobile part of his body. Always searching. First for the Man, then for the Mark; constantly nervous that the Man *was* the Mark; always wary that he might be walking into a sting; into a deal where the buyer turned out to be an undercover cop.

Like any good businessman, Lionel knew most of his buyers. They were his regulars, the main source of his income. But he was a street dealer and to earn his commission he had to push the stuff constantly. Which meant risk, the hazard of new, unknown punters. Yet necessary risk. For if he didn't find fresh customers he'd be out of business. Fats would give the concession to someone else.

Lionel admired Clapham Fats almost as much as he admired Linford Christie, though for different reasons. And it was on an errand for Fats that he was engaged now.

His bleeper had gone off earlier that morning as he was driving home from his girlfriend's flat. He hadn't heard it at first. His car windows had been all the way down and his Pioneer, 240-watt, quadraphonic CD in-car sound system had been all the way up, erupting enough metal-bending, mind-wrecking decibels of Buju Bantum to blast the babies out of their prams and send the geriatrics staggering across the pavement of Tooting High Street.

Lionel had thought something was wrong with the upper register of the sound system and had started frantically punching buttons, trying to eliminate the distorted note that was infiltrating the pure clarity of the music. Angrily he had turned the music down and found that the off-key tone was coming from his pocket. It was a code twelve.

Straight away he had pulled the bright red, 2.8E Quattro into the kerb close to a call box, praying that the locals hadn't smashed it into plastic fragments, ripped out the cash box or totally turned it into a toilet. Code twelve was the most important of them all. It meant he had to call the house in Peckham Rye. Now.

Like everyone else in his line of work, Lionel carried a mobile phone. And like everybody else he had stopped using it for business after press revelations about regal eavesdropping and deficient security in the networks' systems. Everyone in the business had gone back to using bleepers and public phones, just like some of them had gone back to using condoms. It was the safe method.

He spoke to one of Fats' people who told him he was wanted at the house right away. His heart leapt in alarm. He'd been to the house a few times before but had never been ordered there so urgently. He broke out in a sweat. He couldn't think what he had done. Nothing, as far as he knew. But if Fats *thought* he had done something, or if he had crossed Fats in some way without knowing it, then . . . The last guy to have been summarily ordered to the house had lost all the toes off his right foot. Fats had taken an electric carving knife to them.

There was no way that Lionel could disobey the summons, but he drove slowly to Peckham Rye. With the music off.

The house was filled with a sound which Lionel recognized as Luther Vandross. The security shutters were down and all the lights were on. Fats was waiting for him in one of the brightly lit living rooms, wearing a red, yellow and violet kaftan and lounging on a sofa. Two girls were playing a one-arm bandit in the corner. They were white. Lionel had flashed them a fast glance. Young, not bad bodies, faces like galvanized iron. Toms. He kept his features expressionless. It was well known around south London that Fats liked playing sandwiches; a fat slab of black meat between two pieces of soft, white flesh.

'You know a user called Jimmy Pierce?' Fats demanded.

After twenty seconds in the room Lionel was street-sensitive enough to have sussed that Fats wasn't angry at him. His relief was mingled with surprise. Surely Fats couldn't have demanded his instant attendance to enquire about a craphead like Jimmy Pierce.

'Yeah, I know him. Piece of whitey shit.' Lionel shot an assertive glance at the girls. If they heard the remark they ignored it. So did Fats.

'He deals, yes?'

Lionel shrugged. It was an idiot question. It was like asking if a pig grunts. If you used you either stole, tommed or dealt. How else could you pay for the habit? Rule number one in Lionel's business – if you use you lose.

'Yeah.'

'And you supply him?'

'Yeah.'

Fats nodded. 'Okay. I want you to watch him.'

'Yeah? What for?'

'There's word he may be trying to score on his own; that he

wants to be a big man broker. He could be setting up a meet with someone to buy some stuff.'

Lionel let out a sharp, barking laugh. He caught Fats' look and stopped. 'Jimmy Pierce?' Despite Fats' scowl he couldn't keep the incredulity out of his voice. 'Jesus, that shitheap couldn't meet himself in a mirror. He's jacking off the spike. Mahn, he's halfway down the toilet.'

'Maybe. But the word is he's setting up to peddle independent. So I want you to keep a lookout. Watch him close.'

Lionel made a face which said that he thought watching Jimmy Pierce was a waste of time.

Fats ignored the dumb impudence. 'How often does he score off you?'

'Three, four times a week.'

'Today?'

Lionel frowned as he thought about his day's business schedule. 'Yeah.'

'Okay. Go there now. Straight from here.'

Lionel was surprised. 'I can't. I'm not carrying.'

Lionel kept his supply of narcotics in safe locations close to his flat and when he was on the street his girlfriend carried the bundles of tiny white and brown bags in a specially designed pouch between her legs.

Like every pusher in the country, Lionel knew that the police had limited powers to stop on suspicion and even more limited powers of street search. The most a copper could do, if Lionel's girlfriend was ever stopped on suss, was to pat her down. No copper, male or female, would ever dare put their hand between a girl's legs. There would be race riots and questions in the House.

The law, and the sanctity of his girlfriend's snatch, made Lionel's technique for dealing on the street as safe as he could make it. He never carried the stuff himself, not unless he absolutely had to. Lionel was a natural businessman, and, like all businessmen, he took pains to minimize risk.

'There's some stuff there.' Fats jerked his head at four one-gramme balloon bags sitting on a glass-topped coffee table.

Lionel's eyes widened in surprise. 'You want me to tote that?' Fats nodded. 'But it isn't enough. I do ten kites with Pierce.'

'So take some more tomorrow. And the day after, and the day after that. Tell him supplies are tight and that he has to score with you every day. That way you can watch him better.'

'But—'

'Do it,' Fats had snarled.

So Lionel was doing it.

The four small bags of heroin were nestling in a condom dangling on a length of nylon string inside the left trouser leg of his purple shellsuit. The shellsuit, along with his big, black, Nike, air-cushioned basketball boots, was exactly the kind of outfit Lionel thought his hero, Linford Christie, would sport. And when he was wearing those basketball boots, Lionel could sprint like the wind.

His loose-limbed, bouncing lope brought him quickly to the entrance of the council estate. Three fifteen-storey tower blocks stood in the middle of an acre of sparse, faeces-splotched grass. Surrounding them on all four sides were long blocks of flats, five storeys high, fronted by open concrete walkways like galleries in a prison. Much of the concrete of the buildings was stained a light brown colour, like the inside of unwashed coffee cups. Rows of battered lock-ups, with bleached paint peeling off their thin, sheet-metal doors, ran alongside the long blocks.

Lionel made for the far side of the estate, towards the

five-storey block backing onto the railway line, taking care to sidestep the dog turds as he went. He could have driven onto the estate but, as usual, he'd opted to leave the Quattro a couple of streets away. A car like that was as safe in a place like this as Clapham Fats at a National Front rally.

Pierce lived on the fourth floor. Lionel took the stairs at the end of the block in rapid bounds and moved swiftly down the exposed concrete walkway to the flat. It was about halfway along. The green door, the colour of corrupting vegetation, was uninviting. It sported four five-lever mortice deadlocks and the letterbox was boarded up from the inside. With the exception of his giro cheque, Jimmy Pierce had long ceased to receive any mail that mattered.

Lionel banged vigorously on the door. It was hard and solid, with none of the shaky, thin-timber feel of the other flats' doors along the exposed, draughty landing. Some time before, Pierce, who must once have been clever with his hands, had braced it on the inside with cross members of four-by-two. It would, Lionel thought, have taken a strong man with a sledgehammer ten minutes to break it in.

At his first blow on the door the barking started. Dogs. There were two of them; two distinct cacophonies of mad sound. Which told Lionel that Pierce was home. When he went out to deal, Pierce left one dog in the flat to protect his stash and took one dog out to protect him. Both dogs going apeshit behind the door meant that Dr James Pierce was in residence and at home to visitors.

The dogs were pit bulls. Seventy-five pounds of smooth-haired bone and muscle, with short stubby legs and fearsome, ripping jaws. Seventy-five pounds of snarling, fearless, totally aggressive, psychopathic animal. Killer dogs. And there were two of them. They scared Lionel shitless.

A curtain twitched at a barred window close to the door.

'Hey, it's me,' Lionel shouted. He could hear the dogs leaping at the inside of the door, frantic to get at him, to rip him to pieces. 'For Christ's sake, get rid of the dogs.' From inside the door he heard a quiet word of command and the barking petered out. A few seconds later came the sound of bolts snapping back. The locks were unfastened. The door opened.

'Dogs?' It was always Lionel's first enquiry.

'They're in a room. The door's closed. You're okay.'

The voice was low and hoarse, as if its owner was in pain, though its hollow intonation couldn't disguise the fact that the man behind it had once had a good education.

Pierce was tall and in his early thirties. He was cadaverously thin, with a sheet-white face, cheeks as deep as saucers and dark, hollowed eyes. He looked half dead. He *was* half dead. He knew he was half dead.

He had started using morphine at medical school. Later, as an intern, he had also got into popping amphetamines, to help him cope with the 120-hour working week. By the time he qualified he was heavily into cocaine. He'd practised medicine for a year before his addiction had become obvious and he had been quietly removed. By then he was doing five grammes of coke a day and had begun mainlining heroin. Now, a few years on and deeper down the sewer, every accessible vein in his body was covered in needle marks. These days he was shooting up into the dorsal vein at the base of his penis.

Pierce closed and bolted the door as Lionel loped down the hall, his Nikes slapping onto bare floorboards. There wasn't a thread of carpet in the flat. The room Lionel bounced into, the one other residents of the block called the living room, had a low, rickety plastic table, two kitchen chairs and a bare lightbulb hanging from the ceiling. Nothing else. In terms of interior decoration Dr Pierce clearly favoured the minimalist.

'You got my money?' Lionel demanded.

'In the kitchen. Where's the stuff?'

Lionel hiked the nylon string out of his trouser leg, untied the double sheet bend and dropped the floppy condom onto the plastic table. He jaunted out of the room and into the kitchen, acutely aware that all that stood between him and the pit bulls were the wafer-thin wooden panels of the bedroom door. The dogs were quiet. He could hear them sniffing at the crack at the bottom of the door but they weren't barking. Pierce had them trained.

There was nothing in the kitchen beyond what the men who had built the flats had originally put there. Not even a cooker. The place was filthy, though the air was filled with the clean, astringent smell of lemon juice. Scattered around on the dirt-encrusted work surfaces were a few yellow plastic lemon-juice squeezers.

Lionel picked up the thick wad of dirty notes lying on a chipped work-top next to the sink and slapped it a few times on the formica. A couple of cockroaches scampered out of the bundle and darted across the draining board to join others of their brethren running towards the grimy, foul-smelling sink. A cockroach fell to the floor and Lionel stomped it into the floorboards with his baseball boot.

'Jeeesus.' The money was crawling.

Lionel pulled a pair of rubber household gloves out of a pocket in his shellsuit and put them on. In the days of Aids, the gloves were an essential part of a clean dealer's working clothes and although Lionel knew they were a dead give-away to any drug cop who patted him down, he never went to work without them.

He began counting the money. It came to over a thousand.

'What the fuck is this?' Pierce was holding up the condom with the four small balloon bags nestling in it. 'There's only four shots here.'

Lionel turned to face him. 'That's all I got right now.'

'But this isn't enough.' Pierce's voice was close to panic. There was a sheen of perspiration on his forehead and upper lip. 'How am I supposed to deal? I need more H than this. I also need a lot of snow. I've got people waiting. If I don't supply, they'll buy elsewhere. How can you expect me to make a living?'

Lionel didn't like James Pierce. He didn't like him because he was a junkie whose lights were going out. He didn't like him because he lived in shit and kept killer dogs. He didn't like him because he was white. And he didn't like him because, despite his terminal condition, despite his tone of whining hostility, Dr Pierce always spoke with clear diction and perfect grammar.

'Hey, what the fuck,' he erupted. 'I was carrying that stuff. For you. Me. Taking all the risk. The Man's out there, looking to scurf me. Feds everywhere, trying to tuck me up and you're fuckin' bitching.'

'But I need more than this. This isn't sufficient.' Pierce wasn't to be put off.

'Well, fuck you, mahn. If that's—'

Suddenly Lionel recalled Clapham Fats' instructions. He was supposed to be getting alongside Pierce, close enough to keep an eye on him. It wasn't part of Fats' instructions to start a fight with him.

'Hey look,' he grinned, 'don't get into no sweat about it. There's no problem, junk's a bit short is all. Tomorrow I'll bring more. No problem. You got 'nuf stuff there for today, okay. Tomorrow you'll get more. Anyway, how's it going? What's happening with you, mahn? What's the story?'

Subtlety had never been part of Lionel's social repertoire. Pierce was obviously shocked by the sudden change in the tenor and direction of their conversation. He blinked rapidly and moved his head back and forth, like a drunk trying to read a bus timetable.

'What?' He looked confused.

Lionel was still grinning. 'What's happening? What's going down? How're you doing?' For a moment he thought he saw a glint of suspicion in Pierce's heroin eyes. Then the look turned to anger.

'What is this,' Pierce demanded, 'a social call? I'm not bloody well organizing soirées. You didn't come here for that. Just get me my stuff. That's all I want.' At his last words his tone changed back to whingeing aggression. His dilated pupils, floating in a pair of watery eyes like dark, bloated corpses in a stagnant pond, filled with anxiety and panic.

'Hey, what the fuck, I'm only trying to be friendly.' Lionel tried to keep his voice affable but the grin had faded from his face. The guy was a piece of shit; a smart-assed whitey bastard trying to shine him with a lot of smart-mouth whitey talk. If it wasn't for Fats and his dumb idea that Pierce was trying to go independent, Lionel would have decided not to come back for a couple of days. Let the piece of shit do some cold turkey.

'I don't need you to be friendly,' Pierce retorted. 'I just need you to bring my supplies. I've got a living to make. I have expenses to meet.'

Lionel looked at him contemptuously. Expenses. What kind of whitey craptalk was that? The piece of shit had a giant habit to feed. Without a word he turned back to the money on the worktop, gathered it up and stuffed it into a couple of ziplock bags which he zipped into two inside pockets of his shellsuit.

141

'You'll be here tomorrow. Early. Yes?' Pierce was pleading.

'Maybe,' said Lionel cruelly. 'If I've got some junk. If I feel like it.'

He pushed past Pierce and bounced down the hallway, past the fearful sniffing at the bottom of the closed door. Pierce followed him and shot back the bolts of the locks on the fortified front door. 'Tomorrow,' he said hoarsely.

Lionel ignored him and stepped out onto the galleried walkway. He heard the bolt of the locks cracking home behind him.

He loped rapidly along the gallery and down the stairs. He was in a hurry. Carrying money was almost as incriminating as carrying junk.

Fats, he thought as he headed out of the estate, was crazy. Pierce wasn't trying to find a new supply. There was no way the guy could put together a drug buy. Not without someone behind him. Someone with money and connections. And who would go into business with a shithead like Pierce? The guy's body was destroyed and his brains were fried. And even if there was some dumb bastard stupid enough to go in with him, Pierce couldn't organize a major score. He was so far gone he couldn't organize himself to go to the toilet.

For a moment Lionel remembered the strange look in Pierce's eyes; that quick flash of what might have been suspicion. Or could it have been guilt? Could Pierce be worried about something? Could he be trying to go independent?

He came in sight of the bright red Quattro. No. No way. Whatever the look meant, it didn't have anything to do with any deal Pierce was setting up. There wasn't any deal.

Ten yards off the car, Lionel buttoned the alarm system. He climbed in behind the wheel.

Pierce wasn't going independent. The only place Pierce

was going was to the cemetery. And pretty soon. The guy was more than halfway dead already.

Lionel fired up the engine, punched the sound system up to absolute maximum, hit the button to slide down the windows and gunned the car out into the stream of traffic.

Jimmy Pierce made the other half of his inevitable journey sooner than Lionel expected.

An hour and forty minutes after Lionel's visit he was no longer half dead. He had made it all the way.

By then, Dr James Pierce was dead. As stone-cold dead as the cockroach smeared across his kitchen floor.

Chapter Eight

A third of a mile further on she hit the brakes and slewed the car into the kerb.

She sat for a while, staring at the big industrial buildings lining the road, drumming her fingers on the steering wheel.

Why, she asked herself, was she running away? She hadn't done anything. It was the man who had done something. Back there in the warehouse he had mugged her with his eyes.

She took a couple of deep breaths, trying to calm her mind. Maybe she had imagined it. Maybe he hadn't been staring at her. Maybe he had been watching Richard Jamieson. It didn't work. She knew it was her he had been exploring with his probing, malignant stare. And she was damn sure she hadn't imagined him a moment ago, taking the number of her car. To do that he would have needed to hang around the car park for almost an hour. Waiting for her to leave. Why would he want to do that? Shifty, probing, lecherous stares were one thing, but hanging around her car, waiting for her . . . for God's sake, that was something else. Something a lot more serious. A lot more menacing.

Her long fingers beat a louder tattoo on the wheel. And what use could the car number be to him? she fretted. He couldn't trace her through that; it wasn't possible. Or was it?

'Face it.' She said it loudly, firmly. 'Face it. Face him.' That was the answer. Confront the problem. Attack it, eradicate it, excise it like a malignant cyst before it turned into something worse. Like fear.

The powerful, growling CRX, hunched like a bunched muscle, gave her confidence. Deftly she swung it around in the road and opened it up, roaring back the way she had come. Within seconds she was at Drumanon's building.

The man was gone.

She turned the purring motor into the executive car park. Apart from a few expensive cars dotted about, it was deserted. Slowly she prowled past the cars, checking that the man wasn't cowering behind one of them. Nobody was there. Glancing about her, she gently piloted the car over to the broad apron of asphalt at the far side of the warehouse where the depot workers parked. An early-eighties Volvo sat sagging in a far corner. Otherwise it was empty. She drove around twice. Nothing.

Yet she felt better. The man must have hustled like hell to have got out of the area so quickly. Which meant to Eleanor that he was the one who had run. She took one last glance around, then accelerated out of the car park with a small sense of satisfacftion.

The white Honda powered away with a bubbling roar.

Dan Lassiter, standing discreetly close to the windows of his office, watched it disappear. His hard eyes were narrowed and suspicious.

Philip Passmore turned up at Hagerty Clark the following morning. He looked only slightly better than he had at David's funeral. He was seated behind his large desk, riffling through the accumulated mail that Alice had opened and piled in his in-tray. Eleanor wandered in and leaned against a filing cabinet. It was a dull, windless day and through the window behind him the harbour waters were sombre and still.

'Are you sure that you ought to be back yet?' Eleanor asked sympathetically.

'I'll be all right.'

'What is it, anyway?'

He looked up at her, puzzled. 'What's what?'

'Your virus.'

'I don't know.' He said it brusquely, not at all in his usual suave, well-modulated tones.

'Haven't you seen a doctor?' He shook his head impatiently. 'God, Philip, it could be catching. You could have the whole office out with some unknown bug, just because you came back to work too early.'

'It's not catching.' His voice was definite, dismissive. 'I'm fine. There's nothing wrong with me.' Eleanor begged to differ, though she kept her opinion to herself. The virus was chewing the edges of his urbanity, making his manner jagged and his voice sharp.

'What's happening with Drumanon? How's the audit going?' he demanded.

Eleanor let out a small sigh. She had suspected that Drumanon was the reason he had come back so soon. He was as protective as a mother hen about the company. Fearful to let it fall completely into her hands; concerned that she couldn't cope. It wasn't at all like him. She put it down to his illness. And his gender.

Men, she had discovered, changed their personalities when they fell ill. Especially men at work. They started worrying about things they wouldn't think twice about when they were well. Frightened that someone could cope perfectly well without them; worried that they might not, after all, be indispensable. Philip was typical of the species. All she needed to do was give him a few days and he would be back to his customary, charming, easy-going self. In the meantime . . .

She smiled. 'Everything's fine, Philip. I went over there yesterday and met Richard Jamieson. Took a couple of clerks with me. They spent the afternoon going over what David had done.'

Passmore frowned. 'Why are they checking on work already done? We'll never get the audit finished at this rate.'

Eleanor's smile thinned. It was Philip who had failed to reassign the job quickly after David's death; who had left the whole thing in limbo. Now he was griping about the time-scale.

'Anyway,' he demanded, 'what's wrong with David's work? Why are you checking up on it?'

'We're not, Philip. We're just picking up the threads. We need to know what's been done and where we go from here. As far as I can see, David had worked through most of the asset register. He'd finished the physical checks and had started on a couple of other things. Once I'm absolutely clear exactly how far he had got, I can re-plan the assignment.'

He stared at her morosely, his broad, normally polished face pale and strained. 'All right, but don't forget. I want you to keep me informed about how it's going and to bring any queries, anything you don't understand, straight to me. And for God's sake, let's hurry it up, Eleanor.'

Her smile died completely. She straightened up off the filing cabinet and walked abruptly out of his office. Ill or not it was really too much; Passmore was acting as if she was still serving her articles.

Back in her office she emptied her attaché case of the papers and the handwritten notes she had made in her meeting with Richard Jamieson. She switched on her PC, put on her spectacles, and went to work on Drumanon's figures, sifting through the documents, the ledgers and the computer printouts on her desk, checking figures, transferring calculations and punching them up on her screen.

The documents and printouts were liberally annotated with auditors' marks; small, neat signs and symbols in green ball pen. David had made them, just as he had created the long, orderly columns of figures she was working on. It hurt to look at them and be reminded that the person who had compiled them was dead. Eleanor sought to keep her mind fixed firmly on the business; it was too painful to think about David, though as she worked through the documents one thing became increasingly obvious. He had been tackling the Drumanon audit in an organized and professional manner. From what she was seeing of the work he had done, he appeared to have been well on top of it.

She straightened up from the keyboard, swivelled her chair and looked out over the harbour. The day remained dull but the wind had risen and now the waves were arching their backs in a freshening swell. She frowned. What was it that had made her suspect that David wasn't coping with the audit? What had made her think that it was all beyond him? She couldn't remember.

She turned back to the papers on her desk. She noticed that David had made a number of short notations on scraps of paper and on the copies of Drumanon documents; aide mémoires, action points, short comments, that kind of thing. The notes were useful, they showed the direction in which his mind had been working. Some of them could have been written by herself. She grimaced mournfully. Yet more proof that David had been more on top of the job than she had thought.

A couple of the notes mystified her. One, on a scrap of

paper merely read 'Canadian Company?' Another, even more mysterious was on a copy of a contract with Van Dameer, Drumanon's Dutch distributors. It read 'Asset? How prove?' She puzzled over it. It didn't make sense. Why the question mark?

A contract was an asset, any first-year articled clerk knew that. And if the contract was working, there was no need to prove it. The contract with Van Dameer, who distributed the kitchens, conservatories and industrial equipment for Drumanon, had been working for over twelve years. That was all the proof an auditor could want. The only other way to prove a contract would be to talk to a lawyer. She frowned at David's notation and put the copy of the contract to one side. Maybe David hadn't been *quite* so on top of the job as she was beginning to think.

She worked through the morning, stopping to take phone calls from clients but otherwise concentrating on catching up with the work on Drumanon. At twelve thirty she asked Alice if one of the girls would go out and get her a sandwich. She worked through lunch and finished the job in the middle of the afternoon.

She stood up, hollowed her aching back and punched the print button on her keyboard. Moving close to the window she read through the printouts of her day's work with a quiet satisfaction. Now all she needed to do was button up a few loose ends at Drumanon's. She called Richard Jamieson. He wasn't there. She told his secretary that she would be coming over for a couple of hours.

She wandered along the corridor to Passmore's office taking off her spectacles as she went. She hated being seen wearing them, even by someone like Philip. She knocked on the door and walked in. He looked up from his desk.

'Just to tell you that I'm off to Drumanon's for the rest of the afternoon,' she said brightly.

'Is there a problem?' He looked worried.

'No,' she laughed, 'no problem. You'll be pleased to know that we're practically back up to speed on the audit. I worked through lunch. In fact I've spent the entire day catching up on David's work. Now all I need is to tie up a few queries at Drumanon's and we'll be completely up-to-date.' Her voice was bright, chipper with self-satisfaction.

'Do they know you're going over?' he growled.

The smile faded and she frowned. 'Yes, I've told them,' she said frostily.

He nodded and for few seconds looked up at her with a glowering, sombre stare. 'Good,' he said finally and dropped his eyes to the work on his desk.

For the second time that day Eleanor stalked out of Passmore's office. She swept into her room, shot the papers, notes, calculator and everything else she needed into her attaché case, gathered up her laptop computer and stormed out, catching Alice's startled face as she clattered down the stairs and marched out of reception. She let the door crash loudly behind her.

'Thanks a lot, Eleanor,' she muttered. 'Thanks for working through lunch. Thanks for breaking your back all day to get up-to-date on the Drumanon audit so I can bloody stop worrying about it. Thanks, I appreciate it.'

She rounded the corner of the building, marching towards her car parked in the small car park on the other side of the narrow sidestreet. Suddenly she became aware of a couple of passers-by and abruptly stopped her muttering. She stared at the strangers malevolently. She was close to the car and pressed the button of the remote control to release its security systems.

Why, she thought, are men all the same? They use you,

abuse you and only appreciate you when they want something. She opened the car door. 'Just because he's ill,' she hissed, 'that's no reason to treat me like sh—'

She stopped herself. Standing by the side of the car with the door open, she took a deep breath. This, she told herself, was not the reason she had come to Dorset. If she was going to get angry and uptight about work; if she was going to revert to using bad language, she might as well have stayed in London. She took another deep breath, the salty air tanging the membrane at the back of her throat, the ozone vaporizing the outrage in her head. She took her time getting into the car and closed the door calmly and deliberately.

It was her own fault, she reasoned, as she slid the CRX out of the car park. She had got the job at Hagerty Clark by acting dumber than she actually was. Neither Philip nor anyone else had yet caught on to how bright, how adept at the job she was. So it was scarcely surprising if, as she supposed, Philip didn't think she *really* had got the work up-to-date.

By the time she was halfway to Ferndown she had revised her opinion.

Philip's behaviour *wasn't* her fault. That had been her problem with Alec. For the first couple of years of their marriage she had believed that every setback in his career, every commission he didn't get, every tantrum he threw, every frantic drinking fit she'd endured, was, somehow, her fault. It had taken a painful period of time for her to realize that she had married a spoiled, neurotic boy and that his behaviour and misfortunes were his own responsibility. She wasn't going to fall into that trap again.

It wasn't her fault that Philip didn't feel well. It was true he hadn't actually *asked* her to work flat out to get the Drumanon audit up to date, but he *had* said that he wanted it finished as soon as possible. Which was why she'd worked through lunch.

If Philip couldn't notice and acknowledge the effort she was making, that was his problem. As he was usually kind and appreciative, it must be because he was ill. Which was also his problem. She would, she decided, forget about his lack of appreciation and wait for him to return to his normal, polite and considerate self.

Though, she thought, it had better not take too much time. She wasn't prepared to put up with that kind of shitty behaviour for very long. Damn, why *did* she keep swearing?

By the time she arrived at Drumanon's building she was back in control and feeling adult. She locked the car, walked across the car park slowly and elegantly and climbed the stairs to the first floor. Brenda, Richard Jamieson's secretary, was waiting for her.

Chatting amiably, Brenda clicked down the stairs with her to the accounts office, where they collected more of the papers and documents that David had been working on. They remounted the stairs to the boardroom and dumped the reams of computer printout and piles of ledgers onto the walnut board table. Brenda asked if she wanted a coffee as Eleanor opened her attaché case and spread the papers out over the table's long, glossily polished surface. She said yes. By the time the girl came back, carrying an elegant, bone-china cup and saucer on a small silver-plated tray, she had plugged in her laptop and was busily punching numbers.

She worked doggedly, concentrating on the digits on the small screen; riffling through the printouts to find the next piece of data to input to the laptop. She was only faintly aware of the building emptying at five thirty, then, later, of the occasional solitary slamming of a car door, the sound of a vehicle firing up and driving out of the car park.

Finally, there was silence.

The brilliant glow from the fluorescent lights in the boardroom, though diffused, was hard and unyielding. As the hours passed it made the figures on the screen shimmer and blur. Her head began to ache and after a while she put on her spectacles. Beyond the opened Venetian blinds the dull day had grown duller. Heavy black stormclouds were boiling up in the south west, making the evening light murky. Hunched over her little computer and surrounded by papers, she was unaware of time passing.

The door of the boardroom opened slowly.

Suddenly Eleanor was conscious of someone standing in the doorway. She looked up, startled.

'Hello, dear. I didn't know any of you was left.' It was one of the cleaning women. Eleanor let out a relieved sigh and smiled.

'I'm working late,' she said.

'All right dear. We'll leave this place 'til tomorrow.' She made to close the door.

'No, leave it open,' Eleanor told her.

For the next hour she was half-aware of movement and the distant sound of vacuum cleaners. Then they too ceased and the place returned to silence.

The boardroom was a pool of light. In the corridors the cleaners, forgetting her presence, had turned off most of the lights. Outside, though it was eight thirty and late May, it was so dull as to be practically dark. A spatter of rain hit the windows. Eleanor looked up. It was then she heard the noise.

Somewhere along the executive corridor a door was being opened. She cocked her head to one side and listened carefully. Nothing. No other sounds, except those of the building settling down for the night. She leaned forward, straining to hear. Still nothing. Had she imagined it? Maybe she had. It wasn't the usual sound of someone unselfconsciously opening a door. It had been more muted. Cautious. Spooky.

She stood up and quietly moved around the table. She went to the doorway and peered out. The dim, carpeted corridor was empty. Only one light was switched on at the far end, close to the swing doors. She moved further out from the boardroom, took off her spectacles and peered through the shadows. All the doors on both sides of the corridor were closed. She had imagined it.

She returned to her work. Another half an hour and it would be finished.

She had no idea how long she had been absorbed in the job when she heard it again. This time it was nearer; much nearer. The same eerie sound. A door slowly moving back on its hinges.

She jerked back in her seat, staring at the bright rectangle of light made by the open boardroom door. She sat perfectly still, breathing deeply, keeping control. Again she listened intently. This time she knew she hadn't imagined it. But as before, now there was only silence. No, maybe not. Maybe she could hear something; something or someone, quietly moving about in one of the rooms along the corridor.

She thought back to the previous day's tour with Richard Jamieson. Dan Lassiter's office was on the same side of the corridor as the boardroom, close to the head of the stairs. Then came Graveson's, the marketing director, then Richard Jamieson's, then another office and then the boardroom. She listened hard. The slight, almost indistinct sounds weren't coming from the room next door. They were coming from the one beyond. Richard Jamieson's.

Was someone quietly moving about in Jamieson's office?

Eleanor heard something humming. It took her a moment to realize it was the blood, rushing crazily inside her head.

She took another deep breath and told herself she was being stupid. She'd heard a noise and it had frightened her. Ridiculous. And yet . . . she was a woman on her own in an office. And office buildings got broken into.

What was stupid was to sit there and let herself take fright. 'Right.' In the silence of the building her voice seemed very loud. 'Let's take a look.'

She expelled the air in her lungs in one great rush and stood up quickly. She strode around the table. She reached the open doorway and turned into the corridor.

He was moving quickly down the corridor towards her doorway. She crashed into him.

'*Aaarrrrrgh.*'

It was him. HIM. The man in the warehouse. The man with the probing eyes; the one who had taken her car number. His face was less than eighteen inches from hers.

'*Aarrgh. Uuh, uuh.*'

The impact of crashing into him bounced her spectacles onto the tip of her nose. She scrabbled at them, pulling them off with both hands.

'Oh my God, oh my God.' Her voice was loud, uncontrolled. His face was still there, still close to hers.

'Christ, you gave me a fright.' His voice was strained.

'What? What?' She was practically screeching.

The face moved back from hers. The little bit of her brain which wasn't seized up registered that the face was startled.

'What? I gave *you* a fright? I gave *you* a fright? You gave *me* a fright. You frightened *me*. What do you want? What do you want?' Her voice was high contralto, hitting the upper register as the breath rocketed off her soft palate like a typhoon. Her arms were outstretched, as rigid as railway lines, ready to fend him off.

His face was strained with surprise. He backed off from her screeching voice and stared at her in shock. 'I don't want anything.'

'What do you want with me? Why are you following me? What do you want?' Her shrill repetitions oscillated along the dim, deserted corridor. The man looked at her in stunned astonishment.

They stared at each other for some moments, frozen in the wedge of light streaming out through the boardroom doorway. Beyond them were shadows. Gradually the man's expression changed. He looked uncomfortable, unsure, almost shifty. 'I don't want anything with you,' he protested. 'I'm not following you.'

Warily Eleanor lowered her arms, crossing them across her breasts, close to her body. She was beginning to regain control, even though her heart was banging like a Bofors gun and the hand holding her spectacles shook uncontrollably.

'Yes you are. You were staring at me yesterday. In the warehouse. And you took my car number. Why? I want to know.'

'I wasn't staring at you.'

'Yes you were. And you took my number. Why?'

He shook his head. To Eleanor, fast unfreezing from the fear and even faster hotting up at the cause of it, he looked guilty. 'No I didn't. I didn't take your car number. It wasn't me.'

Close up he didn't seem threatening at all. He was about her age, slim, a few inches taller than her, with dark hair and brown eyes. There *was* something about his eyes. They were hard and darting; penetrating. Like a hawk's. But even they weren't especially menacing. She guessed from his voice that he was from London.

'It was you.' She was shouting. 'I know it was you. And if you don't bloody stop bothering me I'll report you to the police. To the management.'

'All right, all right. Take it easy for God's sake. Nobody's bothering you. Nobody's gonna bother you. Okay.' They stared at each other. He was breathing hard. So was she.

Eleanor contracted her diaphragm, sucking breath deep into her lungs. She sought to control her voice, scrutinizing the man with narrowed eyes. 'Anyway,' she demanded, 'what are you doing here? At this time of night?'

'Well, what are *you* doing here?' He was regaining his composure too.

'I'm bloody well working,' she said heatedly. 'I'm the company's auditor.' She jerked her head in the direction of the boardroom doorway.

He glanced at the table strewn with papers. 'Oh, I see. Well, I'm sorry I frightened you. You gave me quite a shock too.' He grinned at her. It was shallow and unconvincing. 'Well, I'd better go. I'm sorry about the fright.' He half turned away from her.

'Wait. You haven't answered my question. Why are you here? The warehouse finished working hours ago.'

He shook his head as he backed away. 'We're working overtime. I had to drop something off in one of the offices.'

'What? What did you have to drop off?'

He shrugged, giving her the insincere grin. 'Just an envelope with some papers in it. That's all.'

'Which office?'

'The guvnor's. Lassiter.' He began to walk away.

He was halfway along the corridor, walking rapidly, when she thought to ask the final question. 'What's your name?' she called. He seemed not to hear. Keeping up his fast pace he was close to the swing doors at the corridor's far end.

Eleanor shouted. 'I said, what's your name? I want to know.'

He called a name over his shoulder as the doors crashed shut behind him. It sounded like John.

Eleanor leaned back against the corridor wall, closed her eyes and tried to capture her hammering heart.

After a while she came off the wall and walked slowly and unsteadily back into the boardroom. She slumped into her chair.

All of a sudden she was tired. No, not tired, exhausted. The excess adrenalin that had pumped into her blood was curdling and turning sour. She felt nauseous. She stared at the papers and the glowing screen of the laptop. She had no stomach for the work. Not any more.

She started clearing up, piling the papers and printouts into a neat stack on the boardroom table. They would be safe enough there. She put her things into her attaché case, unplugged and closed the laptop and, carrying them both, walked wearily out of the room. She didn't turn off the lights.

A few yards along the corridor she stopped. The door to Richard Jamieson's office was ajar. Earlier, when she had checked the office doors, it had been closed. If the man from the warehouse had been dropping off an envelope in Dan Lassiter's office, then what the hell had he been doing in Jamieson's? She was positive it was from there she'd heard the noises.

She stared at the door for a few seconds then gingerly pushed it open. Putting down her case she reached in and switched on the lights. The large room was as she remembered it from the previous day, except that now the desk, apart from a couple of telephones, was perfectly clear. All the filing cabinets were shut tight. As far as she could tell nothing was missing, nothing different. She moved further into the office and tried one of the filing cabinets. Locked. She guessed the desk would be the same. Jamieson's security was good. She left, switching off the lights and closing the door properly.

She picked up her case and made her way down the corridor. Maybe, she thought, she had imagined the noises in Jamieson's office after all. No, she hadn't. She knew she hadn't.

She reached the pool of light close to the swing doors. Dan Lassiter's door was closed. She had a sudden thought, and again put down her attaché case.

Cagily, she opened Lassiter's door and turned on the lights. The big room, like Jamieson's, was uncluttered. The filing cabinets were closed and the surfaces of Lassiter's enormous desk and the couple of occasional tables were clear of papers, files, printouts . . . and envelopes. She stepped into the middle of the room and took a careful look around. Nothing. There was no sign of any envelope.

She jabbed at the switch to kill the lights, closed the door, picked up her case and pushed her way through the swing doors.

A man was walking up the main staircase.

'*Haaahhhhhh.*'

The man's face shot up at her startled cry. He was wearing something dark; dark trousers, a dark jacket. The jacket had flashes and emblems and badges. Badges. A uniform. The man was a security guard.

Eleanor staggered back against the still swinging doors. 'Christ, I can't take much more of this,' she moaned.

The man's face was concerned. He came up to her. 'Are you all right, miss? I'm sorry, did I startle you?'

She straightened up and shook her head. 'No,' she mumbled, 'no, it's all right.' She hung her head in exhaustion, staring at the floor, at the bright shine on the man's boots. 'I just want to get out of here. I want to go home.' Her voice was drained flat by fatigue.

'I'm not surprised,' the man said cheerily. 'It's past nine o'clock. Long day. I'll have to let you out now, I'm afraid. The alarms on the main door are switched on.'

She looked up into the man's red, fleshy, jovial face. 'Thanks.' They made towards the head of the stairs. 'By the way,' she said in her tired voice, 'I'm the auditor. I've been working in the boardroom.'

He nodded. 'I know. They left me a message to say you were in there and that you might be working late.'

'I've left the lights on and all the files on the table, I'm afraid.'

He smiled at her. 'Don't you worry about that, miss. I'll fix the lights and lock the door.'

They were silent for a moment as their footsteps echoed down the stairs. 'Do you usually lock the doors along the executive corridor?' Eleanor asked.

He shook his head. 'No. No need. Everybody locks everything away in their desks and cabinets. Company rule. If they don't I snowflake 'em.' He grinned. 'Even Mr Lassiter. Not that I've ever had to, mind. Not him. Or Mr Jamieson.'

'It's good security here then?'

'The best. The alarm systems are state-of-the-art. And I come round every two hours.' They had descended the stairs and were in the large reception area. The man moved to a control panel close to the entrance doors.

'By the way,' Eleanor addressed the man's back, 'are they working overtime in the warehouse?'

'Yup. They've just finished.' The man returned from the control panel. 'That's it, miss. I can let you out now.' He went to open one of the glass doors.

Eleanor moved slowly towards the opened door, then stopped. She was frowning. 'Can they come through from the warehouse into the office block? I mean, after close of business.'

'They can if they've got a key. And before I activate the alarm systems at that end of the building. Not after that. No. Why?' He smiled at her as he held the door.

'Oh, nothing. But someone coming to the offices from the warehouse would come from the other end of the executive corridor, wouldn't they?' The man nodded. 'They'd have to walk past the boardroom. They couldn't come from this end of the building. Could they?'

'Well, they could. But it would be much better to go up the stairs in the warehouse to the gallery and along the directors' corridor. Coming this way is the long way round.'

Eleanor recalled the exposed glass gallery in the warehouse. She was willing to bet that the long way round was the unobtrusive way round.

'Why do you ask?' said the man.

She smiled at him wanly. 'Oh, no reason. I'm just trying to get my bearings. That's all.' The guard nodded. Eleanor moved past him into the gloom. 'Well, thanks very much,' she said. 'Goodnight.'

'Goodnight, miss.'

Although it wasn't quite dark, the lights in the car park were switched on. It was raining steadily. Eleanor hurried to the car, eased herself behind the wheel and made it back to her flat in fifteen minutes. The first thing she did was fix herself a very large vodka.

By eight forty-five the following morning she was back at Drumanon's offices and by ten she had finished the rest of the job. She drove to her office. Philip Passmore was out meeting a client. Eleanor arranged with Wendy to see him after lunch.

'I need to ask you a few questions about Drumanon,' she told him as she seated herself in the chair on the opposite side of his desk. 'Technical stuff mainly. A few minor queries about the stock control systems in their warehouse. It's stuff I've come across in the last day or so.'

'Ask away,' Passmore said. He seemed in a better humour.

He dealt with her queries quickly. She wasn't surprised. She had thought it judicious to involve Passmore; to let him feel that he was still involved; still in ultimate control. All the questions, all the problems she was raising were ones which she could have easily solved herself.

All except one.

'And finally,' she said after about an hour, 'there's the arrangement with Van Dameer.'

'What about it?' Passmore's voice was serious.

'Well, I understand how it works. I've come across a number of similar deals before. What I don't understand is why. I don't understand the rationale behind it. It's unnecessary and it looks to me as if Drumanon are losing out on the deal.'

Passmore frowned. 'You think so?' He looked at her thoughtfully. 'I think maybe I should arrange for you to talk to Dan Lassiter about that. He set the contract up. He knows it best. I'll arrange for you to meet with Dan.'

Eleanor couldn't see why she shouldn't fix a meet with Lassiter herself but she said nothing. Better to let Passmore set it up, she thought. Now that she was easing her way into the exclusion zone she had to be careful not to look as if she was trying to break up the brotherhood. 'Fine,' she said.

She didn't hear anything from Passmore for a couple of

days. In the meantime she sent Lindsey and a couple of clerks over to Drumanon's to get on with more number crunching whilst she attended to the work piling up from other clients.

Passmore caught her as she was on her way to lunch.

'We've been invited out to dinner,' he told her with a grin. He appeared to have recovered from his viral infection; his mood and manner were back to normal.

She smiled at him. 'Really? Who by?'

'Dan Lassiter. Drumanon has had a record first quarter and they want to take us out to celebrate. Friday night at Lavenham Manor. Should be a good night. Lavenham Manor is a very posh, elegant restaurant in an old Jacobean house in the middle of the New Forest. They'll send a car to pick you up at your flat. Seven thirty. Oh, yes,' he added as he turned to go, 'Dan asked me to tell you that he'll explain that contract over dinner.'

'Philip,' she called to him as he walked towards his office, 'how sophisticated *is* this place?'

She decided to wear a little black evening dress that had cost her an arm and two legs in a boutique in Knightsbridge. She hoped it would be appropriate. It was low-cut and had a handkerchief hem at the knee. Eleanor had a good body and good legs and the dress showed both off to advantage. She wore a simple gold chain, no earrings, bright lipstick and a little eye makeup.

She was relieved to discover that she had been wise in her choice of what to wear. Lavenham Manor was dripping with provincial ritz. The bar was dark, with old oak panelling and hunting scenes in oils hanging below picture lights. The restaurant had three stars and was full of pink tablecloths, fresh flowers and subtle, diffused lighting. Muted strains of Vivaldi wafted from hidden speakers.

There were seven of them: Philip Passmore and his wife, Dan Lassiter and his wife, a thin woman with grey hair and a smoky, Canadian voice, Richard Jamieson and, a surprise to Eleanor, James Hagerty. She wouldn't have thought that the evening was his kind of scene. In fact Hagerty turned out to be relaxed and amiable and although he talked less than the others, his hunting, fishing and shooting stories over drinks in the bar were amusing.

Eleanor found herself seated next to Jamieson who was wearing an expensive, buttermilk-coloured mohair jacket, dark slacks, a blue shirt and a paisley tie. She thought he looked gorgeous and for the first time in what she realized with a start was a long time, she felt something inside her stir. The shock must have shown on her face.

'Are you all right?' Jamieson leaned toward her, a touch of concern in his voice.

'Yes, yes I'm fine.'

He grinned his appealing, boyish grin. 'It takes a bit of getting used to, doesn't it? We're all so different outside the office. I think it's really important for people who work together to get to know each other, to discover each other's interests. Don't you?'

Eleanor remembered Raymond. 'Well, maybe. I suppose so.'

He didn't notice her guarded response. 'So, what are yours?' he asked, broadening the grin.

She laughed. 'Oh, nothing very dramatic. Tennis, theatre, good books, good music, working out, that kind of thing. Nothing spectacular like rock climbing or anything like that.' She nodded across the table in the direction of James Hagerty. Jamieson laughed.

'Do you like sailing?'

She thought back to her student days and grinned broadly.

'Yes, I like sailing. Though I haven't done very much.'

'Plenty of opportunity to put that right in this part of the world. And music, you like good music. You know there's a fine symphony orchestra in Bournemouth?' She nodded. 'Have you been to hear it yet?'

'No.'

'I go quite often. Perhaps next time you might like to come with me.' His hazel eyes were warm and intense. The thing inside her fluttered for a moment.

'I'd like that a lot,' she said quietly.

They were a surprisingly noisy table. The wines were superb and Eleanor's glass was replenished constantly. The food was delicious. Over the *bombe au chocolat* she looked across the table at Dan Lassiter. 'Dan, you were going to explain the Van Dameer contract to me.'

'Sure. What don't you understand?' She thought about it for a moment, trying to remember. 'You think it's too complicated?' Lassiter went on with his hard smile.

'No, not at all. I've come across similar deals before. You have the sole European distribution rights from Campanalla SA for their kitchens, conservatories and air-conditioning equipment. As Van Dameer has agents selling throughout Europe, you have granted the company sub-distribution rights for the whole of the EC.'

Eleanor noticed that everyone at the table had stopped talking and was listening to her.

'The agents in this country,' she continued, 'remit a large percentage of the monies they receive from the sale of the Campanalla products direct to Drumanon's bank account. That money is payment against the amount owed by Van Dameer to Drumanon for the supply of the products in the first place.'

Lassiter bobbed his head to acknowledge her succinct

description. 'You got it. That's it. In a nutshell. So, what's your problem, Eleanor? You gotta admit it makes your life as Drumanon's auditor simple.' Again he flashed her his superficial smile. 'Only a few suppliers' invoices from Campanalla to tie up with our sales invoices. Hell, we've made it easy for you. Which is why I don't understand,' he looked across the table at Passmore, 'how come Phil hits us with such big audit fees.' Everyone laughed.

Eleanor couldn't see Passmore's face but she guessed that although he had laughed with the others he wouldn't be too pleased by Lassiter's last remark. Friends or not, Lassiter was making the point that he paid the piper. Eleanor was beginning to wish she hadn't raised the subject; she was in danger of embarrassing Philip. And, come to that, James Hagerty. She glanced across the table at him. Hagerty was watching her intently.

She shrugged. 'The thing I don't understand is why you have the contract. Three-quarters of your turnover comes from the Campanalla deal and it seems to me that you could more than double your profits if you undertook sales and distribution of the products yourselves.'

Lassiter was lighting a large cigar. He took his time, then shook his head slowly. 'No, we don't want to get too involved in that side of the business, Eleanor. It's not our thing. Van Dameer have a good distribution set-up. We feel more comfortable letting them handle that side of things.'

She couldn't let it go. 'Yes, but they must get millions every year from you for doing it. Most of that could be yours. As profit.'

'Sure. They take about seven mill a year off the top,' Lassiter said affably, 'but they sure as hell earn it. We, on the other hand, make five million gross profit just through moving a few pieces of paper.' He got an even bigger laugh for that one.

Eleanor smiled and relaxed back into her seat. Lassiter had headed her off at the pass. Probably, she thought, he didn't think it was any part of an auditor's job to question corporate strategy. He had made it clear that he wasn't prepared to talk to her about the Van Dameer contract. Had made it plain by making her look silly.

Not that she felt too bad about that. She knew she had pushed it; knew Lassiter was not the kind of man who liked having his commercial decisions questioned. Especially not in public.

Anyway, what the hell. She was feeling good. Better than she'd felt in ages. And she knew she was looking good from the expression in Richard Jamieson's eyes. He was asking her about her family.

'How's the audit doing, Eleanor?' Lassiter's voice from the other side of the table cut across Jamieson's. She noticed his tones were honeyed . . . conciliatory. He didn't want her to feel upset by the put-down.

She smiled at him. 'It's going well. We've had three of our people working on the figures over at your place for the last couple of days.'

'I saw them. Doing the grunt work eh?'

'Eleanor says that she's caught up,' Passmore announced. 'Won't be long before it's completed.'

'Good.'

'I hear you were working late yourself a couple of days ago,' Jamieson said warmly.

She turned and smiled at him. 'Who told you that? Your secretary?'

He shook his head. 'One of our security guards reported it. They have to make a report on anything out of the ordinary.

He was a bit concerned. He thought that he'd given you a fright.'

She nodded. 'He did. But he wasn't the only one.'

Jamieson frowned. 'What do you mean?'

'One of your fellows from the warehouse frightened me half to death.'

Jamieson's frown deepened. She saw him glance across at Lassiter. She looked around. Lassiter, waving away his cigar smoke, had obviously overheard the conversation. He too was frowning. 'One of the guys from the depot?' his voice was troubled. 'What time was that?'

'About nine.'

'What was he doing there?' Jamieson asked.

'They were working overtime in the warehouse and he said he was dropping some papers off in Dan's office. In an envelope. I walked out of the boardroom and smacked right into him. The corridor was dark and –' she let out a short bubbling laugh '– I thought I was going to have a coronary.'

She caught Jamieson's look of confusion. He was staring at Lassiter. She glanced across the table and then back at Jamieson. She wondered if she should mention that the man had been eyeing her in the factory and had taken her car number, but decided against it. The story would make her sound feeble. And anyway, she had handled it.

She turned and looked at Lassiter. His face was showing serious concern. For a moment she thought to add that she'd checked his office and seen no sign of any envelope. She thought better of that too. A chief executive who didn't like having his contracts questioned wouldn't like having his office inspected either.

Lassiter's next words puzzled her. His face cleared and he said, 'That's right. I'd forgotten. I get a bunch of reports from the depot when they're working overtime. I had a whole slew of them that night.'

Eleanor wondered where the hell the man could have put a whole slew of reports. She hadn't seen any sign of them.

'Which one of the guys was it, Eleanor?' The concern had left his voice.

She described the man who had frightened her. It was a good description; she had cause to remember him. 'I'm sure he said that his name was John,' she added.

Lassiter nodded vaguely. He seemed almost indifferent now. Passmore's wife leaned across the table to say something and he turned to her. He had lost interest.

Eleanor stared at him, still trying to figure out where the man could have left an envelope full of reports. After a moment she gave up; it wasn't her problem. She took a sip of wine and turned to Jamieson.

Unlike his boss, Jamieson's face remained clouded in confusion. He was staring at Lassiter with mystified eyes.

She glanced across the table at James Hagerty. He was still gazing at her in an intent, slightly absorbed manner, as if she was one of his foxhounds whose behaviour wasn't quite right. She caught his eye. His leathery face broke into a guarded smile.

They left the table at eleven and retired to the manor's chintzy lounge for coffee and liqueurs. The cars collected them at twelve.

'I'll call you,' Jamieson told her as he saw her into the car. 'I'll get some tickets for the next concert. If you like, we'll have dinner afterwards.'

She told him she'd like that a lot. Leaning back in her seat, with the dark trees whooshing past and the smell of summer mixing with a faint whiff of the sea through the open driver's window, Eleanor decided it was the best night she'd had for longer than she could remember.

She had to wait almost a week for Jamieson's call. She'd begun to think he'd forgotten, when one evening, soon after she arrived back at the flat, the phone in the lounge warbled.

He was apologetic. He hadn't called earlier as he'd been away on business. She knew that. She had been at Drumanon's offices twice since the dinner party and each time she had been disappointed to find that Jamieson wasn't there.

He had got tickets for a concert on Saturday. It was a good programme, he told her; Mozart, Brahms, Scarlatti, and afterwards he knew a little place where they could have dinner. He knew it was short notice but was she free?

She was, but she put him on hold and made a pretence of checking her diary. Yes, she was free, she told him. She gave him her address.

He said he'd pick her up at seven.

She put the phone down, kicked off her shoes, put her feet up on the sofa, leaned back and smiled. The feeling deep down in her belly was warm and bubbling.

She picked up the late edition of the *Evening Echo* she had pulled from the letterbox and thrown onto the couch when she'd arrived home. Casually she turned the pages.

It was a small item on page five.

She would have missed it, except something about the picture caught her eye. It was a full-face shot of a man. A young man. There was something familiar about him. She looked closer. Although the image was sharp, the man's face was rigid and slightly unnatural. She stared at it.

Then it hit her. The last time she had seen that face it had been inches from hers in a darkened corridor of Drumanon's offices. It was the man from the warehouse.

Eleanor stared in shock.

Below the photograph a few words of print said the picture was of an unknown man found drowned in Poole harbour.

Chapter Nine

Lionel didn't see him until it was too late.

The man's clothes – his grey anorak, crumpled dark trousers, even his bleached face – blended into the dull, urban concrete perfectly; consummate camouflage in the drab landscape of the street. He emerged as if out of the pavement and seized Lionel's arm like a striking snake, crashing him into a doorway between a dry cleaners and a betting shop.

'Whoa, hey what the fuck—'

Lionel had been dealing all morning and was carrying over £1600. His first thought was that he was being turned over by undercover fuzz, then, that it was a mugging. Neither notion stayed with him any longer than it takes for lightning to vanish. He looked down at his assailant and his blood froze. Donnie Boyle. This was far worse than any mugging or shake down; this was his worst nightmare come true.

'I want youse, blackie.'

The little man from Barrhead stared up at him, his dirty yellow eyes glinting with ethnic enmity. Lionel felt sick. He looked for his girlfriend who had been following him on the other side of the street. She had taken off like a rabbit at the sight of a gun.

Lionel tried to shake his arm free. 'Hey, whaddaya want?

Leggo. What the fuck you want?'

'Hudya still ye black bastard.' The little man's grip was like a metal clamp on Lionel's arm. 'Hud still or I'll gie ye a kicking.'

Lionel looked down. The bleak grey light of morning glinted on the sharpened steel edging the toecaps of the man's boots. Despite the fact that he was seven inches taller and at least thirty pounds heavier than his assailant, Lionel abandoned all thoughts of resistance. He held still.

'You know a dealer called Jimmy Pierce?' Boyle kept his grip on Lionel's purple shellsuited arm.

Lionel nodded. 'Yeah, I know him.'

'Take me to him.'

'Why? What do you want with him?'

Boyle moved his right leg back, lifting his heel off the concrete of the doorway. 'Don't you question me, blackie,' he hissed. 'What I want with Pierce is my business. Understand? You just take me to him.'

'What? You mean now?'

'Aye, now. Whaddaya think I mean, ya shitheid coon, next New Year?'

For a moment Lionel's face hardened. The guy was a little piece of white shit. Racist, Scottish shit. He tried to keep his voice neutral. 'I don't know, mahn,' he said, 'Fats may not like it. I mean, I gotta check with Fats first.'

Donnie Boyle's grip tightened. 'Fats isn't fucking here, is he? So ye canna check. And anyways, what's it got to do with him? I work for the Profit. Not for that lump of black crap. I need to talk to this bastard Pierce and I need to do it now. Fats knows why.'

Lionel looked down into a pair of demented eyes. They were vibrating with hate. He shrugged, doing his best to keep the fear and loathing off his face. 'Okay.'

They stepped out of the doorway together and the little man let go of Lionel's arm. For a moment Lionel had ideas of getting up onto his Sebastians and doing a Linford. He could have left the little runt standing. But though Boyle would have had no chance of catching him, Lionel also abandoned all thoughts of running.

Lionel could run but he couldn't hide. Maybe Boyle wouldn't catch him today, but he would catch *up* with him tomorrow. Or the next day. Or sometime. And then, what he would do to Lionel . . . Forget it.

He reached the Quattro and buttoned the control. The doors unlocked. He slid in behind the wheel and Boyle got in beside him. Almost immediately Lionel noticed the smell. Body odour. The little Scotsman was reeky. Lionel was particular about his personal freshness. He spent a lot of money on expensive colognes. He wrinkled his nose. Boyle lit a cigarette.

'Hey, mahn, I don't like people smokin' in my car.'

Boyle gave him a sour, malevolent look. 'Drive the fucking motor and shut your mouth,' he ordered.

In a perverse way Lionel was glad of the cigarette. It helped mask the rank aroma of dirty clothes and unwashed flesh. The journey to Pierce's flat took less than ten minutes. Despite his protests, Boyle made Lionel drive right into the estate and close to Pierce's block. He parked the car on a strip of cracked concrete a little way off from a row of shabby lock-ups.

'Hey,' he wailed as they got out of the car, 'if I leave the car in this place, even for five minutes, they're gonna be coming like rats outa their holes to trash it. They're gonna wreck my machine.'

Boyle hawked at the back of his throat and spat a gob of phlegm onto the Quattro's nearside rear wheel. He shrugged. 'Who cares about the fucking car.'

Lionel agonizingly eyed the glob of glistening mucus drooping off the alloy spokes. 'Sheeet, mahn,' he cried, 'don't do that to my 'chine.'

He looked back at the car as he led the way towards the concrete staircase. The bright red Quattro sat in the middle of the urban desolation as obvious and enticing as a hard red nipple on a naked breast. He went up the stairs at a run, pausing on the fourth-storey walkway to look down at the car. Boyle pushed him in the back. 'Forget the bloody car. Get on with it.'

They reached Pierce's doorway and Lionel banged on the door. Immediately the dogs started up.

'Dugs,' Boyle exclaimed. 'No one said anything about fucking dugs.'

It was Lionel's turn to shrug insouciantly. 'Whaddya expect, gerbils?'

Boyle pierced him with a poisonous glare. 'What are they? Pits?' Lionel nodded. 'Fuck.' Boyle said it with feeling. He was silent for a moment, then, 'What's he do with 'em when you come here? Does he lock them up?'

'Sure. That's 'cos he knows me. He needs to score off me. But he won't lock 'em up when he sees you.' Lionel waited a while then banged on the door again.

'Is the bastard in?'

Lionel listened to the mad racket inside the flat, shrugged again and made a face. 'Two dogs. That oughta mean he's home.'

In fact Lionel had begun to wonder if Pierce *was* home. He wasn't sure, but there seemed to be something different about the dogs. Every time he had knocked on Pierce's door before, the ferocious, barking dogs had sprinted down the hall and hurled themselves high against the door's timber bracing, avid to get at him, desperate to rip the intruder to pieces. This time he could hear the pads of their paws as they ran down the bare hallway and *then back again*. He'd never known them do that before. And there was something different about their barking. To his untutored ear it seemed more manic than usual. As if the dogs were going beserk. Maybe Pierce *had* left them on their own.

He pounded on the door, pleased to see that Boyle was looking decidedly unhappy. 'If he's there, he ain't answering.' He said it with relish.

The little Scotsman turned his back and kicked the door savagely with the heel of his boot. He glanced at Lionel sharply. 'Shit. Is this reinforced?' Lionel nodded. Boyle's pasty face looked even more sick. He turned and stared at the door, surveying the series of locks and listening to the demented baying beyond. He made a decision. 'Right. Come on.'

He led Lionel down the stairs and around the back of the flats. There was a narrow strip of wasteland between the long prison-like block and the railway line. Boyle picked his way along it, followed by a cautious Lionel, conscious of the easily torn fabric of his shellsuit. The ground was a garbage tip. Scattered about in the waist-high grass were skeletons of abandoned prams, forsaken refrigerators and large, rusted chunks of metal which might once have been bits of cars. Dog turds, bottles and rusty cans were everywhere, along with a fair number of used condoms and hypos with broken needles. Lionel trod carefully, just managing to miss stepping on what the rats had left of a dead cat.

Lionel was a city boy who liked the feel of pavement beneath his feet. He hated the countryside. 'Jeeesus, mahn, whadada fuck we doin' here?'

'Shut your black face.' Boyle stopped, turned and stared

up at the rows of little square windows set in the sullen concrete. Behind them, up on the embankment fifty feet away, a train clattered noisily past, heading towards London Bridge. 'Which is Pierce's place?' Boyle demanded.

Lionel took a moment to work out how many flats he passed to get to Pierce's front door. He pointed up to the fourth storey. 'There. Those three windows.'

Boyle frowned. 'That window there, on the left, the one with the frosted glass, that'll be the bathroom then?'

'Yeah, that's right.'

Boyle stared a moment longer. 'Aye, that'll do,' he muttered. 'Come on.' He led the way back through the sour grass and rusted detritus to the car. 'Get in,' he ordered.

He made Lionel drive to Lewisham where they went shopping. 'You got money?' Boyle held out a hand.

'Hey, mahn, it ain't my bees. It belongs to Fats.'

'Gimme.'

With a pained face Lionel handed over a hundred pounds.

At the first hardware store Boyle bought a fifteen-inch, heavy-duty screwdriver before going in search of his next purchase. He found what he was looking for in a shop in a sidestreet and emerged carrying a fat, seventeen-inch, bright green BCF-Halon cylinder. He placed it on the floor of the car between his feet.

Lionel eyed it. 'What's that for?'

'For to fix the fucking dugs.'

'You reckon a fire extinguisher's gonna stop those pits?'

'No problem.'

Lionel gazed speculatively at the Halon cylinder. 'That's not the right one. You want the other one. The black one. Black's best.'

Boyle looked at him sharply, his eyes narrowed. 'You trying to be funny?' Lionel said nothing. Boyle turned his gaze back to the green cylinder. 'This is the one I want. I can carry this one on my back.' Lionel had no idea what he meant. 'Anyways, a fire extinguisher is a fire extinguisher. It's what the polis use to sort out dugs.'

'Not any more. The feds use those high-pitched, ultrasonic whistles. With one of them, either the dogs take off or they start whimpering and shit themselves.'

'Oh aye, and where do youse think I'm gonna find one of those around here?' Boyle shook his head. 'Niggers. Always trying to get clever.' He patted the cylinder. 'These things are noisy when they go off. They frighten dugs. And if I get the little bastards in the face, like as not they'll suffocate. Whatever. I'll push 'em into a room and shut the door. Then, Jimmy Pierce and me will have a wee chat. And if I have trouble from him, he can have a blast of Halon too.'

A rictus leer which might have been a smile passed across Boyle's face. His mouth looked like a chainsaw. His teeth were broken and stained brown by decay and nicotine. Lionel shivered and felt something inside which was rare enough to be noticeable. Pity. All of a sudden he felt sorry for Jimmy Pierce.

Lionel started the car as Boyle lit a cigarette. The vee-sign fingers of his right hand were the colour of yellow ochre.

'You won't get no trouble from Jimmy Pierce,' Lionel said quietly.

'No? Well, he isna answering his fucking door, is he? That's trouble enough.'

'Maybe he's not there.'

Boyle looked at him suspiciously. 'Maybe not,' he said cautiously, 'so in that case we'll get in there first and wait for him to come back.'

'We,' Lionel yelped, 'whaddaya mean *we*? I ain't going up against no pit bulls.'

Boyle cackled. 'Dinna worry. I'll handle the dugs. You'd be no use. Blacks havna any bottle. Everyone knows that.' He paused. 'I think the bastard's there, only he's not answering. There's two pits in the place and that means he's more'n likely home. Hiding behind the dugs. Big mistake.' He touched the Halon cylinder with his foot.

On the drive over, Lionel had been puzzling over why Pierce hadn't answered his door. Or at least appeared at the window. It could be he wasn't there but he thought that unlikely. So, if he *was* inside, why hadn't he shown himself?

There was one explanation. Maybe Pierce had taken the big fix. Jacked his final spike. A number of Lionel's customers did that. Pierce odeed would explain the strange behaviour of the dogs. If Jimmy Pierce was still inside the flat maybe he was beyond anything the crazy Scotsman could do to him.

Not, Lionel concluded, that he was going to tell Boyle his suspicions. Let the white-arsed bastard find out for himself.

They arrived at the estate. Boyle told Lionel to bring the Quattro's tyre lever.

'What for?'

'Just do it. And stop asking fucking questions.'

Back on the fourth-floor walkway, Lionel, who was carrying the fire extinguisher, shot a worried look down at his car. 'Forget the car for Christ's sake,' Boyle rapped from behind. 'I haven't got all bloody day.'

Lionel stopped at Pierce's door but before he could knock Boyle walked past him and began banging insanely on the door of the next flat. The noise set the dogs off again.

'Whaddaya doing?'

Boyle ignored him.

The door of the flat was opened by an old, stooped man wearing carpet slippers. He had a dark brown, leathery face.

Boyle pushed the old man hard in the chest and sent him staggering backwards into the hallway. 'Inside, you Paki piece of shit.' He followed the old man into the flat.

Lionel, standing in the doorway, was alarmed. 'Hey mahn, what the fuck you doing?'

'Get inside here and shut the door,' Boyle ordered over his shoulder.

Again Lionel felt the urge to run; to leave Boyle to do whatever he meant to do alone. He thought better of it. No matter what, Boyle would remember. And find him.

Sweat was beading Lionel's forehead and his throat was dry. He felt himself shaking. It wasn't as if he was unused to violence. In Lionel's line of work violence was a part of the job and in his time he had slashed a few faces, cracked a few skulls and broken a few arms. He'd even used a sawn-off once.

But, Lionel reasoned as he stepped quickly into the hall and shut the door, all his violence had been in the course of business. It had been *necessary*. What was happening here was different. Boyle was a madman who lusted after blood. A crazy Scottish bastard who loved violence for its own sake and who was now about to vent his demented ferocity on some poor old shrivel-dick Paki.

And Lionel was stuck with him; an unwilling accomplice in an obscure and insane enterprise.

Boyle turned the old man around and, gripping his arm, crashed open the doors of the flat, checking who else was at home. In the living room was a woman in a sari. Clinging to her as tightly as they could were two young, whimpering children. The woman was paralysed by shock, her fearful eyes dark and rounded like railway tunnels.

'Is this everyone, all the people in the place?' Boyle glared at the old man insanely. The old man nodded. Boyle turned to Lionel. 'Money. Gimme money.'

'What? More?'

'Shut your mouth and gimme.'

Lionel pulled out a wad which Boyle snatched off him. He peeled off fifty pounds and thrust them at the old man. 'Fifty punds now,' he snarled, 'and the same later on if you don't make trouble and do as youse're told. If not, I'll slice the bairns. So help me if I don't.'

From nowhere a long bayonet appeared in his hand. The old man jerked back and the woman let out a squeak of terror. Boyle moved towards the woman and her children.

'Jesus, mahn, whaddaya doing?'

Boyle walked past the shuddering woman and her clutching children to the telephone. He picked it up and with a flick of his wrist cut the connection. 'Okay,' he announced, 'bring them.'

'What?'

Boyle hurled himself across the room in a sudden, frenzied rush and jabbed the point of the bayonet up under Lionel's chin. Lionel yelped and kept very still. He could feel the steel tip pricking his flesh, drawing blood.

'If you say "what" again,' Boyle hissed, 'I'm gonna slice off one of your ears. That way you'll have a fucking excuse for not hearing me. Gettit?'

Lionel, his eyes wide, nodded. A thin sliver of blood was trickling down the blade of the bayonet.

'Now, bring them.' He indicated the old man, the woman and the children with a flick of his head. 'I want them where I can see them. I dinna want them running to the law while I'm getting in next door.'

Boyle led the way, followed by a frightened Lionel carrying the fire extinguisher in one hand and holding a handkerchief to the bloody puncture beneath his chin with the other. He shepherded the family in front of him, noticing that the dogs next door had quietened down.

Boyle walked into the bathroom which, Lionel realized, was the closest room to Jimmy Pierce's flat. The two bathrooms were adjoining, separated only by a thin wall.

The bathroom was clean, neat and decorated in pink and blue. It was small; with six of them in it there was scarcely room to move. The children were quietly keening. Boyle opened the window. It opened out and upwards. He stood on the toilet seat, leaned out and examined the space between him and the window of Jimmy Pierce's bathroom. 'Aye, that'll do.' He said it to himself.

He pushed the window up as far as it would go and examined the size of space it made. He smiled, the same evil, infected, broken-tooth smile. 'I can get through that, no problem.'

He clambered down from the toilet seat, turned to Lionel and nodded at the window. 'Jimmy that off.'

Lionel didn't know what he meant but he was too scared to ask. He stared at Boyle.

'Fur Christ's sake; the tyre lever,' Boyle snarled. 'Jimmy the window off the frame.' He slipped his bayonet into some kind of scabbard inside the sleeve of his anorak and the tension in the bathroom eased.

Lionel was baffled. He squeezed past Boyle and inserted the tyre lever between the wooden windowframe and the window's hinges. He heaved. The wood splintered at his second effort and the window parted from one of the hinges with a loud crack. The window hung drunkenly at a shallow angle. The old man began protesting; first in Punjabi, then broken English.

'Shut yer mouth,' Boyle told him, 'youse are getting paid.'

Lionel moved to the other side of the window, jammed the

lever into the gap and yanked hard. Without warning the window snapped away from the frame, dropped four storeys and smashed loudly onto the narrow strip of concrete at the foot of the block.

The old man complained louder. Boyle glowered at him and made a move towards his left sleeve. The man shut up.

Boyle climbed back onto the lavatory seat and peered through the windowless gap as Lionel leaned back against the bathroom wall, dabbing at the cut beneath his chin. Speckled lines of blood ran across the cheap blue enamel of the lavatory seat and wash basin. Lionel was grateful for the cool June breeze which, four storeys up, was now blowing through the small room. The place had been hot and reeking with the smell of fear.

Boyle turned back from the window and looked down at the others, his eyes searching. He saw what he wanted. 'Get me the old man's belt,' he commanded.

The old man understood sufficient English to get the drift. He made to protest but looking up at Boyle thought better of it. Muttering under his breath, he pulled his belt from around his waist.

'Loop it onto the extinguisher.'

Lionel looped the belt through what looked like a trigger guard, set beneath the nozzle at the top of the cylinder, and buckled it at the furthest notch of the belt. He noticed that what might have been the trigger guard had no trigger. The extinguisher was operated by holding the handle at the top of the cylinder, and exerting pressure with the heel of the hand on a black lever set below the nozzle. Above the black lever was a red safety catch which, when down, prevented pressure on the lever. When the safety was flicked up, the extinguisher was ready to fire.

Lionel handed Boyle the Halon cylinder and watched him

snake his head and an arm through the loop of the belt. Now the belt was like a sash, and – Lionel shook his head in wonder – the green cylinder hanging heavily at Boyle's hip . . . like a weapon. Only Boyle could have done that, he thought. Take a common, everyday object and make it exactly into what he intended it to be – a piece of artillery. Boyle pulled the screwdriver with the long stainless-steel shaft out from beneath his anorak. He looked down at Lionel.

'You wait outside Pierce's door,' he ordered. 'If the bastard hears me getting in and tries to run for it, stop him. You'd bloody better not let him go. You hear?' He jabbed the screwdriver towards Lionel like a sword. Lionel nodded. 'And don't let any of this lot out of the flat. I don't want them running to the polis. Tell the old bastard I'll give him the other fifty when I've sorted Pierce. That'll keep him happy. Gottit?'

'Yeah, I gottit.'

Boyle grunted and turned back towards the window. Lionel watched in amazement as the little runty Scot clambered over the windowledge.

The dude was completely off his trolley. They were fifty feet up in the air with over six feet of blank concrete wall between them and Pierce's bathroom window. Who the fuck did Boyle think he was? The Flying Scotsman? Spidermac?

Boyle was now out of the window and hanging onto the frame on its left side. Lionel moved closer and peered out. Then he saw it. Running along the wall between the two flats was a narrow sill, scarcely more than a crinkle on the face of the concrete. It was three, maybe four inches wide. Leaning further out, he saw similar ledges stretching the entire length of the block, all set at about the level of the interior floors; some architectural device necessary to the erection of the flats. Boyle must have seen them when they'd surveyed the rear of the block.

But even so. Three or four inches, for Christ's sake. The stupid Scots bastard was insane. Lionel stared at the grey, grubby figure spreadeagled against the grey, grubby concrete and was mesmerized.

Boyle was edging along the ledge with his right arm outstretched, inching the long, steel shaft of the screwdriver towards Pierce's bathroom window. *Closed* bathroom window.

Lionel noticed Boyle's feet on the ledge were turned out at 180 degrees. *Jesus.* The guy was fifty feet up in the air, hanging onto a windowframe by his fingertips, balancing on a four-inch ledge, with an eight-pound cylinder swinging against his hip and *he was worried about blunting the blades in his boots against the concrete*.

Lionel frowned. It was difficult to believe what he was seeing. The guy was a one-man assault battalion, a single, killer blitzkrieg, seething with rage and aggression. He was a churning psychopath: without sentiment or concern. The man was completely fearless.

It wasn't something to admire. Even Lionel knew that. Boyle was an animal. An alien, a non-human; so bereft of normal mortal emotion, so lacking in compassion, sensitivity and imagination, so mad in his desperation to attack the dogs and inflict pain on Jimmy Pierce, that he would take any personal risk. Any goddam, lunatic, life-threatening risk.

Boyle didn't have fear because he didn't have feeling. Only a lust for blood. He shared with the bayonet sheathed along his left forearm a common purpose in life. And the same range of human emotions. He was nasty, brutish and short. Like the pit bulls on which he was about to make war.

Lionel wasn't witnessing bravery, he was watching madness.

He found himself staring at the hand clutching the wooden frame at the side of the window. It was grimy, its nails bitten down to the quick, their jagged edges thick with ingrained dirt. He was fascinated, fixated by the flexed fingers holding on for dear life. All he had to do was reach out and pull the hand away from the windowframe. It would be that simple. One quick tug and he could rid the world of Donnie Boyle, the source of his fear and humiliation. Revenge himself on the motherfucking piece of whitey shit.

A fifty-foot fall, he figured, would almost certainly kill the bastard. Either that or Boyle would break his back, falling on top of the fire extinguisher or onto one of the pieces of rusty metal on the waste land. That, Lionel thought, would be fitting. Just another piece of crap in a wilderness of garbage.

He gazed at the hand, imagining Boyle's last agonized moments impaled on one of the rusted car parts. Suddenly he sensed he was being watched. He looked up. Boyle's mad yellow eyes were riveted on him, gazing silent and unblinking at his face, lasering into his brain.

Jesus Christ, *Boyle knew*. He knew what Lionel was thinking. The madman could read his mind. Boyle was staring him down, daring him to try it, daring him to make a grab for his hand. Lionel stared into the mad eyes . . . and saw the soul of Satan.

He looked away in dread and slowly, as if retreating before an imperial presence, moved back. Back from the hand gripping the windowframe. He flickered a final glance at Boyle. The monster in a man's shape still stared at him. Their eyes locked once more, and then, as Lionel dropped his gaze, Boyle turned his face, slowly and carefully, towards the other window.

Lionel fell back into the room. He was shaking. He'd had Boyle's life in his hands, and without a word Boyle had prevented him doing anything about it. Boyle had won. Boyle was the devil and nobody could kill him. He was indestructible.

Slowly, Boyle edged towards Pierce's window. Behind and below a train rattled past. Boyle ignored it. He knew the few passengers who noticed him would do nothing. They wouldn't break their journey merely to tell the police they'd seen a man climbing into a window four storeys up. They wouldn't want to get involved. The train's passengers were no more a threat than that stupid coon who'd thought about pushing him off the ledge. Boyle had seen it in his eyes. Only the black bastard had bottled out. They all did that. It was like he said. None of them had any guts.

He was close enough now to ease the screwdriver between the outer and inner frames of the window. The dogs, somewhere inside the flat, heard him jemmying at the window and returned to their manic baying.

Boyle shoved the screwdriver further under the frame and levered outwards, exerting as much pressure as his precarious position allowed. It gave easily. The softwood frames had been cheap when the flats were built and hadn't been painted much since. He eased his body further along the wall and slid the shaft of the screwdriver under the wood until he felt its tip come up against the soft metal of the windowlock.

He was stretched to his fullest extent, the fingers of his left hand barely grasping the frame of the window from which he had climbed.

He jabbed at the windowlock as hard as he could. And jabbed again. And again. His right arm trembled with the exertion. His legs were shaking, his calf muscles unused to the maximum angle of his feet. The weight of the Halon extinguisher was pulling him away from the face of the wall. He couldn't hang on much longer. Any moment now he was going to drop off the ledge. He was going to fall.

He pressed his face against the wall, his breath rasping. The roughcast concrete scraped his cheek bloody. He jabbed once more and heard a click. The windowlock moved. Cautiously he eased his extended right arm outwards, away from the wall. The shaft of the screwdriver moved the window out and upwards. The window was open.

Now came the hardest part. His right hand was at least six inches from the ledge of Pierce's window. To get closer he needed to release the grip of his left hand. Yet at the same time he had to keep his right arm rigid and extended – to grip the screwdriver like a rapier and use it to hold Pierce's window open.

Without a hold by either hand, he was bound to fall.

He figured he had about a second after he let go with his left hand. A second to madly shuffle the few inches along the ledge and grab the frame of Pierce's window.

And if during that second his right arm wavered . . . if he lost his strength . . . or his nerve . . . or his hold on the screwdriver . . . if he couldn't hold the window back . . . couldn't stop it from closing on him . . . couldn't make the windowledge in time . . . then he would find himself scrabbling at a pane of frosted glass. With nowhere to go but down. A two-second plummet onto a strip of cracked, dirty concrete.

He reckoned the odds against making it were about three to one.

Boyle didn't think about it. He just did it. He let go with his left hand and crabbed madly to his right, sweeping his arm out from the wall, pushing the window back with the screwdriver. At the furthest extent of the sweep he let go of the screwdriver. He grabbed for the windowledge. Now it was a race. His hand or the window arcing down towards its closed position. Which?

His hand won.

His fingers clutched the wooden windowframe. An instant later the swinging window cracked the back of his hand. He swore foully but hung on. Dimly, above the noise of his rasping breath and the barking dogs, he heard the sound of the screwdriver hitting the concrete below. That could have been him. He didn't give it a second thought.

He pulled himself closer towards the window, pushed it up with his left hand and leaned inside. It was definitely his lucky day. The bathroom door was closed and the dogs were outside it. At least he wouldn't have to fire the extinguisher at them whilst hanging onto the windowledge. Boyle slipped the old man's leather belt over his head and carefully dropped the extinguisher inside the room. A few seconds later he was picking it up off the bathroom floor. He was inside the flat.

The dogs were hurling themselves against the door. Already one of its wafer-thin panels, the one closest to the top, was cracked. Boyle saw it wouldn't take long for them to break into the room. That, he calculated, would have been his best strategy; to let the dogs come to him. But he didn't have time. Pierce would have heard him breaking into the flat and would probably be doing a runner out of the front door right now. Boyle couldn't rely on the coon to stop the bastard escaping.

He flicked up the red safety catch on the Halon and moved to the door. He gripped the extinguisher firmly in his right hand, took a breath, and yanked open the door.

The crazed barking of the demented pit bulls was hammering against the walls of the hallway. The dogs, trapped in the flat with the corpse of their lord and master, had gone mad. At sight of Boyle they went berserk.

They leapt at him. The hard, solid body of one knocked the Halon cylinder up and sideways as Boyle hit the firing lever.

Sssssssssst. The gas ejected from the cylinder – and sprayed the ceiling. It was a soft, sibilant noise. Boyle scarcely heard it above the noise of the dogs.

For Christ's sake, the extinguisher wasn't supposed to be muffled like that. It was supposed to be noisy – noisy enough to frighten dogs.

The Halon was too quiet.

The other dog hit Boyle square in the chest, crashing him and the extinguisher back against the wall. Its fangs closed over Boyle's cheek. It hung for a moment then fell back, ripping a bloody crater from his nose to his jaw.

Boyle screamed. He kicked at the dog savagely and it squealed as the Stanley blades sliced into its neck. Boyle straightened up and aimed the cylinder nozzle at the dogs. He had to spray them on the floor. The Halon gas excluded all oxygen; in a confined space at low level, one burst and they would be suffocating. Desperately he clenched the firing lever.

Nothing.

He clenched it again, savagely jabbing the heel of his hand against the lever. Nothing. It was rigid, solid, unyielding. He looked down. The safety was on; the red safety catch was *down*. The knock against the wall had smacked it back into place.

The dogs, sensing Boyle was not holding an effective weapon, leapt at him together.

Boyle screamed again. It was no longer his lucky day.

Lionel stood in the hallway of the flat with his eyes wide

and his face rigid. The old man and the woman were further down the narrow passage, their faces, like his, immobilized by horror. The children clutching their mother looked to be in a catatonic trance. The ghastly, inhuman sounds coming through the wafer-like walls were beyond anything that any of them could comprehend. The sound of beasts killing each other. The baying, shrieking, snarling of animals in their death agonies. Lionel and the little family stared blindly at each other down a few feet of hallway, traumatized by the noise.

Lionel knew he had to get out, get away. Donnie Boyle wasn't going to survive the horrific nightmare next door. And even if he did, even if he came looking for Lionel . . . it didn't matter. He had to get out.

He jerked himself out of his paralysis. Dragging a wad of money from his pocket, he rushed down the passage towards the old man.

'Here, here.' He thrust the notes at the old man. 'You never saw me, okay? Forget about it. You don't know nothing. Right. You never saw me.' The old man didn't move. Lionel grabbed the man's hand, shoved the money into it and turned, making for the door.

The noises beyond the wall had changed. The snarling of dogs over raw meat remained but the half-human, high-pitched screeching had been replaced by a new noise. It was worse. It stopped Lionel in his tracks. It was the sound of a man trying to scream under water. An obscene, gurgling shriek.

'Oh Christ.' Lionel charged down the hallway, crashed open the front door and hurled himself along the walkway and down the concrete stairs.

A group of kids were gathered around the Quattro. They scattered like sparrows the moment they saw the tall, purple-shellsuited figure racing towards them. Lionel reached the car, pressed the control, yanked open the door and threw himself into the driving seat. Both his wing mirrors had been smashed and deep gouges ran the length of the Quattro's red paintwork, from the bonnet to the back bumper.

It didn't matter. None of it mattered.

All that mattered was to get away. As far away as possible from that monstrous, horrific sound. The sound of a man drowning . . . flooding in his own blood.

Chapter Ten

She sat in the car, thought about it for a while and guessed she was probably wasting her time. Yet running through her mind was a favourite expression of her father's: 'civic duty'.

Her father talked a lot about civic duty. He also talked a lot about responsibility, and citizenship, and all sorts of other stuff like that. In fact, her father talked a lot about most things. She smiled as she thought about him. He was a man with definite views. Most of them pretty old-fashioned. Still, she thought, his opinions were interesting. He wasn't boring about them, or pompous, and he was always ready to listen to her or her brother put the other side of the argument. And, she recalled fondly, he was always ready to give them plenty of help and advice. Though she'd noticed over her last few troubled years, he'd been careful to offer her counsel only when she asked for it. She was grateful to him for that.

She didn't doubt that if her father had known of her present dilemma he would have advised her to report the matter. Even though she was convinced it would be a waste of time. Even though someone else would probably have already contacted the police.

She had phoned Richard Jamieson the day after he'd called her. She had wanted to talk to him about it, but his secretary had said that he was away on business. He was in

Europe, somewhere en route between Holland and Switzerland. He wasn't due back until the weekend. Eleanor was surprised. She hadn't realized when he'd called that he had been phoning from outside the country. She'd asked to be put through to Dan Lassiter and had been told that he was on his way to Spain, to visit the company's suppliers. After that she had given up. She had decided to report it herself. Even though she figured it would be a waste of time.

She got out of the car. At least, she thought, it was Saturday morning and it was her own time she was wasting. It probably wouldn't take long. She hoped not; she had some important shopping to do. And, she concluded, once she had reported it, she could sleep easily, knowing that she had done the right thing. Her civic duty.

The police station was disappointing. In a town of some fine architecture it was ugly and utilitarian. Recently built of dull red brick and duller grey slate, it looked like a Norman keep.

One of the few advantages she had gained from her marriage to Alec had been that, as an architect, he had taught her to look at buildings. She recalled him telling her that police stations in earlier times had been built to impart authority to the community. Now, he'd said, they were built like fortresses, to be defended against an alienated and riotous populace. Alec, in his usual cynical way, had thought that was amusing. She had not. She had, she supposed, quite a lot of her father in her.

There was a sergeant at the counter. He looked younger than she was. She had got used to the policemen on the street looking young but *desk sergeants* for heaven's sake! Already she was beginning to wish she hadn't bothered coming into the station. Not if police sergeants were going to remind her that she was close to thirty.

'Yes, miss?' He gave her an appreciative smile. It wasn't every day he got such a classy good-looker coming to the desk.

Eleanor had the copy of the *Evening Echo* under her arm. She laid it on the desk, open at page five. 'I've come about the man found drowned in the harbour. It says here that he was unidentified. I think I know who he is.'

'You think, miss?' The sergeant's voice was pleasant but there was an edge to it.

'Well, no. It's more than think. I'm pretty certain, as a matter of fact. Though I expect you've already had people tell you about him.'

The sergeant shook his head. 'I don't know if we have or haven't. Nobody's told me if we have. Anyway,' he drew a pad across the counter and found a pen, 'perhaps you can start by telling me who you are.'

Eleanor quietly sighed. The problem with civic duty was that it was swamped in bureaucracy. There was no way that she could walk into the station, tell the police what little she knew and leave it at that. No. She had to give them her name, her address, her telephone number . . . She wondered why she was required to give her telephone number and eyed the young sergeant suspiciously for a moment. She had to tell them all her details before she could get started.

'Now, Miss Lambert, you know this man, you say.'

'Well, not exactly know him. I just know where you can find out about him.' The sergeant frowned. 'He works in the shipping depot of a company called Drumanon Consolidated, out towards Ferndown. I think his name is John. Anyway, if you contact the personnel people there, they should be able to give you details from his personnel file. Although I expect someone from the company has contacted you by now.'

197

'Do you work for this company, miss?'

'No. Well, not exactly. I'm the company auditor.' She watched the sergeant writing it out, slowly and deliberately. At school, Eleanor had learned to read upside down; she noticed that he misspelled auditor.

'Can you give me the address of this company?'

Earlier that morning she had copied Drumanon's details off one of their letterheads. She passed them to the sergeant. 'There. I'm sure that if they've not already done so, the personnel people at Drumanon will tell you all you need to know about him. Poor man. It must be awful for his family. I mean, not knowing what's happened.'

The sergeant nodded. 'Can you wait there please, Miss Lambert. I want to find out if anybody else has reported the identity of this man.'

He disappeared with the newspaper and the details he had taken down. He was gone for more than five minutes. A few people came into the station and were dealt with by a constable who looked scarcely sixteen. Eleanor sat down on a padded benchseat and waited. Her hope that reporting what little she knew about the drowned man wouldn't take much of her time had been ill-founded. She should have known better. Civic duty was never simple.

The sergeant finally returned. 'That's all right, Miss Lambert. We've had a couple of people phone and tell us who this man is. But my inspector wants me to say that we're very grateful to you for coming in and reporting it.' He gave her a broad, hope-to-see-you-again smile. 'Thanks a lot.'

She smiled back. It *had* been a waste of time. From the outset she'd been sure that either the man's friends, or someone at Drumanon, would have seen the paper and told the police about him. But at least she had done the right thing.

'You're welcome.' She said it brightly.

She turned and walked elegantly across the station lobby, conscious of the sergeant's gaze. At the door she realized that he hadn't returned her newspaper. She shrugged. What did it matter? She didn't need it any more. She wanted to forget about the man and his tragic death. Still, her father would have been pleased. She'd been a good citizen. She'd tried to help the police with their inquiries.

She heard the distinctive sound of the flat six at exactly seven o'clock. It was not a noise she greatly cared for. It brought back memories. Alec had once owned a Porsche. He had bought it as soon as he'd learnt he was on the short-list for a hospital extension in Bahrain. Eleanor had protested they couldn't afford it, but Alec had been so arrogantly confident he would be awarded the commission he'd ignored her. After the job had been awarded elsewhere he'd hung on to the 911 like a kid to its dummy. He'd kept it for months, even though the work was drying up. Which was more than Alec had been doing.

He'd written the Porsche off on a rainy night when he was almost three times over the limit. He had been lucky to escape with no more than a few cuts and bruises. Eleanor thought he had been even luckier to get away with only losing his licence for a year. The crash had been the beginning of the end. Alec's childish paranoia, his delusion that the world in general and Eleanor in particular was against him, had snowballed – along with his drinking.

Jamieson rang the bell and the thing inside, just below her navel, leapt. It was warm for early June and he was wearing a lightweight suit in pale lilac with a blue shirt and dark tie. Eleanor thought he looked great. She was hoping her own efforts in that direction might have the same effect on him. She had decided on a long dress in blue chenille. After a design by Ralph Lauren, its severity was moderated by its body-hugging cut, which allowed it to be both decorous and sexy. Her tailored crêpe jacket was in midnight blue.

'You look fantastic.' He sounded as if he meant it.

She fixed him a drink and he admired her flat. She had ditched most of the furniture from the London house, keeping only what would blend in with the flat and its decor. The result was an understated look of spare elegance; slightly Nordic, with polished floors and cream-coloured walls and vivid splashes of colour in the rugs and soft furnishings.

Her heels were higher than she was used to and she teetered slightly on the gravel drive as he accompanied her towards the car. The whale tail spoiler proclaimed it a top-of-the-range, 3.6 Turbo; £85,000 worth of motor car. Despite her unhappy memories of the marque, Eleanor was impressed. Richard Jamieson was doing well. Which meant that Drumanon Consolidated was doing well. She smiled quietly to herself. Of course she already knew that. Anyway, tonight was not a night to think about Drumanon. Tonight she wanted to think about Drumanon's director of finance.

Jamieson opened her passenger door. Another of the few advantages she had gained from her marriage was knowing how to get in and out of a Porsche 911 elegantly. Even when she was wearing a close-cut dress.

Jamieson drove the car well. He let it fishtail once as they accelerated out of the drive, but his crafty, adolescent grin told her it was a deliberate ploy. Just to let her know that, though the car was a raging beast, he had the measure of it. He was its master. She smiled at him. Boys! After that, he held the car as steady as a rock all the way to the centre of town. Eleanor remembered that the rear-engined 911 was definitely a driver's car and that Alec had never really mastered it. Sitting beside Richard Jamieson she felt safe.

They parked close to Lower Gardens. In the shimmering pink light of the seaside summer evening, the gardens were a blaze of colour, the flowerbeds a profusion of begonias, nemesias and Californian poppies. The motionless, balmy air was heavy with their scent. The gardens were busy, with well-dressed holiday makers and young people making their way towards the Pavilion.

Jamieson had managed to get two of the best seats in the house. The music was delightful: light, sweetly melodic, mainly *rococo*; sublimely right for the enchanting summer's night. Eleanor glanced at Jamieson's profile as the closing notes of the Jupiter died away and wondered if this was the start of something.

The feeling fluttered in her stomach and she let her breath out slowly. Nothing ever really changed. She had always been reckless about men. And she had paid for it – with a lot of pain. But she was too old to alter now. She knew that sooner or later she would throw herself off the cliffs of caution and plunge into a new affair with a man she didn't know nearly well enough. She just hadn't expected it to happen so soon, that was all. And in Bournemouth of all places.

But this time, she resolved, she would take it carefully. Ease her way into the affair instead of grabbing at it. Get to know something about the guy before she committed herself. This time she would withhold her affections and her body until she was sure.

After the concert they walked a short distance to the restaurant. It was intimate and sophisticated and unencumbered by the usual pretensions of French restaurants. Warm and subtly lit, it was the kind of place to inspire romance.

Eleanor ate sparingly but found herself drinking extravagantly. Jamieson had ordered a couple of bottles of *Château d'angludet, Margaux.* It was a vintage '89, full-bodied and fruity and described on the wine card as having a juicy appeal. She soon had a good idea what that meant. The rich, ripe Medoc went to her loins. Her head was beginning to spin, her heart to race and the thing deep in her belly to flutter like a caged linnet. With her raging blood betraying her cautious resolve, Eleanor's body began to vibrate with lust. She was surprised that Jamieson couldn't see it.

They talked – mainly about her, although she was able to establish that Jamieson was unattached; that there wasn't a wife somewhere in the background he had forgotten to mention. No, he told her, no wife. He had been married once but it hadn't worked. He had been divorced for more than nine years.

She also managed to learn how he had come to work for Drumanon. He had met Dan Lassiter, he said, in London, in the early eighties, sometime after Dan had bought the company. Shortly afterwards Dan had offered him the job as finance director.

Most of their conversation was about her and Eleanor did most of the talking. She liked that. It was a change. Frequently on dates with new men she'd found herself marble-eyed and apathetic, her ear-drums exhausted by the sound of the guy droning monotonously on about himself and his career. Jamieson didn't do that. He was different; he seemed interested in her. He got her to talk about her childhood in Gloucestershire, her parents and older brother, about Alec and her marriage, about the job at Karding Hillier Longland, even a little about Raymond.

She drank as she talked, the rich, red wine damping down her tension and stoking up her desire. At the end of the evening, after she had said yes to a large Remy Martin, she was hazily surprised to find that they had consumed both bottles of the Medoc.

She wondered if the alcohol was having the same effect on Richard Jamieson. If it was, it didn't show. He drove her back to the flat as adeptly as he had driven her away.

He opened the car door and helped her out of the Porsche.

She smiled. 'Coffee?' she enquired and made for the front door, trying her best to walk steadily.

Jamieson remained by the car. 'Well, maybe not tonight, Eleanor. I've really enjoyed this evening and I'd like us to do it again. Soon. Perhaps I can come in for coffee next time.'

She turned. Oh God, she thought, he's being coy. Acting the gallant gentleman. Well, to hell with all that. She gave him what she hoped was her sexiest smile. 'Why wait until next time, Richard? I'd like you to come in for coffee *now*. It's all right. I don't bite, you know.'

That was a lie. Bite? She wanted to devour him.

Eleanor found herself suddenly, urgently, yearning for the feel of a man's – this man's weight on her breasts, for the hot enclosing of his mouth on hers, for the thrusting, pulsing feel of his penis inside her. Oh God, did she want that.

He frowned. 'Well, I'm not sure. We've both had a bit to drink and, well . . . I like you. I wouldn't want anything to happen to spoil that. If you see what I mean.' He seemed faintly embarrassed.

She walked back to him, as elegantly as she could on the treacherous gravel. She stood close to him. 'I don't think anything is going to spoil it, Richard.' Her voice was low and hot with wanting. 'In fact we may even . . .' she wanted to say 'cement it', but it seemed inappropriate, the wrong expression . . . 'make it better. Anyway,' she put her hand on his arm, 'nothing is going to happen that I don't want to happen.'

He stared at her for a moment then, suddenly, bent his head and kissed her hard and passionately, his tongue sliding inside her mouth. She reached up and pulled him close to her.

They shuffled their way into the flat and up the stairs, clutching each other and kissing ravenously. She manoeuvred him towards the bedroom, nudging him in the right direction with small but urgent thrustings of her belly. Blindly she reached out to switch on a lamp as they clung together next to the bed, locked at their loins and lips. They pulled at each other's clothing, the close cut of her elegant gown making it difficult in the anxiety of passion. Jamieson was breathing heavily and somewhere in the room Eleanor could hear a low animal moaning. Through the jittery, electrified mist of alcohol and longing inside her head, she realized it was her.

They were naked. She saw that he had a good body; lean and well-muscled. His penis was gorgeous. She fell back on the bed, pulling him onto her. She heard a hoarse, incanting voice she recognized as her own. 'Oh God, Oh God.' She closed her mouth on his, kissing him voraciously, gorging herself on him.

Then she remembered. She pulled her head back, disengaging their hungry lips and pushed him up off her breasts. 'Do you have anything?'

'What?' His voice was as hoarse as hers. He stared at her, his eager eyes clouding with puzzlement.

'A condom.'

'No. No. I hadn't thought – I didn't think – we would. Not first time.'

'Oh God, God.' She wriggled out from under him and stood up. He turned and sat up on the edge of the bed. 'Don't move,' she told him, 'don't go away. Stay here.' She caught sight of the crimson column standing between his tanned, lithe thighs. 'Oh God, don't let anything happen to that.' Her voice was pleading. She brushed her fingers lightly along it and he moaned.

She scuttled into the bathroom and rattled around in the cabinet above the sink. She was sure she had brought some with her when she'd moved from London. Had she thrown them out thinking she wouldn't need them? Please God, no. She wouldn't have done that, surely not. Surely she knew herself well enough to know that she would need them one day? No, not one day. Now. Now. She needed the bloody things *now*.

She raked through the shelves, jars, combs and pillboxes clattering into the sink. Please God, let there be some. Somewhere.

She found one, lying flat at the bottom of the cabinet. Christ, only one. Well, it was better than none. She squinted at the use-by date. She couldn't make it out. She needed her spectacles. For God's sake. Forget it. She wasn't going to wear her spectacles in front of Richard Jamieson. Not ever, if she could help it. But certainly not now. Not stark naked.

It didn't matter; the bloody date didn't matter. Only one thing mattered right now. The trembling inside her, the churning, turning, boiling ache in her breasts and her belly and between her legs.

She hurried into the bedroom, ripping open the little packet. Her eyes immediately went to his penis. It was still rigid and engorged. 'No, no, let me,' she whispered. She slid the gossamer sheath onto him as delicately as if he were made of fine bone china. Lightly she caressed his testicles with her fingertips. He shuddered and let out another small moan.

She pulled him onto the bed and on top of her, feeling the

movement of rippling muscles in his powerful back. 'Now,' she croaked. 'Now. Do it. Don't stop. Do it.'

They were her last coherent words before she lost her mind to the wanton longing of the moment. She arched her back and abandoned her body.

The light was streaming through the half-closed curtains when she woke up. He was already awake, his hands behind his head staring at the ceiling. He smiled at her. 'Good morning.'

She smiled back and moved close to him. 'Hello.'

It had been a wondrous night. She had climaxed almost immediately the first time, hoarsely crying out as the atom bomb orgasm had billowed up her body like a mushroom cloud. Later they had done it again and for her it had been a raucous, flailing second coming. She seemed to remember a third time; a dreamy languorous affair in which she had signified her climax by a faint whinnying before drifting away into a sated, tranquil sleep.

Three times. It had been a long time since she had done that in one night. She wondered what had become of the condom; she couldn't remember. They had made love twice without one. She closed her eyes; she didn't want to think about that. Not now. All she knew was that Jamieson was great in bed and that she felt marvellous; content to lie in his arms and say nothing. After a while she got up and put on a cream silk kimono. 'Coffee?'

He smiled at her. 'You asked me that last night and look where it got me.'

She laughed. 'This time I mean it.'

She returned with two mugs on a tray. She had cleaned her teeth and combed her hair and done her best to bring some order to the ravaged apparition that had startled her in the bathroom mirror.

She slipped into the bed beside him. After a while she said. 'You know, I didn't really mean this to happen.'

He glanced sharply at her. 'What do you mean?'

'I didn't mean this to happen the first time we went out together. I had planned to get to know you first. I'd thought that maybe we'd go to bed on the third or fourth date.'

He chuckled. 'Even the best laid plans go astray.'

'You're right. Still, it was the best lay I've had for a long time.'

He laughed loudly. 'I didn't realize that you'd got it all worked out.'

'I thought I had.'

'What went wrong?'

She grinned. 'I couldn't resist you. And, frankly, I haven't made love in over a year.' She looked at him apprehensively and her voice matched her expression. 'It's all right, isn't it? Doing it on the first time we date? I mean, all right with you?'

He was puzzled. 'Yes, of course. Why do you ask?'

'We work together. I'd always promised myself that after Raymond I wouldn't get into a relationship with anybody I work with. Now look at me.' She put her mug on the bedside table, moved her hands below the lightweight duvet and caressed the thin line of dark hair running down his belly.

'We don't exactly work together, do we? I mean you're the company auditor. It's not as if we'll be seeing each other in the office every day.'

She gazed at him. 'But it's a fine line, isn't it? I mean, we may not work together all the time but you *are* a client. Sometimes I don't think I'm very good at learning from my mistakes. Still,' she grinned at him and moved her hands down to the most exciting part of his body, 'there's not much point in thinking about that. I'm here now.'

'Don't worry about it. You'll have finished the audit soon. After that we won't be seeing each other professionally for months.' She grunted, concentrating on what she was doing with her hands. 'When will you finish by the way?'

She glanced at him in surprise. 'I don't know. Soon.'

He frowned. 'Is there a problem with it? The audit? Is there something wrong?'

She stared at him. She couldn't comprehend how he could be talking about the auditing of Drumanon's financial affairs when she was doing what she was doing to his body.

'No, no major problems. No more than any other audit I've ever done. But who wants to talk about that? There are other things you know, Richard. Much more interesting and exciting things than thinking about work.' She smiled wolfishly, threw back the duvet and climbed on top of him.

He left about lunchtime. He'd told her that he had to be in London that evening for a meeting with some Swiss business people who were flying in especially. Before he went they arranged to have dinner the following Thursday.

After he had gone she took a long, leisurely bath, pulled on a tee shirt and a pair of faded jeans and set about cleaning up the flat. Normally she hated the mind-numbing chore of housework but today it was a cakewalk. Today it was easy. Almost fun. Today she felt marvellous. Already she was looking forward to Thursday.

The bell rang at about five thirty. She had finished the ironing and was making a cup of coffee. She had considered fixing herself a drink, but decided that she'd had enough alcohol for one weekend.

She tripped down the stairs in her well-worn pumps and peeked through the spyhole.

There were two of them. The older, bigger one was closest to the door. He had a stern, stone-grey face. The other one, younger, slimmer and slightly less menacing, hung back.

She put the door on the security chain and opened it cautiously. 'Yes?'

'Miss Lambert?'

'Yes.'

'I'm Detective Chief Inspector Winchcombe. This is Detective Inspector Malin. May we come in?'

'Why? What do you want?'

The big man's voice was quiet and flat. 'We'd rather talk about that inside if you wouldn't mind.'

Eleanor frowned at him through the narrow gap. 'Do you have any identification?'

The way he presented it convinced her he was who he said he was. He neither smiled nor frowned but, with his stony face blank, produced a laminated card in a small leather binder. He held it close to the door and allowed her plenty of time to inspect it. The warrant card looked official. The likeness in the small photograph was good. She took the chain off the door.

'Thank you.' Winchcombe moved carefully past her, followed by Malin who gave her a small, almost shy smile. They waited for her at the top of the stairs.

'This way.' She led them into the lounge. After her efforts it was looking particularly good. Which, she realized, was more than could be said for her. 'I'm sorry but you must excuse my appearance,' she said hurriedly. 'I've been cleaning.'

Winchcombe's face didn't alter. 'That's quite all right.' Eleanor noticed that Malin gave her a slightly larger smile.

'Please sit down.' She was confused and added, nervously. 'Would you like some coffee?'

'No thank you.' Somewhere far back in Winchcombe's voice was a trace of the Dorset downs, but his tone was as expressionless as his face.

The policemen sat in the armchairs. Seated they seemed slightly less intimidating. Eleanor settled herself in the middle of the sofa and gave them an anxious smile. 'So, what can I do for you?'

'You went to Bournemouth police station yesterday, to report the identity of a man drowned in Poole harbour,' Winchcombe began.

She nodded. 'Yes, that's right.'

'Can you tell us how you came to know this man, Miss Lambert?'

'I didn't know him. I told your sergeant. I just knew who he was.'

'You knew who he was.' Winchcombe repeated the words slowly, as if translating them out of Latin.

For no reason, Eleanor felt herself reddening. 'Well, I knew vaguely who he was. What I mean is, I knew where you, the police, could find out about him.' She could hear herself gabbling. She took a deep breath and slowed her words. 'The newspaper said the man was unidentified. I happened to know where he worked, so I gave your sergeant the information. He said that someone else had already reported the man's identity.' She paused and added lamely, 'So I suppose I needn't have bothered really.'

She gave Winchcombe a weak smile. He didn't respond. She glanced at Malin. He was staring at her intently. She noticed he had rather a nice face. His eyes were dark and solemn. She turned her gaze back to Winchcombe. Looking at him was like looking at the north face of the Eiger. He made her uneasy and she wished she'd fixed herself that drink. She felt uncomfortable in her own home – not a feeling she liked. It irritated her. 'Your people already know all this,' she said brusquely. 'Your sergeant took long enough to write it down.'

'How did you know where the man worked?' Winchcombe asked.

'I told him that too.' Her irritation was growing. 'I'm an auditor. I work for a firm of accountants in Poole. Hagerty Clark. Currently I'm working on the annual audit of Drumanon Consolidated. That's where the man worked.'

'In the warehouse?' It was the first time Malin had spoken.

'Yes. You see, you know all this already.'

Winchcombe ignored her irritation. 'Have you been working at Drumanon long?'

'I've been supervising the audit for nearly two weeks.'

'What does that entail, exactly? Does it mean that you're working at Drumanon all the time?'

She shook her head. 'No. I go in for a couple of hours, every other day or so. I have a couple of articled clerks who spend most of their time there. Doing the legwork.'

'Legwork?'

'Checking up on the physical assets, going through the ledgers and books of account, checking on the computer programs; basically crunching the numbers. I come along and make sense of it all. Put it all together into a series of financial statements: balance sheet, profit and loss, source and application of funds, that kind of thing.'

'I see,' said Winchcombe. Eleanor wasn't sure that he did. She felt rather pleased about that. He was silent for a moment. 'So, do you know many of the people who work in the warehouse at Drumanon?'

She frowned. 'No, I don't know any of them. All my contacts are with the directors, the senior management.' She frowned. 'I'm sorry, that sounds pretentious. I don't mean it to be. That's just how it is.'

She noticed Malin's face soften into a smile. Winchcombe continued to stare at her. 'So if you don't know anybody in the warehouse, how did you come to know this man?'

'I told you, I didn't know him.'

Winchcombe's gaze was as bleak as a prison gate. 'But you knew who he was. You knew *something* about him. You told the sergeant that his name was John. You knew that, Miss Lambert.'

She was getting flustered. 'Well, that's right. But that's all I knew. I mean, I didn't know anything else about him.'

'His name was John Adams.' Malin's voice was low and gentle. He could sense her discomfort.

Eleanor stared at him, grateful for his concern though somehow shocked at the disclosure of the dead man's name. 'Oh.'

'What I'm getting at, Miss Lambert,' Winchcombe's voice was as hard and ponderous as rolling logs, 'is, if you don't know anyone else in Drumanon's warehouse, how did you come to know this man? How did you know he was called John?'

'I'd noticed him.'

'You'd noticed him.' Winchcombe was back to translating her words as if from some foreign tongue.

'I'd noticed him looking at me.'

'You'd noticed him looking at you.'

Eleanor closed her eyes and took another deep breath. Christ, it was so maddening, this slow, deliberate repetition of everything she said. She opened her eyes and looked as impassively as she could at Winchcombe. 'On my first visit to Drumanon I was taken into the shipping depot, to see the operation. The man Adams spent his entire time staring at me.'

There was a moment's silence. Eleanor noticed the late afternoon sun burnishing the lounge's polished pine floorboards and picking out the vivid Aztec colours of the rugs and cushions.

'If you don't mind me saying so, Miss Lambert, you're a very good-looking woman.' Malin's voice remained soft. Like his eyes. 'Being stared at can't be an entirely unknown experience for you.'

'It isn't, as a matter of fact.' She said it more haughtily than she had wished. 'But he was different.'

'Different?' queried Winchcombe.

She wanted to scream. 'Yes, that's what I said. Different. I was on a gallery, looking out over the warehouse operation. I was there with one of the directors of the company. Most of the men in the place gave me a fast once-over then looked away quickly. This man Adams, he didn't. He kept looking. A lot of men will give a girl a long letch, but normally they'll look away as soon as you catch their eye. He kept looking. He seemed well . . . sinister. Then he took the number of my car.'

Winchcombe glanced at Malin. 'What do you mean?' She recounted her experience coming out of the car park.

Winchcombe was frowning deeply. He seemed troubled. 'How did you know his name was John. Did you ask around?'

'I was working on the audit in Drumanon's office. It was late, about nine I think. I heard a noise and walked out into this dimly-lit corridor and bumped straight into him. It frightened me to death. I thought he was after me.'

Winchcombe didn't seem bothered that the man could have been intent upon attacking Eleanor. Again he glanced quickly at Malin then looked back at her. 'Late at night. In the offices. What the hell was he doing there?'

'I don't know. He said he was delivering an envelope to the managing director's office.'

'What happened after he bumped into you.'

'He seemed embarrassed. He left pretty quickly. I was

213

shaken up but I did think to ask him his name before he disappeared. He said it was John.' She paused. 'That's all I can tell you, I'm afraid.'

There was another long silence as the two policemen scrutinized her. Then Winchcombe stood up. It was a surprisingly agile action for such a large man and the sudden movement startled Eleanor. She and Malin stood up at the same time.

'Well, thank you for your time, Miss Lambert,' Winchcombe said, 'you've been very helpful.'

'Have I?' She was genuinely surprised. She couldn't see what use anything she'd told them could possibly be. Not in an accident enquiry. It was obvious they already knew all about the man John Adams. So, she wondered, what difference did it make to learn how *she* had come to know what little she knew of him?

Malin gave her a solemn smile. 'Yes, you've been very helpful. Thank you.'

'But how? I mean why . . .'

'There's one other thing, Miss Lambert.' Winchcombe's voice cut across hers. 'It's important that you keep our visit this afternoon absolutely confidential. We would rather you didn't talk about it with anyone. Not whilst we are making our enquiries. Is that understood?'

She was startled. 'Well, yes, if you want.'

'We don't want anybody to know we've been to see you. So we would like you not to mention it to anyone. Do you agree?'

She felt unnerved. 'Yes, yes, I suppose so.'

'Good.' Winchcombe turned towards the door of the lounge, followed by Malin. Eleanor trailed them down the stairs, her face puckered in confusion.

Winchcombe opened the front door and he and Malin

stepped out into the bright sunshine. Eleanor followed them onto the gravel drive. She could feel the roughness of the stones through the thin soles of her pumps. 'Wait.'

The two men stopped and turned. Close up, Winchcombe seemed as big as a block of flats. 'I'm sorry, but this isn't good enough.' Eleanor's voice was determined. 'You've come here to ask me a lot of irrelevant questions about some poor man drowned in the harbour and then you tell me that I've got to keep quiet about it. I don't understand. It doesn't make sense.'

Winchcombe fixed her with a look. 'I'm sorry, Miss Lambert, but that's how it is I'm afraid.'

'Look, I'm not a child. If you wish me to co-operate with your bizarre schemes then I want a reason. And if you're going to start giving me orders in my own home, then I want a bloody *good* reason.' She noticed a brief grin flit across Malin's face.

The policemen glanced at each other and something significant passed between them. Behind their heads sunshine was glittering through the heart-shaped leaves of the big silver lime, standing in the centre of the old house's drive.

Malin took a step towards her. His voice was subdued. 'The fact is, Miss Lambert, that we don't think this man's death was an accident.'

'What do you mean?'

'Just that. His death wasn't an accident.'

She heard the words but they didn't connect in her head. 'I don't understand.'

Malin's voice was grim. 'The man found in the harbour was a policeman. He was working undercover on a case. His real name wasn't John Adams. We believe that he was murdered. *That's* why we want you to keep quiet.'

Chapter Eleven

Dunaff took the call late in the afternoon.

'Kevin?'

'Yeah.'

'Bob Woodall at Eltham. We've got something over here that you might want to take a look at.'

'Yeah? What?'

'I dunno, Kevin. I think it's better if you come over and see for yourself. It's a mess, that's for sure. And it doesn't add up.'

In Dunaff's experience, messes never did. 'So what have you got?'

'For a start we've got an odee and a couple of dead pit bulls. Plus a lot of other stuff.'

The big, raw-boned DCI was not amused. 'You must be bloody joking? You want me to punch my way through rush-hour traffic just to take a look at an overdosed junkie and a couple of dead dogs? What's so special about any of that?'

'It's just . . . different, Kevin. There's something not right here. I think you ought to take a look.'

Dunaff thought about it for a moment, staring at the mess of papers on his desk. Woodall was okay. He wouldn't ask Dunaff to take a look at something on his manor unless there was a reason. He made up his mind. Anything to escape the paper.

'All right. Where?'

'Brockley.' Woodall gave him the address. Normally it was a twenty-minute journey; it took him fifty-five.

'Jesus, what the hell happened here?'

The young constable at the doorway stepped aside as Dunaff walked into the flat. The hallway looked as if a demented decorator had splashed dirty red paint over its bare walls and floorboards. Dunaff knew it wasn't paint. The place was beginning to smell.

Woodall appeared from a room off the hallway. 'Kevin. Thanks for coming.' He led Dunaff into a small sparse bedroom, more like a cell. A couple of threadbare, stale-smelling blankets covered an iron bedstead. They were indented, as if someone had been lying on them.

Woodall jerked his chin at the bed. 'That's where we found Jimmy Pierce. He'd been dead more than a day. Did you know him?'

Dunaff shook his head. 'No. It's not a name I know. Should I have?'

Woodall shrugged. 'He was only a minor dealer – though a major user. Which is probably what killed him. It looks like a classic odee. There's a syringe in another room. He probably felt sick, came in here to lay down, and . . .' he turned away from the bed, 'shuffled off to the great poppy field in the sky.'

Dunaff's granite face didn't change. 'So why all the blood out there?'

The two men walked out into the hallway and Dunaff frowned at the bloodstained walls. A couple of detective constables were mooching about the flat, unsure what to do, yet careful not to disturb anything.

'That's the interesting bit. We got a call from one of the neighbours about a terrific row going on in here; dogs going bonkers; someone screaming. The local nick thought it was a domestic. They sent a young copper round who found the door half open.'

'Just as well,' Dunaff eyed the timber bracing on the inside of the door.

'The lad walked in and damn well near threw up. There were a couple of pit bulls. Here, in the hallway. Dying. Stab wounds all over them. Blood everywhere. One of the bloody dogs was virtually disembowelled; dragging its entrails around on the floor behind it. Even then,' Woodall shook his head, marvelling at the dogs' aggression, 'even though they could scarcely crawl, the dogs tried to have a go at the lad. They died soon afterwards.'

Dunaff was frowning. 'I don't get it.'

'Nor did the rookie. He called in and I and my lads came over to take a look. We did some checking around with the neighbours. Someone had seen a couple of blokes knocking on the door. One was a tall black dude, been seen around here a lot. The other was a little skinny guy. White. Looked like a tramp, apparently. We went next door. Asked the Pakistani family there what they'd seen or heard. They wouldn't tell us anything. Terrified. Said they hadn't heard a thing. From what the other neighbours said, you'd have to be as deaf as a cemetery wall not to have heard what was going on in here. We asked to take a look around the flat. Found their bathroom window unhinged and smashed on the concrete below.' Woodall paused. 'Come and take a look at this.'

He led Dunaff into the small bathroom. They peered out of the open window. 'We've had a report from a train passenger about a man trying to break into a window in a block of flats somewhere around here. If that report is about this place, and I'm willing to bet it is, then somebody edged their way along the wall from the bathroom of the flat next door and got in here. Whoever it was, the Pakis aren't saying. Too damn scared. But I'll tell you, Kevin, the bloke must be bleeding crazy. Look at that ledge. There's nothing of it. And look at the drop, for Christ's sake. Whoever he was, he wanted to get in here bad.'

Dunaff nodded. 'And the dogs surprised him.' They walked back out into the hallway.

'No. That's what makes this thing even more iffy. He knew there were dogs here. The bloody nutter brought that with him.' Woodall indicated a green fire extinguisher lying on its side halfway along the hall. It was smeared with blood.

Dunaff raised his eyebrows. 'He was going up against two pit bulls with a Halon extinguisher?'

Woodall looked surprised. 'Isn't that what you blokes in the squad use for dogs? Fire extinguishers?'

'Not any more. And we never used Halon. The stupid bastard got it wrong. He should have used CO_2, the black one. That's the one that makes the noise and freezes 'em out.' Dunaff motioned at the extinguisher. 'That wouldn't have scared a couple of poodles.'

'Maybe it didn't. But the bloke also had a knife. And he knew how to use it. He's obviously a lunatic. I wouldn't go up against pit bulls with nothing but a knife. He must have been desperate to get his hands on Pierce's stash. And after all that, he didn't get it. Or at least not all of it.'

'What do you mean?'

'He missed three wraps. In here.' They walked into another bare room. Sitting on a low, lopsided plastic table were three small balloon bags.

Dunaff eyed them. 'That's all the stuff you found?'

Woodall nodded. Dunaff stared around the ugly bare room, lost in thought. 'The bloke was desperate all right.' He spoke quietly, almost to himself. 'But what for? He would have known someone like Pierce wouldn't have a big stash. Not big enough to risk breaking his neck over; not worth getting savaged to death by a couple of pits. Whoever broke in here was after something else. But what? Anyway,' he glanced at Woodall, 'you were right to call me. You sent for Soco?'

Woodall shook his head. 'Not yet. This lot's hardly a priority. Apart from the break-in, where's the crime? Pierce is almost certainly an overdose and killing a couple of dogs, well – is it worth calling in Soco? I thought I'd talk to you first.'

Dunaff gave him a suspicious smile. 'And if I call in Soco, it goes against *my* budget, eh?'

Woodall gave him a surprised look. 'It never crossed my mind, Kevin.'

Dunaff laughed. 'Bollocks.' Followed by Woodall he wandered back into the hallway and along to the kitchen. On the wall above one of the filthy formica work surfaces was a telephone. The bare, grubby plaster surrounding the phone was decorated by scores of pencilled telephone numbers.

Dunaff surveyed the numbers for a while. 'I get the feeling that your young copper has stumbled across something here, Bob.' He stared at the wall a moment more then turned to Woodall. 'Get your lads to take away whatever evidence you've got; the extinguisher, the balloon bags, anything else they find, then seal this place off. We'll wait for the post mortem on Pierce. After that we should know if anything's worth following up. Okay?'

'Yeah, okay.'

Woodall called him the following day.

'It's a can of worms, Kevin. Pierce died of an overdose at

about midday two days ago. He had enough heroin in him to kill a herd of hippos. Close to a hundred percent pure, the pathologist reckons. What's more, we've had the shit analyzed in the three wraps we found. Guess what? They're the same. All close to a hundred per cent pure. So, now, it looks like murder. That stash on the table was meant for Pierce. It wasn't to deal, it was to use. Whoever supplied him the stuff wanted him dead.'

'So if it was murder, then what was the break-in all about? I don't get it.'

'Nor me. But as it's a murder enquiry,' Woodall continued, 'it'll be down to us at Eltham. It's my case. I've got Soco going in now. I've told them they're investigating a murder and that it's drug related. They're going to take the place apart; give it the works. We'll also check out the telephone numbers. I'll keep you posted on progress. Okay?'

'Yeah. Thanks.'

Dunaff was called to a meeting at Eltham four days later. Woodall's guvnor, a DCI called Sommersby, was there. Woodall did most of the talking.

'It's not so much a can of worms, Kevin,' he began, 'more a sackful of snakes. We've got a good set of prints off the balloon bags. They belong to a local tearaway called Lionel Montrose.'

'I know Lionel,' said Dunaff. 'We've snatched him for dealing a couple of times. Never been able to make it stick.' He was thoughtful. 'Lionel fits the description of the black guy seen banging on Pierce's door. He was probably Pierce's supplier. But,' he frowned, 'murder isn't his style. He hasn't got the balls for it. And anyway, why knock off a good customer and then go banging on the bloke's front door the day after you've topped him?'

'Maybe he was just the bagman,' suggested Woodall. 'We

found some more prints. On the inside of the wraps. Not many, just a couple, but they're clear enough to know they belong to one of London's all time great scumbuckets. Clapham Fats.'

'Shit.' Dunaff sat up in his chair. Suddenly, Woodall had his entire attention. 'Clapham Fats. He's a different pot of poison. Fats would murder his mother if there was money in it.' Dunaff's grey, craggy features crumpled into deliberation. 'But Pierce was small time. He wasn't a threat to Fats. In fact, he was probably one of Fats' minor distributors. So, if it *was* Fats who fixed him to odee, the question is why?'

Woodall grinned. 'I dunno for sure, Kevin, but I think maybe we have an answer. We've checked out the telephone numbers on the kitchen wall. Some of them belong to old medical colleagues of Pierce's; people he knew at med school and at the hospital. We've been interviewing them. It seems Pierce had been trying to persuade them to supply him heroin.'

Dunaff raised his eyebrows and glanced from Woodall to Sommersby.

'As they're all respectable medical men,' Woodall continued, 'they told him to piss off. All except one. This guy is a GP called Kensale. He has a practice out in Middlesex. The bloke has got himself into a lot of debt; big mortgage, heavy gambling, a couple of expensive mistresses, all that kind of shit. Pierce told him he could make ten thousand if he brought two kilos of H into the country. So he did it.'

Dunaff looked at Woodall in astonishment. 'This doctor, Kensale, he told you all this? Just like that?'

Woodall laughed. 'Yeah, just like that. We went along to his surgery, after hours, to talk to him about Pierce and he coughed the lot. Straight away. He was scared shitless.' He laughed again, a hard jagged sound. 'He thought we already knew about it. So, we arrested him, brought him back and interviewed him. We've had him here overnight.' He laughed again and shook his head. 'He said he wanted to make a clean breast of it. I haven't had anyone say that to me in years.'

Dunaff's expression darkened. 'He'll change his story when his brief has a go at him.'

'Maybe, but at least we know the story.'

'Yeah? So, what is it?'

'It seems that Kensale goes out a couple of times a year to Eastern Europe. On those mercy missions. He and a group of others hire a few light trucks and take food, medicines, baby clothes and that kind of stuff out to Bosnia and Croatia and other places. Four weeks ago he went to Rumania. Pierce had fixed for him to meet up with a Turkish business-man in Bucharest. This Turk supplied him with a couple of one-kilo packages of heroin. Kensale hid them in the truck and brought them back to this country.' He laughed cynically. 'Some mercy mission, eh?'

'That's been happening for a while,' Dunaff told him. 'But it doesn't explain why Fats snuffed Pierce.'

'Maybe Fats got to hear Pierce was setting up to deal on his own,' suggested Sommersby, joining in the conversation. 'So he decided to eliminate the competition.'

'That's the kind of thing Fats would do, Kevin,' Woodall agreed.

'Yeah, but not by odeeing him. Fats would make an example. Chop Pierce into bits and leave the pieces in a skip as a warning to the others. And before he topped him, Fats would want to know where Pierce had stashed the stuff. Fats wouldn't pass up the chance of getting his hands on a buckshee two kilos of skag. Where is the stuff by the way?'

'We've got it here. As evidence.' Sommersby told him.

224

Woodall grinned. 'Kensale had the packages in a glass cabinet in his surgery. Hidden behind some medical text-books. He got back from Rumania about ten days ago. He says the day after he returned he met Pierce in a pub. Pierce wanted him to hand over the stuff straightaway but, as he didn't have Kensale's ten thousand, Kensale told him he wouldn't part with the stuff until he got paid.' Woodall laughed again. 'Nobody trusts anybody, do they? Anyway, Pierce told him that he would have his money in about a week. He told Kensale he'd phone and tell him when he was to go round to the flat, deliver the stuff and pick up his ten thousand.' Woodall pulled a face. 'Kensale never heard.'

'Did Soco find any money in the flat?'

Woodall shook his head. 'No.'

'Could whoever broke in have taken it?'

'Soco says that there was no sign of anything disturbed, no indication that the place had been turned over. The intruder would have had his hands full with those bloody dogs; he wouldn't have had any chance to go searching for cash.'

Dunaff was staring at the floor, slowly shaking his head. 'It doesn't add up. Pierce would have had to pay at least £50,000 for two kilos of H. Plus the ten thousand to Kensale. Where would a bloke like Pierce find that kind of money? Pierce didn't have two pieces of paper to wipe his arse. He didn't have anything. Somebody was funding this deal. If Pierce had been using his own money, he would have paid off Kensale straight away. Maybe Pierce had a backer.'

Woodall shrugged. 'Okay, so Pierce had backer. So what? All the more reason for Fats to eliminate him. Maybe Fats has done for the backer too, only we don't know about it. That's what happens in narcotics, isn't it? Anyone dealing independently usually comes to a violent end.'

Dunaff was unconvinced. He stared at the other two. 'I

dunno. It doesn't add up.' He was silent for a while then went on, 'We've got a saying in the drug squad. "Follow the money." Did you ask Kensale how he paid for the delivery in Bucharest? Did he take the money out with him, or what?'

Woodall shot a quick glance at Sommersby then looked sheepishly at Dunaff. 'We never asked.'

'Okay, well, why don't you ask him? And ask him if Jimmy Pierce ever talked about who was funding the deal.' Dunaff stood up. 'By the way, have you found out who broke in and killed the dogs? I'll bet good money it wasn't Lionel. He's too smart to do a crazy thing like that.'

Woodall shook his head. 'No, not yet. The extinguisher was pretty well smeared with blood but we've got a couple of good prints. And you're right, they're not Lionel's. We're checking them out now. One thing's for sure, whoever they belong to was badly savaged by the dogs. A lot of the blood is human, and it wasn't Pierce's. There's a trail of it, all the way down the stairs and out of the estate. It gets lost in Brockley Road.'

'Don't worry about following a trail of blood, Bob,' Dunaff told him as they shook hands, 'you worry about following the money.' Woodall and Sommersby laughed.

He didn't hear from Woodall for two days. The call came through in the middle of the morning. 'You're right about the money, Kevin. Kensale told us that £55,000 was wired from a bank in London to an account in a bank in Zurich on the morning he met the Turk in Bucharest. The Turk was very twitchy. Wouldn't hand over the stuff until he got a call to say that the money was safely deposited.'

'It wasn't Pierce who wired the money?'

'No. As far as we can tell he didn't even have a bank account.'

'Did Pierce talk to Kensale about who was funding the deal?'

Dunaff heard Woodall chuckle down the line. 'Yeah, and you're never going to believe it. He told Kensale that the backer lived in Peckham; told him that the guy had more money than he knew what to do with. Told him that the backer was a bloated slob.'

'Fats? The backer was Fats?'

'Looks that way, Kevin. So maybe Fats didn't top Pierce after all.'

Dunaff frowned, his brain churning this latest piece of information. He was barely listening to the voice at the other end of the phone. 'I mean, why should he? There's no point, not if they were in business together. Especially as he hadn't got his hands on the dope.'

Dunaff dragged his mind back to the conversation. 'I don't know,' he said cautiously, 'maybe not. Anyway, thanks for letting me know.'

'One other thing,' Woodall continued, 'the prints on the extinguisher. Strathclyde police came back on them. They belong to a nutter called Donnie Boyle. He's done a lot of time in Barlinnie . . . got a file thicker than the London telephone directories. The guy's been done for murder, attempted murder, GBH, aggravated assault, you name it. He's a psychopath; very dangerous. He's off their patch now, believed to be in London.'

'Description?'

'Little and skinny. A runt. And scruffy with it.'

'The other guy,' Dunaff declared. 'With Lionel. Knocking on Pierce's door.'

'Looks that way. You know him?'

'The name doesn't ring any bells. Anything else known?'

'Something that ties in with the death of the dogs. It seems his trademark is one of those old-fashioned bayonets. He carried it up his sleeve.'

'Right.' Dunaff's voice was suddenly filled with understanding.

'You do know him.'

'No. But I know *about* him. The word is that the Profit has got a new minder for his money men. Boyle and his bayonet fit with what I've heard. But he isn't the kind of bloke that Lionel would choose to go knocking on doors with. So why were they together?' he paused. 'Something doesn't add up. I'll call you back.'

Dunaff replaced the receiver, put his feet up on the corner of his desk and stared sightlessly at the large black-and-white group photographs decorating the walls of his office.

He called Woodall a couple of hours later. 'I'm coming over. Now.' He put down the phone.

Woodall and Sommersby were waiting for him in Sommersby's office. Dunaff came straight to the point. 'You were right the first time, Bob.' Woodall raised his eyebrows. 'I reckon Fats *did* murder Pierce. But you were right for the wrong reason.' Woodall laughed. 'Fats didn't murder Pierce because the poor bastard was trying to source his own independent supply of H. He murdered Pierce to stop him talking. To stop him ratting out that *Fats* was trying to set up an independent supply.'

'How do you know that?' Sommersby asked.

'I don't *know* it. But I reckon it. It fits the facts. Fats is supplied by the Profit, right? It's an exclusive contract. Now, if the Profit finds out that Fats is doing a deal on the side, what's he going to do?'

'Something very nasty to Fats,' Woodall said laconically.

'The least Fats can expect is to have an arm amputated. While he's watching. Or maybe lose an eye. Maybe the Profit would have *Fats* chopped into bits and left in a skip. Whatever, Fats isn't going to like it. So, he has to shut Pierce up.'

Woodall looked puzzled. 'But why would Fats have gone into business with a poor pathetic druggie like Jimmy Pierce?'

'Simple. Pierce had a source of supply. His old mate Kensale. Pierce gets Kensale to agree to bring the stuff in then goes to Fats and asks him to bankroll the deal.'

'And Fats is too greedy to say no,' Sommersby commented.

'Right.'

'And you think the Profit got to know about this.'

'Only about Pierce's end of it. Maybe the Profit knows the Turkish businessman Kensale met in Bucharest. The Turk tells the Profit what's happening and one of the Profit's people follows Kensale when he gets back to England. He sees Kensale meet with Pierce and, bingo! there's the connection. Everyone knows Pierce hasn't got a pot to piss in, which means somebody must be funding the deal. So the Profit sends this demented jock to see Pierce, to make him talk. I reckon Boyle was going to torture Pierce until he gave up who was bankrolling the buy and where the heroin was hidden. Somehow, Fats got to know about what was happening and got to Pierce first.'

For a moment no one spoke. The sound of the traffic on Shooters Hill drifted into the sunlit room. 'That poor, pathetic bastard.' Woodall's voice was filled with sympathy. 'He didn't stand a chance. I suppose Fats did him a favour; at least Boyle didn't get to him.'

'It's a good story, Kevin,' Sommersby's voice was cautious, 'and it could actually be true, but I don't see how we could ever prove it in court. All we've got are a few fingerprints on those balloon bags. We could maybe make a case against Lionel, although he probably didn't know that the stuff he supplied Pierce was lethal. We've got almost no case against Clapham Fats. And nothing that'll stand up on this guy Boyle either. So where does that leave us?'

'It leaves the drug squad with a great chance of nailing Fats.'

'It does? How?'

'Fats lives in a fortress in Peckham Rye. The squad has been planning on going through his doors for a while. The problem is that by the time we actually break into the place, Fats and his crew could have got rid of any drugs on the premises. And if we find firearms, Fats will deny all knowledge. He'll say they belong to one of his henchmen.' Dunaff scowled. 'Unless we're in there like lightning, Fats gets off scot-free.'

'So what's different now?' It was Sommersby's turn to be puzzled.

'I *may* have solved the problem of getting in quick,' Dunaff replied cautiously, 'but even if it doesn't work, even if Fats destroys any evidence, at least this time we can go in there with a warrant for murder. Whatever else happens, we can lift Fats. And hold him. Have him in the nick and refuse him bail. This time we can rattle Fats' cage. You never know, something might fall out.'

'But,' Sommersby protested, 'we've hardly got any case against Fats. Just a couple of prints. A good brief will explain them away easily.'

'So, what we'll do is get hold of Lionel and frighten him. Tell him that we think *he* murdered Pierce. Lionel wouldn't normally grass on Fats, but if he thinks he's facing a murder charge he might just say who supplied him the dope that killed Pierce. That's what we need. Lionel to say that Fats supplied the stuff. That way we'll get Fats banged up in Brixton on remand.' Dunnaff's face broke into a hard, predatory grin. 'It's a start.'

Sommersby nodded. 'So we lift this Lionel and tell him we're going to charge him with murder.'

Dunaff, still grinning, shook his head. 'No. The squad will lift him. He's a slippery bastard and we don't want him going to ground. After that, we won't *say* we're gonna charge him. We'll charge him. That'll make his bowels revolve. Okay?' The others nodded.

Dunaff got to his feet. He seemed elated, the wolfish grin spreading across his face. 'We'll get him, you sweat him. Then we'll stick it to Fats. Thanks for your time. I'll be in touch.' He walked out of the room and the door crashed shut behind him.

Sommersby gave Woodall a puzzled look. 'What's got into him? It's not often you see DCI Dunaff looking so bloody cheerful.'

Bob Woodall laughed. 'He's been wanting to crash Fats' place for ages. All he needed was the right reason. Now he's found it. He's over the moon. Kevin is a man who loves breaking down doors.'

Chapter Twelve

She heard the tyres scrunching on the gravel as she finished her drink. She moved to the big bay windows of the lounge and looked down. She didn't recognize the car, a well-worn, four-year-old Granada, but she did recognize the man in the dark slacks, pale green open-necked shirt and ivory-coloured linen jacket who emerged from it into the early evening sunshine.

The dulcet, two-tone note of the doorbell echoed around the flat and for a moment she thought of not answering. She didn't want to talk to Malin. Not again. It was all his fault. The shock of his last words had broken her resolve and in the last hour she had poured herself a couple of large vodkas.

The bell rang again and Eleanor had the feeling that Malin wouldn't go away. Maybe he had seen the white CRX parked discreetly along the side of the house and knew it was hers. So soon after his previous visit, he probably guessed she was still home.

'Hell.' She descended the stairs slowly and deliberately and opened the door. 'Yes.' She was abrupt. 'What do you want?'

He seemed slightly taken aback by her harshness. His troubled expression reminded her of the way her brother used to look when her father told him off. She had a sudden desire to laugh. She suppressed it.

'I was hoping to talk to you.'

'You've already done that. What else have you got to say?'

'Well,' his tone was even, 'quite a lot as a matter of fact. Can I come in?'

She hesitated for a moment then sighed and opened the door wider. 'I suppose so.'

He didn't walk straight into the lounge but, as before, waited for her at the top of the stairs. Close up she noticed he was three or four inches taller than her and slim, though quite muscular. She guessed he was in his early thirties. He followed her into the large lounge, its walls and polished floorboards burnished by the tangerine glow of the evening sun. He remained standing until she invited him to sit, and chose the chair he had used previously. She placed herself once more in the centre of the sofa.

'Where's your colleague, Inspector Winchcombe?'

'Chief Inspector Winchcombe,' he corrected her with a small smile. 'He's gone off duty.'

She didn't like the sound of that and fixed him with a narrow stare. If, she thought, this was a ruse . . . if this policeman was also off duty and was using his office to get inside the flat and put the moves on her . . . if he had come back to make a date, she would be bloody annoyed. She'd throw him out, telephone the local station and make a loud and very forceful complaint.

It was as if Malin could read her thoughts. 'I'm still on duty,' he told her. 'This is not a social visit.'

'I didn't imagine for a moment that it was.' She said it coldly, though she wondered if he'd guessed what was going through her mind. Then it struck her. The thought crashed through her skull like an axe. Maybe he had returned to interrogate her about the murder of John Adams. For God's sake, maybe Malin thought that *she* had murdered him. She felt her heart surge into turbo charge and stared wide-eyed at the policeman, trying to hide any sign of its manic hammering. Malin's next words puzzled her.

'Although,' he continued, 'it is unofficial.'

She frowned. 'I don't understand.' Her voice wavered.

'I'm here on police business but it's unofficial. And,' he added, 'pretty unusual.' Her frown deepened. 'I'd like to ask you some questions about Drumanon Consolidated.'

'Drumanon? Why?' Confusion was adding to her fear.

'Firstly, it occurred to me that you might have been a bit shocked when I told you that our man had been murdered.'

'Shocked? I was completely stunned. But you said you *believed* he was murdered.'

'We're pretty sure.'

She swallowed hard. 'Have you any idea who did it?'

'No.' He returned her fearful gaze with a candid look and she began to realize that he did not suspect her of murder. 'He was unconscious when he went into the harbour,' Malin went on. 'He'd taken a severe blow to the back of his head.'

Eleanor shuddered. 'It could have been an accident.'

Malin's tone was dry. 'We don't think so.'

'Do you think he was murdered because he was a policeman? Working undercover?'

'It's possible.'

'But what has Drumanon got to do with it? You can't mean that he was working undercover at Drumanon?'

Malin was studying her with dark, intense eyes. 'Look, before we go any further I need your agreement that everything we say here will remain absolutely confidential.'

Eleanor grimaced. Whilst her confusion remained, her fear was rapidly being replaced by resentment. She didn't understand why this man had come back to see her. And what the hell gave him the right to put the fear of God into her? And why, like his colleague before him, was he so bloody determined to make a drama out of the visit? 'Your friend Winchcombe said that the last time you were here,' she announced icily. 'As a matter of fact, he bounced me into agreeing to keep quiet before I'd had a chance to think about it. I don't usually say yes to something until I know exactly what I'm saying yes to.'

'I understand. But I do have to ask you again. This is an exceptional situation, Miss Lambert, and what I'm doing is very unusual. It's also risky. So it's important you understand that secrecy is vital.'

Something cold inched its way up the nape of Eleanor's neck. 'What exactly *is* it that you are doing?'

'For a start I'm involving you. You're a civilian and we don't normally involve—'

'A civilian? I'm a civilian?' Eleanor's voice was querulous. 'What the hell does that mean? So what are you, Inspector, some kind of soldier? What is all this? A war?'

'No, I'm not a soldier.' His voice was level. 'But it is a kind of war.' Eleanor frowned. 'And up to now you've been outside it. You've not been involved at all. We know because we've checked.'

'What do you mean you've checked? Have you been checking up on me?'

Malin met her enraged gaze without flinching. He nodded. 'Yes,' he said quietly, 'we have.'

'You can't do that. You can't just check up on somebody like that.'

'Yes we can.' Malin's voice was quiet. 'If we have reason to believe that a person is, or has been, involved in criminal activities, we can check up on them.'

'Criminal activities?' Eleanor's voice moved up an octave.

'How dare you. I'm not involved in criminal activities.' She heard her voice arcing even higher and realized she was sounding shrewish. She paused, taking a long, controlled breath. She stared angrily at Malin. 'You can't go around accusing me of being mixed up in anything criminal. That's a serious charge. I'm a chartered accountant for God's sake. I could lose my job. That kind of accusation could ruin my career.'

Malin shook his head. 'I'm not accusing you, Miss Lambert. I didn't say you *were* involved in anything. In fact, I know you're *not*. But we had to check first.'

'Check? How?'

He smiled the same smile as before; serious, thoughtful, almost hesitant. 'We lifted your fingerprints off the page in the *Evening Echo*, the one reporting the murder.' Eleanor stared at him, appalled at what she was hearing. 'So now we know you haven't got a criminal record. And since yesterday morning, when you went to the police station, we've been investigating your background. Your home in Gloucestershire, university, your job in London, the job down here.'

She was too stunned to be angry. 'For God's sake. I suppose now you're going to tell me that you know all the intimate details of my life.'

'No, Miss Lambert, we don't. That's not what we were after. We were not trying to uncover personal details about you. Only facts about your activities and associations. We did find out you were married, so we ran a check on your ex-husband. We know he hasn't got a record either.' He paused, then added softly, 'Not unless you count his driving. What we know about you is what we needed to know.'

'Which is what?' Her voice was steely.

'Which is that you're clean.'

'Thank you very much.' Icicles hung off her words. 'The

last person to take it upon themselves to tell me that was my mother . . . when I was about six.'

'Look, all I'm trying to tell you is that we know that you're not a criminal, that you have never, knowingly, associated with criminals and that in fact you've never had anything to do with the police. We're as sure as we can be that you are honest and above board.'

'You mean that I'm a good citizen. That I do my civic duty.' Her tone was loaded with sarcasm.

He frowned and replied hesitantly. 'Yeah. I suppose so. If you want to put it that way. What it really means is that we can trust you.'

'You can trust me,' she repeated. 'What exactly do you mean?'

'Just that. We can trust you to keep everything I tell you absolutely confidential.' He fixed her with a look. 'Will you? Will you agree to keep what we say here private?'

They had come full circle and Eleanor had the feeling that Malin had led her around it like a Cotswold farmer in her parents' village leading a prize heifer round a show ring. She studied him. He had a good face; thoughtful, slightly serious, sincere. It was the kind of face she could learn to trust. And yet she was pretty sure that he had manoeuvred her into this position. Inspector Malin, she decided, was more complicated and devious than his honest, open face led her to believe.

'Very well.' She was disdainful. 'I will agree to keeping everything we say here confidential. What I will not agree to is continuing this conversation beyond the moment I decide to terminate it. I'm not sure that I like you or this situation very much, Inspector Malin, and any moment now I may choose to throw you out.'

He chuckled warmly. 'Fair enough.'

'I mean it.'

His face straightened.

'Now.' She had the feeling that she was back in control. 'You wanted to ask me some questions about Drumanon.'

'Yes. What exactly does your work as auditor involve?'

'I thought I'd explained that to your Chief Inspector.'

'Tell me again.'

She shrugged. 'It's quite straightforward. Basically I have to make sure that the financial statements presented by Drumanon's directors are in accordance with the underlying accounting records.' She noticed Malin's face furrowing, as if he didn't understand. She spoke more slowly. 'What I'm supposed to do is provide an opinion as to whether the balance sheet and profit and loss account, as drawn up by the company's directors, give a true and fair view.'

'A true and fair view of what?'

'Of the company's reported financial position. Is the company worth what the balance sheet says it's worth? Did the company achieve the level of sales disclosed by the profit and loss account?'

'So you check all the figures.'

'No, not all of them. But quite a lot. The auditor verifies the company's systems and a random sample of its transactions.'

'Does your work take you all over the company? Into the warehouse, for instance?'

It was Eleanor's turn to frown. 'The only reason to go into the warehouse is to watch the annual stock count and to follow through systems tests. To check the physical existence of people against the payroll. That kind of thing.'

Malin seemed disappointed. 'So you don't go into the warehouse very much.'

'I told you the last time you were here. I've only been in

the place once and that was to take a quick look at what goes on there. That was when I noticed your man, Adams, staring at me. A colleague of mine had already done all the physical checks in there a couple of weeks previously. He should have completed the whole audit but he had an accident and I took over.'

'An accident?'

She nodded. 'He was killed in a car crash on the Dorchester road.' She made a face. 'He was only twenty-four.'

'I'm sorry.'

Eleanor stood up. 'Would you like a drink?'

'Yes I would, but I won't, thanks all the same. I'm on duty.'

'You don't mind if I do?'

He grinned. 'No, go ahead.' She moved to the drinks cabinet and began fixing herself another vodka and tonic.

'What was your colleague's name?'

'Rudge. David Rudge.'

Malin nodded. 'I remember the report.'

Eleanor dropped two cubes of ice into her glass and, returning slowly, flopped onto the sofa. She was suddenly tired. Malin's questions about her work and the unhappy memories of David they prompted irritated her. She took a long sip of her drink. 'Look, frankly, I don't see what all this is about. Why should my job as an auditor at Drumanon be of any interest to the police?'

Malin fixed her with his serious, intense look. It lasted for some moments. Finally he replied. 'We were hoping you might be in a position to keep an eye on what goes on there for us.'

'What goes on there? I don't understand. Why should the police want to know about what happens in Drumanon? Drumanon is a commercial company. What goes on there is exactly the same as in any other company. They buy and sell things. They make money. That's it.'

'We don't think it *is* all that happens, Miss Lambert.' He paused. 'We believe someone is using the company to bring massive amounts of cocaine into this country.'

She stared at him stupidly for a moment then began to laugh. 'You're joking. Drumanon? This isn't Miami you know. We're not living in the middle of Florida. This is the south coast of England. Bournemouth, for God's sake. People come here to retire. It's respectable, that's why they come.'

'A lot of people go to Florida to retire,' Malin growled. 'And where they go is pretty respectable too.'

'Oh, but come on. What earthly reason could make you think that Drumanon is involved in drug smuggling? It's bizarre.'

'The reasons don't matter. Whatever, they were good enough to make us plant an undercover drug squad detective in the company's warehouse. To check out what was going on.'

'And did he discover anything?'

Malin looked sheepish. 'No.'

'There. What did I tell you.' Eleanor was triumphant.

'Yeah, okay, so he didn't find anything. But no one is going to make what they're doing obvious, are they? Not everyone in the company will be involved. It only needs two or three to make it work; someone at the right level to take advantage of Drumanon's import operations – all those trucks arriving from Holland and Italy and everywhere else. Easy enough to bring the stuff in on them. No, just one person close to the top, plus a couple of workers in the warehouse. That's all it takes.'

'But your cloak-and-dagger man didn't find anything, did

he? No sign of any drug smuggling.' Eleanor found it difficult to keep the scorn out of her voice.

'No. No sign of anything. He even took the car numbers of all the people who work there. Including yours.' Eleanor scowled as Malin continued in a despondent voice. 'Their owners check out. No one in the place is known to the police.'

'I'm not surprised. I know this company, Inspector, and I know the people in it. Or at least, I know the directors. In a way, Drumanon Consolidated is like Bournemouth. It's solid and respectable. In fact, between you and me, it's a bit boring. Drumanon isn't some high-flying, high-risk City finance house, or hi-tech computer operation, or go-go pharmaceutical company. It isn't really an interesting commercial venture at all. It's a trading company, importing everything from up-market household furnishings to industrial equipment. But it *is* very successful. It makes a lot of money, and if somebody is using it to bring in illegal drugs, it won't be anyone at the top. They're all making too much money. They don't need to resort to anything like drug smuggling. Anyway they're not that kind of people. I think you've got it wrong.'

'Maybe,' Malin agreed darkly. 'Except for one thing.'

'Yes, and what's that?'

'Our man was murdered.'

Again the nameless, cold thing scampered up Eleanor's neck. She had forgotten that. She frowned. 'What makes you think it's connected?'

Malin shrugged. 'I don't know. It's just too much of a coincidence. He was a policeman, and drug dealers don't think twice about killing policemen. I told you, it's a war. Our bloke was young. It's possible he took unnecessary risks. Maybe something gave him away. Maybe he got himself noticed. You noticed him.'

Eleanor laughed harshly. 'I see. You've got this crazy notion that someone in Drumanon murdered your policeman, and now he's dead you want me to go sniffing around in his place. Like some tracker dog. Christ, no wonder you said it was risky. It's bloody crazy.'

'No.' Malin's voice cracked like a gunshot. Eleanor jumped in her seat and her vodka slopped over the rim of her glass. 'There's absolutely no way I'd want you taking any risks.' His tone was stern and demanding. 'The last thing any of us wants you to do is to go *snooping*. All we'd ask you to do is keep your eyes open as you go about your ordinary business. We don't want you to do anything unusual. Just your job. You're not a trained policewoman, you're only—'

'A civilian,' she said icily.

'I was going to say an auditor.'

'*Only* an auditor,' she said bitingly.

'I didn't mean it like that. What I meant—'

'I understand what you meant. But the fact is, Inspector Malin, that as an auditor I don't think I can help you. You see, an auditor is a watchdog. Not a bloodhound.'

Malin frowned. 'I don't understand.'

'It's simple. Years ago, a judge summing up a big civil case said that an auditor is a watchdog and not a bloodhound. It's not an auditor's job to go digging around a company looking for dishonesty or wrongdoing. As an auditor I don't *investigate* the company. What I do is check the company's figures, its internal controls, its financial status. *If*, and I don't believe for a minute that it's happening, someone was using Drumanon to smuggle cocaine into the country, I wouldn't know about it. Not unless the transactions were being openly recorded in the company's computer and its ledgers; not unless this mythical drug smuggling was being reflected in the company's trading activities. And I don't think that's very likely, do you?'

'If they were paying for the stuff out of the company, would you be able to pick that up?'

'Certainly. A company can't just go paying for anything it wants. The money has to be accounted for. Invoices and receipts have to match. The items purchased have to be for the benefit or use of the company.'

'But supposing they were buying the stuff and calling it something else. Say they bought £50,000 worth of snow –' Eleanor raised her eyebrows – 'it's what they call cocaine,' he explained, 'and called it ceramic tiles or whatever. Couldn't they get away with that?'

She shook her head. 'There would be purchase invoices for the tiles. There would also be sales invoices, showing how many had been sold and to whom. And the difference, what was left, would show up in the stock ledgers and in the stock count. If the company was buying something other than what it said it was buying, any auditor, even an articled clerk, would pick it up very quickly. You see, that's what we do. Auditors check and double-check, we analyze, we make things balance. We reconcile everything. We even circularize the debtors.' It was Malin's turn to raise his eyebrows. 'Check that the people who bought the ceramic tiles *did* actually buy them and are going to pay for them,' she explained.

'So you don't think there's any way they could be using the company to deal in drugs?'

'Not without me finding out about it, or at least noticing that something was very wrong; that things didn't add up. People watch a lot of nonsense on television about companies using drug money, but it isn't that easy, believe me. Companies have to be audited. I don't think the people who write for television remember that. Even loans have to be accounted for; you can't just have a chunk of money appear on the company's books without a reason.'

'But it does happen sometimes,' Malin pointed out, 'in real life.'

'Sometimes,' she conceded, 'but capital flight, international tax evasion, drug money, all that kind of thing usually involves insurance brokers or investment companies or international banks headquartered in Luxembourg. Not medium-sized trading companies on the south coast. No, I think you're wrong. I just can't see anyone using Drumanon Consolidated to smuggle drugs.'

His voice sounded depressed. 'So you've not come across anything you think strange or suspicious?'

She smiled. 'I'm sorry, Inspector, but I'm not in a position to discuss my client's affairs, not even with you. Every audit has its share of problems and puzzles and items that take a bit of tracking down. But I can tell you that there's nothing in the work I'm doing that makes me think that Drumanon is not trading perfectly legally. Certainly nothing that makes me believe that the company is involved in smuggling drugs.'

It was impossible for him to keep the dejected look off his face. Again she was reminded of her brother. 'I'm sorry.' She meant it.

'Maybe you're right. Maybe we've had the wrong information. Maybe there is nothing in it. I just thought that if you helped us you might come across something that our bloke wouldn't have noticed.'

She shook her head. 'I don't think there is anything to notice. And even if I decided to help you, I don't see how I'd be much use. I'm at Drumanon's offices for, at most, two days a week and then only for a few hours. I spend most of my time supervising the articled clerks, or with people in the accounts department, or with the finance director. In a couple of weeks' time I'll have completed the audit. After that,' she shrugged, 'I won't be going near the place for another year.'

He nodded. 'Yes, I see.' His voice was gloomy. 'Well,' his tone lightened, 'I'm sorry to have bothered you, Miss Lambert. And I hope I didn't shock you too much by telling you about John Adams.'

She smiled at him. 'You did, as a matter of fact. When you came back I thought you suspected me of his murder.'

He laughed. It was a rich, bubbling sound. He seemed genuinely surprised. 'It honestly never crossed my mind.'

'Really? Then what I don't understand is why you told me in the first place.'

He shrugged. 'You might have seen something at Drumanon that connected with the murder. And I was pretty sure that if I told you, you'd keep it to yourself. You seem to be the type that helps the police.'

'What makes you think that?'

He smiled warmly at her. 'You went into the station to report what you knew. I don't know . . . there's just something about you, about what we know about you, that made me think . . . well, you know.'

She felt something pang somewhere inside her. It was the same sensation she felt when she told a lie. Guilt. She looked at Malin's guileless face and wondered if he was doing it deliberately . . . trying to make her feel guilty. She couldn't tell. 'Look, I haven't said I *won't* help you. Only I'm sure there's nothing that I can help you with. I'm absolutely convinced that Drumanon isn't involved in anything. But, if I do come across something I think supports your notions, then I'll let you know. Is that okay?'

He smiled his serious smile. 'That would be great. We couldn't ask you for more than that.'

'But I still think you're wrong. It's quite possible your John Adams met with an accident, you know.'

'Maybe.' Malin wasn't convinced.

'Didn't you say that wasn't his real name?'

'It wasn't. Drug squad officers use assumed names when they work undercover. It goes with the job.'

For a moment Eleanor considered enquiring what the man's real name had been. She thought better of it. It was only morbid curiosity. If Malin had wanted her to know he would have told her. She was silent for a moment, unsure what to say next, then asked, 'Are you sure you don't want a drink?'

'No thanks. As I said, I'm still on duty.' Malin stood up and Eleanor followed suit. He fixed her with his solemn look and she met his gaze. With his dark hair and eyes he was, she supposed, not a bad-looking guy . . . of course not as good-looking as Richard Jamieson. With a shock she realized it was the first time she'd thought about Jamieson for a while. Her thoughts earlier had been overflowing with him.

'There's just one more thing . . .' he began.

She laughed. 'I know, I know. It's absolutely essential I keep it all confidential.'

He grinned. 'But it is.'

'And I've told you I will. Don't worry.'

'You see, if we are right about Drumanon then . . .'

'But you're not.' She smiled and shook her head. She led him down the stairs and walked with him towards his car. The last of the sun's rays felt good on her face.

'By the way, how did you find out I had been married?'

He turned as he was about to open the door of the Granada. 'We got the number of your driving licence from vehicle registrations in Swansea. It had been recently renewed. In the name of Lambert. We checked the details of the previous licence and got your married name.' He smiled. 'Most women change their licences to take on their husband's name. You did it the other way around.'

She shrugged nonchalantly. 'As I've no intention of having any more to do with my ex-husband, there was no way I was going to carry on using his name. If I have to adopt a man's name, I prefer it to be my father's. Are you married?'

He shook his head. 'Never found the time.'

She smiled at him. 'Then you wouldn't understand.'

'Maybe I wouldn't. We are on opposite sides of the fence when it comes to using our parents' names.'

'What do you mean?'

'You've gone back to using your father's name. I'm using my mother's.'

She frowned. 'Your mother's name?'

'Yes. Malin is my mother's family name. She's Irish. It isn't my real name.'

'So you're working undercover too.'

'In a manner of speaking.' He grinned at her. 'Like I said, in the drug squad it goes with the job. Well, thanks for your time, Miss Lambert. If you come across anything, anything at all, call me.'

He took out a pencil and a notepad and wrote down a number. He tore off the sheet and handed it to her. They shook hands. He had a strong grip. He turned towards the car.

She looked at the paper. Below the words, 'Inspector Malin', he had written a Bournemouth number.

'Wait.' He turned back to her. 'You couldn't tell me your real name, could you?' As soon as the words were out she felt a fool. Like a teenage girl trying to get a date. She had no idea why she'd asked. She felt her face reddening.

He stared at her for a moment. 'Yeah, I guess that's okay. It's John. John Shephard.' He smiled and turned to the car.

She watched the Granada swing around the big silver lime in the centre of the circular drive and disappear between the tall stone pillars at the entrance.

The sun was still warm on her face, but at the back of her neck she could still feel an icy crawling.

Chapter Thirteen

Lassiter hated Galicia. He flew to Spain often and lamented his luck that in a land of modern cities, glittering nightlife and foxy, hip-churning whores, he had to do all his business on its Celtic fringe.

As the Airbus throttled back on its approach into Santiago he moodily scrutinized the countryside slipping beneath the wings. At least, he thought, it was summer and the lush hills, covered in pine and eucalyptus trees, seemed warm and inviting. In the winter, when it rained, the bloody country looked like the west of Ireland.

Alonso had sent his driver, and a few minutes after the A320 had landed, Lassiter was in the back of the stretch-limo speeding southwest towards the city. It was close to midday, with the temperature a comfortable twenty-four. Heathrow, which he had left two hours before, was eight degrees cooler.

A fine, warm drizzle had just stopped and faint trails of vapour were spiralling up from the dark surface of the road as the sun burned off the moisture. The air was filled with the fragrant, tangy smell of pine and eucalyptus. Lassiter lit a cigar and helped himself to a large Courvoisier from the limo's bar, ignorant, inside the air-conditioned Cadillac, of the warm sun and vibrant, redolent aroma beyond the dark-tinted windows. He leaned back in the deep leather of his seat and stared impassively at the passing scenery. The short, twelve-kilometre journey into the centre of Santiago gave him just enough time to finish his brandy.

As always, Alonso had booked him into the Hotel de los Reyes Catholicos, the parador on the north side of the plaza de España.

The hotel had five stars and was rated one of the best in Spain. Lassiter hated the place. It had been built in the fifteenth century as a hostel for pilgrims. It was laid out around a series of cloisters, with a Gothic chapel, baroque balconies and a heavily ornamented entrance façade. The public rooms were filled with antiques, oil paintings and old, heavy pieces of Spanish furniture, and in the hotel's renowned restaurant there was a low, vaulted ceiling. It looked like a medieval crypt. Which is what it had once been.

Whenever he stayed in the hotel, Lassiter had the sensation that he was sleeping in a museum. In fact, as far as he was concerned, the whole of the beautiful medieval city of Santiago de Compostela, with its ornate Romanesque cathedral and stuccoed, moss-speckled façades, its old buildings and narrow streets, myriad squares and long arcades, its innumerable gargoyles, statues and fountains, was an irrelevant anachronism; a film-set city built by Disney.

A boy showed him one flight up to his room. It was big and well-appointed, with expensive furnishings and a couple of vases of fresh-cut flowers. Huge casement windows opened onto one of the cloistered courtyards below. The bedside telephone rang. It was Alonso.

'Dan, my good friend. Welcome again to Santiago.' As ever, Alonso was effusive. Lassiter wasn't moved. Alonso's warm, welcoming hospitality was as thin as tissue; beneath it was a personality as hard and dark as the heavy Spanish furniture filling the hotel lobby. 'You had a good journey?'

Lassiter told him that he had. They fixed to meet in the hotel bar in thirty minutes.

Alonso arrived on time and found Lassiter staring gloomily at the antiques furnishing the bar. They had a drink. 'Why don't we eat outside,' Alonso suggested. 'I know a place, in a square just off the rua Nueva. I think the rain has gone for the day.'

'That's okay with me.' Lassiter was heartened to hear Alonso's forecast; it rained a lot in Santiago. Whoever, he thought, had said that the rain in Spain falls mainly on the plain, had been full of crap.

Outside the elaborately embellished entrance of the hotel the temperature had risen and the sun was beating down fiercely on the stones of the plaza. 'Is it far?' Lassiter asked.

Alonso grinned. 'It is just a short walk, Dan. There are no cars in the old city, so we may walk in peace and enjoy the sights.' To their left, across the huge expanse of the city's main square, the twin towers of the cathedral glowed warmly in the sun.

'Santiago is a city for walking,' he added, then caught Lassiter's look. He laughed. 'Dan, my friend, for more than a thousand years men and women have been walking to Santiago de Compostela. Making the pilgrimage. Walking. All the way. From every corner of Europe. Just to see', he gestured, 'our beautiful cathedral and the bones of the saint. One day I must take you inside and show you what they walked so far to see.'

Lassiter snorted and Alonso laughed again. 'It is a great pity that you do not appreciate our historic city and its cathedral; such a shame that I cannot persuade you to pass through the Portico de la Gloria and kiss the mantle of the Saint.'

As they sauntered across the square, Lassiter gave his

long-time business associate a swift, sideways glance. Considering what Alonso did for a living . . . what the guy was . . . he could never figure out what was with all this religious and guidebook shit that he talked. Sometimes he wondered if the big Galician was putting him on. He eyed him speculatively. Alonso was about six two, with a heavy gut and a swarthy, deep-grooved face. The dark hair at his temples was turning the colour of sour milk. Lassiter guessed they were about the same age.

'Is it because you come from Toronto,' Alonso continued in a lighthearted voice, 'that you do not appreciate history and the tradition of our culture?'

'I appreciate it all right,' Lassiter growled, 'I just don't like living in the middle of it.' He stared around the square. 'It's like being in a time-warp. I'm a businessman. I live in the present, in the modern world, where it's real. None of this is real.'

Alonso shrugged. 'It was all modern once. And it is still real.' He smiled. 'The men from Miami, they too are businessmen. They deal with the real world. Yet they like to come to Santiago.'

'Sure, it's their culture. Part of their past.'

Descending the flight of broad stone steps in the plaza de Quintana, Lassiter noticed the squares and narrow streets were filling with tourists. He mentioned the crowds to Alonso, who reminded him that in a few weeks the city was due to hold its annual religious festival.

Lassiter had once made the mistake of coming to Santiago in late July and had found the place filled to capacity with thousands of Jesus freaks. There had been parades and religious processions and fireworks in the plaza de España. It might have been New Orleans at Mardi Gras, except he had noticed there wasn't any jazz.

And the hookers had been haggard and scraggy.

This year, Alonso told him as they strolled across another bright, colourful plaza and through an arched walkway of warm, golden granite, the festival was even more special; the Saint's day fell on a Sunday, which made it a holy year. In which case, Lassiter retorted sourly, he wouldn't be returning for their next meeting until sometime in September. After it was all over.

'Then we must make sure we cover everything at this meeting,' Alonso murmured, 'all the points on the agenda.'

Lassiter wondered what he meant. He and the big Galician had been meeting regularly for years and usually their discussions covered pretty much the same ground. Alonso, who didn't seem inclined to expand on his remark, spent the rest of their walk pointing out, as he invariably did, various sights of historical significance. Lassiter did his best to feign interest.

They arrived at the restaurant and sat down beneath a bright parasol. They ordered *camarones*, *vieras*, and a couple of bottles of white Rioja. They talked business.

Alonso was el Presidente of Campanalla SA, a company headquartered in Santiago with subsidiaries throughout Galicia. Campanalla's commercial activities covered a broad spectrum, ranging from fish processing and canning plants on the Galician coast, to the manufacture of a range of high-class, Spanish-style kitchens and conservatories as well as industrial products.

Like Drumanon, Campanalla was a highly profitable mini-conglomerate. And like Lassiter, Alonso was a seriously rich and successful entrepreneur. It was as natural as drawing breath for the two businessmen to talk of product deliveries and payment procedures.

Some of their conversation was about kitchens and

conservatories and industrial equipment – more was about a higher-margin and much more profitable commodity.

Cocaine.

Not that they gave it a name. They didn't need to. *They* knew what they were talking about.

Like all businessmen, most of their talk was about money. And contracts.

At the beginning of the year, Drumanon's Dutch distributor, Van Dameer, had terminated its contract and Lassiter had been forced to source a new distribution agent in Geneva to market the kitchens, conservatories and industrial equipment. Over the *tetilla* cheese, coffee and brandies, Alonso and Lassiter discussed in detail how the new distribution arrangements were working out.

They talked money and numbers until well after three, by which time the sun was drumming the surface of the small square. The air above the flagstones shuddered in the baking haze and the square was almost deserted.

Throughout the lunch Lassiter had been covering the sheets of a notepad with lightly pencilled figures. At last he closed the pad and put it into an inside pocket of his lightweight suit as Alonso scraped his chair backwards over the stones, moving further under the shade of the parasol.

The big Spaniard swirled his brandy in his glass before giving Lassiter a long hard look. 'I hear you have been having some difficulties,' he said quietly.

'Oh yeah. Where did you hear that?' Lassiter was non-committal.

'They tell me you have had some trouble.'

'Who? Your people in Miami?' Alonso nodded and Lassiter frowned. It astonished him how quickly news of what was happening in his part of the business got across the Atlantic. He had never met the men from Miami; didn't know anything about them. But they seemed to know a lot about him. 'How did they get to know?' His voice was flat and guarded.

'Would it be from your Mr Profit?' Alonso posed it as a question. Lassiter shrugged. He guessed that the Profit was the source of the information. He had to be. As far as Lassiter knew, the Profit was the only person in the British end of the organization who had direct dealings with the men in Miami. Whether the Profit was actually one man or a group of men, he didn't know; all he knew was that he – or they – knew a lot about his business affairs. Just like the men in Miami.

Lassiter often wondered how the Profit could know so much so quickly. The man he reported to wasn't the Profit. He was certain of that. The Profit would be a long way up the chain of command. Yet Lassiter had the feeling that, who-ever the Profit was, he was close enough to know in detail what was going on.

He made a non-committal face. He didn't like Alonso knowing his affairs. He hated like hell for people to know any more about his business than absolutely necessary; even long-standing associates like Alonso. Lassiter had learned long before that the best way to survive in business – any business – was to minimize the distance between his cards and his chest. His voice was neutral. 'Sure, we had a problem. There were a couple of small difficulties which could have caused some trouble. But they're sorted now. I identified the problem and found a solution. That's my job. That's what I get paid for.'

Alonso narrowed his eyes. Maybe it was to guard against the glare of the sun. They glinted in the light like slivers of polished black marble. 'Ah yes, but have you solved *all* your problems?'

'What the hell is this, Alonso?' Lassiter kept his voice low but the tone was sharp. 'I don't report to you. Why are you so interested in my business? I told you. There was a little trouble, a couple of complications. I told the man I report to. Soon after that my troubles went away. Problem solved. That's it. End of story. Now I'm getting on with the business. Which is what I'm paid to do.'

'Dan, Dan, my friend,' Alonso's voice was smooth and conciliatory, 'please don't be offended. It is because you do what you do so well, because you have done such good business for us, and for so many years, that my friends in Miami are a little concerned.'

'About what, for Christ's sake? If your buddies over there are so anxious, why don't they communicate their worries like businessmen? Tell the Profit, or whoever's their contact in Britain, who'll pass their concerns down the chain to me. Do it through the proper channels. Not slip messages to me through you. Christ, Alonso, that's a Mickey Mouse way of doing things. It's not the way to do it. It's not professional, not businesslike. And we're supposed to be an international organization. Shit.'

Even as he said it, Lassiter was wondering why he'd heard no word of the Americans' concerns from the man he reported to back home. Communications in the organization were usually very good. If the Americans had voiced their fears to the Profit, the message would certainly have been passed on to him by now. The thought bothered him. Why hadn't he heard anything about this from his own people?

Alonso's dark, fleshy face creased into a scowl. 'My friend, it *is* an international organization. And you have a very important part in it. That is why the men in Miami are worried. They have a right to be concerned. I know they have told your Mr Profit of their fears.'

'What fears? Christ, Alonso, I keep telling you, there's nothing to be worried about.'

'There's the woman.'

Lassiter frowned. 'Woman? What woman?'

'The accountant woman. The one working in your company right now. The one who is . . . what do you call it?'

Lassiter stared at the man across the table and wondered how in hell he knew about Eleanor Lambert. 'Auditor,' he said bleakly.

'Ah, yes. The auditor. My friends in Miami think she could be a threat also.'

Lassiter frowned. 'I don't think so. Anyway, I'm watching her. Carefully.'

'Why did you let her become the company auditor? That was not a smart move. Couldn't you have found someone less dangerous?'

'For Christ's sake, Alonso, somebody has to do it. In Britain all company accounts must be audited. That's the law. It's not like here, in Spain, where you guys can get away with three separate sets of accounts.' He realized he was getting heated and stopped. When he spoke again his tone was colder. 'You're gonna find it much tougher now, Alonso. Now you're in the European Union. No more rinky-dink accounting.' He glanced around the square, scarcely changed in four hundred years. 'This place is gonna be dragged into the twenty-first century . . . into the real world,' he added acidly.

Alonso ignored the gibe. 'But why her? Why this Eleanor Lambert? I hear she is well qualified; that she is clever and intelligent. She may discover something.'

Lassiter shook his head in wonder. Alonso and his friends even knew her name. 'Jesus Christ, Alonso, there was nothing I could do about it. She practically turned up on the doorstep, ready to get on with the job. If I'd said I didn't want her, if I'd told Jamieson, my finance director, I didn't want her auditing Drumanon's accounts, it would have looked suspicious.'

Alonso shrugged. It was a distinctly Latin gesture, sinister, filled with menace. 'But now she is there, she is a threat. One you may be forced to,' he paused, 'eliminate.'

Lassiter felt his scalp prickle. 'Right now,' he said huskily, 'there's only a small chance she's a threat. She's not a problem. She's not going to uncover anything. I've made sure of that. She'll be finished in a couple of weeks. Next year I'll make sure we get somebody else from the accountants. Somebody a lot more junior.'

'How can you know she won't discover anything?'

Lassiter leaned across the table and stared hard at his companion. 'Because,' he said icily, 'I've fixed it. She won't, don't worry.' The big, swarthy Galician did not seem convinced.

'Look,' he continued, 'she's a twenty-nine-year-old divorcee. She came to our part of the world to get over a bad marriage. She's working for a small, two-bit accountancy practice on the Dorset coast. This woman is definitely not crazy to make a name for herself . . . not into building a big career. If she was into all that, she'd have stayed where she was, in London. She may have been a shit-on-wheels accountant once but not now. Now all she wants is to do the job, go home and forget it. She's not gonna go looking where she's not supposed to go looking. What she's most likely looking for right now is a new man.' Lassiter smiled evilly. 'She's an attractive woman, she needs a man. She can't get her rocks off on a column of figures.'

'But my friends tell me she has already been digging into things? Asking questions?'

'For Christ's sake, Alonso, how the fuck would your friends know what's going on in my business? They're three thousand miles away, in Miami. And you're here, in Santiago. None of you know what's happening from day to day. As long as I do the business for you, what the hell do you care? Lambert isn't asking any more questions than I'd expect. She's not doing anything out of the ordinary. So tell your people in Miami to stop worrying. She won't find anything. The whole business is set up so that an auditor can't find out what's going on.'

'Maybe. But she is intelligent, yes? Clever?'

He thought about it. 'Yeah. I'd say so.'

'So she *is* a risk.'

'I didn't say she wasn't a risk. Only that I've got it under control. I'm a businessman, I'm used to risk. Lambert is around for the next couple of weeks. After that she's gone – out of the picture. No more risk.'

Alonso was shaking his head. 'My friends in the States would prefer it if she was out of the picture now. They don't like it. This woman, so close to our business, digging into our affairs. She could uncover things. It would be better if she was not there. Better for us if she had an accident. One that would keep her out of the picture permanently.'

'Just tell your friends I'll take full responsibility. I've run my side of things long enough without any hitches.'

'Except for your recent troubles,' Alonso pointed out dryly.

'Okay. So every business has some trouble occasionally. I handled it, didn't I? I know what I'm doing. And I don't want any more . . .' he paused, 'accidents. Not to people working at Drumanon. You can have too many coincidences. I don't want any more trouble unless it's absolutely necessary.'

261

'It may become necessary,' Alonso's tone remained arid. 'If this Eleanor Lambert discovers something then you will have to take action. Quickly. Do something unpleasant.' A faint smile crossed his lips. 'In the real world such things are sometimes necessary.'

Lassiter stared at him silently for a few seconds. 'I know,' he said softly.

Alonso reached into an inside pocket and put on a pair of sunglasses. He nodded slowly. 'Good. So long as you understand that, then I can tell my friends in Miami that everything is under control. You must watch her very carefully, my friend. Until she finishes her work this woman is dangerous to us.'

'It's only another couple of weeks. There won't be any problem. I guarantee it.'

The big, dark Spaniard shook his head. 'Dan, my friend,' his voice was as sharp and cold as the steel of a Toledo blade, 'you cannot guarantee it. There is only one way you can guarantee this woman is no longer a threat to us. When she is lying on a slab in the morgue.'

Chapter Fourteen

'You've switched the deal.'

Jamieson looked up from the spreadsheet on his VDU. Eleanor was standing in the doorway of his office wearing a light, close-fitting cotton dress and a cream-coloured jacket. She'd found out that Jamieson was planning to be in the office for the next few days and she had taken extra pains with the way she looked.

He frowned. 'What?'

She moved further into the room, stood opposite his desk and put her attaché case on the floor. It was mid-morning and sunny and she had just arrived in the building. 'I was going through some papers I had in a file in my office. I couldn't make sense of them. Then it suddenly dawned on me. You've renegotiated your distribution contract. With some people in Geneva.'

'Lubbenau. Yes, that's right.' He was frowning. He seemed distracted.

She was disappointed. He didn't seem especially pleased to see her. She looked down at his tanned face with the dark tongue of hair slanting across his forehead and her generous mouth broadened into a wide, warm smile. It held a hint of intimacy. He smiled back briefly.

'That's not a problem for you, is it?' he queried. 'You're

auditing *last* year's figures. The new contract with Lubbenau came into force in January, at the start of our new financial year. It's not something you need to worry about.'

'Yes, but it is a material event, Richard. Even though it's outside the scope of this audit. It affects the company. It will have to be noted in the audit report.'

He gave a slight shrug. 'If you say so. Though it doesn't really affect the company at all. It's still business as usual.'

'Perhaps, but you've ditched a contract with a company you've come to know and which worked well for twelve years, in favour of a new deal with a completely unknown entity. That could affect Drumanon. The shareholders have a right to know about it.'

It was Jamieson's turn to smile. 'As Dan is the majority shareholder and as he negotiated the new deal in the first place, don't you think that's a little academic?'

She chuckled. 'Are you trying to tell me I'm pedantic?' He didn't speak, although his smile broadened. She laughed louder. 'Well, maybe I am. A little. But it's the right thing to do. It ought to be noted. For the sake of good order.'

'Okay,' he said lightly, 'if you say so.'

'Why did you change distributors anyway? You seemed to have a good thing going with Van Dameer.' A thought struck her. 'God, Dan Lassiter must think I'm a total moron, going on about the Van Dameer contract that night at dinner. No wonder he was curt with me. He probably wondered why I was discussing a deal that died months ago.'

Jamieson, still smiling, shook his head. 'I don't suppose Dan thought that at all. You weren't to know.'

'So why did you make the switch?'

'Lubbenau offered us a better deal.'

'So you fired Van Dameer . . . cancelled the distribution agreement?'

'No, it was all pretty amicable. In the end, Van Dameer gave us notice, saying they wished to terminate our agreement.'

'I see.' There was a long pause. Jamieson seemed anxious to get back to the work on his computer. 'Are we still on for dinner Thursday?' she asked hesitantly.

He gave her his boyish grin. 'Of course.'

Something inside leapt and she felt relieved. 'Casual, yes?' He nodded. 'Great.' She picked up her attaché case. 'Oh. I'll need to see the new contract. And Van Dameer's letter cancelling the old one.'

'You will? Why?' He looked perplexed.

'Just to make sure they're in order; that the change doesn't affect the company. It's only a formality, really.' She laughed. 'Me being pedantic.'

He gave her a wan smile. 'You'll have to see Dan. He keeps all the papers relating to contracts in his office.' The telephone on his desk warbled.

'I will. See you soon.' Eleanor turned away from his desk and gave him a brief wave at the door. She strolled along the executive corridor, carpeted in thick Berber, to Lassiter's office. Nancy, his secretary, was filing papers, standing at the row of veneered cabinets running along one wall of the big room.

'Is he here?' Eleanor asked.

Nancy shook her head. Like the rest of the directors' secretaries she was young; Eleanor guessed about twenty. She had been with Drumanon since she had left school. 'No. He was supposed to have come back from Spain at the weekend, but he phoned this morning to say that he was flying to Geneva and would be there for a couple of days.' She caught sight of Eleanor's grimace. 'Can I help?'

'It was about Geneva that I wanted to see him. Actually,

Nancy, all I wanted was to get hold of a copy of the company's new distribution contract with Lubbenau. And a copy of Van Dameer's cancellation of the old contract.' Nancy looked troubled. 'Something wrong?'

'Mr Lassiter usually keeps all the stuff about contracts and such locked up.'

Eleanor smiled, recalling her nocturnal survey of Lassiter's office a couple of weeks before. The place had been shut up tighter than the Kremlin. 'I'm sure he does,' she said affably. 'Security is very important. But are they all locked away now?'

Nancy glanced at a filing cabinet at the end of the row. A small key was in its lock. 'No,' she said hesitantly. 'But I'm not sure if I can let you have any of the papers. Mr Lassiter is very careful with contracts and anything to do with Van Dameer.'

'I know. And he's absolutely right. But all I want are copies, Nancy. Just to check. I won't be discussing them with anyone except the directors. If you find them for me, then you and I can go to the photocopier and you can watch me make one copy of each. That should satisfy Dan.' The secretary remained hesitant. 'Didn't he ask you to give me all the help you could?' Eleanor queried gently.

Nancy stared at her a moment longer then moved to the far cabinet. Pulling open the top drawer, she riffled through the files until she found the one she wanted. She pulled out a document. 'That's the new contract with Lubbenau.' She handed it to Eleanor who put her attaché case down close to Lassiter's big, polished mahogany desk. The contract comprised half a dozen sheets of close-typed legalese. Eleanor scanned the densely worded clauses as the secretary reverted to picking through the files.

'Here's the Van Dameer file.' Nancy lifted a brown

manilla folder out of the cabinet and laid it on the desk. It was surprisingly sparse. In Eleanor's experience, company files were almost always bulging to bursting with ancient history; stuffed with letters and memos and other irrelevant rubbish which should have been thrown out years before. Nancy sorted through the papers in the folder. 'I can't see anything here.'

'It would be a letter from Van Dameer, giving notice that they wished to stop acting as Drumanon's distributors. Did you get anything like that?'

'I suppose so.' Nancy looked puzzled. 'I can't remember. If we'd received it, I would have filed it by now.'

'Could it be in another file?'

Nancy frowned. 'This is the only file for Van Dameer we've got.'

Leaning across Lassiter's desk. Eleanor gave the young woman an encouraging smile. Nancy was a nice girl but she was hardly directors' secretary material. Eleanor was mildly surprised that Lassiter, who was known as a hard boss, employed her. 'Could you have misfiled it?'

'Maybe. I'll check.' Nancy moved back to the cabinet as Eleanor sorted through the file again.

Close to the top of the bundle of papers was a copy of a fax from Lassiter to Van Dameer in Amsterdam. It was a request for confirmation that a bulk shipment of kitchens and conservatories had arrived from Campanalla in Santiago. The consignment, crated and packed in flatpacks, was said to have arrived by ship in Rotterdam two days previously. Eleanor read the fax and allowed herself a smile. She was wrong. It wasn't a request from Lassiter. It was more of an order. There were no niceties in the narrative, no mention of please or thank you; merely the instructions. The next document in the file was the confirmation from Van Dameer.

It used the same wording as Lassiter's original instructions. Eleanor's smile broadened. It was easy to see who had been driving the bus in that particular partnership.

She sifted through the rest of the papers, then stopped and frowned. At the back of the file was a small stack of black letterheadings. Van Dameer letterheadings. Eleanor stared at them. Why, she puzzled, would Lassiter want to hold a supply of a distributor's – an ex-distributor's – blank letterheadings? She stared at the sheets of paper. She knew there could be a number of entirely innocent reasons for them being there . . . maybe Lassiter had used them as scrap paper and forgotten they were still in the file. Certainly, she thought, there were plenty of good reasons.

There were plenty of bad ones too. Like Lassiter had been using them to fabricate false numbers in the orders and deliveries from Van Dameer, to evade corporation tax. Or perhaps he had been using them to manipulate the size and timing of deliveries and so minimize VAT. Eleanor had come across plenty of similar things before. It wasn't her job as the auditor to *look* for them. But, if she discovered them . . . well, then she had a duty to report them to the board and the shareholders. Which would mean confronting Dan Lassiter. And Richard Jamieson. She couldn't believe that Richard was into anything like evading tax, not now that she had . . .

She shook her head irritably. No, she was being hypersensitive. By themselves, the blank letterheadings meant nothing. She was just looking for problems, seeking to uncover mysteries that weren't there. It was because of that bloody policeman and his . . .

'I can't find it.' Nancy's voice interrupted her thoughts. 'If we received a letter of cancellation, then Mr Lassiter must still have it.'

'Okay, Nancy. Thanks for looking anyway. I'll ask Mr Lassiter for it when I see him. Let's go and photocopy this Lubbenau contract.' Together they went to the photocopier in Nancy's office and returned a few seconds later. The Van Dameer file was still spread over Lassiter's desk, the small pile of blank letterheadings on top. Eleanor frowned at them.

'Here.' Eleanor handed Nancy the original contract. Nancy moved towards the filing cabinets as Eleanor looked around for her attaché case. 'Can you pass my case, Nancy?' she asked. 'It's on your side of the desk.'

Nancy lifted the case off the floor and passed it over the desk. Eleanor reached for it. As her fingers touched the handle Nancy let go. The case slipped between their outstretched hands and crashed noisily onto the desk. It clattered over onto its side.

'Oh, Christ,' Nancy yelped, staring at the case lying on the desk's polished surface. 'He'll go raving mental if his precious desk is marked. He'll go spare.' She was close to tears.

Eleanor gingerly lifted the case and placed it on the deep-piled carpet before peering closely at the place where it had landed. Almost immediately she looked up and grinned. 'We're in luck, Nancy. Look, the bloody thing fell on the papers.' Nancy moved closer. The corner of the case had fallen on to the stack of Van Dameer letterheads, making a distinct identation . . . a mark like a curved scar on the surface of the paper immediately below the address at the top of the page. The mark was visible on the top three letterheadings.

'God, what a piece of luck.' Eleanor smiled encouragingly at the panicky, wet-eyed young woman.

Nancy's face remained the same. 'Yes, but look,' she wailed, 'there, just there. The case must have hit the desk when it fell over. Look, it's scratched it. Oh my God.'

Eleanor followed the direction of Nancy's finger. A few inches from the pile of papers was a tiny mark; a new, pristine nick about a quarter of an inch long in the dark, glossy wood. Though small it stood out like dandruff on a dinner suit.

'Damn.' Eleanor cast a quick glance at Nancy's anguished face. 'Okay, now look, don't worry. I can fix that.' She reached into her shoulderbag, found her spectacles, put them on and then scrabbled around inside the bag for her mascara. Nancy watched with a face filled with dread and fascination as Eleanor leaned across the desk and began delicately painting over the mark with her mascara brush. Afterwards, she gently smoothed the area around the small scar with a Kleenex. When she had finished she stood back from the desk, cocked her head to one side and appraised her handiwork. 'There, what did I tell you, Nancy? You can't see a thing. Not unless you're looking for it.'

Nancy inspected the surface of the desk. 'That's great. I can hardly see it.' She straightened up and tittered. She wasn't completely over her fright. 'God, wherever did you learn something like that?' Eleanor shrugged and took off her spectacles. 'Anyway, thanks a lot. I would be in dead trouble if he saw it.'

'That's okay,' Eleanor said graciously, putting her mascara away, 'I think it was probably my fault anyway.'

'I don't think he'll see it, do you?'

'No, and if you have a word with the cleaners they'll probably be able to polish it up so he'll never know.'

'I hope to God he doesn't. He's dead fussy about this desk, even though he does put his feet up on it.'

'Bosses are like that,' Eleanor observed dryly.

Nancy's face changed. 'You won't tell him, will you?'

'No, of course not. In fact the best thing is not to tell him I've been in here this morning. Just say that I asked for a copy of the Lubbenau contract and that you made one and gave it to me. That's the truth anyway, isn't it? I wouldn't say anything about looking in the Van Dameer file. Just don't mention it.'

Nancy sounded relieved. 'Yeah, that's best. If he thinks I've been going through files in here, he might start looking to see if I scuffed his precious desk.' She giggled once more before gathering up the Van Dameer papers, slipping them into the manilla folder and dropping the file into the cabinet drawer.

Eleanor accompanied her into her little office next door, thanked her again for her help and walked out into the corridor. Slowly she made her way back towards the board-room and the two articled clerks working there.

She was glad that Dan Lassiter wouldn't know that she had seen the Van Dameer file. She wasn't exactly sure why. Maybe it had something to do with that small cache of blank letterheads.

It was possible, she thought, that the directors used them to jiggle the figures; to indulge in some creative accounting. She knew from past experience that some companies did that kind of thing; especially private companies. She hoped it wasn't true of Drumanon. The last thing she wanted was to find an unholy mess like that coming up in her face. Not now that she and Richard were . . . well, whatever she and Richard were. Suddenly she realized it wasn't Lassiter she was bothered about. It was Jamieson.

She was busy for the next couple of days, catching up on tax work for another of Hagerty Clark's clients. Since she had taken on the Drumanon audit, Philip had been like a dripping tap, reminding her that the practice did have other

271

clients and that she couldn't devote all her time to just one of them. She knew that, but she took Philip's gentle pestering in good part.

Halfway through the morning he stopped by her office to discuss a small company takeover that the practice was advising on. After he had finished he began, as usual, nudging her to complete the audit as quickly as possible. 'You're too senior to be spending time on basic auditing,' he moaned. 'Let Steven or Lindsey take it on. I need you here. For the stuff they can't handle. There's a lot of other work on, you know.'

She gave him a steady look. 'I'm keeping up with the workload, Philip. None of the other stuff I'm handling is falling critically behind. I've got Lindsey circularizing Drumanon's trade debtors to verify the year-end balances. With her help I reckon I'll be finished in just over a week. It would look bad if she or Steven took over management of the audit now. With what happened to poor David, Drumanon has already had one change of auditor. Another one would look bad. Don't worry.' She switched on a broad, reassuring smile. 'It's all quite simple and straightforward. Everything is going according to plan. It'll be finished soon.'

'I hope so,' he grunted irritably. Smiling, Eleanor watched his broad back as he peevishly retreated to his own office.

That afternoon she put in a call to Dan Lassiter. 'Hello, Dan, how was your trip to Europe?' He told her it had been fine. She had the impression he wasn't in a chatty mood. 'I asked Nancy for a copy of the new contract with Lubbenau whilst you were away.'

'Yeah, she told me.' His voice was cool and distant.

'I hope that was okay.'

'I guess so. What I don't understand is why you need it.'

Eleanor laughed softly. 'Richard thinks it's because I'm

pedantic.' Her lighthearted mood seemed to have an effect on Lassiter and she heard him let out a sharp laugh. 'But why I'm phoning is because I also need a copy of Van Dameer's letter terminating the old contract.'

'Van Dameer's letter?' His tone switched.

'Yes. You must have had one. The contract said that either party had to give six months' notice and Richard tells me that you parted company with them quite amicably.'

Lassiter was silent for a moment. 'Did he? Well yes, I guess that's true.'

'So they would have written a formal letter, terminating the contract.'

'Of course. It's in the file.'

'No, it's—' She stopped. She had just remembered her agreement with Nancy.

'What?' Lassiter snapped.

'—it's, it's, bound to have been written sometime in the middle of last year.'

'Sure, I know that.' Lassiter's voice was metallic. 'But what I don't get, Eleanor, is why you need all this stuff.'

She was slightly surprised. Lassiter had been in the mainstream of commercial life long enough to know the reasons why. 'It's standard procedure, Dan. I have to check that no contingent liabilities are likely to fall on the company because of the change in contracts. If there are any possible liabilities, I'll have to note them on the balance sheet.'

'Hell, that's all textbook stuff, Eleanor. I'm the chief executive for God's sake. Do you think I'd enter into a contract that would saddle this company with ongoing obligations?'

She was surprised at his intensity. 'Well, no, of course not. But it's my job to check, Dan. You know that.'

She heard him swear softly under his breath and she

smiled. Dan Lassiter was a typical chairman and managing director; he did not like auditors; did not like having his actions examined. 'Yeah, well, okay,' he said reluctantly. 'I'll have Nancy dig the letter out of the file. You want me to mail you a copy?'

'No, that's all right, I'll pick it up when I'm next at your offices.' Lassiter grunted and hung up.

She put down the receiver, turned in her seat and stared out over the harbour. Lassiter had been harsh and abrupt but that didn't matter. There had been a note of respect in his voice; he had talked to her as if she were a man . . . an equal. She grinned. There was no doubt about it. She was gradually being accepted. She was inside the exclusion zone.

Richard picked her up at the flat early on Thursday evening. Eleanor appraised him as they walked across the drive to the Porsche. As always he looked great. He was wearing a navy blue windcheater, white cotton trousers and a pale blue, casual shirt. Eleanor, as it had been a hot day and promised to be a warm evening, had put on a cotton blouse, a patterned skirt and sandals. She was carrying a lightweight jacket over her arm.

Despite Jamieson's distinctly nautical appearance he headed north. They drove inland, to a secluded country pub which boasted a small, low-beamed, highly recommended restaurant. It was beyond Blandford Forum, out in Cranbourne Chase and close to the Wiltshire border.

The food was simple but superb and Jamieson was in good form. He had her laughing throughout the meal with stories of his past life. The subject of work came up only once when, halfway through dinner, he asked how the audit was going.

'Don't you start,' she laughed. 'I've got Philip desperate for me to finish and Dan grouching because I keep asking for documents.'

'That bad, eh?' he chuckled.

'Thank God it's nearly done. I should have the draft accounts ready in just over a week.'

'That's excellent.'

She nodded. 'I'm working mostly on the easy stuff now. I've got one of our people checking trade debtor balances and the after-date cash received and I have to verify the new contract with Lubbenau. I'll do that when Dan lets me have Van Dameer's letter of cancellation.'

'Is that one of the documents he's been grouching about?'

'Yes.'

He gave her a sympathic look. 'I wouldn't worry about Dan. His bark is far worse than his bite. I'm sure he'll let you have the letter.'

'Yes he said he would, though—'

'Though what?'

She had been about to say, 'though God knows where it is,' but thought better of it. She didn't want Richard knowing she had been into the Van Dameer file. She didn't want to raise the subject of those blank letterheads. She frowned at the handsome, rugged face across the table. If there was some fraudulent reason for them being in the file, she was sure Richard knew nothing about it. He was staring at her inquisitively. She smiled at him. Behind his eyes she could see his desire.

Her smile broadened. ' . . .though God knows when he'll get around to it,' she added.

'Oh, I wouldn't worry about that. If Dan says he'll do something, what he means is that he'll do it right away.'

It was still light when they left the restaurant, a soft, diaphanous light which had only minutes to live as the dusk crowded in over the chalk downs and the sun smudged the sky violet and dusky pink beyond the western slopes of the Chase. The car sped through the rolling lanes. Across the grassland the beech woods were dark and mysterious in the expiring light.

South of Winbourne Minster, Jamieson took the road towards Poole. Eleanor was surprised; she had been looking forward to getting back to the flat in Bournemouth and luring him into bed. 'Where are we going?' she asked.

'Poole harbour. It's a surprise.' She shot him a puzzled glance. His face, in the gloom of the car, was impassive.

It was late and they were able to park close to the quay in the old town. The vast harbour was calm, with just enough of a languid swell to create the gentle, incessant sound of rigging slapping against the steel masts of boats moored out on the water. Night had fallen and the darkness of the harbour was pricked by lights rippling on the shadowy waves; glaring arc lights at the ferry terminal over to their right, soft twinkling lights way out at Sandbanks on their left. A number of the craft out in the harbour had lights on in their cabins. The quayside was quiet. There was scarcely anybody about.

'Come on,' Jamieson led the way down some stone steps at the edge of the quay and helped her into a small inflatable. He got the outboard motor started on the second pull and after casting off, nosed the dinghy out into the harbour. Eleanor put on her jacket, for though it was a warm night there was a breeze out on the water. She vaguely wondered why Jamieson hadn't offered her a life-vest. Maybe, she thought, the dinghy didn't carry them. She shook her head vigorously and felt the breeze tease deliciously at her hair. Jamieson steered the small craft away from the lights at the quay.

Gradually Eleanor's eyes grew accustomed to the darkness. From the low angle of the dinghy she could make out the dark, distant bulk of Brownsea Island silhouetted against the star-spattered sky. As they passed, the dinghy's wake gently rolled the moored yachts, the tips of their masts tracing arcs across the stars.

Jamieson headed for a yacht moored at a buoy some distance out. As they drew closer Eleanor could see that it was a long, sleek craft sitting low in the water. They came up on its stern. Jamieson cut the engine and turned on a powerful torch. There was a small step platform and a short, three-rung transom ladder up onto the yacht's afterdeck. Jamieson secured the dinghy's painter onto a fairlead. 'Climb aboard,' he said. His voice was low.

Eleanor swung herself easily onto the platform and up onto the deck. Jamieson followed her up and checked the securing of the dinghy before leading the way forward. They climbed into the cockpit where he unlocked the companionway entrance. Climbing down he flicked a switch and the cabin lights came on. Eleanor followed him down the companionway – and gasped.

The yacht's interior was luxurious. Forward, there was a large saloon with a curved, deeply upholstered benchseat circling halfway around a polished wood table, whilst aft she could see a superbly appointed galley which had everything, including a microwave. From where she stood at the bottom of the companionway she could see the bulkheads, all clad in a light, polished oak which gleamed opulently in the warm glow of the concealed lighting.

'My God.' She was astounded. 'I didn't know yachts could look like this.'

He grinned at her. 'You like it?'

'Like it? Are you joking? It's fantastic. It's like a luxury hotel.'

'So it ought to be. It cost me close to half a million.'

'Christ. Did it really?' She stopped and silently admonished herself. Astonishment was no excuse for bad language, nor for sounding like a star-struck teenager. 'Well,' she continued in a more measured tone, 'it certainly looks like it, Richard.'

'How about a drink?' he asked.

'I'd love one.' Already she was adjusting to the gentle sway of the boat beneath her feet.

He took a bottle of Remy from a polished wood locker and poured two generous glasses as Eleanor sank into the bench seat.

'Cheers.'

After a while he asked. 'Would you like to see the cabin aft?'

'The cabin aft? What's that?'

'The bedroom.'

She grinned salaciously at him. 'I thought you were never going to ask.'

He led the way aft, pulled aside a wooden sliding door and ushered her inside. It was surprisingly large, with a big double bed, recessed bookshelves and a few sailing prints on the oak-panelled walls. The lights gave it a warm, intimate look.

She put her glass down on the fitted dressing table. 'I think I ought to tell you,' her voice was slightly rasping, 'that there's something about the rocking of a boat that does things to me.'

'Oh, yes? What?' He grinned and moved towards her.

She grasped him, encircling his broad back with her arms and pulled him close. Through the thin material of her skirt she could feel the hard, solid knot of muscle at the top of his thighs pressing powerfully into her belly. She groaned, and raising herself on her toes, ground her loins against the pulsing organ. 'Get these clothes off,' she croaked, 'and I'll spend the rest of the night showing you.'

Pale tangerine light, seeping through the rectangular portholes of the cabin, woke her. Delicately she disentangled herself from his body and the bedclothes. She got up and peered out. The sun had just cleared Sandbanks. Jamieson stirred. 'What time is it?' he mumbled.

'Just after five.'

'I suppose we had better get moving.'

'What, already?'

He eased himself up onto an elbow and stared at her blearily. ''Fraid so. I have to be in London at ten.' She was disappointed. She had expected to do it at least once more before they parted. 'Do you want to shower here or would you prefer to get back to your place?' he asked.

Although there was a small ensuite shower room, which Jamieson called 'the heads', she opted to clean up at home. He found her a spare toothbrush which she used whilst he made coffee in the galley.By five forty-five they were in the inflatable, chugging across the water towards the quay. The sun was too young to be warm and Jamieson had found her an anorak to put around her shoulders. They reached the quay, and as Jamieson secured the painter Eleanor stared back over the glistening water to the sleek, white-hulled yacht, majestically riding the gentle swell of the waves.

'Thank you,' she said as he mounted the stone steps. 'It was really a magical time.'

He smiled. 'You said that as if you meant it.'

'I do.'

They walked to the Porsche. Jamieson, fumbling for his car keys, smiled at her over its roof. 'How would you like to come sailing with me one weekend? Maybe pop across to France or the Channel Islands.'

She could scarcely contain her excitement. 'I'd love to. When?'

He laughed at her eagerness. 'I don't know. I'd need to look at my diary first. But sometime soon.' They climbed into the car.

'That would be absolutely marvellous.'

'Good.' Jamieson fired up the engine and accelerated along the quayside.

He dropped her at her flat before going on to his own place near Christchurch. He promised to call her over the next couple of days. She had half hoped that he might want to see her again immediately, maybe over the weekend. After all, she thought as she shrugged out of his bulky anorak and peeled off her clothes, she had nothing planned. But as he hadn't seemed inclined to make a date there and then, she had been careful not to push it, not to drop any hints. She had got it wrong so often with men in the past; this time, she would try to get it right.

She arrived at Hagerty Clark early and spent the morning working at her PC, pausing every so often to stare out over the harbour and smile. Halfway through the morning she slipped out and bought herself a powerful and expensive pair of binoculars from a shop in the town centre and felt strangely guilty when Alice walked into her office and caught her focusing on a yacht moored out in the middle of the harbour.

After lunch she drove over to Drumanon, to sort out a couple of queries the articled clerks had got caught up on. She knew there was no chance of seeing Richard; he had said he would be in London all day, at meetings with Dan Lassiter. The clerks were in the boardroom, surrounded by files and computer printouts. One of them handed Eleanor an envelope with her name on it.

Inside was a copy of a letter from Van Dameer, giving notice that it wished to terminate its distribution contract with Drumanon. Eleanor recalled Richard's words of the previous evening. He was right. When Lassiter agreed to do something, he got on with it.

She read the letter quickly. The date was in May the previous year. It appeared to be in order; allowing Drumanon more than the contractual six months to find itself another distributor.

She reached for the file containing the Lubbenau and Van Dameer contracts and made to slip the photocopy inside. She stopped. Something on the paper caught her eye. She drew the letter back across the table towards her, peered at it then reached into her bag and put on her spectacles. Yes, she was right. She stared at the piece of paper, frowning deeply.

She knew that the photocopier in Nancy's office, like all the other copiers in Drumanon Consolidated, was state-of-the-art. It was the kind that would faithfully reproduce everything, down to the smallest detail; every mark, every spot, every blemish.

Eleanor screwed up her eyes and squinted at the sheet of paper. There was no mistake. Faintly but perceptibly reproduced on the copy letter was a mark immediately beneath Van Dameer's address. It was a faint, curving line . . . a mark which she knew on the original would look like a curved scar.

Chapter Fifteen

They lifted Lionel as easily as an eagle snatches a rabbit on the run. It was illegal, but it was effective.

The girl was short and solid and dressed in a stained anorak and creased, shabby jeans. Her hair was lank and greasy and there were dark rings under her eyes. She looked strung out. Lionel didn't know her but he had her marked down as a score as soon as he saw her. She called to him quietly from the boarded-up doorway of what had been a Greek restaurant.

'You got anything?' she croaked as he passed the doorway.

He stopped and eyed her hard. 'Whaddaya want?'

'Skag.'

'Cost you seventy-five.'

'Jesus.' She made a bitter face before digging her hand into a pocket of her anorak and pulling out a bunch of dirty, crumpled notes. Lionel shot a glance up and down the busy street. His girlfriend had stopped about fifty yards away and was pretending to look in a shop window. Two young blokes wearing paint-blotched overalls were hurrying past.

'That's all I got,' the girl said.

'Whaddaya mean that's all you got? The price is seventy-five.'

'Maybe I got that much there.' Lionel could see the girl

was coming down hard. Her eyes were watering and she was constantly scratching her scalp. The notes she held were old; well-used tens and twenties. The crumpled bunch looked to be at least seventy-five. The girl proffered him the money and Lionel reached for it.

The girl let go of the notes and grabbed his wrist.

'Hey, whaddaya doing?' She was strong and fast. Keeping hold of his wrist she whipped in close to his body and brought her knee up into his groin. 'Urghhh.' Lionel doubled over in agony.

The men in paint-marked overalls grabbed his arms and bundled him backwards across the pavement as if he were a sack of laundry. The girl scooped the money up from the shop doorway and followed. At the kerb was a painter's van which Lionel hadn't noticed. As the men rushed him back, the van's rear doors sprang open and he was thrust inside. The two men climbed in with him. The last thing Lionel saw before the men turned him face down onto the van's cold metal floor was his girlfriend being roughly hustled into the back of a dark blue Mondeo. Then, as the van doors clanged shut, his arms were pulled behind his back and he felt the handcuffs snap around his wrists.

They pulled him upright and sat him on a seat running along the side of the van. Opposite was a big grey-haired man with a face like a prison gate. The man had the build of a highland hill farmer. Lionel knew him.

'What the fuck is this?' he yelped. 'You can't take me like this. It's a heap of shit. This is an illegal arrest. I'll sue you for assault, Dunaff. Bastards.' Lionel's testicles hurt like hell and there was a dull monotonous ache in the region of his kidneys. His breath was rasping.

Dunaff leaned over and placed a hand the size of an elephant's foot on Lionel's chest. Gently he pushed Lionel back against the side of the van. 'Shut up, Lionel. You haven't been arrested. Not yet.'

'You fucking beat me up,' he screeched. He looked around for the girl from the shop doorway but she wasn't there. 'You snatched me off the street. That's illegal. You can't do that.'

'Yeah, tell me about it.' Dunaff's voice was indifferent.

'You ain't cautioned me nor nothing.'

Dunaff gave him a faint smile. 'I'm not standing around in a draughty street giving you a caution, Lionel. Like as not you'd start screaming racism and police brutality and all that shit and we'd have a riot on our hands. No, this way is better . . . leastways for us.' The smile turned into a grin like a hungry shark's.

'This is police brutality,' Lionel screamed. 'It's a heap of shit. It's a—'

Dunaff surged across the van like a bull and stuck his face close to Lionel's. 'Shut up, Lionel. We're doing you a favour, so just shut it. Right.' Dunaff eased back onto the benchseat.

Lionel frowned and pondered Dunaff's words. What the hell did he mean? He needed a favour from Dunaff like he needed salmonella poisoning. He eyed the big policeman suspiciously but kept his mouth shut.

Dunaff lit a cigarette, took a long drag and expelled the smoke slowly out of his nostrils. 'At the moment,' he said in a matter-of-fact tone, 'we're taking your girlfriend to Eltham where she'll be charged with possession.' Lionel threw his head back in a sneer. 'And,' Dunaff continued, 'conspiracy to murder.'

'What?' Lionel's voice was falsetto. 'That's a load of crap. Murder. She ain't murdered no one.'

Dunaff nodded his head in carefully considered agreement.

'Yeah, I expect that's what she'll tell us. She'll say that *you* did it.'

'Hey, hey.' Lionel was shouting. 'What you giving me here? This is a heap of shit. I ain't murdered no one and you know it. You're trying to stitch me up. You bastard. You're fitting me up.'

Dunaff stretched out a long arm, grabbed the front of Lionel's shellsuit and pulled him close. 'If you don't shut up,' he said pleasantly, 'I'll get my driver to find a nice, fast stretch of road and tell my blokes to throw you out the back door.' Dunaff nodded at one of the men in overalls sitting next to Lionel. The man turned his head and smiled as Dunaff let go of Lionel's shellsuit.

'Bollocks.' Lionel wasn't intimidated. Even so, he slumped back against the wall of the van, took a deep breath and waited for Dunaff to speak. The van shuddered as the driver changed down. It struck Lionel that it was taking a long time to get to Eltham.

'Jimmy Pierce is dead,' said Dunaff.

'Oh yeah?' Lionel sounded cocky. 'Who's Jimmy Pierce?'

'Don't waste my bloody time. You know who Pierce was. You supplied him. A couple of weeks ago you went to his flat with some nutter called Donnie Boyle and broke into the place.'

'Hey, I didn't break in anywhere.'

'Okay, maybe *you* didn't break in. It was probably Boyle. But you were at the scene.'

'You can't prove that.'

Dunaff nodded his head slowly. 'Sure I can prove it. Your fingerprints are all over a bathroom window we found smashed on the ground at the back of the block. It belonged to the flat next door to Pierce's. What's more, the old man who lives there has all of a sudden agreed to help us. We reckon he's illegal, which means he's more frightened of the Home Office than he is of you. He can pick you out, Lionel.'

Lionel shrugged. 'So what? So I went there. You still ain't got anything on me. I didn't break into the place. And I got nothing to do with Jimmy Pierce being dead. He most likely odeed. The guy was a stone junkie, a total hophead. He was a long way down the toilet anyway.'

'Maybe he was. Maybe that's why you decided to pull the chain and flush him all the way, eh?'

'I don't know what you're talking about.'

'No? Then I'll remind you. The day before you turned up at the flat with Boyle, either you or your girlfriend supplied Pierce with four balloon bags of H.'

'You can't prove that either,' Lionel said quickly.

Dunaff ignored him. 'Each one of those balloon bags contained ninety percent pure heroin. Enough to kill a horse. They were lethal,' he added quietly. 'Whichever one of those bags that poor sad bastard used, it was going to kill him.'

Lionel's eyes widened in shock.

'The bags are covered in your fingerprints. You took Pierce the stuff. That's murder, Lionel. You murdered him.'

'Shit, shit. That's crazy shit.' Lionel was yelling, the sound crashing around the thin steel walls of the van. 'What the fuck are you handing me here? Jesus Christ, I didn't murder the little whitey bastard. Why would I want to murder him? He was nothing to do with me.'

Dunaff, unmoved by the hysterics, stared at the frightened man. His craggy face was set and immovable. 'He had a lot to do with you. You're a dealer and Pierce was scoring off you. For some reason you decided to top him. So you took him four lethal doses of skag and,' Dunaff made a motion with his thumb and forefinger like a hypodermic syringe, 'whack, he's dead. That adds up to murder. We can put you at the scene and we can prove you did it.'

Lionel attempted to calm himself. 'Jesus, but why would I kill him? I got no reason to kill him.' There was a new note in his voice. Pleading.

Dunaff shrugged. 'Who cares why? In your business people kill each other for no reason at all. You know it, I know it. Whatever the reason, we're charging you with murder.'

'Wait a minute. You can't do this to me. I didn't kill him.'

'Yes I can. And yes you did.' Dunaff dropped the stub of his cigarette onto the floor of the van and ground it out. He looked up, directly at Lionel. 'Your girlfriend will be arriving at Eltham just about now. In another hour's time she'll have turned you in. The moment she's told that she's facing a conspiracy to murder charge is the moment true love will go flying out of the fucking window. She'll drop you in the shit quicker than you can say it, Lionel. She'll stand still for possession but she won't stand still for anything else. She'll point the finger at you for trafficking. She'll say you forced her. So, now I'm going to have you on two counts. Murder and trafficking. I've got you, boy.' Dunaff made the motion of squeezing Lionel's testicles.

Lionel looked at the bleak face opposite and knew that it was true. He could feel the perspiration standing out on his forehead. He was staring down both barrels and could see the hammer coming down. 'But you gotta listen,' he pleaded, 'I didn't kill him. I got no reason. Okay, I was supplying him a little dope. But why would I want to kill him? He was a customer.'

'I told you, reasons don't matter.'

'But it wasn't me.'

'Sure it was you. You took him the stuff.'

'But I didn't know the shit was pure. I didn't know it would kill him.'

Dunaff was silent. Lionel noticed the noise in the back of the van as it rattled over the road. 'So, what are you telling me?' Dunaff asked finally. 'Are you saying that you were delivering the heroin for someone else?'

Lionel needed to think. He was in trouble and he needed time to figure it all out. He shot a glance past the man in the overalls on his left and out of the van's rear windows. He didn't recognize the receding road. They seemed to be taking forever to get to Eltham. It occurred to him that they were driving around in circles.

'Well?' Dunaff's voice was like a whip.

'Yeah, well, maybe I was,' he admitted cautiously.

'Were you or weren't you?'

'Yeah, okay, I was.'

Dunaff nodded. 'That makes a difference, Lionel.' He sounded animated; cheerful. 'If you say you were delivering the stuff for somebody else and that you didn't know it was pure, then you wouldn't be guilty of anything. Would you?' He gave Lionel another piranha grin. 'That is, if we believed you.'

Lionel stared back at him. He felt sick. Suddenly he could see where all of this was going. 'You'd just be an innocent messenger, wouldn't you?' Dunaff continued. He sounded almost sympathetic. 'It would be the bloke who gave *you* the stuff that we would want to talk to. He'd be the murderer. He'd be the bloke who wanted Jimmy Pierce dead.' He paused again. 'So,' he announced sweetly, 'you want to tell me who that was?'

Lionel stared around at the blank metal walls of the van. He was trapped. Every which way, they had him by the balls. He glanced at Dunaff and swallowed hard.

'Come on, Lionel,' Dunaff's voice changed. Now it was more businesslike. 'You know the score. You know what this is all about. Why do you think we're bouncing around south London in this poxy van? It's because I'm offering you a deal. That's the favour. But once we're at the station it'll be too late for deals and favours. The tape recorder will go on and you'll ask for a brief and it'll all be formal, according to the rules. We both know who gave you the stuff. So come on, give him up. Give us the name.'

'If you already know, why do you want me to tell you?'

'Because I want to hear it from you. And afterwards, when we get to the station, I want you to give me a statement saying who it was.'

'Christ. You want me to grass up Fats. You must be crazy.'

'So it was Fats? Clapham Fats?'

'Yeah, it was Fats. Who else? But I swear he didn't say anything about the stuff being pure when he gave it to me. That's the truth.'

Dunaff nodded. 'I believe you.'

'But look, I ain't going to make any statement. No way. Fats would kill me.'

'Not if he's inside, doing life, he wouldn't.'

'Yeah, you won't get Fats. He's too clever for you.'

Dunaff shook his head. 'Not this time. He'd have probably got away with it if Boyle hadn't broken into Pierce's place and killed the dogs. If he hadn't done that, we'd have thought it was a straight odee. But, what with all the blood and everything, we took an interest. It's not only your fingerprints on those balloon bags. We've got Fats' dabs on them too. And we know why he murdered Pierce. So all we need now is a statement from you, Lionel. A nice, simple, voluntary statement, telling us that Fats gave you the stuff.'

'Hey, listen,' Lionel's voice was anguished, 'you can't ask

me to testify against Fats. You know what he'd do to me?'

Dunaff's voice was low and ominous. 'If you don't give me Fats, Lionel, I'll have you. But I don't want you. I want Fats . . . and I'm gonna have him. I've been wanting to put him away for a long time and this is the best chance I've had. So if you don't give him to me, Lionel, then I'm going to take it personally. So personally that it'll be you who does life for the murder of Jimmy Pierce.' He shrugged, and his voice grew lighter. 'It's your decision. It's a simple choice. You or him. If you give me Fats, then you're out of it. Free as a bird.'

'Whaddaya mean?'

'We've got nothing on you, have we? I mean, you didn't know what was in those wraps, did you? And you're not carrying now. So there's nothing we can charge you with.'

Lionel frowned. The noise in the back of the van was giving him a headache. 'You mean if I give you a statement I can walk away?'

'No. You give us a statement and then we'll keep you under wraps somewhere in the country until the trial. You'll have to testify against Fats. And you'll have to swear that nobody did any deals with you . . . that you weren't,' he stopped, searching for the word, 'induced to testify. After that, after the trial, you'll be free. We might even be able to fix for you to have a little money.'

'Fats could get to me before the trial,' Lionel wailed.

'Fats will be in Brixton. On remand. Everybody else will be too busy trying to take over the territory. You'll be surrounded by armed policemen. We'll keep you safe. Afterwards you can go back home. To Trinidad or Barbados or wherever.'

Lionel glowered at him. 'I come from Lewisham.'

'Well, you can go and visit your granny in Jamaica.

Whatever, you'll be free to go where you like.' He grinned. 'Only if I were you, I wouldn't hang around south London. So come on, Lionel, are you going to give us a statement?'

Lionel stared at Dunaff with hate in his eyes. A few minutes before he had been gainfully employed in his chosen profession, making a lot of money. Now his world was blown apart. Now, he was facing the prospect of being a hunted man. Of having to find a new career.

'You bastard', he croaked, 'what choice have I got?'

Dunaff grinned. 'From where I'm sitting, Lionel, you got no choice at all.'

Suddenly he was blind.

One moment the small room was filled with the blue-tinged flickering light of the monitors, the next it was deepest black. Sightlessly the watchman stared at the unexpected blackness and let out a small involuntary cry. He could feel the panic bubbling in his chest. Then he caught sight of the glowing electron spots fading in the centre of the screens and knew that he hadn't gone abruptly blind. The video monitors had cut out.

Which meant that the house had gone blind.

The watchman cursed quietly and moved to the window. Outside was as black as the interior of the small room – no garish orange sodium glow illuminated the street. Again the young man cursed quietly. It was a power cut.

He scrabbled around for the torch he knew was on a shelf. He found it and clicked the button. Nothing. Someone had taken out the batteries.

The man peered at his watch. The small green glimmering figures registered four thirty-one. Outside there was still the occasional passing car; even a heavy lorry trundling past. But inside, the house was still and silent.

There had been music and a lot of noise from the slot machines downstairs until well after two; before everyone had either gone home or gone to bed. Including Fats, there were about half a dozen of them in the house, plus a few assorted women. For a moment the watchman thought about the women. He finished his shift at six and if he was lucky he might find one of them wandering around, looking for a bathroom. He smiled at the thought of pulling a woman into his room. The long watches of the night were silent . . . and celibate.

In the meantime he wondered what he should do about the power cut. Should he wake Fats? The man edged his way to the door and hesitated. Power cuts had happened before and Fats would not be pleased if he was disturbed for nothing. Supposing he woke Fats and then the lights came back on. On the other hand if he didn't wake Fats then . . .

Thummmp.

The house shook crazily. The watchman staggered slightly as the floor shuddered beneath him.

Thuummmp.

The metal shelving holding the video monitors rattled against the walls. From all around the house came the sound of glass breaking, furniture shuddering and things – pots and clocks and china plates – smashing onto the floor.

The watchman yanked open the door. 'It's a raid,' he roared. 'We're being hit. We're being hit.' He stumbled along the dark passage to the top of the narrow staircase.

Unbelievably, men were already swarming into the house; scrambling through a dark hole where once the heavy metal front door had stood. The men had spotlights clipped to the shoulder-straps of their dark uniforms, the lights dancing and jigging in the blackness like fireflies. They were carrying what, even in the darkness of the stairwell, the watchman knew were automatic weapons.

A bunch of them came charging up the staircase. They were shouting; all of them were shouting. The sound was unbearable. The watchman put his hands close to his head; a gesture half of surrender, half to shut out the noise.

'Stand still. Armed police. Stand still,' they bellowed. The first man reached the shocked watchman and crashed him against the wall. Something – a fist, a knee, maybe the butt of a gun – hit him low in the stomach and he doubled over. Hands shoved him to the floor and a heavy boot cracked down between his shoulderblades. Other boots, scores of other boots, thundered by, close to his head. He felt something cold, round and hard pressing into the back of his neck and knew that, for him, the difference between life and death was the discipline in a policeman's trigger finger.

Everywhere in the darkness of the building doors were crashing, men were shouting and women screaming. Lying with his cheek pressed roughly into the carpet, the watchman found it hard to believe how easy it had been for the police to break into the terraced houses. In the end none of the surveillance stuff had been any use at all. As a watchman he had been found dismally wanting.

Dunaff eased himself past the JCB and over the pile of rubble which had once been the doorframe of the terraced house. The heavy metal door hung at a dangerously drunken angle. Dunaff surveyed it briefly in the light of a torch. 'Get the digger to knock that door over before it falls on someone,' he instructed a sergeant.

'Yessir.'

'And get onto the electricity people. Tell them we want the power back on.' The sergeant immediately began muttering into his radio.

Dunaff spoke with all the quiet elation of a man who had

just indulged himself in something he really enjoyed. He turned to Bob Woodall who was standing behind him. 'I reckon we were inside within thirty seconds,' he said contentedly. 'With any luck we caught them before they could get their pants on.'

Woodall smiled in the darkness. Dunaff and his love of going through the doors was renowned throughout the Met. In Woodall's opinion, drug squad blokes were as addicted to busting down doors as addicts to drugs.

Inside the darkened hallway an armed sergeant of SO19 was waiting to report. 'The house is secure, sir. We've been through all the rooms and found seven of them. Plus five women.'

'Weapons?'

'Four sawn-offs, two self-loading pistols . . . Steyrs, and an Ingram MAC 10. So far.'

'Christ, a right little arsenal,' said Woodall.

'This lot would use them, too,' Dunaff observed sourly.

At that moment the streetlights came on, casting a dull orange radiance over the wreck of the front door. Immediately lights started going on inside the building.

The armed sergeant moved away as one of Dunaff's drug squad inspectors approached from along the hallway. 'Any product?' demanded Dunaff.

The grinning man nodded. 'Plenty. The place is a crack factory. We hit them before they could make a move, sir. They've been cooking crack in one of the rooms. So far we've found a stack of barbies, bennies, ganja—'

'Any class A?' Dunaff asked impatiently.

The inspector's grin broadened. 'They've just taken a delivery of smack. They were cutting it with talcum. There's more than a kilo there. We were lucky to get in quick, though. They've got buckets of bleach and hydrochloric acid everywhere. Any longer and they'd have destroyed the lot.'

Dunaff nodded. 'Good. Keep on looking. There'll be more. First thing in the morning I want forensics here and I want this place taken apart. I've got the feeling Fats got complacent.'

'Yessir.' The inspector turned away. An armed constable led Dunaff and Woodall upstairs to a large bedroom with a king-size bed. The room's ceiling and walls were lined with mirrors, reflecting light from a few tacky, mock crystal sidelights. Fats, sitting up in the middle of the bed like a big black Buddha, was being watched by two constables from SO19, their carbines trained on his enormous belly. The duvet was pulled up as far as his loins and his hands were on his head.

Two young girls were hurriedly dressing in a corner of the room, close to a couple of uniformed policewomen.

'Take them down to the station.' Dunaff indicated the girls with a nod of his head. 'Keep them there until I arrive.'

'Hey, what the fuck is all this?' screamed Fats. 'You can't do this.'

'What do you mean I can't do this?' Dunaff responded evenly. 'I've just bloody done it, Fats.'

Fats scowled at hearing his nickname. 'This is illegal entry,' he snarled. 'You gotta have a warrant. You supposed to knock and say it's the police. You gotta *ask* to come in here.'

Dunaff laughed. 'How come all you bastards think you know the law? I don't have to ask anything. Not if I think there are drugs in the place. And there are a lot of drugs here, Fats.'

The two girls shuffled past him, led by the policewomen. Dunaff looked hard at one of them. 'How old are you?'

The girl tossed her head. 'Eighteen.'

Dunaff looked sceptical. 'When you get to the station find out how old she really is,' he ordered one of the police-women. 'If she's as young as I think, then . . .' he turned to Fats, 'I've got you on something else.'

'You ain't got me on shit,' Fats responded. He sounded confident but he didn't look it. Sweat was sheening his obese face and his eyes were wild.

'Sure I have, Fats.' Dunaff's voice was low and menacing. 'I've got you on trafficking and possession of illegal weapons. Those two add up to a lot of time. Maybe I've got you for sex with a minor. But best of all, Fats, is what my colleague has got you on.' He indicated Woodall who had been standing silently by his side. 'This is Inspector Woodall. He's been investigating the murder of Jimmy Pierce. And he's got you all tucked up on that one, Fats. Motive, fingerprints, even a couple of sworn statements. He's got you nailed down and put away.'

He looked at the gross figure in the middle of the bed for a moment, then added quietly, 'That's the last comfortable bed you're going to sleep in for the next twenty years.' He nodded at Woodall who stepped forward to issue the caution.

The sergeant overseeing the forensic search of the terraced houses in Peckham arrived at his office a couple of days later.

'I thought you might like to look at these, sir,' he announced, 'before they go to the Confiscation Unit.' The sergeant opened a manilla envelope. In it were a number of papers, bank statements and chequebook stubs. 'We found the cheque stubs in a bank deposit box Fats had under a false name,' he explained, 'and the papers and bank statements were sewn into the bedroom curtains. The stuff is years old but it might help the Unit trace Fats' money.'

'What about his organizer?'

'We passed it to code section, M15. They came back this morning. They've cracked the code. Said it was easy. Fats had itemized all his product deliveries and payments. And there's some kind of record of where he's been putting his money.'

Dunaff grunted and told the sergeant to leave the file on his desk.

'They reckon Fats has got more than three million stashed away,' the sergeant continued as he was leaving. 'I hope the Confiscation boys can find it. Take it off the bastard.'

Dunaff didn't get around to the file for a couple of days. There were plenty of other things to do and he had never considered hunting drug dealers' money to be one of his priorities.

When he finally got around to opening the file he shuffled through the papers quickly. It was an entry on one of the cheque stubs that caught his eye. He frowned at it, then went back to the bank statements he had glanced over. He began examining the rest of the documents minutely.

An hour or so later he flicked the switch on his intercom and called his secretary. 'There's a detective inspector attached to a special drugs unit working on the south coast,' he said. 'He's called John Shephard. Get him on the phone. I've got a whole bunch of stuff here that's gonna interest him.'

Chapter Sixteen

She waited until just before everyone was due to go home.
On Friday afternoons Drumanon's offices closed for business
half an hour earlier, and as the fine weather looked like
holding, the building buzzed with expectations for the weekend. She sauntered along the corridor and leaned against the
upright of the open doorway.

'Hiya, Nancy. Looking forward to the weekend?'

Nancy glanced up from watering the pot plants on top of
the filing cabinets. 'Can't wait.' She said it with feeling.

Eleanor smiled. 'By the way, Dan found the letter from
Van Dameer cancelling the contract. He gave me a copy.'

Nancy frowned and put down her small green watering
can. 'Well, where was the original? I couldn't find it.'

Eleanor shrugged. 'I don't know. He just sent me a
photostat. Look.' She waved the copy letter at Nancy, who
came to the doorway and examined it briefly.

She shook her head. 'I've never seen that before. The
original wasn't in the file when we looked. Was it?'

'Maybe Dan forgot to give it to you. Perhaps it was in his
case or his in-tray.'

Nancy grunted. 'He doesn't usually forget things like that.
In fact, he doesn't forget anything.'

Eleanor giggled. 'Shall we see if it's there now? In the file,

I mean. Maybe he's sneaked it in, hoping you wouldn't notice. Let's take a look. He's not due back from London till later, is he?'

Nancy looked doubtful before catching sight of the bright, mischievous smile on Eleanor's face. She grinned. 'Yeah, okay.'

Eleanor followed her into her office and through the side door into Lassiter's room. 'No problem with the desk, then? He hasn't discovered anything?'

'No, thank God. If he had, I'd have heard about it by now. You really saved my neck. I'm ever so grateful.' Nancy unlocked the filing cabinet and pulled open the top drawer. She took out the Van Dameer file and opened it. 'Well, look at that. The sneaky ba—' she stopped and gazed at Eleanor. 'You were right. It's in the file now. He must have put it here.' She withdrew the letter and gave it to Eleanor.

One glance at the original was all it took. Beneath the Van Dameer address was a mark, a score in the paper like a curved scar. She handed the letter back to Nancy without a word.

'Hell,' Nancy sounded indignant, 'if I'd have told him I couldn't find it, he would have bawled me out. He'd have said it was my fault. Christ, you can't trust them, can you?' She put the letter back in the file, placed the file in the drawer and locked the cabinet.

'I wouldn't mention that you've found it now,' Eleanor said quietly. 'You don't want him thinking that you're checking up on him.'

'I'm not going to, don't worry. I don't know anything about the Van Dameer file and I don't know anything about any marks on his bloody, precious desk. I was never here.'

Eleanor smiled. 'Right. That's the way to play it.' They retraced their steps to Nancy's office where Nancy picked up her watering can. Eleanor moved to the door. 'Okay, Nancy. Well, thanks. Have a good weekend.'

'Yeah. You too. Thanks again about the desk.'

Eleanor didn't hear her. She was walking back towards the board room deep in thought.

Hagerty Clark, Practitioners in Accountancy, didn't close for business half an hour earlier on Fridays, but she let the two articled clerks go at the same time as everyone else. It seemed unfair to keep them working when the entire staff of Drumanon's offices were noisily pouring out of the building. She told them she would pack away the working papers. They said thanks and left quickly. Within ten minutes the building was deserted.

Eleanor stared at the computer printouts and files on the boardroom table. They needed at least another couple of hours' work before the clerks came back to them on Monday, and more work was piling up back at the office. She looked out of the window. Sunshine was filling the boardroom with bright golden light. She didn't feel like doing any more. She was tired. Which, she thought with a small smile, was hardly surprising. Not after last night's love making. What she really wanted was to go home, eat a light supper, take an early bath and go to bed. She wanted to forget about Drumanon Consolidated for a while. And, she reflected, to forget about that letter from Van Dameer.

She couldn't understand it. Why hadn't Van Dameer written the letter cancelling the contract in the middle of last year? Or, if it was an oversight, why hadn't Dan Lassiter simply asked them for the letter now? Why, instead of all that, had he forged it? It didn't make any sense.

On an impulse she sifted through the computer printouts for the records of Van Dameer's transactions. That part of Drumanon Consolidated, the sale of the kitchens, conservatories and industrial equipment supplied by Campanalla, had been the easiest part of the audit to work on. All she'd had to do was balance twenty-four pieces of paper; twelve monthly suppliers' invoices from Spain, with twelve monthly sales invoices to Holland.

After that, she'd had to reconcile the payments into Drumanon's bank account by Van Dameer's salesmen. That had been more complicated, but as David Rudge had done most of the work before his accident, even that had not been too difficult. It had all stacked up; everything had balanced.

She found the printout and again noticed the neat, precise auditor's marks which David had made on the pages. There was a comment at the top of one of them. It read 'Round sum amounts?' She hadn't noticed it before. She smiled sadly at David's little penchant for putting comments on the working papers. She wondered what it meant. She began checking the figures on the printout.

She saw it immediately. David had picked up something she hadn't. All the invoices, both from Spain and to Holland were for round sum amounts in sterling. Always to the nearest thousand pounds. She frowned. Surely that couldn't be right? There had to be something wrong.

She started working her way through the printout, reworking the reconciliation of the invoices that David had made weeks before. It took her less than an hour. When she had finished she screwed up her face, trying to make some sense of what she was looking at. Everything balanced perfectly. Too perfectly.

She knew business wasn't like that. It wasn't that ordered. Particularly business involving exchange rate fluctuations. Commerce was almost always disorderly, inexact, untidy. Payments for goods and services were made in odd sums; numbers got lost; mistakes were made. Eleanor's job as an auditor was often bloody irritating. Trying to balance the books, to make sense of the mess, was a hard task. But this . . . this? It was all too neat.

She scrabbled among the papers on the board table, searching for the schedule of payments from Van Dameer's agents in the UK, who paid most of the sales price they received for the kitchens, conservatories and air-conditioning equipment direct into Drumanon's bank account. It was a thick printout, with hundreds of pages of payments recorded on it. David had done a good job. It had clearly taken him a lot longer, but he had completely reconciled the monthly totals with Drumanon's invoices to Holland.

Yet, she noticed, even on this schedule the payments were for round sum figures; every sum paid in had clearly been rounded to the nearest hundred. All the payments were for sums somewhere between twelve and fifty thousand pounds.

Did no one, she wondered, ever buy extras or add-ons to the products; items which would create the payment of odd numbered sums? Could *everything* the salesmen sold be in multiples of a hundred? Round sum amounts sure made life as an auditor easier, but it was unique in Eleanor's experience to come across them with such consistency.

There was a noise at the open door. She looked up and her heart walloped into the wall of her chest. Dan Lassiter was standing in the doorway. 'Working late?' There was an edge to his voice.

Eleanor felt herself flushing. She couldn't account for it. He hadn't caught her wearing her spectacles. She looked at her watch quickly. 'Just a couple of hours or so, Dan. Tidying up.'

He strolled into the boardroom. 'You work too hard,

Eleanor. In this kinda weather you want to get out. Enjoy yourself.'

'I'm about to.'

He moved round the desk to peer over her shoulder. Casually, Eleanor turned the page of the printout so that he wouldn't see David's remark.

'You got a problem with Van Dameer?' His tone was sharp.

'No. Checking that the sales and purchases reconcile.'

'I thought David Rudge had already done that.'

'He did. I'm just making sure he did it properly.' She smiled up at him. 'Richard thinks I'm picky. But, you know how auditors are.'

He didn't smile. 'So no problem with Van Dameer?'

'None at all. Everything balances perfectly.' She wondered if she should raise with him the puzzling subject of round sum amounts. She figured Lassiter would have an explanation. Something stopped her. Something, somewhere inside her head, decided her not to. 'Well, I think you're right, Dan,' she said brightly, 'I think I'll call it a day.'

She stood up, closed the printout, stacked it with the others and placed them in a low, polished wooden cupboard at the other end of the boardroom. Lassiter watched her as she put away the rest of the papers and locked the cupboard. She gave him the key. 'Can you give that to Nancy, please? My clerks will pick it up from her on Monday morning.'

'Sure.' He sounded happier now.

'Oh, by the way,' she said casually as she collected her things together, 'thanks for the Van Dameer cancellation letter. It looks perfectly in order.' She glanced up, watching him for any reaction. His face was impassive.

'You're welcome.' He followed her out of the room and closed the door. 'Okay, Eleanor, have a good weekend.' He followed her along the corridor before turning into his office.

She drove home with the curious feeling that she was back at school and had narrowly escaped being caught smoking behind the lavatories. What was it about Lassiter, she wondered, that made her feel creepy; that gave her the feeling that he had some kind of malevolent control?

In her previous job she had dealt with CEOs of organizations far bigger and richer than Drumanon. Presidents of powerful multi-nationals; men with enormous authority. Yet she had not been intimidated. She had known that she was good at her job, a competent professional who could deliver the goods, who could hack it with the best of the men. She had been confident. She was *still* confident, still good at her job. There was nothing different about *her*. It had to be Lassiter. There was something about *him*. The forged letter . . . the regular, round sum amounts in the accounts . . . something was wrong somewhere.

Back at the flat she fixed herself a large vodka and tonic, took a sip, then put her glass down. A drink was not what she needed. She needed something else to quieten her mind; some alternative to alcohol to pacify the jagged anxieties. She wanted something rigorous . . . physical.

Despite her tiredness she decided to go for a workout; a couple of hours of intense aerobic exercise to get her heart pumping, her lipids moving and her blood racing. Enough activity to exhaust her muscles and empty her head. She changed quickly into a lycra leotard and cycle shorts, put on a hooded shellsuit top and grey jogging trousers and threw a few things into her sports bag. Minutes later she was at the health club.

Outside it was a warm, glittering Friday evening. Inside, the vast expense of green nylon carpet was almost entirely unoccupied by the club's customary throng of grunting, iron-pumping humanity. The fluorescent lights bounced silently off the long expanse of mirrored walls and off the stainless steel bars of the power towers and weight-training equipment.

Eleanor worked vigorously for ninety minutes; the last thirty on the running machine at a steady ten miles an hour. By then the big room was a little busier. A few of the regular fitness fanatics had drifted in and were working out. When the small display screen registered that she had completed eight kilometres, she switched the running machine to slow mode and a few moments later turned it off and stepped down. She grabbed her towel and dabbed at her face and neck. She felt good; her mind was calm and her limbs tingled with a warm, languorous glow.

'Hello.'

For a moment she didn't recognize him. He was wearing a grey tracksuit emblazoned with the name and motif of an American athletic club. The tracksuit had seen better days. Then the face clicked with the name.

'Inspector Shephard.' Suddenly she remembered and glanced around hurriedly. 'Oh God, I'm sorry, I should call you Inspector Malin, shouldn't I?'

He chuckled quietly. 'I wouldn't worry about it. I'm not on duty, so why don't you call me John?'

She shrugged. 'Okay, I'm Eleanor, by the way.'

He smiled. 'I know.'

She began towelling the back of her neck. 'I didn't know you were a member here.'

His smile turned to a sheepish grin. 'I am. Though not so as you would notice. I don't come very often, I'm afraid.'

She caught him appraising her body in the black lycra leotard and the red, thigh-hugging cycle shorts. She didn't mind. He wasn't sly about it, nor lecherous, and anyway she guessed she was looking good. Her body felt tight and compact and her skin was glowing with a sheen of perspiration.

'You look great.' He said it simply.

She smiled. 'Thank you.'

'Actually I was coming to see you this weekend. Maybe you might prefer it if we talked now. I mean, after you've had a shower. Maybe I could buy you a drink. Or an orange juice, at the bar here.'

She was surprised. 'Wouldn't you rather work out?'

The sheepish grin returned. 'Not especially. I've done about forty minutes. That's about all I can handle.'

She agreed to have a drink with him after she had showered, electing for a fresh orange in the club's juice bar. In a shellsuit top and jogging trousers she wasn't dressed for anywhere else.

They sat at a corner table. Though the small bar was deserted, Shephard kept his voice low and toneless. 'I wanted to know if you'd come across anything at Drumanon. Anything you might think was suspicious?'

She shook her head. She hadn't dried her hair properly. It hung to her shoulders in long ringlets, glistening with a myriad drops of water. 'No. Nothing. Nothing that would be of any interest to you, anyway.'

He frowned. 'I see.' He seemed disappointed.

Eleanor looked puzzled. 'To be frank, what I don't understand – what you haven't told me – is what makes you think Drumanon is involved in drugs? I mean, you must admit it's completely bizarre.'

'It's not so bizarre, Eleanor. You'd be shocked at how many respectable people and organizations get themselves involved in the business.'

For some reason she couldn't fathom, she liked him calling

her Eleanor. 'But *I* think it's bizarre. I mean I *know* Drumanon. It's just not possible. What on earth can make you think it is?'

He gave her a long appraising look. As usual his deep brown eyes were serious. 'Can I trust you?' he asked.

She laughed briefly; a low gurgling sound. 'For God's sake, don't start all that again. Yes, you can trust me. In my business, people have to rely on me quite a lot. I've not let any of them down so far.'

He smiled. 'Fair enough.' He was silent for a few seconds before going on. 'One of Drumanon's directors has been spotted a few times in Spain. In the company of a Spanish businessman suspected of smuggling huge amounts of cocaine into Europe.'

Eleanor felt her heart drop like a brick. She sucked in her breath. 'Which one? Which director?' Her voice quavered.

'The boss. The managing director.'

'Lassiter?'

'Yes.'

Eleanor let her breath go in a silent, controlled rush. 'This Spanish businessman,' she asked, 'what does he do? What line of business is he in?'

Shephard frowned, trying to remember. 'He does a lot of things. He's got fishing boats and a fish canning business. And he makes Spanish-style kitchens and things like that.'

'His name is Alonso and he runs a company called Campanalla SA. Right?'

Shephard leaned forward in his seat. 'Yeah, that's right. You know him?'

'No, I don't know him. But I know the company. Drumanon Consolidated does a lot of business with Campanalla.'

'I know. That's what makes us think Drumanon is involved in trafficking.'

'But *what* makes you think that?'

'Drumanon imports a lot of products, doesn't it? I mean, apart from the merchandize from Spain. It gets ceramics and tiles and up-market light fittings from Italy, as well as a lot of furniture from Holland, Belgium and Germany. Now, what's interesting is that those are all countries from which hard drugs are smuggled into Britain. That, along with the Spanish connection, makes us think that Drumanon may be importing narcotics. Between you and me, Customs have been searching some of the products the company receives. The flatpacks of furniture, the deliveries of tiles and ceramics . . . a few of the container lorries hauling the stuff from Europe have been pulled over at the docks and searched.'

'And?'

'And nothing.' He pulled a lugubrious face. 'Bugger all. The problem is that we can't search everything without making someone at Drumanon suspicious. That's why we put Adams into the warehouse.'

'Your undercover man.'

'Yeah. With jobs the way they are, we were lucky to get him in. He'd only been there a couple of weeks before he . . .' Shephard paused, 'before he drowned.'

'Did he find anything?'

Shephard shook his head. 'No. He kept his eyes open but he said that everything coming into the warehouse looked absolutely legitimate. He was pretty sure that no drugs were coming through with the merchandize. The thing is, during the time he was there the warehouse hadn't received any deliveries from Spain. And that's where we think the stuff is coming from.'

'What?' Eleanor's voice was incredulous.

He looked surprised. 'Spain. We're waiting for a delivery from Spain. As Lassiter does business with this character

309

Alonso, that's where we think the coke is coming from.'

Eleanor laughed sharply. Shephard looked confused. 'You're going to wait a long time, John.'

'What do you mean?'

'Drumanon never receives deliveries from Spain. It doesn't get anything from there.'

'But you said it does a lot of business with Spain.'

'It does. But nothing is ever delivered directly to the UK. The company has a sub-distributor.'

'A what?'

'A sub-distributor. All the goods from Campanalla go by sea to Rotterdam. Then a European distributor ships the goods over here against firm orders from its own sales organization here in the UK.'

A thought flashed into her mind. It was important, but it was too quick for her. First it was there, then it was gone.

Shephard looked shocked. 'They never get anything directly from Spain? Ever?'

She shook her head. 'No.'

He leaned back in his seat and moaned. 'Jesus Christ.'

'So you see, if this man Alonso is smuggling drugs, Drumanon would never know about it. Maybe Van Dameer in Amsterdam might have been involved. But not Drumanon.'

He stared at her, scarcely able to grasp the significance of what she had said. 'I don't believe it,' he said softly, almost to himself.

'I'm afraid you have to. It's true. It looks as though you're barking up the wrong tree. It may be possible that the death of your undercover man was an accident after all.'

He shot her a hard look and made as if to say something. Instead he stared silently at her. A couple pushed through the swing doors of the club bar, took a look around and decided to find somewhere with a little more life. The doors clattered behind them as they left.

'This deal with Campanalla,' his voice was low and stony, 'you say the Spanish company sends the goods to Holland and then this Dutch company, Van – what was it?'

'Van Dameer.'

' . . .Van Dameer sells the stuff over here?'

She nodded. 'That's the arrangement I'm auditing right now.'

'Yet Campanella's original contract is with Drumanon.'

'Yes, that's right.'

'Isn't that very complicated?'

'No, not especially.'

'It seems a funny way of doing business to me.'

She smiled. 'That's because you're a policeman. You wouldn't think it was complicated if you were a businessman.'

He wasn't convinced. 'I don't know. It sounds very –' he searched for the word – 'elaborate.'

'Would you think it was elaborate if the goods from Campanalla were being delivered to a distribution agent in Birmingham, or Manchester, or somewhere like that?'

He frowned. 'No, I don't suppose so.'

'So, you only think it's complicated because the goods are delivered to Holland and sold on Drumanon's behalf by a European distributor.'

'Yeah.'

'But don't you see? That's why we've got this thing called the European Community. It's supposed to be a free market. And the whole point of the EC is to allow the kind of business that Drumanon is doing.' She stopped.

There it was again. The thought. It was significant . . . to do with what she was saying. But she couldn't catch it. It was past in an instant.

She frowned. 'I'm sorry, I must sound as if I'm delivering a lecture.'

He grinned at her. 'No, not at all. But this Dutch distributor, what exactly does it do?'

'Van Dameer,' she went on in a lighter tone, 'has a regional sales organization over here, with salesmen selling the kitchens and conservatories and ventilation equipment. Van Dameer's salesmen pay eighty-five percent of the price of everything they sell directly into Drumanon's bank account and remit the rest, Van Dameer's commission, to Holland.'

Shephard screwed his face up. 'God, it's a different world, isn't it? That sounds involved. Why do they do that?'

'Well, there would be no point sending *all* the money to Holland, would there? The Dutch would only have had to pay eighty-five percent of it back to Drumanon in Britain and that would mean currency exchanges costs. Changing guilders into sterling. With the sums involved, that would amount to a lot of money.' She laughed. 'That's one of the reasons why a lot of business people in Europe want a single currency in the Community.'

'To hell with that,' Shephard growled. He looked at her enquiringly. 'You wouldn't want us to give up our own money, would you?'

'I don't really know.' She smiled. 'I have to admit I'm attached to sterling. But,' she shrugged, 'business isn't run on sentiment.'

'What *are* the sums involved?'

'Between Drumanon and Van Dameer?' He nodded. 'In the last fiscal year about forty million.'

'Christ,' he said softly. He thought about it for a moment. 'It must be hell for you to audit. All that money going backwards and forwards to Holland.'

'No, not really. In many ways it's the easiest part of the whole job. A lot of the work had already been done before I got there. By David Rudge.'

'The guy killed in a car crash?'

'Yes. So you see, John, Drumanon's business is perfectly legitimate. Whatever might be going on in the company, it's got nothing to do with drugs. There's no way that Drumanon is smuggling drugs from Spain. Maybe Campanalla and Van Dameer are up to something. I couldn't say. But not Drumanon.'

He wouldn't concede defeat easily. 'Even though they have these complicated deals? I mean, why doesn't Drumanon sell the stuff from Campanalla directly? Why subcontract it out to someone else?'

'Good question. I've already suggested that. But, as Dan Lassiter pointed out, Drumanon makes a profit of more than five million from the deal. And all for shifting a few pieces of paper. Five million for doing nothing. Lassiter reckons that's good business.'

It came and went in a flash. A connection – an insight – an intuition. Something vital. Gone.

Shephard grunted. Eleanor had the impression he didn't approve of Drumanon making easy money.

She drained her glass. She was beginning to feel tired; tired of the questions. 'That's it, I'm afraid,' she said. 'I haven't seen anything because there is nothing to see.' She gave him a tight, tired smile. 'As I told you, auditors aren't bloodhounds. There's nothing there. Not that would interest you. All Drumanon's contracts are perfectly straightforward and legal. The distribution arrangement isn't particularly complicated. It isn't even unusual. I've come across similar deals before.'

He looked defeated. Slumped back in his seat, he had an

unhappy look on his face. 'So you think Drumanon's perfectly straight?'

She thought about Lasssiter's forged letter and the curious round sum amounts. Whatever they were, she knew they were nothing to do with the drug squad. And anyway, she had a duty of confidentiality to her client. Her work at Drumanon was no business of the police. She was beginning to wish Shephard would stop asking her all these questions about the company. He seemed so intense about it. 'Yes I do,' she said wearily.

'Who owns it?' His voice was as flat as hers. He was gazing fixedly at her but the question seemed an afterthought.

She sighed. 'It was owned by a local family, the Drumanons. In fact most people around here think it still is. But actually Dan Lassiter bought the company from them in the late seventies. The family still owns a few shares but Dan owns most of it.'

'What about Richard Jamieson?'

She was surprised to hear Shephard mention Richard's name. 'What about him?'

'Does he own any of it?'

'I think maybe he owns a small amount of stock.' Her tone was quick, irritable. 'I'm not sure. I haven't checked the share register. David did that before he died.'

'What's Jamieson like? Is he close to Lassiter?'

Something in his tone, the way he asked the question, bothered her. Her voice grew edgy. 'Why are you asking me?'

'You're seeing him, aren't you?'

'How the hell do you know that?' Suddenly she was indignant. 'In my flat, you said that you weren't interested in my personal life. Now, all of a sudden, you know who I'm dating. Have you been following me?'

He shook his head. 'No. Him.'

She glared at him suspiciously. 'Are you sure?' He nodded but he didn't look sure. Something came to her. 'Wait a minute. How did you turn up here so conveniently? That's a hell of a nice, neat coincidence. I've never seen you in here before. Are you really a member of this club?'

He looked embarrassed, like a small boy caught stealing sweets. 'Well, actually, I joined this evening.'

She stood up quickly. 'So you *are* bloody following me.'

'No, not really. I was on my way to see you and—'

'Spare me the lies, Inspector Shephard.' She was furious. 'If you want to know what Richard Jamieson is like, I suggest you ask him. Now, if you'll excuse me.' She grabbed her bag.

He looked up at her. His face was baffled and disturbed: startled by her outburst; shocked by the sudden change in her manner. 'Jesus Christ,' he groaned. 'Look, believe me, I'm not trying to pry into your private life.' He stood up. 'The last thing I want to do is offend you.'

'I'm not offended, Inspector.' Her tone was high and icy, as remote as the stratosphere. 'I've done my duty, co-operated with the police, told you what I know. Nothing is happening at Drumanon that could be of any interest to the drug squad. So that's the end of it. You've told me your secrets and I've told you mine. We're quits.'

'Secrets?'

'Certainly. I've told you how Drumanon conducts its business. As an auditor I'm not supposed to do that. But don't worry, I'm not going to tell anybody about our conversation. Or about the fact that you asked me to spy on my client. That is, so long as I'm assured that you're not spying on *me*. That you're not going to follow me around for the rest of my life. Now, as there's nothing for you to know about Drumanon, there's really no need for us to meet again.

Is there?' She turned sharply and strode across the bar, crashing the swing doors noisily behind her.

Shephard watched her go, his face disordered by confusion.

By the time she was halfway to the car park she regretted it. Her reaction had been totally over the top. Shephard, she thought, wasn't a bad guy. He seemed almost . . . well, gentle. She felt like an idiot, going so far out of her tree just because he knew she was sleeping with Richard Jamieson. Why should she care if he knew? Yet, strangely, she did.

She let out a sigh. The outburst had done her no good. All the physical wellbeing her workout had induced had gone; evaporated in a rush of indignation. Now she'd probably have to take a Temazepam to get to sleep.

She swore violently under her breath. 'Damn, blast and fuck.' She thumbed the button on the car's remote control, got in and sat staring at the concrete wall of the multi-storey.

Something else was bothering her too.

Those thoughts. Those fleeting, shadowy notions that had flashed through her brain. For an instant they had been as revealing as flickers of bright lightning. And as impossible to hold.

Chapter Seventeen

She got the call early. The phone warbled as she was watching the Business Breakfast Programme. The little yellow clock at the bottom of the screen showed six thirty-five. She knew immediately it was the Laundryman. He always called early.

'I've got work for you,' he said. 'You're going for a drive.'

She pulled into the underground car park behind Harley Street at a little after eight and parked on the second level. Close by, nose out from the wall, was a BMW 750i. The Laundryman emerged from the passenger side and approached as she got out of the car.

'Any problems?' He meant had she been followed. She shook her head.

'What's happening?' she asked.

'There's been some trouble. A big dealer has been hit. Nobody knows whether he's talking or not but the Profit wants to move the money straightaway. There's a lot of it.'

'Where am I going?'

'Somewhere near the south coast. He'll tell you where.' He nodded in the direction of the driver of the BMW who had got out of the car and was standing by its open door. She looked him over. He was about her age; blond, tall and well-built. He was wearing some great clothes.

'Who's he?'

'It doesn't matter. Come on.' The Laundryman led her towards the BMW.

The young man eyed her coldly as he pushed the car door shut. 'Does she know what to do?'

The Laundryman shook his head. 'No, I haven't told her anything.'

The young man stared dispassionately at her for a few more seconds. 'Come with me,' he ordered.

They walked around to the back of the BMW, squeezing in between the rear bumper and the roughcast concrete wall of the car park. The man opened the boot of the car. It was filled with cheap nylon holdalls and plastic sports bags. She counted six, no, seven, all stuffed to the limit. She shot a glance at the man. Sitting in the car boot was close to two million pounds.

He slammed the boot shut. 'I've got four more of them, in full bleeding view on the back seat. They need to go in your motor.' The man opened the rear door of the car and pulled a rug off another set of holdalls. He and the Laundryman carried them to the Astra and put them out of sight in the boot. She watched them pack the bags away carefully. It was standard procedure. When the money men had to move a lot of merchandize they divided it between at least two couriers. That way, if one was stopped or tailed, the other still had a chance of getting through.

'Okay,' said the man, 'you got a road atlas?'

'Yeah.'

'Get it.'

She brought him the atlas and he instructed her on the route. 'Take the M3 down to Southampton, then the M27, west towards Ringwood.' He was tracing the route with his index finger. In the dull light of the car park she noticed the fingernail was manicured. He looked up and scowled at the GSi 16v. 'Don't drive too fast. Keep it below eighty.'

'I have done this a few times,' she told him coolly. 'I know the SP. I've been told what to do before.'

'Well, I'm telling you again.' He glanced at the Laundryman. 'There hadn't better be any fuckups with this. There's too much involved.'

The Laundryman gave him a sickly grin. 'Don't worry, K. She's the best I got.'

He grunted and went back to the atlas. She wondered why the Laundryman called him Kay. Maybe he's a fruit, she thought. She appraised him out of the corner of her eye. He didn't look like one; he looked like a straight. But these days, who could tell?

'There's a Little Chef along here, after you come off the motorway,' he continued. 'Pull in there for coffee. I'll come in but don't act like you know me. Another bloke will come in. He might be with a woman. They'll sit at my table. The bloke will be carrying a copy of last Saturday's *Financial Times*. Got that? Last Saturday's.'

'Yeah, I got it.'

'He's our contact. When he goes out, so do we. He'll drive off and we'll follow. We'll switch the stuff to his car when and where he stops. Right?'

'Right.' There was a moment's silence. She looked at the Laundryman. 'What's my manda?'

He shrugged. 'The usual.'

'Hey, that's not right. This is a big trip. I'll bet I'm carrying close to a million there. That's a lot of risk. I ought to get more than the usual.'

The man called K gave her a hard look. 'Shit,' he hissed, 'I haven't got all day to stand around this sodding car park talking about your fucking take. I'll pay you a grand. That's it. Okay.'

319

She gave him her innocent look. 'Yeah, that's okay.'

'Right. Then let's get on with it.'

She walked back to the Astra and followed him as he drove out of the car park. They passed the Laundryman walking up the ramp. He didn't look at them.

It was the rush hour, but they were driving against the flow of traffic and they made good time. The day was bright and dry, though not sunny; the big ball of orange light was diffused behind a low, filmy curtain of cloud. They crossed the river at Hammersmith, drove through Barnes and headed west on the Upper Richmond Road. The man, K, wasn't in any hurry and it was easy for her to keep up. She didn't get too close. It was important not to appear as if they were in convoy.

She locked on to the Jaguar at Twickenham. She had first noticed it four or five cars back on Hammersmith Bridge. It had stayed with her since then. She slowed down and allowed a few cars to overtake. The Jag hung back. From her rearview mirror she could see two men inside. Her heart began banging like a hammer on an anvil. Had she picked up a police tail? Did the law know what she was carrying in the boot?

She was on the Chertsey Road, doing fifty. She shoved her foot to the floor and slewed the Astra out into the fast lane. She stayed at eighty for half a mile, roaring past K in the BMW who shot her an angry, confused glance. Closing up on the stream of slower moving traffic ahead she eased off the accelerator. The Jag was right behind her.

She reduced her speed to little more than a crawl and, despite the blaring horns from somewhere behind the Jag, allowed the traffic in the left lane to overtake. She saw the BMW coming up in her nearside mirror and whipped across in front of it. The Jag followed her across, cutting up the BMW.

She reckoned if the Jag was an unmarked police car, they were making a bloody mess of trailing her; about as subtle as a rhino at the Ritz.

She watched the men inside the Jag in her rearview mirror. The man in the passenger seat turned round and gave K in the BMW behind some kind of acknowledgement. It was no more than a nod but it told her all she needed to know. No, they weren't the police; they were the minders.

She allowed herself a small smile of relief and settled down in the driving seat. Minders made sense. It was obvious that the Profit wouldn't allow two million in cash to be transported to its point of departure for some foreign bank without protection. It was necessary, when they were on the move or when they were parked. The men in the car were there to guard against the unexpected. A mechanical breakdown, joyriders, a kid trying to lift the stereo system.

Most of all they were there for her. Just in case she made a run for it; tried to take off with a million in used notes. One or two girls in her line of work might have thought about it; maybe even tried it. They had shit for brains. Not her. The men in the Jag had guns; automatic weapons probably . . . and they'd use them. Without thinking about it. They'd catch up with her and then – then it would be a shotgun blast in the face or two 9mm bullets in the back of the head. That was the way they dealt with anybody who tried to cross them; who got out of line; screwed up; let them down. The professional hit . . . execution by the organization . . . it was their solution to every problem.

She shuddered. No. No way she was going to cross them. She was happy to drive with a few bags of dirty money in the boot to wherever she was told. She wasn't going to make a run for it. Or get cute and start asking dumb questions. Not her. She would be perfectly happy to pick up her pay and forget everything that happened.

It was an easy drive. On the motorway the BMW overtook her and remained a few cars in front. The Jag dropped back a couple of cars. They reached the Little Chef just after ten thirty. The car park was almost full. She noticed that, apart from the usual quota of salesmen's cars, there was a fair sprinkling of the kind of vehicles she would expect to see in the rich, rural south: a muddy Land Rover towing an empty horsebox, a traditional Range Rover, a few Japanese Off Roaders.

K found a place to park, then waited as she got out of her car and walked towards the restaurant. The Jag arrived and found itself a slot in clear view of both the BMW and the Astra. The two men remained in the car.

The place was busy. She waited to be shown to a table and asked for one in the smoking section. She had it to herself. K came in and asked for something in non-smoking. He was forced to share a table with a young couple. The woman was reading the *Daily Mail*. The girl ordered coffee and a Danish; travelling made her hungry.

She looked around, surveying the roadhouse's customers. No one was reading the *Financial Times*. The people in the restaurant reflected the vehicles outside. A few men and women, mostly around her age and formally dressed, were obviously between appointments. Most of the others were older; suburban, even rural, with fresh, open-air faces and old-fashioned clothes.

The waitress brought her order. She wolfed the Danish and lit a cigarette. Something made her glance over her shoulder. At the entrance, close to the till, a short, tubby man and his short, plump wife were waiting to be seated. In their late fifties, dressed in casual but expensive clothes, they looked like a retired couple with plenty of money; like a pair of well-heeled Munchkins.

The man was carrying a copy of the *Financial Times*. She watched him shoot a quick glance in the direction of K whose table was still occupied by the young man and his avid, Nigel Dempster fan of a wife. A waitress led the Munchkins to a table further along the row.

She stood up and headed towards the lavatory. Passing the couple's table she glanced down at the pink newspaper the man was reading. It was Saturday's edition. She paused at the lavatory door and gave K a brief nod.

Afterwards, she lit another cigarette, ordered another coffee and waited. The couple had tea and toast. When they looked about ready to leave, she paid her bill and strolled across the car park to the Astra. The men in the Jag watched her.

The Munchkins emerged a few moments later. The girl expected K to follow immediately but it was a couple of minutes before he showed, by which time the Munchkins had climbed into a silver-grey Volvo 800 estate. As soon as K got into his car they started the engine and sedately exited the car park. The others, led by the BMW, followed.

They drove westwards for a few miles. The road was slightly elevated, with views in both directions over what had once been the New Forest and was now scrubby heathland. Bushes of mustard-coloured gorse lined its edges.

Finally the convoy turned off the road and headed north into rolling, lightly wooded countryside. The lanes grew narrow, though the man in the Volvo drove surprisingly fast.

They powered up a long, sweeping hill. On the right, at its brow, was a layby, shielded from the narrow road by a high hedge of gorse and bordered by a small, dense wood. The Volvo slowed, pulled into the layby and stopped. The other two cars followed suit. The Jag stayed on the road, pulling over onto the verge. The two men got out. From where they were standing they could see the road in either direction for almost a mile. It was the perfect spot for a switch.

The Munchkins moved surprisingly fast. They were out of the car and had the Volvo's tailgate open in a flash. K was already humping a couple of holdalls out of the boot of the BMW. The girl did likewise, struggling across to the Volvo under the weight of the money in two sports bags. The man and woman were stuffing the bags inside large wickerwork hampers. The girl noticed that the interior of the car was filled with fishing and sailing tackle which, with the wickerwork baskets, made it look like the back of a typically untidy sportsman's Volvo.

The switch was completed in less than forty-five seconds. The Munchkins, who hadn't said a word throughout the proceedings, slammed the rear door shut, clambered back into the Volvo and drove off, heading in the same direction the convoy had been driving.

The girl closed the back of the Astra as K walked towards her. 'What the hell was all that business on the Chertsey Road?' he demanded. 'You trying to get us fucking noticed?'

She nodded her head in the direction of the hedge. 'I picked out the Jag. I didn't know if it was the law or what. I needed to see if I could pull it out.' She shrugged. 'How was I to know it was your guard car?' He grunted irritably.

She was silent for a moment, waiting. Behind K the Jaguar purred into sight around the end of the high, yellow-speckled hedge. The driver was alone. He stopped the car, got out, went to the back and opened the boot. He lifted something out.

She had waited long enough. 'You got my money?' she demanded.

He put a hand inside his jacket. He pulled out a neat, squat-looking gun.

She jerked backwards in alarm. 'Hey, what's this? Shit, it's only a grand. Jesus, you can afford that. You can't rip me off for a measly thou.'

The driver of the Jag was close now. She could see what he was carrying. It was a roll of black, heavy-gauge polythene sheeting. He dropped it onto the dusty surface of the layby and spread it out with his foot. Then she knew.

'Oh no,' she cried. 'Oh no. Christ no. Please no.' K moved behind her and pushed her forward towards the black sheeting. 'Wait,' she wailed. 'Why? why?'

She heard his voice behind her as if from a great distance. 'You shouldn't have been so nosy.'

She didn't know what he meant. 'I didn't see anything. Jesus Christ, I promise I didn't. I won't talk,' she sobbed. 'Please, no, not this. God, please no.'

She stared boggle-eyed and quivering at the man standing in front of her on the edge of the polythene. He was short and runty with dirty clothes and an appalling set of raking, livid scars, like jagged tracks, down one cheek. He grinned at her. His teeth were black and broken.

'Nooooo, pleease, no.' She was screaming. K chopped the back of her neck with the edge of his hand and she sank to her knees.

The man to her front pulled a pistol from the waistband beneath his jacket and walked behind her. She heard K step back. She lived long enough to hear the first sharp crack before the bullet blew her brain apart. She didn't hear the second.

The man with the dreadful scars bent down and wrapped the little, twitching body tightly in the polythene. He and K lifted the black bundle and trundled it to the boot of the Jaguar. 'Watch my fucking suit,' K said.

The man shut the boot lid and got into the Jaguar. Without

another word K walked back to his car, got in and drove out of the layby, heading back the way he had come. The driver of the Jag stopped at the verge on the road to pick up his companion before setting off in the opposite direction.

They had been parked on the brow of the hill less than three minutes.

Richard didn't call. She was in or around the flat for most of the weekend, and even when she wasn't the answering machine was switched on. But there was no message. Men. Eleanor hated that about them. They would promise to call and then . . . nothing. She should have known by now. A man's promise to call wasn't worth the bloody breath it took to make it. She had wasted her weekend, passing her time suspended in some half-world state of anticipation, waiting.

She got into work early on Monday morning. She thought about calling Richard at his office but gave it up. Let him come to her. Instead she put a call through to the two clerks in Drumanon's boardroom. They were already hard at it and reckoned two days at most to finish. That put her in a better frame of mind. Almost all the items on the audit checklist were complete. By the end of the week she should be ready with the first set of draft financial statements.

She leaned back in her seat. She would, she thought, be glad when the audit was finished. It would make her relationship with Richard so much easier to handle. If they continued seeing each other, it wouldn't be for business reasons. And if they didn't, well, she wouldn't be bumping into him in Drumanon's offices.

She had already decided that she wouldn't do the audit next year. She'd only undertaken it this year because of David's death and to prove a point: that she could break into the male preserve of *important* work; that she could cut the mustard. She smiled. She'd proved she could do that. It hadn't been a difficult audit at all. Except . . .

She thought about the discoveries of Friday afternoon; the round sum amounts and the Van Dameer letter. No, it hadn't been difficult. But there were bits of it that bothered her. Made her uneasy. Things that didn't quite stack up.

Remembering the Van Dameer letter prompted her to shuffle through the files on her desk. She found what she was looking for, a plain manilla folder. In it were copies of the two contracts; Van Dameer's, and the contract with Lubbenau which replaced it. Though she wasn't a lawyer, Eleanor had read enough commercial contracts to know her way around one. She studied the contracts carefully. The brilliant light, streaming through the windows from the harbour, enabled her to read the cautious, stilted prose without her spectacles.

Afterwards, when she had finished, she laid the two documents side by side on her desk and stared at them. They were the same. In every essential clause and provision they said the same thing. It didn't make sense. She frowned. Dan Lassiter had replaced one well-tried and tested commercial agreement with another exactly like it. Where, then, was the advantage? She couldn't understand it.

Eleanor was a commercial animal; she knew and understood business. She knew that business was all about getting an edge. And, having got it, improving on it. On the surface of it, Dan Lassiter had lost an edge, lost the advantage of more than twelve years' experience when he replaced Van Dameer with Lubbenau. There had to be a reason. Lassiter was too astute to do something like that without a reason.

She picked up the phone and asked the girl on the switchboard to get her Dan Lassiter at Drumanon. A few seconds later he was on the line. There was one good thing about Lassiter, she thought. He always took her calls.

'Eleanor,' his voice was cheery. 'Good morning.'

'Morning, Dan.' Her voice was equally cheerful but she was mindful that she would have to watch her words. 'Dan, I've just been through the Lubbenau contract, comparing it with the one you had with Van Dameer.'

'Oh yeah.' His voice wasn't so bright.

'Dan, I'm a little puzzled and I thought maybe you can help me. On the surface of it, the Lubbenau contract is exactly the same as Van Dameer's. The same terms, the same deal, the same everything.'

'Yeah,' Lassiter's voice was cautious. 'So what? What are you getting at, Eleanor?'

'Well, I was wondering, where's the advantage? I mean, isn't it a bit like replacing a two-year-old car that you know with a ten-year-old car you don't?'

'Ah, okay, I see what you're driving at.' His voice was back to its original animation. 'Well, what you don't realize, Eleanor, is that Van Dameer had been getting troublesome. All of a sudden they wanted to renegotiate the deal; wanted to up their volume discounts.'

'I see,' said Eleanor.

'Of course, we wanted to keep the contract with them. We negotiated with them for over a year. The file is thick with correspondence: offers from us, counter-offers from them. We tried to hold them down to the existing terms but it was no good, Van Dameer wouldn't have it. So, in the end I figured to hell with them and found Lubbenau. Lubbenau said they were prepared to distribute for us on exactly the same terms as the original Van Dameer agreement. So, that was it. Van Dameer lost, Lubbenau won. And so did Drumanon. Van Dameer was too greedy. And that doesn't always pay.'

'Yes, you're right.' She was staring at the documents on her desk. Now she understood. 'Okay, Dan, thanks very much. I'll make a short note to the financial statements.' Lassiter grunted his approval. 'Oh,' she added as an afterthought, 'I wouldn't mind a word with Richard, if he's in.'

'No, he's not here. He's not due in until tomorrow.'

'Okay, thanks.' She put the phone down. It was probably just as well that Jamieson wasn't there. First she'd resolved not to call him at the office and then, the first opportunity she'd got, she'd tried to talk to him. She made a rueful face. She never learned.

She wondered where he might be. She got up from her desk, turned to the window and, picking her binoculars off the windowsill, trained them on the line of buoys where Richard moored the yacht. It wasn't there. She swept the harbour with the glasses. There was no sign of it.

She put the binoculars back on the windowsill. So, she thought, he'd gone sailing. Without her. Well, why not? After all, he hadn't promised to take her sailing that weekend. All he'd promised to do was call. She wondered if he'd taken someone else with him. Some other woman. She turned back to the work at her desk. It was stupid thinking like that. She didn't own Richard Jamieson. Something struck a chord.

Owning and Jamieson – where had she heard the two connected? She remembered. Friday evening at the sports club. The policeman, John Shephard. He had asked if Jamieson owned any shares in Drumanon. Why the hell would he want to know that?

She found the audit checklist, glanced at it quickly and saw that David had inspected all Drumanon's statutory records early on in the audit. She buzzed Lindsey on the intercom and asked her to come into her office.

'Lindsey, didn't you do some work with David when he started on the Drumanon audit?'

'Yes.' She flicked her hair back. She was as tall as Eleanor, with long mousy hair and a pale, birdlike face. She was young, eager and helpful but not particularly talented and Eleanor had the impression that she wasn't especially serious about her career.

'Did you examine the share register?'

'Me personally?'

'Yes.'

'No. David did. He was muttering about checking something out.'

'Checking what out?'

Lindsey shrugged. 'I don't know. He didn't tell me. He only mentioned it once, so I don't think it was very important.'

'Okay, thanks.' Lindsey turned to go. 'Oh, by the way, how are you getting on with circularizing the trade debtors?'

'I've almost finished. Most of the replies are in and they've confirmed our figures. The only important one I'm waiting to hear from is Van Dameer in Holland.'

'But Van Dameer was Drumanon's biggest debtor. If we don't get confirmation of the year-end balances from them, we may have to qualify the audit report. Are they being bloody-minded, because they lost the contract?'

'No, nothing like that.' The girl made a face. 'I can't get through. On the phone or the fax.'

'Damn, Okay. Keep trying. I'll talk to someone at Drumanon to see if they can help. What about Campanalla? Have you confirmed their supply figures?'

Lindsey giggled. 'I've got through on the phone a couple of times but all I get is someone who speaks Spanish.'

'That's not too surprising in Spain, Lindsey.' Her tone was

mildly caustic. 'What about faxing them?'

'I was going to do that next.'

'No, it's okay. I'll do it.' She sighed as she watched Lindsey leave the office. It was at times like now she missed London and the sharp, driving professionalism of Karding Hillier Longland.

She drafted a fax and took it down to the main office on the ground floor. Most of the girls were busy at their desks, the big room quietly humming with the sound of computer cooling fans and the click of keyboards. Philip was standing in the middle of the office scrutinizing a clutch of tax schedules. He looked up as she walked in and his broad, fleshy face broke into a warm smile. 'Morning, Eleanor.'

She smiled in return. 'Hello, Philip.'

She saw Alice leaning over one of the girls' desks. 'Alice, can you get someone to send a fax for me?' Alice came over. 'It's to Campanalla in Spain. I'd like it to go this morning.'

'Yes, of course.'

Philip wandered over. 'Faxing Campanalla?'

Eleanor nodded. 'I need them to confirm the figures on Drumanon's purchase ledger. And the outstanding balance owing at the end of the last balance-sheet date.'

Philip looked over her shoulder at the draft. 'I hope they understand it. Apart from the president, I don't think many of the company officers speak English.' He read it swiftly. 'Yes, that seems okay.'

'Do you think I should ask them to send copies of the shipping documents too? We ought to see some proof that the goods were actually despatched and that they arrived in Holland. Otherwise, how do we know that a debt has been established between Campanalla and Drumanon?'

He pulled a wry face. 'That *will* make it difficult. Van Dameer distributed for them in all the other EC countries as well, you know. It would put at least another week on the audit. You've got the goods received notes from Holland to prove the stuff arrived. I don't think you need belt *and* braces.'

She smiled at him. 'Don't *you* start telling me I'm pedantic now.' Alice laughed.

Philip frowned. He didn't understand. 'Here, give me the fax. I'll make sure it goes.' Alice gave him a peevish look.

She handed it to him. 'Thanks.'

She drove over to Drumanon in the afternoon. By now she was getting used to the journey; it was even beginning to become something of a chore. The clerks were busy, their heads down in the piles of printouts and files in the boardroom. They seemed as eager as she was to finish the job. After a while she left them to it and walked along the executive corridor to Richard Jamieson's office. Brenda, his secretary, was there.

As Jamieson was both the financial director and company secretary, Eleanor knew that it would be his responsibility to take care of Drumanon's statutory records. They were kept in a fireproof safe in his office. Brenda had a key.

'Brenda, I need to check something in the share register,' she announced. 'Can I take a quick look?' Brenda unlocked the safe without demur. Eleanor, standing close to the small nest of sofas in the corner of the office, watched her. The girl brought her the register. She put it on the glass-topped table and sat down on one of the sofas.

Controlled by five or fewer persons, Drumanon Consolidated Limited was a close company. There were three names on the register of shareholders. One was Edmund Drumanon who, at over seventy, was one of the last of the original owning family and the company's non-executive chairman. Eleanor was surprised at his modest shareholding. Five per cent. Yet it was Edmund Drumanon who was quoted in reports about the company; his picture that always appeared in the press. He was the face of the company, giving the impression that the company was still a family concern. She remembered Philip telling her that he was a hunting and shooting friend of James Hagerty.

Eighty percent of the shares were owned by Dan Lassiter through a company called Lassiter Holdings Limited. Lassiter Holdings' parent company was Lassiter Enterprises Inc of Toronto which meant that Dan Lassiter's Canadian company was the ultimate majority shareholder in Drumanon.

The remaining fifteen per cent of the company was owned by Richard Jamieson. She closed the register, stood up and handed it back to the secretary. 'Thanks, Brenda.'

She walked back to the boardroom. Jamieson's shareholding was in line with what he had told her on their first date. Lassiter had induced Jamieson to come to work for Drumanon by offering him a piece of the action. A small stockholding in a close company was a common enticement for a good accountant. Fifteen percent wasn't an enormous amount, though it was substantial enough. It didn't prove that Jamieson and Lassiter were especially close; in fact, Eleanor concluded as she reached the boardroom door, it could mean quite the opposite. When it came to control of the company there was Lassiter and nobody else. Lassiter, at eighty percent, effectively had total control. Richard and old man Drumanon didn't have enough stock to make any difference.

She didn't know why it was important for her to establish that the two men weren't close. She stopped at the boardroom door. Who, she wondered, was she kidding? Sure she knew why.

She was sleeping with Jamieson and she was suspicious of

Lassiter. About what, she didn't know. But she knew he was up to something. She recalled his words earlier in the day about the Van Dameer file; about how thick it had become with the letters of negotiation between the two companies.

Bullshit. There hadn't been any negotiation. Lassiter didn't know it but she had *seen* the Van Dameer file. There was virtually nothing in it. Except those blank letterheads.

A ghostly notion flitted across her mind. The same thought she'd had when she was with Shephard. Something to do with Van Dameer. Something she should know . . . understand. What the hell was it . . .?

'Hello.'

She spun around, startled. Richard Jamieson was standing right behind her.

'God, you gave me a shock.'

He smiled. 'I'm sorry.' He stared at her for a moment. 'What were you doing?'

'What do you mean?'

His smile broadened. She noticed that he was looking especially tanned, as if he had been out on a boat all weekend. 'You were standing here,' he nodded at the closed boardroom door, 'looking as if you were contemplating the nature of the universe.'

She laughed. 'Was I? Well, I was thinking about something, but it wasn't the nature of the universe. Just some minor accounting matter.' She looked up at him with a puzzled expression. 'Anyway, what are you doing here? I spoke to Dan earlier. He said you weren't coming in today.'

'I had some business in town. I got through it quicker than I thought.'

She nodded, remembering the absent yacht. She appraised his smiling face and there was a moment's silence. 'I thought you said you were going to call me this weekend.' Her voice was low and level.

'Did I?' His face puckered. Then he said, 'No I didn't. I said I'd call you in the next couple of days.'

'That's right. That was on Friday.'

He gave her his winsome, boyish smile. 'Well, you know how it is. When one says a couple of days, it can mean longer.' He looked concerned and flicked the cowlick of hair off his forehead. 'I'm sorry if you were expecting me to call over the weekend. Anyway I was going to phone you this evening.'

'Oh yes.'

'Yes. I wondered whether you might like to come sailing next weekend? Across to France or the Channel Islands.'

In spite of her reserve she felt her heart leap. 'I'd love to.'

She'd blabbed out the words before she'd even considered whether she was just one of a succession of women with whom he spent the weekend on his boat. What the hell, she thought. 'Though I ought to tell you,' she said, 'I'm not a very experienced sailor. Not for all that deep sea stuff.'

He laughed. 'It's not deep sea. It's the Channel. We'll try and get away on Friday afternoon. Is that okay?'

'Fine.'

'Good.' He turned to go. 'I'll call you before Friday. I promise.'

She walked into the boardroom and sat down. The two articled clerks, immersed in the paperwork, ignored her. After a moment she stood up and stared out of the window into Drumanon's car park.

The prospect of a weekend's sailing with Richard was exciting. She could feel the customary buzzing in her stomach. Yet something else resonated inside her head. A memory. Of the early days of her marriage. Of the way Alec, whenever he hadn't done what he said he was going to do, would weasel out of it by switching on the charm and the engaging, naughty-boy smile. Laughingly, he would tell her that his words at the time of the promise had not meant what she had taken them to mean. After which he would follow up on her confused irritation by promising something else, something even more exciting.

Richard had used the same manipulative trick. In the old days, married to Alec, she had fallen for it. But she'd been too much exploited by bullshit boyish charm to be taken in by it now. It was a dishonest trait . . . one to make her wary.

She worked well into the evening, making up for the time she hadn't put in the previous Friday, and left the offices after seven.

She drove onto the gravel drive of the big old house and parked the car in its usual place. She walked to the door of the flat and put her key in the lock.

A voice said, 'I need to talk to you.'

She spun round with a yelp. 'Oh my God.'

It was John Shephard. 'For Christ's sake.' She put a hand on the doorpost to steady herself. 'Don't do that,' she cried.

'I'm sorry.' He frowned. 'Did I startle you?'

'You damn near gave me a bloody heart attack. You're the second man to creep up on me today. If it had been dark, I'd have probably kicked you in the crotch before I realized who you were.'

He allowed himself a brief, serious smile. 'I would have deserved it. I'm sorry I gave you such a shock.'

'Anyway, where the hell did you come from?' She looked around the drive for his car. She couldn't see it. 'And what the hell do you want?'

'I need to talk to you.'

'We did all our talking on Friday. There's nothing else to

say. So please go away. I don't want to talk to you.'

His face changed in an instant. Suddenly it was firm and forceful. Something about it scared her. Its intensity. 'You don't have any option, Eleanor. This is police business. And *I* want to talk to *you*. Now, let's get inside and get on with it, shall we?'

She stared at him a moment longer, then opened the door of the flat. She led him upstairs and into the lounge. She put her bag and attaché case on a table and sat down on the sofa. Shephard sat in the same seat as before. She glanced at him. His face remained unchanged. 'Well?' Her voice quivered a little.

'The accountant who was working at Drumanon before you. David Rudge.'

'What about him?'

'Do you know exactly what he was working on?'

'The audit of course. What else?'

'No, I mean *exactly*. Was he working on anything special, anything in particular, before he died?'

'I don't know. I don't think so.' She was getting flustered. His voice was hard; his questions fired at her like bullets. 'He was just working on the audit. He wasn't doing anything special.'

'How would you know?'

'We have an audit checklist.' Her voice was hurried. 'It's a kind of standard procedure. David was working his way through it. Look, what is this? Why do you want to know about David?'

'There wasn't anything different on it? Anything unusual David might have been doing?'

'No. I'm going through the list now. Following up everything David did.'

'Do you know if he spent a lot of time in the warehouse?'

'He would have spent time in there during the annual stock count. And when he was following through systems and verification terms. Why do you want to know?'

'Would he have moved around the building a lot?'

'No. No more than I'm moving around it now. But for God's sake, why are you asking me all this? Why do you want to know? Tell me.'

He was silent, staring intently at her. When he spoke his voice was low. 'I and some other detectives have been through the file on David's death. We've all come to the same conclusion. We don't think it was an accident.'

Chapter Eighteen

She had a sudden desire to laugh. Or was it to cry? She didn't know, couldn't tell. What she did know was that a compelling, irresistible urge was surging up her backbone and into her lungs. Her chest began to heave. She realized what it was. Hysteria. For God's sake, she was close to becoming hysterical.

She stood up. 'Excuse me.' She kept her voice to a whisper. She walked as steadily as she could to the bathroom where she splashed cold water in her face. Afterwards she stood for a while and stared into the mirror, breathing deeply.

When she emerged he was standing in the middle of the lounge, his face furrowed in concern. Without a word she went to the drinks cabinet where she poured herself a large whisky. She noticed her hand trembling. She sat on the sofa and took a long swallow. The liquid scorched her lungs and she coughed. Shephard was watching her.

'I'm sorry,' he said, 'I handled that badly. I didn't mean to upset you.'

'Well, you did. What is it about you, Inspector? What are you? Some kind of bloody herald of death? This is the second time you've turned up here to tell me that someone is dead in mysterious circumstances. Someone I knew. Or at least had met.'

'At Drumanon Consolidated,' Shephard emphasized quietly. 'They both worked there.' He sat down. '*That's the connection.*'

'*I* work at Drumanon for Christ's sake.' Her voice was loud. She stopped and shook her head. 'I'm sorry. I didn't mean to yell at you. Or use bad language.'

He shook his head and smiled. 'That's all right. But that's the reason I'm here. Because, right now, *you're* working at Drumanon.'

She moved back quickly in her seat. 'Why?' Despite the whisky her throat was suddenly dry. 'Do you think I'm in some kind of danger?'

He stared at her. 'Eleanor, I don't know. To be honest I've got absolutely no idea what's going on. Two men are dead. They both worked at Drumanon. We're positive they were murdered. But why? We've no idea. Except we think the deaths are drug related.'

She shook her head in disbelief. 'What makes you think David's death was murder? The coroner said it was an accident. Everybody believed it was.'

Shephard shrugged. 'There was no reason to think otherwise. Though, even at the time, the officers investigating the incident said it was bizarre.'

'Why? What happened?'

'He was coming back from his girlfriend's in Dorchester. On the Wareham road. It was late. After midnight. He was driving one of those four-wheel-drive vehicles. At the inquest it was presumed he had taken a bend too quickly. The vehicle was found lying on its side in a ditch. David Rudge was inside. His neck was broken.'

'God.' Eleanor shook her head miserably. 'But, could he have been drunk or something?'

'No. His girlfriend told the local police that he'd had two

half pints of bitter all evening. Apparently he was very careful about drinking and driving. The post mortem confirmed it. David had less than forty mils of alcohol in his blood. Under half the limit. And he was known to be a good driver; careful, not a lunatic like some people his age. The vehicle was in good condition, the weather was fine, the roads were dry. It wasn't even a sharp bend. There was no reason for him to go off the road.'

'But it still *could* have been an accident.'

'Yes,' Shephard conceded, 'and the coroner thought it was. But what else was he supposed to think? The investigating officers had done some checking. They couldn't find any reason why somebody should want David dead. They didn't expect to. Yet there were some peculiar things about the crash. Firstly, there were no skid marks. It looked like David had driven straight off the road without touching the brakes. Secondly, there was no bruising on David's body. His neck was broken but there was scarcely another bruise on him. There should have been. Even though he was wearing his belt he should have been banged about a bit. All of which now makes us think that somebody who knew what they were doing broke David's neck, turned the vehicle over and put him inside it.'

She stared at him. 'God, how awful.'

'We're dealing with awful people, Eleanor. People involved in drugs. They're the scum of the earth; not worth the blood in their veins.' He said it quietly, his voice low and filled with fierce intensity.

She was slightly shocked. At their first meetings Shephard had seemed a gentle, sensitive man. A man, she'd thought, who could be tender. She'd been surprised to find those qualities in a policeman. Now she was learning there was another side to John Shephard. A vengeful side. He seemed pitiless. Somewhere inside this gentle man was a hard, implacable core. It scared her. Disturbed her.

'Oh, come on,' she protested, 'they can't all be that bad. I mean, a lot of people who turn to drugs are poor, depressed, they just can't cope any more. I mean, I'm not defending them, but you can understand why some of them . . . well, why they use drugs.'

'Sure. Some users are just pathetic; dumped on by the world. Either that, or they can't make it any more. But a lot of addicts are mean and vicious, Eleanor. A crack addict will kill you for the change in your purse. They'd do anything to get that stuff. It's the devil's candy. Most people involved with drugs live like animals . . . a lot die like them too.'

'We should do more to help them.'

'Maybe we should. But there are some you just cannot help. They're beyond it.'

'I can't believe that.'

He considered her. 'I hope you never have to.'

'What do you mean?'

He gazed around, taking in the simple elegance of the gracefully furnished lounge. 'Look at this place,' he said quietly. 'It's clean, it's neat, it's beautifully done. Everything around you is clean. You live in a different world, Eleanor. You're smart, good-looking, intelligent, you have a great career.' He smiled affectionately at her. 'The most serious confrontation you're ever likely to have is with a parking meter attendant.' His face grew darker. 'You've no idea what it's like down there. In the sewers. What kind of people live in the world of narcotics . . . what they do to each other. What I mean is, I hope that you never have to come face to face with the kind of person I'm talking about. You can't conceive what they're like. You don't even believe they exist.'

342

She felt a shiver run up her backbone.

'And even worse than the addicts and the pushers and the dealers,' he added, 'are the people behind them. The fat cats who make a big living out of importing and handling drugs. The bastards who are never called to account.'

'Why not?'

He shrugged. 'They're too damn organized. They've built it into a business. A big, powerful business. Just like a legitimate enterprise. One of *The Times* Top Thousand. Only it's bigger.'

She let out a quiet guffaw. 'Oh, come on.'

'It's true. The business is structured into regions based in the big cities. The enterprises have their own territories; no one encroaches, everybody sticks to their own turf. They get most of the drugs from a central supply and they have a separate organization to process the dirty money.'

'You make it sound like a franchise operation.'

'That's exactly what it is. Each area has its own bosses; boards of directors, if you like. And each board has a managing director. Usually called the Profit.'

She shook her head. 'I didn't think narcotics was so organized.'

'Well it is.' He appraised her for a moment. 'Which is the biggest business in the world? Come on, you're an accountant. You ought to know the answer to that.'

She frowned. 'I don't know. Sumitomo? Mitsubishi? One of the big Japanese conglomerates.'

He laughed sharply. 'Not by a long way. The biggest business in the world is organized crime. It produces about 250 *billion* dollars a year.'

She was shocked. 'But that's unbelievable.'

He nodded. 'There are so many illegal billions of drug dollars swilling about the world that the economists call them narco-dollars. All that money in the world's financial system causes the economies a big problem. If organized crime was a country it would be in the world's top twenty. About the size of Belgium. Think of it. Think of all that power. No wonder we're losing the bloody war.'

She stared at him. 'But you can't possibly think that someone at Drumanon is involved in all that.'

'Well I do.'

'But why?'

'Because two men who were working there are dead.'

'But why?' She was insistent. 'That's what you haven't answered. Why should they be murdered? You said yourself that your man Adams hadn't discovered anything; hadn't seen any drugs. And what could David have possibly discovered? He was only the auditor. What would he come across that I wouldn't find?'

His eyes, searching her face, were filled with concern. 'That's what worries me,' he said soberly.

With a shock it dawned on her that he cared for her. Though right then she was in no position to examine her feelings; to discover if she liked the notion of his attraction to her.

'Their deaths could be coincidence.' The confidence had gone from her voice.

'There's something else.'

'What?'

'A friend of mine called me last week. I went to see him in London on Saturday. He's in the Met, a chief inspector in the drug squad. A few days ago he and his men hit a crack factory in south London. They found a lot of product.' He saw her eyebrows pucker. 'Drugs,' he explained, 'especially class A – heroin and cocaine – along with thousands of amphetamines, a lot of marijuana, a cache of firearms and, well, you name it. It was a great bust.'

She sensed his excitement as he talked about it. He was like a kid.

'Afterwards the Met sent in a forensic search team. Those guys take the place apart. Literally. In among a lot of other stuff they found bank statements and a few cheque stubs belonging to Fats. That's the dealer's name. He's been running about a dozen bank accounts, some under false names, some in the names of friends or relatives.' Shephard paused. 'Normally all that stuff is passed straight on to the Drug Profit Confiscation Unit, but luckily this DCI looked at it first. The cheque stubs were about ten years old. We reckon Fats must have forgotten they were in his bank deposit box. Naturally all of them were blank. Except two. Written very lightly on them was the name Drumanon. The DCI knew I was targeting the company so he called me.'

'This drug dealer had made out cheques to Drumanon?' Her voice was incredulous. 'I don't understand.'

'Nor do we. Not yet. My guess is that Drumanon was supplying him drugs.'

'Maybe he bought a conservatory or one of Campanalla's Spanish Kitchens.'

Shephard laughed. 'He's not the type. I told you, these people live like animals.'

'So what were the cheques made out for?'

'We don't know. Fats isn't talking. The Confiscation Unit is going through his bank statements and they've had the data he kept in an electronic organizer decoded. As far as we can tell he hadn't had any other dealings with Drumanon. But those two cheque stubs are significant and sooner or later we'll get to the bottom of it. Right now all we know is that someone at Drumanon is involved in drugs and that two people are dead. That's why I'm here, Eleanor, to tell you what we know. And to warn you.'

The cold fingers clutched the nape of her neck. 'So what do you want me to do?'

'Absolutely nothing.' His voice was definite. 'Forget what I asked you before, about keeping your eyes open. That's all out now. What I want is for you to stop working there.'

She shook her head. 'I can't do that. I'm almost at the end of the audit.'

'Can't you go sick?'

'That would only mean someone else from Hagerty Clark being sent in to finish the job. If what you say is right, then they would be in just as much danger. More, probably. At least I know what's supposed to be going on. If there *is* anything to know.'

'You had better believe there is.' His voice was insistent. 'Well, if you can't stop working there, then you've got to stay away from the place as much as you can. And if you do have to go into the building, don't go wandering about the place, don't go digging into anything. Just don't get involved. Okay?'

She stared at him. He meant it. He was serious. He was asking her not to do her job. For a moment she thought to argue with him; to ask who the hell he thought he was talking to. A glance at his determined face made her think better of it. She nodded hesitantly and asked, 'What are you going to do?'

'I'll get onto the Dutch police to check out Van Dameer. I think there may be an unlawful connection between them and Drumanon.'

Connection. That was it. Suddenly, it was there. Or part of it. The connection . . . the association . . . the thing that had been scratching at the back of her mind since their conversation at the health club. Now she had it.

'Not any more there isn't.'

'What?'

'Drumanon and Van Dameer aren't working together any more. Van Dameer cancelled its agreement last year. There's a new distributor now, a company called Lubbenau, headquartered in Geneva.'

'Shit.' He was angry. 'Bloody hell. Why didn't you tell me this before?'

'I only just thought of it,' she replied mildly. He glowered at her. 'Don't forget I'm auditing *last year*'s accounts. When Drumanon's agreement with Van Dameer was still in force. It didn't occur to me to tell you the deal is out of date. I'm sorry.'

He was quiet for a moment then laughed quietly. 'No, it's I who should apologize for getting all worked up. I'm sorry. But you do have a habit of dropping bombshells on me. First you tell me that Drumanon doesn't get direct deliveries from Spain and now this.'

He stared over her shoulder at the light streaming in the window and shook his head slowly. He seemed bewildered. His tone was low, scarcely audible. 'I don't know what to make of this bloody case.' He jerked himself out of his reverie and pulled out a notebook. 'Lubbenau, you say? What's their address?'

'I don't have it here. I'll call you with it tomorrow.' He nodded. They were silent for a while. From outside came the lazy, summer-evening sound of a small lawnmower. 'What will you do now?' Eleanor asked.

'I'll still get the Dutch police to check out Van Dameer. That may take a while, but . . .' he shrugged. 'We'll also try to get someone else into Drumanon, to keep observation. It's risky, but what else can we do? If only we had some idea of what Adams saw.'

'How do you know he saw anything?'

'He was murdered,' he replied quietly. 'Like David Rudge.'

He stood up. 'I'll be staying in close touch with you. At least until you've finished the audit. I'll check with you every day.'

Eleanor put her glass down and stood up. 'You're not going to start following me again, are you?' She said it lightly, trying to bring some humour into the room.

Shephard looked serious. 'I'm sorry, Eleanor, but if I think it's necessary then, yes, I'll have to.'

She smiled at his expression. His face was filled with concern. He really seemed to care about her. She liked that. 'Well, try not cramp my style, eh?' The serious eyes looked confused and she chuckled. 'Don't worry,' she put her hand on his arm, 'I'll be all right. And I promise not to shout at you if I catch you creeping up on me.'

She led him downstairs, said goodnight and watched him walk between the big stone pillars out of the drive. His car was parked down the street.

There was something she liked about John Shephard, though precisely what she couldn't say. And she was too tired to try figuring it out now; too tired and too wound up over what he had told her about David Rudge and Drumanon. She still couldn't believe it. Not really. It was all too far-fetched. Impossible. Yet frightening. She would be sleeping with Temazepam again that night.

Returning to the lounge she helped herself to another large whisky. She weighed the heavy lead crystal glass in her hand and gazed at the misty liquid within it. Lately she had been wondering if she was drinking too much. She grimaced in irritation at herself and took a hefty swig. When she was tired she had a drink; because she was tired she worried about it.

Again she thought about Shephard. Yes, there was definitely something there that attracted her. She wondered if she should have told him about her forthcoming sailing trip with Richard Jamieson. No, she decided. Definitely not. Bearing in mind all that he had said, she didn't think Shephard would approve.

She slept, though her sleep was filled with formless shadows and incoherent fears. And somewhere in her fretful dreams was a curious certainty that she hadn't told John Shephard everything she knew about Van Dameer and Lubbenau.

There was more. Something that had occurred to her in their conversation in the health club. Something that still escaped her . . . eluded her awake and, now, evaded her asleep.

Next morning she checked her incoming mail tray before calling Alice into her office. 'Has Campanella replied to my fax?'

Alice frowned. 'I think so. I'm not absolutely sure. I'll check.' She left the room.

Eleanor was vaguely surprised. Alice usually knew everything that happened in the office. She was back in a couple of minutes, clutching a few sheets of flimsy fax paper. 'Here it is. It was addressed to Philip.'

Eleanor shook her head in exasperation. 'Typical macho Spaniards. *I* send them the fax – they reply to Philip.'

'Maybe it's because he sent it.'

Eleanor was only half listening as she scanned the words and columns of figures in the fax. 'Did he? Well, it had my name on it. Anyway, it doesn't matter. This looks fine.'

The fax's narrative, couched in perfect English, explained the figures set out below. When Alice had gone she checked the figures against the ones from Drumanon's bought ledger.

They matched perfectly. The audit was almost complete.

Now all she needed was the last piece of the jigsaw . . . Van Dameer's confirmation of its monthly trade debtor balances with Drumanon. For a moment she thought of Shephard and their conversation. She shrugged. In the silky light of a sunny day it didn't seem possible that Drumanon, Hagerty Clark's biggest client, was tied up with a Dutch drug pusher. And anyway, she *had* to check the debtor balances; it was an essential part of the audit.

If, and looking out over the sunlit harbour it was a big if – an impossible, unbelievable if – if David and the man, Adams, *had* been murdered, she was sure it couldn't be anything to do with Drumanon. She was convinced of it.

Still, she noticed that when she lifted the phone to dial the Amsterdam number her palm was sweaty. She waited, listening to the unfamiliar ringing tone. Suddenly a mechanical voice came on the line.

Eleanor's voice was unsteady. 'Hello.'

The mechanical voice grated on. With a start, Eleanor realized it was a recording. The message came to an end, the voice clicked off and Eleanor stared at the handset of the phone. The message was in Dutch. She hadn't understood a word. She replaced the handset with a mixture of relief and irritation and went downstairs to the main office in search of Alice.

Alice was seated at her word processor, her fingers flashing over the keyboard. She looked up and her round, homely face broke into a broad smile. 'Hello, dear.' From the start Alice had called her dear. Eleanor rather liked it.

'Alice, have you been trying to get through to Van Dameer on the fax?'

Alice nodded. 'Yes. Lindsey asked one of the girls to send one to them. She tried a few times but couldn't get through. I had a go myself, but still no luck. I don't know, maybe there's something wrong with the line or they've given it up or . . .' She pulled a face.

Eleanor nodded. 'I've just tried telephoning them. There's a message at the other end. In Dutch. It's a pain. I wanted to get their debtor balances checked this week, get the Drumanon audit finished.'

'Why don't you try Philip?' Alice suggested. 'He may know how to get through.'

Eleanor laughed. 'Good idea. When in doubt always delegate upwards.'

Philip was reading the *Financial Times*. 'Philip,' she announced, as she bowled into the office, 'we're having trouble getting through to Van Dameer.'

'Yes?' He seemed guarded. He could probably see what was coming; she was going to lumber him with a job.

'Alice has tried faxing and I've tried phoning. Neither of us have had any joy. I was wondering if you could help. You must have got through to them in previous audits. Are they still in business?'

'I don't know. I'll have to ask Dan Lassiter. Why do you want to contact them?'

'I need to confirm their debtor balances.'

'Ah, yes. Well,' he paused momentarily, 'you'd best leave it with me. I'll phone Dan Lassiter and see if he can help.'

'Great.' Eleanor grinned. Philip was a nice man . . . and a softy when it came to helping her out. 'Thanks a lot.'

She wandered back to her office. The Van Dameer contract was on her desk, sitting on top of a small pile of papers. Three words were written on it. They were small and neat and she put on her spectacles to peer at the handwriting. It was David's cryptic comment – Asset. How prove? She had forgotten about that. Again, she wondered what he had meant by it. She stared at the notation and from nowhere an idea popped into her mind.

There was a way she might find out . . . a way she might discover if there had been anything different or unusual about David's last few days at Drumanon. It was a long shot, an outside chance, but it was worth having a go.

She dug in her bag, pulled out her address book, looked up the number and punched the buttons on her phone. The phone at the other end was answered almost immediately.

'Mrs Rudge? This is Eleanor Lambert at Hagerty Clark. I'm picking up on an audit that David was doing before his . . .' she hesitated, 'his accident. I've come across a couple of queries and I was wondering – well, I was wondering if David had discussed the job he was doing, either with you or Mr Rudge. I'm sorry to ask, I know it's an imposition, but . . . it's just possible he might have mentioned something which would throw some light on a couple of problems I've got.'

'Yes, I quite understand.' The voice at the other end of the line was strong, well-rounded, middle-class. 'As a matter of fact, Miss Lambert, David often talked about you. He admired you a great deal.'

Eleanor was surprised. She felt herself reddening. 'Oh, did he? I didn't know.'

'Actually, David often discussed his work with my husband. He's an accountant too, you know. I think you should talk to him. Why don't you come over to the house?'

'I wouldn't want to disturb you.'

'You wouldn't be doing that. We would be delighted to see you. When would you like to come?'

'As soon as possible.'

'Come for lunch. Today.'

Eleanor was even more surprised. 'Well, if that's all right . . .'

'Of course. My husband has a business in Swanage. He usually comes home for lunch. I'll telephone him now. Come over about twelve thirty? We would be delighted to meet you.'

The Rudges lived south of Wareham, in a big, white, nineteen-thirties house overlooking Studland Bay. The house was set in formal gardens which, Eleanor guessed as she drove up the drive, must have amounted to at least ten acres. Green swards of well-kept lawn swept down to low cliffs flanking the bay and a highly glossed Daimler, glinting in the sunshine, sat close to the front door. David's father was a big beefy man with thinning grey hair. Mrs Rudge was plump, gracious and capable.

They led Eleanor through the house to a large conservatory which ran the entire length of the back of the property. Eleanor watched a few white-sailed yachts beating into the wind, making towards Old Harry and Old Harry's wife at the Foreland. A table was set for lunch.

Mr Rudge offered Eleanor a drink. 'David talked a lot about you,' he told her as he handed her a spritzer. 'I think you had a very good influence on him.'

'Really? I didn't know that.' She felt slightly uncomfortable.

'Absolutely. When he talked about the audit at Drumanon he always said that he was doing it your way.'

'My way?'

Mr Rudge smiled. 'Properly,' he emphasized. 'By the book. I think you'd mentioned something to him about duty of care, told him that everything ought to be checked thoroughly. So that's what he was doing, double-checking everything.' He stared sightlessly out of the conservatory windows, lost in thoughts of his son. 'For a while there,' he said, almost to himself, 'I thought David was going to make a good accountant.'

Suddenly, Eleanor felt cold. Despite the heat of the sun's rays through the sheets of polycarbonate on the conservatory roof, she shivered.

Dear God. If Shephard was right . . . If David had stumbled on something . . . and been killed for it . . . could it have been her fault?

She got a grip on herself and took a sip of her spritzer. But Shephard wasn't right. She was stupid even to consider it. She was being foolish. 'Double-checking everything?' she repeated quietly.

'Yes.' Rudge came out of his reverie and smiled at her. 'As an auditor it's no more than he was supposed to do, of course, but, well, somehow you'd got David to take the job seriously.'

'Did he mention whether he was checking anything in particular?'

Rudge thought about it. 'The ownership. He mentioned that. He said he was trying to establish who actually owned Drumanon Consolidated. I must admit I was surprised when he told me. I hadn't realized it was owned by a Canadian company. Drumanon has always been regarded as a family company. I thought that old Edmund Drumanon was the majority shareholder.'

'I believe most people think that,' said Eleanor.

Mrs Rudge came into the conservatory. She was carrying a serving dish of sliced avocado and smoked salmon. 'Lunch,' she announced, 'come and sit down.'

Even though the food was excellent, Eleanor found it an uncomfortable lunch. Mr Rudge told her what he knew about David's work at Drumanon but nothing he said seemed significant. Apart from her shared profession with

Mr Rudge, the only thing Eleanor had in common with David's parents was David . . . and he was dead.

The Rudges talked of him openly; with regret, with sadness, but without self-pity. They spoke of his accident, but nothing they said gave any hint that they thought it something other than an awful misfortune. Eleanor admired their fortitude, their resolve, their acceptance of the fact that their only son was dead. They reminded her of her own parents; their British resilience in the face of adversity. It overawed her. It was admirable. Yet alien. She was sure that if it had been she who had lost a son, she would have never stopped crying; would long ago have thrown herself into the sea. She was glad when the meal came to an end and she was ready to leave.

After she had said thanks and goodbye to Mrs Rudge, David's father accompanied her to the front door. Walking across the broad, square hallway she asked, 'Did David ever mention a company to you called Van Dameer?'

Rudge frowned. 'Doesn't ring a bell.'

'David seemed concerned about a contract Van Dameer had with Drumanon.'

Rudge opened the door and they stepped out into the sunshine. His frown deepened. 'Is it a Dutch company?'

'Yes.'

'Distributes for Drumanon? Furniture, that kind of thing?'

'Kitchens, conservatories and ventilation equipment. Yes.'

Mr Rudge nodded. 'Yes, I remember now. David's opinion was that the value of Drumanon's contract was only as good as the ability of Van Dameer to do their job. If their distribution set-up wasn't much good, then the contract wouldn't be such a valuable asset.'

Eleanor was surprised. 'Why was he concerned about that? Last year Van Dameer generated forty million in sales revenue for Drumanon.'

'Perhaps so. But David didn't think their marketing was very good. He thought Van Dameer could have done a lot more to sell their products. That's why he went to see them.'

'He went to see Van Dameer? In Amsterdam?'

Rudge laughed. 'No. David wasn't that keen. Van Dameer has a UK office and showroom somewhere in London. David thought that, as Drumanon's auditor, he ought to go up there, introduce himself and take a look around.' Rudge caught the look on Eleanor's face and laughed again. 'I agree it was a bit over the top, beyond his brief, but, as I said, since you arrived at the practice, David had started to take the job very seriously.'

'He didn't tell me he was going to see Van Dameer.'

Rudge shook his head. 'I don't think he mentioned it to anyone.'

'When did he go?'

'To London?'

'Yes.'

Rudge thought about it for a moment, then a brief look of pain passed over his face. 'It was the day before he died.'

Chapter Nineteen

She registered nothing of the return journey to Poole and the office. She drove on auto-pilot, watching the road with empty eyes, her mind churning with what David's father had told her.

She parked in the small car park close to Hagerty Clark's building, hurried through the reception area and up the stairs to the office David had shared with the others. Both Lesley and Steven were working at their desks. What had been David's desk was piled with the overflow of their files and papers. With a grunt of satisfaction Eleanor saw, sitting on a wooden chair in a corner, a stack of magazines. She crossed the office and picked them up. There were a dozen or more fat, glossy periodicals.

Lindsey and Steven looked sheepish. 'I'm sorry, Eleanor,' Steven said, 'we haven't got around to tidying the place up.'

She grimaced under the weight of the magazines. 'That's why I thought I'd make a start.' In her office was a message to call a Mr Malin. It took her a few seconds to remember who Mr Malin was. She dropped the magazines onto her desk and pushed the note to one side. She didn't have time for that now.

Most of the periodicals related to high-class home furnishings and interiors. Two had a tick on the front cover; the rest a cross. She quickly discovered why. In the classified sections at the back of the magazines with ticks were small, single-column advertisements for Campanalla Kitchens and Conservatories. The magazines with crosses carried no adverts for Campanalla. The address for the company was in south London.

The three magazines at the bottom of the pile were industrial and dealt with factory equipment. The one with a tick carried an advert for Campanalla air-conditioning and ventilation equipment with the same address in south London. The remaining two had crosses on their front covers.

Eleanor leaned back in her seat. She was beginning to understand what had disturbed David about Drumanon's contract with Van Dameer. For a company producing forty million in sales revenue it didn't do a lot of promotion.

She tore the page carrying a Campanalla advert out of one of the house furnishing journals and pushed the stack of magazines to one side. There was a knock at the door. Alice walked in.

'We've got the figures you wanted from Van Dameer.' She waved a small clutch of fax papers at Eleanor before setting them on her desk. The top sheet of the fax was from Drumanon; those beneath it were on Van Dameer letterheads.

Eleanor frowned. 'How did we get this?'

Alice looked puzzled. She had expected Eleanor to be pleased. 'I think Philip called Mr Lassiter at Drumanon. He must have contacted Van Dameer. Maybe Philip has another phone number for them. Anyway, the figures came through from Drumanon just after lunch.'

'Okay, Alice, thanks very much.'

Alice left, looking even more puzzled. Eleanor waited until she had closed the door then put on her spectacles and carefully examined the faxes printed on Van Dameer letter-heads. Maybe it was her imagination, but there seemed to be a small, crescent-shaped mark beneath the address on a couple of the pages. Maybe. She couldn't be sure.

She checked that the figures listed on the fax matched those she had taken from Drumanon's sales ledger, then lifted her phone and pressed Philip's internal number. 'Philip.'

'Hi, Eleanor.' He sounded in a good mood. 'Your debtor balances have come through from Holland. I called Dan about you not being able to get through to Van Dameer and a couple of hours afterwards we received a fax. Have you seen it?' Eleanor said that she had. 'Do the figures correspond? Is that what you want?'

She looked at the pages of fax on her desk. 'Yes, the figures match exactly, Philip. And, no, it isn't what I want.'

'What?' Philip sounded baffled. 'What do you mean it isn't what you want?'

'Van Dameer have confirmed their trade debtor balances directly with Drumanon. That isn't good practice. It allows for collusion. Debtor and creditor balances should be con-firmed directly with *us*. We're the auditors. This fax should have come straight to Hagerty Clark, not via Drumanon.'

She heard Philip swear softly under his breath. 'Jesus Christ, Eleanor.'

'I'm sorry, Philip, I expect you think I'm being fussy, but I'm not happy. I think we should fax Van Dameer and have them confirm these balances directly with us.'

Eleanor heard Passmore sigh. She could imagine his face, scrunched up in mild irritation. He would be upset that his easy-going way of doing things was being disturbed. 'Well I know we've not done it exactly by the book, Eleanor,' he moaned, 'but I don't think in this instance it really matters.

After all, I've been dealing with Drumanon for years. Dan Lassiter is a personal friend. I think we can overlook it this time.'

She allowed herself a sardonic smile. It was Philip's usual ploy; to appeal to the old boy network. Well, she thought, *she* wasn't a part of the old boy network. It didn't cut any ice with her. 'No, I'm sorry, Philip, I don't like it. I think we should contact Van Dameer. Have them send us confirmation of the balances direct. We have a number on the fax they sent to Drumanon. We can get in touch with them now. I'll do it if you wish, but we ought to do it. For the sake of good order.'

'All right, Eleanor, all right.' The exasperation in Passmore's voice came through clearly. 'I'll handle it. I'd better call Dan and tell him what we're doing. He's going to wonder what we're playing at.'

'I don't see why.' Eleanor's tone was resolute. 'He should be pleased. His auditors are conducting things properly. We're doing a good job for him.' She heard Passmore's grunt of irritation as he put the phone down and she smiled. Philip was like a bad-tempered teddy bear.

The advertisement she'd torn from the magazine was sitting on the desk in front of her. Without replacing the handset she depressed the cradle of the phone and cleared down the line. She punched nine to get an outside line then tapped out the number printed beneath the address. She was answered by a machine. It told her that no one was available to take her call and asked her to call again. She put the phone down. Eleanor was no expert on marketing, but she knew that asking a prospective buyer to call again was the business equivalent of bad breath. Most buyers would go elsewhere. The machine hadn't even allowed her the chance to leave a message. It wasn't a good way to do business.

She stood up and looked out over the harbour. The sun had disappeared and the sky was the colour of iron. Through the window Eleanor could hear the sharp cry of the gulls, wheeling above the choppy, grey-green waters. She stared at the waves, at a million pitching flecks of white foam, and wondered why the hell she was bothering.

For some reason David had been concerned about the Van Dameer contract. He had checked out their marketing, decided it wasn't up to much and gone to see them. All of which had been well beyond his brief as Drumanon's auditor. Anyway, she thought, Van Dameer was history. They had lost the contract. Lubbenau was distributing for Drumanon now. No doubt making a much better job of selling Campanalla's products. They probably understood how . . .

The thought crashed into her brain like a brick through a window. This was Lubbenau.

Lubbenau had been working for Drumanon since the beginning of the year. She checked the dates on the magazines. They were only a couple of months old. Which meant that the place in south London she'd just called, the place where they didn't seem anxious to sell their wares, belonged to Lubbenau. So, if David had gone to London to check out Van Dameer . . . where had he gone?

And why, for God's sake? Van Dameer were yesterday's men. Keen as David had suddenly become, it was totally over the top to check out a distribution contract that had terminated five months before the audit began. It didn't make sense. None of it made any snse. She grimaced at the sea.

Unless.

Yes, of course. Unless David hadn't realized that Van Dameer had lost the contract.

David hadn't known about Lubbenau. That had to be the

answer. David had gone up to London assuming that the marketing operation there belonged to Van Dameer.

But how could David not have known Lubbenau were the new distributors? *She* knew. David had worked on the audit for at least a month before his death. Longer than she'd worked on it. He *must* have known. Yet she was convinced that he didn't. He hadn't known that Lubbenau had supplanted Van Dameer.

So what?

So what if David, in his impetuous attempt to prove himself good at his job, hadn't realized that Van Dameer had been replaced? What difference did it make? She didn't know. Yet something inside told her that his mistake was significant.

Maybe, she thought, David hadn't gone to the address in south London. Maybe he had found out where Van Dameer's offices and showrooms were and had gone there instead. Presumably Van Dameer was still in business, distributing other products for other people.

She dialled directory enquiries. The operator told her that they had no listing for Van Dameer. So they were out of business.

Or were they? Eleanor was loath to give it up. She wasn't ready to abandon the hunt for Van Dameer, not until she had exhausted all the possibilities. She smiled quietly to herself. The watchdog had become a bloodhound.

There was one way she might possibly track Van Dameer down. She knew it wouldn't be easy, but she was prepared to give it a go; ready to endure a little suffering to get what she wanted. She sat quietly for a moment, mentally preparing herself for the call. Then she picked up the phone and punched up the familiar number. The phone was lifted at the other end. 'Hello, Mother,' she said.

The first five minutes were spent on the minutiae of the latest news: all the current events in the lives of her mother, her father, her brother, his wife, her infant niece, the bridge club . . .

After that it took some time to explain what she wanted. 'You have a stack of them, Mother.' She spoke slowly, deliberately. 'On the table in your bedroom. They go back years. Go up there and pick up the extension. Yes, the bedroom.' Eleanor closed her eyes and tried to relax the tension in her neck. It was like trying to talk down a pilotless aircraft.

She finally manoeuvred her mother into the bedroom and then talked her through what she wanted. 'Yes, anything before December last year. Yes, at the back of the magazine. Yes, it will be a little advertisement, Mother. No, Campanalla. I'll spell it.' She spelled it. Twice.

After twenty minutes of honey-tongued encouragement and heartless bullying, her mother found it. 'Yes, that's it.' Eleanor tried to keep the excitement out of her voice. 'Tell me the address.' Her mother told her. 'What? Tell me that again.' Her mother repeated it. 'What's the date of the magazine?' Her mother told her. It was two years old.

'Mother, that's great. Thanks so much for helping me. I'm sorry I swore. Can you tear the page out and post it to me first class? Yes, the page with the advertisement. Yes, it's okay to tear it out, Mother, it's only a magazine. Yes, yes, if you want to cut it out, that's okay. No, I know, not your sewing scissors.' Eleanor scrunched up her face in agony. 'Yes, I know it makes scissors blunt, Mother. Look, Mother, I'm afraid I have to go. Send me the cutting. I love you. Give my love to everyone and thanks again. Bye.'

She pulled the handset off her ear as if it were a live piranha, banged it onto the cradle and slumped in her seat, traumatized. Dear God. Eleanor had developed a business-man's attitude to the phone. For her it was a mechanism for succinct communication. Not for her mother. Eleanor adored her mother but she had long ago come to realize that after a phone conversation with her, even Freud would have needed therapy.

She stared at the address she had written on her notepad. Thoughts of her mother evaporated.

The address was SE11, the same as the one in the advertisement she'd torn from the magazine.

Lubbenau were distributing Campanalla kitchens and con-servatories from the same address that Van Dameer had used. Which, she figured, suggested that Lubbenau had taken over Van Dameer's distribution network. She gazed pensively at the opposite wall. Well, that wasn't so unusual in business. Although she hadn't got the impression from Dan Lassiter that Lubbenau had taken over the Dutch marketing operation.

The phone bleeped. It was a client. With an effort Eleanor dragged her thoughts away from Lubbenau and Van Dameer and onto the problems of the client's advanced corporation tax.

An hour later Alice appeared with another half dozen sheets of fax paper. 'This has just come in from Van Dameer,' she announced, setting the papers in front of Eleanor. She seemed puzzled. 'It looks the same as the one we received earlier.'

Eleanor was comparing the two facsimiles. 'It is.' She looked up. 'I told Philip that we had to get this information directly from Van Dameer. It's no good coming to us via Drumanon.'

Alice laughed. 'Well, I'm glad to see he's done as he was told. It looks like you've got him well trained.'

Eleanor grinned. 'I like to think so.'

Alice pointed to the number automatically printed at the top of the fax by the transmitting machine. 'That's why we couldn't get through to them. They've changed their fax number.' She headed for the office door. 'Oh, by the way, Mr Malin called again. While you were on the phone. He wants you to call him back.'

'Okay.' Eleanor waited for her to leave then examined the new set of facsimiles. As far as she could see there was no sign of any crescent-shaped mark on them. She lifted her phone and punched out the number at the top of the fax. She got the long, continuous bleep of a fax line. There was another number printed at the head of the fax. She pressed out the digits. The call was answered in Dutch. Satisfied, she put the phone down. Almost certainly the second fax had come direct from Holland.

Probably, she thought, the first one had as well. Her doubts and suspicions were all in her mind. Her imagination was getting the better of her. She was dreaming up conspiracies that didn't exist. She was becoming neurotic. Paranoid. With a sigh she picked up the fax and deposited it in her attaché case which was sitting open on the table at the side of her desk. She would, she thought, be damn glad when she could get this bloody audit finished.

Her phone warbled. It was another client. Eleanor told the girl on the switchboard to put him through.

It was a busy afternoon. The phone never stopped and she spent her time handling one client problem after another. By six thirty she was dying for a drink and her desk was covered in papers. She cleared them away, threw everything relating to Drumanon into her case and abandoned the office, emerging with blinking eyes into the bright, steely light of the English Channel.

A man was standing by her car. As she drew closer she recognized him. It was John Shephard. 'You didn't call me back,' he said. 'I wondered if you were okay.'

'No, I'm not okay,' she snapped. 'I've had a completely useless afternoon answering irrelevant questions and solving pointless problems.'

He grinned at her. 'I have a lot of afternoons like that. Would a drink help? You look like you could use one.'

She laughed. 'Do I look that bad?'

They found a pub in the old town, close to the quay. He bought her a large vodka. She noticed he had the same. 'Not on duty?' she asked.

'Yes, I am, but it's all right here. Drinking in pubs goes with the territory.' He looked around. 'Usually it's in places a lot less appealing than this.'

Eleanor sipped her drink. 'I went to see David Rudge's parents today,' she said. 'They told me that the day before he died he went to London. To check up on Van Dameer.'

He looked shocked. 'Christ, Eleanor, I told you not to go digging into anything. Not to get involved. Now you tell me you've been to see Rudge's parents.'

His tone nettled her. 'Well, what's wrong with that?'

'Supposing they're implicated in drugs? Supposing they had Rudge killed. Or at least know who killed him.'

She stared at him. 'For God's sake. Do you know what you're saying? We're talking about his *parents*.'

He shrugged. 'It's happened before. You have no idea what people mixed up with narcotics will do, how far they'll go. Family relationships – parents, children – none of that means anything to these people.'

She stared at him. 'You really don't like people involved in drugs, do you?' He looked at her and said nothing. 'I mean, it's as if you hate them. As if you're on some kind of crusade.

It's like . . .' she searched for the word, 'a vendetta.'

For a while he didn't respond, then said quietly, 'I wouldn't go that far. But it's true. I don't like pushers or dealers. I don't even like addicts very much. Most of all I don't like the people behind the business.'

'I don't suppose anybody does. But you seem so much more . . .' again she searched for the word, 'intense about it. Why?'

He smiled at her. 'Because I'm a detective inspector in the drug squad.'

She examined his face then shook her head. 'No, there's more to it than that.'

He was silent for a while, returning her gaze. When he spoke his voice was flat and bleak. 'I've lost a couple of good friends through drugs. Killed by people pushing dope. One was a policeman. He was my best friend. I suppose you could say that, as a policeman, he had to expect that he might die violently. But he was only a young bloke . . . full of life . . . laughed all the time. He was shot dead on a drugs bust. The man who did it was a psychopath, trying to import a hundred kilos of heroin into the country on a ship.' Shephard's voice tailed off. 'I was there when he got shot.'

She watched him take a long swallow of his drink. She waited a while. 'You said two people,' she reminded him quietly.

'The other one was my girlfriend,' he went on. 'It was years ago, when I was at college. We all smoked a bit of pot of course, but someone had been pushing speed on her. I didn't realize, but she was doing a lot of it. One night she collapsed at a college disco. She died the next day in hospital; something to do with her heart and the effect of alcohol and amphetamines. She was a kid. Eighteen. The guy who'd been pushing the stuff must have known that he'd helped kill her. Yet the next term another kid overdosed on heroin.' He shrugged.

'Did they ever catch him?'

'Who?'

'The man pushing dope at your college.'

He shook his head ruefully. 'Last I heard he had retired. At thirty-three, for God's sake. Gone to live in the West Indies.'

'Nice.'

'Sure. Nice place. Nasty way to make it there. The trouble is most people think drugs are romantic. Warm sun and golden beaches, fast cars and fast women, hot money and coke. The truth's uglier. Living in the gutter and sharing needles. Contracting TB and dying of Aids. That's how it really is.'

He gave her a long, thoughtful look. 'But I'm not on any crusade, Eleanor. Like I said, it's a war. And I'm on the losing side. In my business you win a few and lose a lot. There's no way anybody could do their job properly if they were personally involved, on some kind of vendetta. They'd go insane.'

'It's insane to believe that parents would have their child murdered.'

'It happens in South America. It happens in Jamaica and the inner cities of Chicago and New York. Why not here?'

'David's parents just aren't like that. I mean they're *devastated* by David's death. They don't show it but I know they are. They're like . . . well, I know what they're like.'

Shephard was watching her carefully. After a moment he nodded. 'Okay, well, there's probably no harm done. But why did you go to see them?'

'I've got a few queries on the Drumanon audit. I wanted to find out if David had said anything to his father about what he had been doing. His father's an accountant too. He told me that David had gone to London, to what he thought was Van Dameer's showrooms. Only they belong to Lubbenau now. Lubbenau must have taken over Van Dameer's distribution network.'

Shephard nodded briefly. Eleanor could see he wasn't interested in the commercial aspects of the new distribution deal. 'Why did he go?'

'I'm not sure, but I think he wanted to check out the marketing. He didn't think it was very good.'

'Is it usual for an auditor to do that?'

'No, not at all.'

'So the people in London would have been surprised when he turned up.'

'Very.'

'Would he have said who he was?'

'Knowing David, yes.'

Shephard was silent for a while, thinking. 'And this was the day before he died.' Eleanor nodded. 'He may have seen something. A delivery. Something like that.' He was talking almost to himself.

'I've got the address of the place if you want it,' Eleanor told him.

He shook his head. 'We know it. A team from the Met drug squad has got the showrooms under observation. The Dutch police tell us that a bulk delivery of kitchen and conservatory units has arrived in Rotterdam from Spain. The shipment is marked for Lubbenau and on its way to the address in south London. It's expected at Harwich the day after tomorrow. Customs will open the flatpacks at the docks and inspect them for drugs.' He finished his drink and smiled at her. 'We might get lucky.'

She looked at his empty glass. 'Would you like another?'

For a moment he appeared tempted. 'I have to get back,' he said sadly, then added hesitantly, 'perhaps we could have a drink some other time. When I'm not on duty?'

'Perhaps,' she said lightly.

Outside, a chilly breeze was coming off the harbour. Shephard walked her back to her car. 'Now look,' his voice was solemn, 'this is serious. Don't go poking around any more. Just finish the audit. Don't get involved in anything you don't have to. You're far too—' he stopped and Eleanor had the impression that he'd changed his mind about what he was going to say. 'You're far too nice,' he concluded lamely.

Driving home Eleanor smiled as she recalled his words. She hated being told what to do and it was irritating when Shephard kept telling her not to get involved. Yet she found it comforting that he cared.

Back at the flat she changed into an old pair of jeans and a sweatshirt, fixed herself a supper of quiche and salad and, afterwards, emptied the contents of her attaché case onto the dining room table. She surveyed the files and printouts, the columns of figures and the scraps of paper. It was the beginning of the end. She was on the home straight of the Drumanon audit. Once she had coordinated all the figures and data, she would have the draft accounts ready.

She worked for over an hour then made herself a cup of coffee. She carried it back to the table. It was past nine thirty and the light had faded from the windows. She switched on the big lamp hanging over the dining table and the soft light of the fat glowbulb gave the room a warm, golden ambience.

A scrap of paper was sticking out from one of the files. Standing at the table and sipping her coffee, Eleanor leaned across and pulled it out of the file. It was one of David's enigmatic notes. It read 'Canadian company?' She screwed up her face. Somebody had mentioned something about the

Canadian ownership of Drumanon. Who was it? What was it?

It came to her. Both Lindsey and David's parents had said that David had been checking on the ownership of the company. Why had he bothered? she wondered. The share register showed quite clearly that Lassiter's Canadian company was the ultimate owner of eighty percent of Drumanon. Eleanor stared at the scrap of paper for a few moments longer then, on an impulse, reached for her address book. She found the number she wanted and pressed it out.

Her call was answered in a few seconds. 'Don Pennington, please.' A voice came on the line. 'Don, how are you? It's Eleanor Lambert. How are things over there at Karding Hillier Longland? Have I caught you at a bad time?'

She spent a few minutes catching up on news of old colleagues and events across the Atlantic, then popped the question. 'Don, I wonder if you could do me a favour? Could you check out a company for me? It's registered over there in Toronto. It's called Lassiter Enterprises Inc. The usual stuff – who the directors are, if there's a holding company, where it's registered. Could you do that for me?'

Pennington told her he would be pleased to. 'Don, that's brilliant. I'm sorry to ask you, but it's the quickest way of doing it. Maybe you could call me back when you've got something.' She gave him her telephone number, agreed that it would be a good idea to get together when he was next in the UK, and rang off.

She worked until midnight. Before going to bed she stacked all her work, the files and printouts, neatly in her case. At the top of the stack she placed the page she'd torn out of the magazine.

She slept soundly, woke early and by seven thirty was showered, dressed and ready for the office. She crossed to the dining room table and made to close her attaché case. The page of advertisements caught her eye. She took it from the case, studied it, then folded it neatly and put it in her pocket.

Outside the air was filled with the smell of the sea and mimosa. The morning glittered as if the sky had been polished. Eleanor fired up the CRX and slowly headed it around the gravel drive. At the entrance, between the big stone gateposts, she brought the car to a halt.

To the right, beyond the gate, was the road to Poole and the office. Left, was the way to the motorway . . . the road to London. Eleanor sat staring out of the windscreen for a few moments then, slowly letting out the clutch, moved the car forward out of the drive. She turned left.

Chapter Twenty

It was in a street off Kennington Road; a double-fronted showroom with offices above and what looked like a small warehouse behind. Eleanor arrived at the place just after nine thirty, having stopped on the way to tell Alice she wouldn't be in the office until lunchtime.

She drove past slowly, eyeballing the place. It wasn't in the most salubrious part of town, she thought, nor would it get a lot of passing pedestrians. It didn't look to her like the London head office of a hot-shot marketing organization with a turnover of over forty million.

Eleanor parked the car nearby and walked to the showrooms. If there were policemen keeping watch on the place she couldn't see any sign of them.

In the dusty windows was a selection of heavy, dark oak kitchen cupboards and cabinets. They were not particularly to her taste but she supposed somebody might like them. There were also colour photographs and scale models of conservatories. She pushed the door. It was locked. For God's sake, they weren't even open. And it was getting on for ten. She looked up. There was no sign of life in the windows above.

She turned and surveyed the sunny street. Eleanor knew that organizations selling kitchens and the like usually used telephone salespeople who called prospective buyers in the afternoons and evenings. Which meant, she thought, that they probably didn't start work until midday. Maybe that was when the showroom opened. Damn, she hadn't thought of that.

At the side of the building was an alley, just wide enough for a truck. Eleanor made her way along it, gingerly stepping in her two-inch heels around the ruts and potholes in its surface. The warehouse stood on the far side of the untidy yard. A couple of old cars were parked in front of its big double doors. Both doors were open, allowing daylight to fall upon two men working inside. Unnoticed, Eleanor watched them. They were opening flatpacks and assembling kitchen units, working to a plan pinned to a board on a wooden workbench.

One of the men looked up and saw her. He looked startled. He murmured to his workmate who turned with a glare. The second man started towards her. He was holding a long screwdriver.

Eleanor began to back away. As the man came closer she kept her eyes on his face. He looked angry . . . menacing. She wanted to run but was too frightened to turn her back, horrifically conscious of the screwdriver clutched in the man's hand.

'Whaddaya want?'

She found it difficult to speak. 'I . . . I wanted to see some of your kitchen units. I went to the showroom but it was closed.' She gave him a sickly smile and her eyes darted to his right hand.

The man frowned at her. He seemed even angrier. 'The showroom don't open 'til later. You'll have to come back.'

'Yes, yes of course. When?'

'How do I bloody know? These bastards don't pay me

enough to know that kind of stuff. When they're bloody open.' The man turned away.

Eleanor felt relief flow over her like a warm Jacuzzi. Her knees had gone weak. From behind came the sound of tyres on the pitted surface of the yard. She turned, slightly tottery. She felt lightheaded.

A red Escort Cabriolet Si with its top down had drawn up behind her. The man who got out was young, short and as skinny as a toothpick. He was wearing an expensive double-breasted suit and a flashy tie. By the time he reached her his eyes had stripped Eleanor down to her naked flesh. 'Can I help you?' His voice was greasy.

'I came to see some kitchen units. I tried the showroom but it was closed.'

The man flashed her a neon grin; on, then instantly off. 'We don't usually open 'til later, but I'm happy to show *you* everything I've got.' The tone was as odious as an oil slick.

Eleanor ignored the innuendo. 'Thank you.'

With the oleaginous little salesman by her side, she retraced her steps along the alleyway, doing her best to avoid the potholes. 'Here, let me help,' the man said and put his hand on her arm. Eleanor pulled away.

Inside, the showroom seemed drab and somehow old-fashioned. There was no carpet and only a couple of uncomfortable chairs for customers to sit on. The walls were covered in dark kitchen cupboards. A display of cabinets, work surfaces and cooker hobs had been erected in the centre of the room and in a corner was a half-built conservatory. A staircase in another corner led to the floor above. The salesman flicked on the lights.

'Do you have any brochures?' Eleanor asked.

The salesman gave her a clutch of cheaply presented promotional leaflets. She looked at them quickly then gazed around the showroom. 'This is all Spanish, isn't it?'

'Yeah.'

'Campanalla,' she was reading from the brochure. 'What's that, the name of the company?'

'Yeah.'

'Where is it in Spain? I mean, where's Campanalla based?' The salesman shrugged. 'Don't know. What's it matter?'

She feigned surprise. 'Don't you work for Campanalla then?'

'Nah. I work for me. Self-employed.'

'But who pays you?'

He stared at her suspiciously. 'The boss pays me. In cash. That's the name of this game. Anyway, whaddaya wanna know for?' A nasty thought occurred to him. 'Here, you from the bleeding social security?'

She could tell she'd got as far as she was likely to get with that line of enquiry. She drew herself up and gazed down at him. 'Do I look like I'm from the bleeding social security?'

His eyes, bright with lust yet cautious, took in the cut of her expensive clothes and the gorgeous, curving lines of the body beneath them. Clearly she did not.

'Do you sell many of these Spanish kitchens?' she asked lightly.

'Yeah, a lot.' His voice was was suddenly chipper, but Eleanor caught a defensive note.

'Only,' she went on in an innocent voice, 'your two men in the workshop didn't seem awfully busy.'

'Nah, we keep them at it for most of the year. Sometimes we even take on an extra bloke, when we've got a lot of orders. I'm on the go all the time, getting out and measuring up.' He smirked. 'I'll come out and measure you up if you want.' Eleanor was tempted to kick him in the crotch.

'How much is this one?' she asked, pointing to a style in one of the brochures.

'Depends on the size of your kitchen.' She gave him the approximate dimensions of the kitchen in the flat and he worked out the costing. It came to close to £10,000. She thought that was expensive.

'Actually,' she told him, 'it's for a new house I'm buying in Yorkshire. Near Leeds. Do you have a showroom up there I could visit?'

'No. But I expect I could get someone to give you a call. Or I could come up and look after you myself.' He smirked again.

The door of the showroom banged. Eleanor looked over her shoulder. A large man, standing just inside the room, was watching them. He had a stony face and hard, suspicious eyes. 'Maybe you would like to serve this customer while I have a browse,' Eleanor said.

The salesman grinned and shook his head. 'He's not a customer. He's the boss. Don't mind him. Just look interested. I've gotta look like I'm doing my job.'

The big man moved across the room and slowly mounted the stairs. Eleanor could feel his eyes on her.

She asked a few general questions about the conservatories, then made to go. The salesman was pushy but she told him she needed time to think about it. 'By the way, what's the delivery time on the kitchens and conservatories?'

'Once we've measured up and got your deposit, about a week.'

'I see. That's very good.'

'Well, come on then,' the little salesman said breezily, 'you gonna give me an order?'

'I haven't finished buying the house in Yorkshire yet.'

'Oh. Okay, well, lemme have your number in London.'

She hadn't thought of that.

Under normal circumstances she would have told the objectionable little turd to get lost. Now she wondered if refusing might make her look suspicious. The telephone number of the house she had owned in West Hampstead leapt into her head and she gave him that.

He wrote it down. 'And what's your name?'

She hadn't thought of that either.

She hesitated then gave him her mother's maiden name.

'Okay, think it over,' the man said, 'and I'll give you a bell. What you gotta remember is that this stuff is the best value around. It'll last you a long, long time. Just like me.'

Outside she took a final look at the premises. A movement caught her eye. Standing at a window above the showroom was the man with the hard eyes. He was watching her. She hurried round the corner to her car.

The journey to the office took over two hours. She thought about what she had discovered at the showroom . . . and about what David may have uncovered when he had innocently turned up to ask questions about Van Dameer and its marketing strategy.

Poor David. It was still impossible to believe that his death was murder, that his trip to SE11 could have triggered his contrived accident. She thought about David a lot. If only she had listened when he had asked to talk to her about Drumanon. If only – no. It was too late for 'if onlys'.

The best way she could make it up to David was to discover what was really happening; finally to make sense of this crazy audit; to find out once and for all whether his death had been an accident. Or something else.

And to do that she needed to do more than make a quick trip to London. She needed to get to the heart of the matter.

She recalled her time at Karding Hillier Longland. Working for a multi-national accountancy practice she'd learned that if you had a problem somewhere else, then you went to that somewhere else and sorted it. It didn't matter if it was in Europe or Asia or wherever. Distances didn't matter. You just got on a plane. That's the way the business worked. Well, she thought as she stared mechanically at the road ahead, part of her problem was Van Dameer and Lubbenau. And they were in Europe.

She drew into the little car park close to the office, locked the car, put her head round the door of the main office to tell Alice she was back, mounted the stairs and closed the office door firmly behind her. She called the number of a travel agent she had used in her previous job.

It was not good news. The flights she wanted were booked solid. She would have to be wait-listed. There was only one other possibility, the girl at the agency told her, and that was to fly that afternoon. Eleanor thought about it. Why not? If she couldn't do it tomorrow, why not do it today? She'd already decided to go for it; she might as well go for it *now*. She told the agent to make the booking.

She called Alice on the internal and asked her to come up. As soon as she walked in Eleanor said, 'I'm afraid I have to be away from the office until tomorrow afternoon. Something's happened. Something personal.'

Alice looked concerned. 'Oh dear. Nothing serious, I hope?'

'No, no. It's just that I have to get it sorted; get it cleared up and out of the way.' Eleanor was deliberately vague. She hated telling lies, especially to someone like Alice. 'I'm sorry to ask, but can you cover for me, Alice? Handle the messages; put the queries on hold?'

'Of course.'

'I'd better tell Philip, I suppose.'

Alice shook her head. 'Don't worry about Philip. He and Mr Hagerty are seeing a client. He won't be in for the rest of the day.' She leaned forward and added conspiratorially, 'They're playing golf.'

'Good. Well, I'll definitely be back by tomorrow afternoon.'

Alice put a warm, comforting hand on her arm. 'Don't you worry, dear. Everything will be all right here. Hagerty Clark will survive for a few hours without you.'

After she had gone, Eleanor made another call; to Josie Koning at the offices of Hillier Karding Longland in Amsterdam. The call took longer than she would have wished, but there was a lot of catching up to do and she had a favour to ask.

She put the phone down and checked her watch. God, was that the time? She was cutting it fine – bloody fine. But there was something else she had to do before she left the office. She scrabbled among the bulky printouts from Drumanon until she found the one she wanted; the schedule of payments into Drumanon's bank account by Van Dameer's salesmen. Her left hand moved rapidly down the amounts recorded on the computer-printed pages as the fingers of her right flew over the keys of her calculator. In twenty minutes she had completed her calculations. She threw her working papers into her attaché case and dashed down the stairs. She didn't stop to say goodbye to Alice.

She kept her foot down all the way back to the flat, praying that no young traffic cop would take a fancy to her and the car and decide to pull her over for a chat.

She was in the flat long enough to throw a change of clothes into an overnight case and grab her passport. The message light on her answering machine was winking but she ignored it.

She averaged over eighty on the M3, softly cursing the multitude of dodderers who pulled out into the fast lane at anything less than ninety. The M25 was in its usual state of thrombosis, with the traffic moving north towards the M4 interchange at the velocity of cold porridge.

She wanted to scream.

At last she made Heathrow. She parked in the multi-storey, dashed onto the departures concourse of Terminal One, picked up her tickets at the check-in desk and made the British Midland sixteen twenty-five flight to Amsterdam with no more than seconds to spare.

Josie, tall, slim and lissom, with her blonde hair over her shoulders, was waiting for her in the arrivals hall. Eleanor saw her straight away. They hugged each other warmly. They hadn't seen each other in over a year. One of the things about having worked for one of the largest accountancy practices in the world, Eleanor thought as she sat at the wrong side of Josie's Passat heading into Amsterdam, was that it left her with an international network of good friends.

They caught up on each other's news. Josie asked Eleanor about her new job and if, after the disasters of Alec and Raymond, she was sleeping with a new man; Eleanor asked Josie about Max and Beth.

The thought suddenly occurred to Eleanor that Josie, who was her age, not only had her career but also a husband and baby daughter. Eleanor merely had a career. She was shocked. She hardly ever thought about things like that. Anyway, she'd tried having a husband, and it hadn't worked. She wasn't going to try again, not for a long while. Definitely not.

A vision of John Shephard popped into her brain. Why the hell, she thought, should she think of him? She shook her head impatiently. After the easy, stress-free life of Dorset, she reckoned all this rushing around was affecting her mind.

Amsterdam was busy. Josie drove into the heart of the city, the Passat shuddering over the cobblestones, and angled the car into a meter bay overlooking Heren Gracht. They strolled over the bridge crossing the canal. Eleanor noticed that in the warm sunshine of early evening the city hummed . . . buzzed with the excitement of being alive. It smelled of the sea; not the sharp, tangy smell of the Channel coast at Dorset but a softer, richer smell . . . the smell of Europe and the city. They found a bodega and Josie ordered a couple of glasses of white wine.

'I checked on the numbers you gave me from Van Dameer's fax,' Josie said after the waiter had brought their drinks. 'They are the numbers of a fax and photocopying bureau in the city centre, near Rembrandtsplein.'

'A bureau? Van Dameer doesn't have its own fax line?'

'Not any more it doesn't. I have done a little checking since you called. Van Dameer is not an NV nor a BV, what you would call in Britain a limited company.' Josie's English was perfect, with only a slight trace of guttural Dutch inflection. 'If the company exits, then it is either a partnership or, more likely, what you call, I think, a single trader.'

'Sole trader,' Eleanor said. 'What do you mean, *if* it exists?'

Josie shrugged. 'I looked up Van Dameer in the phone book and the Business Directory. There is no business listed by that name.'

'But up to December last year, the company was importing more than a hundred million guilders' worth of Spanish merchandize into Rotterdam,' Eleanor's voice was filled with bewilderment, 'and shipping a lot of it to England. It was supposed to have a major marketing and distribution network over there. In fact, all over Europe. Van Dameer would be a sizeable corporation. It must still be in existence, surely?'

Josie shrugged again. 'It was last year's directory I looked up. The company is not there. And it was not listed in the one for the year before that.' She looked thoughtful. 'It is possible to conduct that level of business as a sole trader, but,' she shook her head, 'it would be very risky. If it went wrong the individual would be *personally* liable for all the debts. And anyway, there are more tax breaks as a limited company. But don't worry,' she smiled at Eleanor, 'if it does exist, even as a sole trader, then we will find it. It just takes a little longer, that's all.'

Eleanor smiled warmly at her. 'I'm really grateful for all your help.'

Josie waved an elegant hand. 'It is nothing. Do you have a copy of Van Dameer's letterheading?'

Eleanor took a copy from her attaché case and passed it across the small round table. Josie examined it. 'The address is just around the corner,' she said. 'We shall go there soon. But this telephone number . . .' her voice trailed off.

'What about it?'

'It is a mobile phone.' Josie dug into her shoulderbag and came up with a small phone. She punched a series of numbers and stared at Eleanor as she listened. Whatever was happening at the other end of the line came to an end and she clicked the phone off. 'This number is not available at present,' she repeated in a mechanical voice, 'please try later.' She glanced again at the copy of Van Dameer's letterhead. 'It looks as if they had their own fax line once. But you say you couldn't get through on the number?'

Eleanor nodded. 'Right. A few people in the office tried it. No go.'

Josie dialled the number, listened briefly, then switched

her phone off. 'Discontinued.' She pulled a face. 'This company, Van Dameer, does not make it easy to get in touch. Do not call us, we shall call you, eh?' She chuckled.

Eleanor gave her a wan smile. They finished their drinks and made their way to an address in Prinzenstraat. On a brass plaque attached to the dull red brickwork of a narrow, five-storey building with ornate gables, was a list of company names. 'In this area a lot of small companies rent rooms,' Josie explained. 'They are usually on a short let.'

Eleanor could feel her heart thumping as they examined the names on the plaque. None of them read Van Dameer. Josie rang a bell at the side of the door. A heavy, middle-aged man appeared. The man and Josie began an animated conversation. After a couple of minutes Josie thanked the man and turned away from the door.

'Well?' Eleanor was eager to know what had been said as they started back across the canal, walking towards the car.

'A company called Van Dameer rented a room there for many years. Just one room, with a fax machine.'

'It's not there now?'

Josie shook her head. 'The caretaker says that the man who rented it for Van Dameer gave notice and moved out after Christmas last year. He was called Schmidt. The caretaker says he was German.'

'Is Schmidt as common in Germany as Smith in Britain?' Eleanor asked dolefully.

Josie laughed. 'Yes, I think it is. Schmidt only used the room for a couple of hours once or twice a week. The rooms are rented by the quarter. Schmidt always paid in advance. In cash.' She shrugged. 'So, I do not think Van Dameer exists any more. Maybe Schmidt and the company disappeared to avoid paying taxes. It happens.' She caught sight of Eleanor's troubled face. 'Don't worry. It may take a few days, but I shall find out more for you.'

Eleanor smiled at her gravely. 'Josie, I really am grateful for everything you're doing.'

Josie squeezed her arm affectionately. 'It's nothing. Now let's go home and eat. Max is cooking supper.'

Josie and Max had an apartment south of the city, near Amstel, on the road to Utrecht. The road was clear and the Passat made good time. Eleanor was quiet: thinking; listening to the drumming of the tyres on the surface of the Autosnelweg.

Suddenly she turned to Josie. 'When we get to your place, do you mind if I use your phone? I want to make a few calls.'

'Of course not.'

'I'm changing my plans.'

'What?' Josie gave her a startled glance.

'I'm not flying back tomorrow morning. I'm going on to Geneva.'

At the apartment, Max gave Eleanor a big, welcoming hug. He was a lawyer; tall, with a mop of unruly hair and horn-rimmed spectacles. Eleanor had always thought him quite dishy. Beth was even dishier. At only ten months old she was a warm bundle of softly gurgling baby fat. Eleanor took her in her arms and cuddled her. 'Suits you, Eleanor,' Max observed.

She made her calls. KLM said they could book her a seat on the nine thirty-five flight to Geneva and British Airways was able to fix her return flight to Heathrow. Josie brought her a drink as she was finishing her second call. 'Why don't you call Francine in Geneva?' she suggested. 'She can maybe help. I have her home number.'

'Great idea.'

Francine was at home and delighted to hear from her. As with Josie, Eleanor hadn't seen her in over a year. She listened carefully as Eleanor explained what she wanted. 'It's no problem,' she said. 'Get a cab to the office after you've landed. I may have something by then. I'll rearrange my schedule and we will have lunch together.'

Eleanor put the phone down. Max had finished preparing supper. Lamb casserole with ratatouille. It smelled delicious.

Josie drove her to Schipol the following morning. They hugged warmly and promised to see each other soon.

A gentle grey rain was falling as the 737 touched down at Cointrin. The pilot brought the plane to a halt on the concrete apron about a hundred yards from the terminal building and two stewardesses stood at the bottom of the steps handing out umbrellas. The cab took less than twenty minutes to get her to the centre of the city.

Geneva smelled of the mountains. Despite the showers, the air was sharp, clean and crisp. Karding Hillier Longland's local offices were in a modern ten-storey block on a street between the English church and the Pont du Mont-Blanc; in sight of where the lake gently flowed into the Rhône.

Francine was in a meeting and Eleanor waited in reception. After she had borrowed the phone and called Alice to say she wouldn't be in the office until tomorrow, she sat around and leafed through a couple of copies of *Fortune*, saying hello to a few faces she recognized from the past.

The people were pleased to see her and intrigued as to why she was there, although when they learned her visit was personal, merely to say hello to Francine, they moved politely but quickly on. It was, she discovered, a curious feeling, to be treated as an outsider by an organization with which she had, for so long, been intimately connected.

Francine came bustling into reception. She was about the same age as Eleanor, with dark, elfin good looks; as French in her appearance as Josie was Dutch. 'Darling.' She kissed

Eleanor twice on both cheeks. 'Come into the office.'

From Francine's window Eleanor could see the Jet d'Eau out in the lake. The rain had eased off and with the coming of the sun the thin pillar of water, shooting high into the sky, was falling in a glistening cascade, like a million unstrung pearls, back onto the smooth sparkling surface of the lake.

Francine organized coffee and they talked of old times. Like Josie, Francine wanted to know who Eleanor was sleeping with and what he was like. 'You are very lucky,' she said suddenly, 'Raymond was here visiting only yesterday.' Eleanor pulled a face. 'He looks terrible. The rumour is that his wife has left him. For a younger man.' They both shrieked with laughter.

Francine became serious. 'This company, Lubbenau. I can find no trace of it in any of the Geneva directories. I have tried the telephone number you gave me; it is a mobile phone and there was no answer.'

Eleanor nodded. It was no surprise. 'What about the fax?'

'It works. I sent something on it this morning.' Eleanor looked startled. 'Don't worry, chérie, it was only one of our economic briefing sheets.' She smiled. 'We send them to everyone. But, anyway, I think we will pay a visit to the address you gave me and see if we can find something about this Lubbenau. It is close to where we shall have lunch.'

They left the offices a few minutes later and started towards the old town. The pavements had dried, the sun was high and to the south, facing them in the distance, the snow-capped peaks of the Haute Savoie glinted in the sunlight. Eleanor noticed, as she always did in European cities, how well dressed the people were. They were elegant and fashionable and walked the streets purposefully. There wasn't a grey anorak in sight.

'What time is your flight home?' Francine asked.

'Seven.'

'Ah, then we have time for a leisurely lunch.'

'Do you have to go back to the office this afternoon?'

Francine made a face. 'Regrettably, yes. I am very busy. It is a pity that I have so much work.' They were crossing the Pont des Bergues; Eleanor could feel the breeze off the lake stirring her hair as Francine waved an expressive arm towards the mountain. 'This is the only country in Europe not in, or applying to be in, your Economic Community. Whilst the rest of Europe integrates its systems, its tariffs, its farm quotas, even what you call its VAT, here in Switzerland we still do things our own way. It gives the Swiss office of Karding Hillier Longland much work, much more than everywhere else. Still, I should not complain. It gives me a good living.'

Lubbenau's address was in the Grande Rue, not far from the Hôtel de Ville.

It was an old property. Francine led the way into a cobbled courtyard. In a corner was a flight of black, cast-iron stairs leading to a balcony which squared the courtyard on the first floor. High wooden doors led off the balcony to rooms and offices. Francine glanced at Eleanor. 'This is a chic address,' she said in a low voice. 'These places are expensive. Lawyers and financial consultants rent them.'

She glanced at the address Eleanor had given her and led the way up the staircase. At the top she turned to her right, found the door they wanted and knocked. 'Leave the talking to me,' she whispered. Eleanor was glad to. Her heart was hammering like an animal caught in a trap.

There was no answer. Francine knocked twice more but beyond the solid door there was silence. A door at the far end of the balcony opened and a man in his late fifties stepped out. He asked Francine if he could help. Eleanor, whose French was up to it, heard Francine reply that they were from a city business directory and that they wished to register a company at this address called Lubbenau.

The man said he was the *concierge* and ambled along the balcony towards them with a smile. The building, he said, did not often get such attractive visitors. Francine turned on the eyes, flashed the teeth and simpered. He was very kind, she told him; most places did not have such friendly caretakers.

The man reached them. Eleanor noticed he was carrying a bunch of keys. Francine noticed it too. She smiled coquettishly at him. She was looking for Lubbenau's boss, the *patron*, she said. When would he be back? The caretaker shrugged. He didn't know. The man who rented the offices only came by once or twice a week. He didn't know when the man would show up again.

Francine pouted and moved closer to the caretaker. She had a problem, she told him. She had been faxing Lubbenau for some days, but with no reply. Now her boss was getting on to her. Her problem, Francine told him, was that she didn't know whether her faxes were getting through. That's why she and her colleague were there. Could the *concierge* check for her? Could he see if her faxes had come through? She promised that they would wait outside whilst he had a look.

The man frowned. It wasn't policy to do such things, he said. But, Francine protested, he must be in and out of the offices all the time. Attending to problems, checking security, cleaning. Couldn't he do it just this once? For her? Eleanor fought hard to suppress a grin. Francine was giving the old boy the business. Her boss was a bastard, Francine went on, a tough, middle-aged lesbian who was forever trying to touch her up. If Francine didn't find out why Lubbenau wasn't replying to her faxes then she was in a lot of trouble. Her boss would probably bend her across a desk and . . .

That did it. The old man let out a macho grunt and opened the big, wooden door. 'Wait here,' he ordered sternly. Francine smiled sweetly, waited for a few seconds, then followed him in. Eleanor trailed after her.

The room was large and square with a single, north-facing window. Hanging from the high ceiling was a bare, dusty chandelier. The walls were a smoky-rose colour and the floor was made of large wooden blocks, half covered by a couple of old, expensive carpets. In a corner was a table which served as a desk. It was grand and ornate with gilded cabriole legs curving down to claw-and-ball feet. On it was a large china tablelamp. The room was gloomy. Motes of dust danced in the beams of pale sunshine streaming through the window.

Eleanor stared around. The place had an air of faded elegance; almost like a museum or an unvisited room in an old house.

On a small table in a corner stood the room's only piece of office equipment. A fax machine. The caretaker was standing by it, examining a fax. He looked up. 'Hey, I told you. You can't come in here.' He moved towards them.

Francine stood her ground. 'Is that my fax?' She pointed to a roll of paper hanging from the machine like a long tongue.

'No, no. That's from a firm of accountants. There's nothing from your business directory.'

He hustled them out onto the balcony. Francine and Eleanor waited as he locked the door. 'It was really very sweet of you to help us,' Francine said, 'at least now I know why I'm not getting any reply from Lubbenau. I must have the wrong number. We shall have to come back.'

'Yes, come back,' said the caretaker, 'and next time maybe you would like to have coffee with me.'

Francine smiled. 'That would be nice.'

She turned to go, then turned back as if she'd just remembered something. 'Oh, I almost forgot,' she said, 'what is the boss's name? The man who runs Lubbenau?'

'Schmidt,' replied the caretaker. 'Herr Schmidt. He's German.'

The restaurant was close by. For a while they walked in silence, then Francine said quietly, 'Not much business is done in that room.'

'None,' agreed Eleanor. 'Apart from the fax there was nothing there. No word processor, no filing cabinets . . .'

'Not even a phone. Did you notice that?'

'Yes.' Eleanor lifted her face to the sun. 'I wish I knew what the hell is going on, Francine.'

La Lyrique was close to the Opera House in the old town. By the time they arrived the place was more than half full. A waiter showed them to their table. The restaurant was decorated in the *belle époque* style, with high ceilings, pastel stucco-work and polished wooden floors. It looked like something out of turn-of-the-century Paris. Except that it was filled with quiet, sober, grey-suited Swiss: serious men whom Francine explained were either lawyers or bankers. Eleanor noticed that she and Francine were the only young women in the place.

They ordered a drink and discussed Lubbenau. They agreed it was inconceivable that an international marketing operation could be managed out of that spare, fading room in the Grande Rue. So, if Lubbenau wasn't managing the sale of more than forty million pounds' worth of Campanalla products into Britain, as well as a lot more into the rest of Europe, then, Eleanor mused, who the hell was? Francine gave her a Gallic shrug.

'The fact is that *someone* is organizing the business,' Eleanor went on. 'I'm auditing Drumanon. I know what's going through the bank account. The business is definitely happening . . . definitely there.' She looked at her friend. Francine wasn't listening. She was staring up at something over Eleanor's right shoulder.

Eleanor turned. Two men were standing close to her chair. She started back in shock and grabbed the arm of her chair.

One of the men was familiar. She *knew* him.

It was Richard Jamieson.

'Eleanor, what the hell are you doing here?' He sounded as shocked as she felt.

She took a moment to reply. 'Hello, Richard. What a surprise.'

'Isn't it. But why are you here?'

'I came over to spend a couple of days with an old friend from my previous firm.' She half turned in her seat. 'Francine, this is Richard Jamieson. Richard, Francine.'

They smiled at each other over the table; Richard with his schoolboy grin, Francine with her sultry, I-want-your-body number. Eleanor shot her a look then turned back to Jamieson.

'Well, what brings you to Geneva?'

He shrugged. 'Business, as usual.'

The serious, uncomfortable-looking man standing with Jamieson shuffled. Jamieson turned to him. 'Oh, I'm sorry,' he said, 'I'm forgetting my manners. This is Peter, a business associate of mine. Peter, this is the lady I was telling you about. Eleanor Lambert. And her friend, Francine.'

The man nodded briefly. 'How do you do?' His voice was quiet, cautious, heavily accented.

Eleanor stared up at him. A sudden doubt jumped into her head. 'Peter,' she repeated. 'Peter what?'

'I'm sorry. I do not understand.'

'What's your other name. Your surname.'

'It's Schmidt. Peter Schmidt.'

Chapter Twenty-One

Francine was marvellous.

At Eleanor's sudden, sharp intake of breath she launched into a prattle of perfect German. The men's eyes switched to her. Her face as she chatted was animated and cheerful and although the dour Schmidt didn't allow himself a smile, he did seem to relax a little. Francine asked him a question and he answered her in German.

'I must say, it's a hell of a surprise seeing you here,' Richard said quietly, bending towards Eleanor's chair. 'Do you come to see your friend often?'

Eleanor had recovered her wits. 'A couple of times a year,' she murmured. 'But this is special. She's just broken up with her man. She asked me over to cheer her up. Talk, drink a few bottles of wine, do some shopping, that kind of thing.'

Jamieson looked around. 'I'm surprised you came here. It's not the kind of place you'd expect to find a couple of good-looking women trying to cheer themselves up. It's full of businessmen.'

Eleanor shrugged. 'Her man is a lawyer. He used to come here for lunch. She thought she might see him. You know how it is.' From his face she could tell that he did not. The addictive agony of waiting for a glimpse of a lost lover was something unknown to Jamieson.

'I called you yesterday morning,' he went on, 'about seven thirty. You weren't answering. I left a message.'

Eleanor remembered the flashing light on her machine. She smiled up at him. 'I got started on the day early. I was on my way to the office by then.'

He frowned. 'I called your office. They said you weren't in.'

Francine's proficiency at instant invention was catching. Without missing a beat, she said, 'I'd been and gone by eight fifteen. I was at a client's by nine and on the flight over here by four.'

'Oh.'

Francine had stopped chattering and Schmidt had gone back to looking awkward. 'Well, we had better be going,' Jamieson said brightly. 'It was nice to meet you, Francine. Eleanor, I expect I'll see you at the office in a day or so.' The two men started away from the table. Jamieson stopped and turned back. 'Oh, I almost forgot. About the trip to the Channel Islands.'

Eleanor was startled. 'Pardon?'

'Sailing. This weekend. You remember? That's why I called you yesterday.'

'Oh. Oh yes.' She had forgotten all about it.

'I can't get away as early as I'd hoped. Would it be okay if I pick you up Friday evening about nine? We can spend the evening on the yacht and set off early Saturday morning. Is that okay with you?'

'Yes, yes of course.'

She watched the two men weave their way through the tables and out of the restaurant. She leaned back in her seat. 'I need another drink.'

Francine gestured to a passing waiter to bring two more vodkas. 'So,' she said, 'that is Herr Schmidt.'

'Apparently. God, Francine, you were marvellous. I was completely gobsmacked. Seeing Richard was a big enough surprise, but seeing him with our mysterious Mr Schmidt well . . . thank God you were on the ball.'

'It was nothing. But Herr Schmidt is not too communicative. He says he travels around Europe buying and selling things, but he didn't say what exactly. He didn't mention anything about having an office here.'

'He must be the same Schmidt all the same. He was with Richard and Richard deals with Lubbenau. He *must* be the same one.'

'Perhaps.' Francine was bored with talk of Schmidt. 'But Richard, he is the man you are screwing, yes?' Eleanor nodded. 'He is gorgeous.'

'Yes, I noticed you thought so,' Eleanor said tartly.

'Chérie,' Francine chided her, 'don't be so English. He is big enough for both of us. You should share your men with your friends.' They both laughed loudly as a waiter brought their salade niçoise.

Francine was anxious to know everything about Eleanor's affair with Richard and was impressed with her description of the yacht. 'Rich *and* sexy,' Francine murmured, 'lucky girl.'

After the self-denying salad their virtue evaporated and they egged each other on to have tarte tatin . . . which they ordered with double cream. 'God, I'm stuffed,' moaned Eleanor afterwards.

'Cognac?' suggested Francine with a grin.

Eleanor eyed the carafe of house white sitting empty on the table in front of her. 'Oh, what the hell. Why not?'

Francine opened a pack of Marlboro and proffered it to Eleanor who shook her head. Eleanor watched her blow smoke at the ceiling. 'Francine, what am I going to do?'

Interspersed with their talk of men and orgasms, Eleanor

had told Francine of her work at Drumanon; of her suspicions of Lassiter, the forged letter of resignation from Van Dameer, the lack of activity at the London showroom and the absence of any kind of organization in Amsterdam or Geneva. She had said nothing about John Shephard and his suspicions of drug running, nor about the death of David.

'Something is very definitely wrong. But I just don't know what. Or what to do about it.'

Francine stared at her. 'Chérie, it has to be some kind of tax scam. Or VTA. No, I mean VAT.'

'But what? I mean, if something is going on, exactly what is it? I can't work it out.'

'Why should you? You're not even a partner in Hagerty Clark. Why should you work out what is wrong? Take it to the partner, this Philip Passmore. Tell him what you know. It is sufficient that you have discovered something . . . something that makes you think you will have to qualify your audit report. Let *him* sort it out with Drumanon.'

'But for God's sake, Francine,' she wailed, 'this is my first audit for the practice and already I'm making waves. Philip is a personal friend of this guy Lassiter; he's going to love it when I tell him that his golfing partner is up to something shady.'

Francine was unsympathetic. 'Why should you care? It is only a little practice anyway. What are you doing there, hiding yourself away in the country? You are chic, you are beautiful, you are a big-city girl. You could get another job tomorrow. You should be working for one of the big five, not for a small-town practice. Not for a man and his dog. Poof.' She waved her cigarette violently in the air.

Eleanor smiled lovingly at her friend. 'God, Francine, what would I do without you? But,' her face changed, 'supposing Richard is involved? I mean, he's here with Schmidt. Do you think he's in on the scam?'

'Do you?'

She thought about it. 'I don't know. I don't think so. But I guess I would think that, wouldn't I? After all, I'm sleeping with him. I just don't know.'

'So what if he is? What does it matter?' Francine shrugged as only a Frenchwoman can shrug. 'It's only a tax scam. You are not responsible for your client's behaviour. Just fuck him for as long as you have the hunger, then . . . forget him. Go sailing in his wonderful yacht for as long as it pleases you and then say au revoir.'

She took a sip of her cognac. 'Last year I had some business with a man who was a lawyer. He was very cute so . . .' She shrugged again. 'Anyway, he carried a gun. He kept it with him all the time, under his jacket, in his desk, under his pillow. He said he needed it for protection; he had business with some men in Italy.' She put her head on one side and gave Eleanor a quizzical look. 'You know the kind of man I mean? It was very sexy, the gun. Very scary, very sexy. In fact, I thought the gun was sexier than the man.'

Eleanor shook her head in wonder at her friend. 'You're crazy,' she laughed.

'No, chérie, I am serious. You have found something that gives you grounds for suspicion. So, tell your senior partner. It is not up to you to discover what is going on. You are an auditor, not a detective.' She laughed. 'You worry too much. Let's have another cognac.'

They left the restaurant forty minutes later, teetering slightly as they emerged into the daylight to find the gentle wooziness in their heads turning into something which moved like a ship in trouble.

The walk through the old town in the bright sunshine

helped dispel some of their tipsiness, though Eleanor wondered how much work Francine would be able to do that afternoon. She said as much.

'I am French, chérie. I am only ever as drunk as I want to be. When I get into my meeting I shall be as always: a tough bitch.' Eleanor laughed.

They arrived at the tower block and rode the lift up to Francine's office where Eleanor retrieved her overnight bag and attaché case. They hugged, warmly and for a long time.

'Lunch was marvellous,' Eleanor said. 'It was so good to see you again. You've been such a help, I just can't tell you.'

Outside, she turned towards the rue des Alpes and spent a couple of hours shopping in the boutiques around the Place de Cornavin. Thinking of the imminent weekend with Richard she bought herself some outrageously expensive silk underwear; it was white and lacy and very, very sexy. She smiled as she handed the assistant her Amex card. Francine would have approved.

Towards five she took a cab to the airport. The clouds of cotton wool floating around her brain after lunch had turned to cement. It seemed to be churning around the inside of her skull in a mixer.

She ordered Perrier in the coffee shop and took a couple of paracetamol. An announcement came over the PA system: the flight to London was delayed by an hour. She groaned and ordered a coffee. Afterwards she wandered around the duty-free. At last her flight was called and she joined the herd heading for the departure lounge.

She had a seat on the aisle and hoped she might doze on the flight. Instead she found herself next to a young, tubby Dutchman who started putting the moves on her. He was an economist with one of the big banks. His talk was infused with the clichés of marketing; he spoke constantly of niche players, level playing fields and globalization. Eleanor, distantly polite, wished he would shut up. His deep, guttural voice droned in the background like a distant motorway. He was saying something about European harmonization.

'What? Say that again.'

The Dutchman's eyes behind his spectacles blinked in surprise. 'I said that national borders in Europe are irrelevant. Our trade, our tariffs, even our value added taxes are being integrated.'

She had heard something similar recently. Where? When? The breeze had been blowing her hair. Francine . . . as they were crossing the Pont des Bergues . . . Francine had talked about integrating taxes.

The Dutchman was staring at her.

Of course. That was it. That was what had evaded her for so long. The elusive thought she'd had when she had talked to Shephard at the health club. The vague notion that had evaded her dreams. It all fitted . . . all made sense.

'Oh God,' she moaned.

How could she have been so stupid, so blind? It was obvious.

She grunted loudly as the pieces dropped into place. 'Uhh, uhh, uuhhh.'

The Dutchman's face froze in shock as he watched her squirming in her seat.

The beautiful woman who had been so impressed by his erudite discourse on macroeconomics appeared to be reaching a climax.

Which, in a manner of speaking, she was.

The plane touched down at Heathrow shortly after nine British time, and by eleven the tyres of the CRX were scrunching on the gravel drive of the big house in Bourne-mouth.

A set of headlights followed her onto the drive. She figured it was either the young couple in the flat below or some of their friends. She was tired and she hoped they weren't about to throw yet another of their late parties. She got out of the car and leaned back inside to retrieve her cases and purchases.

'Where the hell have you been?'

She jerked up in alarm and banged her head on the roof of the car. 'Ow, shit,' she yelped.

She put her hand to her head and turned around. Her scalp hurt like hell. 'Fuck.' She muttered it vehemently under her breath. 'Oooh, fuck.'

The voice was hard and demanding. 'I've been worried sick about you. Where the fuck have you *been*?'

A man was standing close to her open car door. It was John Shephard.

His face, in the light of his headlamps, was rigid with strain and fury. 'You didn't come home last night. Jesus Christ. I've been going nuts. I thought . . . I thought something had happened to you. And where were you? Shopping, for Christ's sake.' He stabbed a finger at the expensive Swiss carrier bag she was holding. 'How could you go fucking shopping? When I'm looking all over the place for you. How could you bloody do that?'

It was a nightmare. She felt as if she were being assailed by a maniac. She could barely think. Her head hurt like hell. She said the first thing that came into her head. 'Look, do you mind not using bloody language like that.'

The anxious rage on his face transformed itself into total incomprehension. 'What?' His voice went up an octave.

'Don't keep swearing at me,' she demanded. 'Saying

bloody and fuck – and – and, whatever, I don't like it.'

He gawked at her, dumbfounded. It was as if she had started talking Swahili. 'But you've just been . . .' his voice tailed off. The situation was beyond him. There was a long silence. 'Look, I need to talk to you.'

'Well, you can damn well talk to me tomorrow. I've had a long day, a tiring flight and, thanks to you, I've got a bloody lump on my head.'

He gazed at her in bewildered astonishment for another moment then, with an effort, pulled himself together and overcame his surprise. 'This is police business. You think I've come round here to have a cosy chat? I want to talk to you and I want to talk to you *now*.'

She stared at his face. That frightening look of intensity was back. His voice was edged with iron. It was clear he meant it. 'All right. You can come in for five minutes,' she snapped. 'But,' she jabbed a finger towards his chest, 'I don't want any more bad language. I'm fed up with you swearing at me. My mother says that kind of language is the language of the gutter. So I'd be grateful if you'd stop using it.' He stared at her as if she were unreal. 'And you've left your headlights on.'

She retrieved the rest of her bags as he walked to his car and turned off the lights. They walked in silence to the door of the flat. She put her overnight bag down to unlock the door and he carried it up the stairs. She switched on the lights. 'I need a drink. As you're on duty, I don't suppose you want one.'

'I'd like a cup of tea.'

She gave him an irritated look. He followed her into the kitchen where she put the kettle on. She rubbed her head. 'God, that hurts. I bet I've cut it.'

'Here, let me have a look.' She glanced at him doubtfully.

401

'Don't be silly, let me take a look.'

She bent her head. His hands were warm; his fingers, as he parted her thick hair, strong but gentle. She was sorry when he'd finished. 'No, you haven't cut your scalp. There's a big bruise coming up, though. I'm sorry. It was my fault. It was just that you had me worried. Really worried.'

'Why?'

'Isn't it bloody obvious?' He remembered her instruction. 'Sorry.'

'Obvious?'

'Yesterday morning you went to the Campanalla showrooms. After that, you disappeared off the face of the earth. I was worried. What the hell did you expect?'

'How do you know I went to Campanalla?'

'I told you, there's a drug squad team watching the showroom. They're taking photographs of everybody who goes near the place. How do you think I felt when they faxed a clutch of pictures yesterday afternoon and there's a couple of blow-ups of you coming out of the place?'

'Photographs. I never thought of that.'

'I called your office and some woman said you'd had to rush out and wouldn't be back for a day or so. For the last twenty-four hours I've been going out of my head, wondering where you'd gone. Wondering what the hell might have happened to you.'

'I went to Amsterdam, to check out Van Dameer. Then I flew on to Geneva and checked out Lubbenau.'

'What?' he yelped. 'Jesus Christ are you nuts?'

'No, I'm not nuts. You said it would take a while for the Dutch police to get around to investigating Van Dameer, so I thought I'd do it. That I'd get on with it.'

'But that's madness. It could have been dangerous.'

'It wasn't dangerous at all. That's because you're wrong.

Neither company is involved in what you think. And, anyway, as you see, I'm still here.'

He glowered at her than grimaced. 'I suppose that's an advantage of not being a bureaucracy. You can just get on a plane and do it.'

She grinned. 'This is still the age of the entrepreneur.'

She considered him, putting her head on one side, and after a moment asked, 'Did that shipment of kitchens and conservatories come through from Campanalla?' Her voice was light and playful.

Shephard nodded. 'Into Harwich. From Rotterdam.'

'Did Customs inspect them?'

'Yes.'

'But they didn't find any drugs, did they?'

He gave her a hard, doubtful look. He suspected she was playing with him. 'How the hell do you know that?'

'Simple. Because nobody, neither Drumanon nor Campanalla, Van Dameer nor Lubbenau, is smuggling drugs. You've been wasting your time.'

He glowered at her. 'What the hell are you talking about? How do you know?'

Her grin broadened. 'I told you, I went over to check them out. I know. I know they're not trafficking narcotics. Believe me.'

'So they're all perfectly legitimate, straightforward businesses then?'

'I didn't say that. All I'm saying is that they're nothing to do with you – the police; the drug squad.' She bent down to open the fridge and retrieve a bottle of milk. Sitting on the top shelf inside the door was a yellow squeezer of lemon juice.

'What the hell is that doing there?' Shephard nodded at the squeezer. His voice was suspicious.

The grin left her face and she looked at him in surprise. 'Why do you think? I use it for cooking . . . salad dressings and such. I do cook, you know. I don't eat junk.' She screwed up her face, puzzled at his question. 'Anyway, why do you want to know that?'

He scowled. 'Heroin addicts use that stuff. They mix their fix with it. Before they shoot up.'

'What?' She slammed the fridge door shut. 'You think *I'm* a bloody junkie now? As you've been wasting your time on Drumanon and the others, I suppose you think you'll have a go at me. Implicate me instead.' Her voice was loud, shrill. 'I suppose you want to check my arms for needle marks?' She began pushing up the sleeves of her suit. 'Well come on then, take a look.'

He held up both hands. 'Okay, okay, take it easy. I'm sorry. I'm just tired. I've been going crazy worrying about you for the last twenty-four hours and I guess I'm whacked out. I always get twitchy when I see that stuff.'

'Well, I'm bloody tired too,' she snapped. 'So just drink your tea and go.' She pushed the bottle of milk across the table at him. He ignored it.

'Wait a minute, Eleanor. I need to talk to you. You said that Drumanon isn't trafficking, you said that I'm wrong. I need to know—'

'I am not answering any questions tonight.' She could hear her voice rising to a yell. 'I refuse. I am too tired and I've got a blinding headache. Thanks to you.'

He stared at her. His face was lined with tiredness. After a while he said, quietly, 'Okay, maybe you're right. We've both had it, both dog tired. I guess whatever you've got to say can keep until tomorrow. It'll be better then.' He moved to the kitchen door, his movements slow, like an old man's. He looked worn out. 'I'll call you in the morning, fix a time.

Thanks for the tea.' She noticed he hadn't drunk any.

They walked down the stairs as they'd walked up them; in silence.

Eleanor wondered what it was about Shephard; what it was about this man that seemed so much to annoy her. She knew she ought to apologize. Her reaction to his question about the lemon juice was totally over the top. But she was too tired. Not now, not tonight. Tomorrow. Tomorrow she would apologize.

He turned at the door. 'Your mother's wrong, by the way.'

'What?'

'Your mother's wrong. Swearing isn't the language of the gutter. Not any more. Now it's the language of the street.'

'Well, it's not a very nice street, that's all I can say.'

He shook his head slowly. 'You don't get it, do you? The street *is* the gutter. At least it is in my business. In a lot of businesses. Maybe even yours. That's the way the world's going.' He walked off into the night.

She had no idea what he meant and was too tired to think about it. She trudged back up the stairs and wandered into the lounge. The message light on her answering machine was flicking three times. Ignore it. She would get the messages in the morning, she thought. But old habits died hard. Despite her tiredness she flicked the machine to playback and flopped into a chair.

The first message was the one Richard had left on her machine the day before, saying he thought Jersey would be a good destination for the weekend. But, he continued, his plans had altered and was it all right to pick her up after nine on Friday evening?

She had forgotten about the sailing weekend. Again. The row with Shephard had put it out of her mind. She thought about it; about Richard and that fabulous yacht. Francine had thought she should have some fun and . . .

The next voice echoing around the room was instantly familiar. It was her mother. The message was completely indecipherable. In amongst the snorts and pauses and frequently repeated, 'I do hate talking to these things', was something about arrangements for a wedding anniversary. Finally, after a couple of minutes of gibberish, her father came on and explained. It was her brother's wedding anniversary soon, there was to be a dinner party and everyone hoped she could come. She put her head back on the easy chair. It would be good to go home, back to Gloucestershire, back to sanity and peace.

The machine beeped and clicked and the tape rolled on to the next message. There was a pause, then a voice made ghostly by distance and the stratosphere came on.

'Eleanor, hi, it's Don Pennington. It's three in the afternoon here so I guess it's nine over there, right? I checked on the company you asked about. Eleanor, it's not good news. I don't want to say anything on your machine so call me when you can. Okay? Speak to you soon.' The line went dead and with a series of clunks and clicks the machine re-set itself.

She groaned. What now? She eased herself out of the chair, found her attaché case in the hallway, retrieved her address book and shuffled back into the lounge. She punched Pennington's number in Toronto. It was close to six, their time. She hoped he would still be at his desk.

She was lucky. 'Don, it's Eleanor Lambert.'

'Eleanor, thanks for calling back. You're up late.'

She grunted. 'Tell me about it. What have you got for me, Don?' Her words echoed slightly somewhere in space and there was a momentary pause as Pennington's voice bounced off the satellite.

'Okay. Lassiter Enterprises Inc has a couple of directors

and a registered office here in Toronto, *but*, the company is a wholly owned subsidiary of a corporation registered in the Dutch Antilles. That's not good news, Eleanor. What's worse is, as far as we can figure out, the corporation in the Dutch Antilles is owned by a Panamanian shell company. Which means you ain't ever gonna find out who's in back of it. It could be Colombians, some guys in Miami, who knows?'

'Of course, it could be legitimate,' Eleanor pointed out.

'Hell, Eleanor, the Pope might have tits but I wouldn't count on it. This kind of foggy, complicated corporate structure is there for a reason. The kindest interpretation is that the guys behind it are trying to evade tax. That's the *best*. The real reasons could be a lot worse . . . a lot more sinister. And the guys behind it could be very dangerous. Whatever you have to do with this company, Eleanor, I would do it very carefully. At arm's length. Best of all, have *nothing* to do with it.'

She was so tired the room seemed to be swaying. She closed her eyes. Dear God, what a mess. 'Okay, well thanks a lot, Don. At least now I know the set-up. You've been a great help.'

'That's okay, Eleanor, you're welcome.'

She was about to put the phone down when she remembered the question. 'Don, Don, I almost forgot. You said two directors. Who are they?'

There was a pause, then the flat, soulless voice floated down the line. 'One is a Daniel James Lassiter, the other is, hang on, I've got it here. Yeah, the other is a guy called Jamieson. Richard Keith Jamieson.'

Chapter Twenty-Two

The BMW swung into the huge, crowded car park and purred slowly between the lines of parked cars. K, rubbernecking in the back, searched for the vehicle.

'There it is,' he said, 'over to the right.'

In the front passenger seat Boyle turned to look. Leon, the driver, took no notice but held the car on its stately course to the end of the driveway before turning right.

'Not this one, the next,' K murmured.

Leon turned into the lane between the long lines of parked cars. The rows of vehicles, their bodywork gleaming dully in the sun, disappeared into the middle distance. They drove slowly, eyeing the vehicle as they drew close. It stood out from those around it.

'Yeah, that's it,' K said quietly. 'Okay, check for surveillance.' The 750i continued its slow progress between the cars, the men inside sharp-eyed, looking for anyone seated in a car; searching for an innocuous couple of blokes, or maybe a man and a woman, who might be watching the vehicle. They drove the length of all the lanes around the vehicle. Checking for watchers. There were none.

'That's enough,' said K finally, 'drop me at reception.'

Leon drove to within a few yards of the hotel's automatic plate-glass doors. K got out, followed by Leon. Boyle moved around the front of the BMW and climbed into the driving seat. Inside the big, anonymous hotel Leon would not look out of place. Boyle would.

A 747 lifted off from the runway a few hundred yards away, the noise momentarily drowning out the sound of the motorway nearby. K strolled into the hotel. Leon followed him a few seconds later.

The enormous lobby was busy. Bellboys were pushing wheeled cages of luggage, and groups of arriving and departing guests were milling around the reception desk. The lobby was noisy, the atmosphere prickly with impatience. Flights in and out of Heathrow were delayed and the hotel's systems were backing up.

K ignored the irritable travellers and made for the bar. Partitioned by smoked glass and equipped with subdued lighting, the place was murky. It was almost as busy as reception. K saw the man he was looking for at a small table in a corner and made his way towards him. Leon hitched himself onto a seat at the bar, ordered a beer and watched.

'Any troubles?' asked the man.

K sat down. 'No. We checked around your motor. No one.'

A tall glass of clear, sparkling liquid with ice and a slice of lemon was sitting on K's side of the table. He picked it up, said 'Cheers' and took a sip. It was tonic water. He never drank alcohol when he met with the Profit; he needed his senses needle sharp.

'What about the girl?'

K put his glass down.'Clean hit. They dumped her somewhere in the New Forest.'

The Profit nodded. 'She was taking too much interest. Looking around the diner, eyeing everyone. She was sharp, she might have remembered who was there. She could have identified me.'

K's face was impassive, though underneath he was surprised. The Profit never justified his decisions, especially about killing.

'We have problems,' the man continued in his cold, measured tone.

'Yeah?'

'The authorities are digging into some of our bank accounts. Asking questions. Clapham Fats may have talked.'

K frowned. 'What could he talk about? He doesn't know anything about our end of the business.'

The Profit scowled. 'He did once. In the early days. Before we were properly organized. He could be talking. Either that or the fool left evidence lying around.'

K grunted. Knowing Fats, that was more likely.

'Can we get to him in Brixton? Eradicate him? Is that possible?'

K glanced curiously at the man opposite. Eradicate. What kind of word was that? Sometimes the guy used some strange expressions.

'Yeah, it's possible,' he replied slowly, 'but it will take time to set up. And it'll cost.'

The Profit shook his head impatiently. 'For Christ's sake, the cost doesn't matter. We've got the money, it's the *time* we don't have. There could still be trouble in the operation on the south coast.'

Another surprise. K's eyebrows shot up. Twice in the last few weeks he and his men had been called in to sort out problems in that part of the organization.

'If the authorities connect Fats' evidence with the set-up down there,' the Profit continued, 'it could be serious. We may have to move fast. Close it all down.'

Closing things down meant killings.

K stared across the table. The operation on the south coast had been the Profit's brainchild. It was his great achievement, his jewel in the crown. It serviced the other franchises in the organization; the Profits from Glasgow and Manchester and Birmingham – all of them used it. Closing it down would be a drastic step. K wondered what the men at the American end of the company would think about that. But if it needed to be closed down, then the man across the table was the one to do it. K had worked for him long enough to know that the Profit was a great businessman: cool, pragmatic, unemotional . . . and extraordinarily ruthless.

'Is there no quick way to shut Fats up?'

'Quick way? No. We don't even know if Fats is talking . . .'

The Profit caught the doubt in his voice. 'But . . .?' he queried sharply.

'If Fats has left evidence lying around, the police will be grilling him like he was barbecued steak. He might crack. Especially with a murder charge hanging over him. If he tells them what he knows – well, he knows enough to be damaging.'

'Get word to him. Tell him what will happen if he talks.'

K made a face. 'He knows that already.' He sipped his tonic water.

The Profit stared thoughtfully at him. 'Supposing you find this man Lionel, the one who made the statement. Made . . .' he paused ' . . .an example of him. That would tell Fats to keep his mouth shut. Underline the message. Wouldn't it?'

K nodded. 'Sure. And with Lionel out of the way, the filth would probably be forced to drop the murder charge.'

The Profit gave him an arctic smile. 'That too,' he agreed.

'But the main thing is that Fats would know what happens to people who co-operate with the police. Can you find him? This Lionel?'

K shrugged. 'Maybe. The law will be holding him in a safehouse somewhere. He'll be under armed guard,' he added darkly.

'That doesn't matter. Use whatever resources you need. Do whatever you have to do. Just do it.' He fixed K with a cold, commanding stare.

K returned his gaze steadily. 'Okay.'

'Where will they be holding him?'

'I don't know. But I think I know someone who might.'

'Find him. Find him and get rid of him. Make him an example. *Pour encourager les autres*.'

K didn't understand the last few words. It didn't matter. A lot of the time he didn't know what the old guy was talking about. He stood up. The Profit gazed up at him. 'Keep in touch,' he ordered.

'Sure,' K nodded. Leon followed him out of the bar.

They found the address in Lewisham in the middle of the afternoon. It was a ground-floor flat in a pre-war block close to the High Street. Leon rang the bell. K and Boyle hung back, out of sight. The door was inched cautiously open by a good-looking black woman in her early twenties. 'Yeah?'

Leon kicked the door wide, stepped inside the hallway and, as the girl opened her mouth to scream, smashed his fist into her face. She flew backwards into the narrow hallway and crashed onto her back with a small cry. K and Boyle followed Leon into the flat and K shut the door. Quietly.

Leon moved quickly. He bent over the girl, grabbed her by her long, ringletted hair and, slapping a large hand over her mouth, hauled her cruelly to her feet. Blood was streaming from her nose and mouth, some of it trickling over the dark hairs on the back of his hand. Swiftly Leon propelled the girl backwards into a small living room and pushed her into a seat. Twisting his fingers deeper in her hair he wrenched her head back. K stood in front of her, careful not to let any of the dripping blood fall onto his shoes. 'If you scream,' he said quietly, 'if you make any noise at all, we'll kill you. Do you understand?'

The girl's eyes were huge, wide with shock and pain. She did her best to nod.

'Where's the law keeping Lionel?'

Leon took his hand away from her mouth. She gasped, fighting for breath. 'Fuck.' She put her hands to her face. 'You hurt me. Christ, I think you've broken my nose. You bastards.' Leon pulled her hair savagely and she yelped.

K jabbed a finger at her. 'I told you, no noise. Now, I don't care if the whole of your fucking face is broken. Just tell me. Where are they keeping Lionel?'

'I don't know what you're talking about. I don't know no bleeding Lionel,' she gasped.

Leon slapped his hand back over her mouth as K nodded to Boyle. With a leer, the little Scotsman pulled the bayonet from his left sleeve. The girl's eyes grew wider and she began to struggle. Leon yanked her hair, bending her head brutally backwards. Boyle stepped forward, grabbed the girl's tee shirt and with one deft stroke drew the razor-sharp edge of the bayonet down its front. The fabric split apart and the girl's firm, swelling breasts surged out. Boyle took one of her nipples between his thumb and forefinger and made to slice it with the bayonet. The sound beneath Leon's hand was of the girl shrieking.

K bent forward and put his mouth close to her ear. His voice was quiet and pitiless. 'If you fuck about with me again, he's going to start cutting your tits off. Slice by slice. Starting with that nice, juicy nipple. So no more games. Right? You're Lionel's tart and Lionel kept some of his stash here. So, he would've got in touch with you somehow. And he would've told you where he was. Now, if you don't tell me this time, your new fella's going to have nothing to suck on. Gettit?' The girl nodded imperceptibly. Leon took his hand away from her mouth.

'Woking,' she gasped. 'Somewhere in Woking.'

'Where?'

'I dunno.'

Boyle drew the edge of the bayonet lightly across her nipple.

'I don't know,' she screeched. 'I don't. It's some house.'

'What house?'

'Maplethorpe House, something like that. I wrote it down.'

'Where?'

'On a pad, over there.'

K crossed the room, picked up a pad and flicked through. He found what she'd written. He ripped out the page and returned to the girl. 'Is this all you got?'

'Yes.'

'No street name or anything?'

'No, no, I promise. I asked. He didn't know it. All he'd seen was the name on the gate.'

'How do you know he's there?'

'He called me. There's a couple of armed coppers with him. Once they left him on his own. In a room with a phone. Just for a moment. I don't think they meant to.'

K eyed her speculatively. She was too frightened to be lying. Frightened and wounded. Blood from her face was dripping onto her breasts. 'You'd better be right,' he said. 'If you're wrong, if you're fucking us about, we're gonna come looking for you. And he's gonna do things to you with that knife you can't even imagine.' He nodded at Boyle who, with a surly look, straightened up and sheathed the bayonet. 'You understand?'

The girl nodded. Leon let go of her hair and cuffed her smartly on the side of the head. 'Remember it, bitch,' he said bleakly.

The girl shuddered uncontrollably as the three men silently left the room. Clutching the severed halves of her tee shirt she pulled them over her breasts.

'We should have offed her,' Boyle said as they reached the BMW. 'She might talk.'

'She won't talk,' Leon growled.

'She might. I say we should have done it,' Boyle repeated.

'We didn't have any instructions to kill her,' K admonished him.

Boyle shrugged. 'So what? We should have offed the black bitch all the same.'

K stared at him with the incomprehension of a man who kills for profit for a man who kills for pleasure. They climbed into the car.

'Where now?' Leon asked.

'Woking. Where else?'

They headed west, to Wandsworth, where they picked up the A3.

'How we gonna find this Maplethorpe House?' Boyle enquired as they were driving into Woking. 'This looks a big place.'

K shrugged. 'Find me the public library,' he said, 'I'll start there.'

He was gone for almost two hours. By the time he returned the library was getting ready to close and the others had smoked a pack of cigarettes between them. He had a look of quiet satisfaction. 'Found it,' he told them. 'It was on the electoral register.' He gave them the name of the road.

Maplethorpe House was a large Victorian house at the end of a leafy private road of similar properties. It was detached and had a thick, high hedge around the garden.

Leon drove past it slowly. 'How do we get to him in there?' asked Boyle.

K, slumped in the back, stared at the place. 'I don't know. Not yet. But I will.' He took a final look at the large redbrick house. 'Okay, let's go back. We can't be seen driving up and down here too often.'

Sitting in the BMW a few days later, K said, 'Tomorrow morning we go to Woking.'

'You found a way of getting to that bastard?' Boyle asked.

K nodded. 'I've had the place watched. It's got good security and it won't be easy. We have to get in at the back.'

'What about the coppers?' Leon asked. 'They ain't just going to let us walk in. They'll be armed.'

'I know. We're gonna hit them just after they've changed the morning shift. They'll be relaxed, not expecting anything.'

'So what do we do?'

'They change shifts at eight every morning and evening. On the morning changeover, the two new cops stand around in the hallway for a couple of minutes, yakking with the blokes they're relieving. That means they're all at the front of the house with the alarm turned off. We'll break in at the back.'

Leon frowned. 'How the hell do we get round the back? We'll have to get through that bloody great hedge.'

K shook his head. 'The hedge doesn't go all the way around. There's a fence between the garden and the one next door. The house next door has been converted into a couple of flats. Yuppies. They're out all day. We'll cut the phone lines just in case, get into the garden and go over the fence. We'll break in while the coppers are in the hallway and hit them after their mates have gone.'

'We're gonna hit the polis?' Boyle repeated. There was a note of anticipation in his voice.

'We're going to put them out of action. That's all.' K pointed a stern finger at Boyle. 'No dead coppers. Understand? It's bad for business. So long as neither of those two bastards babysitting Lionel wants to be a hero, they stay alive.'

Boyle scowled.

'Right,' K continued, 'tonight, find a van and nick it. Change the number plates and be ready with the gear first thing tomorrow.'

It was a dark blue, unmarked Citroen C25E. Leon drove. They wore boilersuits and gloves. They had ski-masks in their pockets.

At ten minutes to eight they were driving slowly down the private tree-lined road in Woking. Leon stopped halfway along, close to a telegraph pole. Boyle climbed into the back of the van and started up a chainsaw. The noise of the saw's motor against the metal walls was horrific. Leon got out, walked to the back of the van and opened one of its doors. Boyle, grasping the chainsaw, stepped out, moved a couple of feet to the pole and with one deft movement cut through the thick black plastic cable guard running up the pole and severed the clump of cables beneath it. He killed the saw's motor and got back into the van. It had taken him six seconds.

Leon drove off and, a hundred yards further on, turned the C25 into the driveway of the property next to

Maplethorpe House. He parked at an angle, allowing Boyle, crouched in the back, a good view of the house's doorway from the van's rear windows. K and Leon got out. Leon was carrying a workman's canvas toolbag.

They walked down a narrow passageway at the side of the house and waited close to a corner of the garage, out of sight of anyone in the house or any neighbours. K was holding a short-wave radio. A couple of minutes later Boyle's voice came through. 'There's a car turning into the drive of the house. A couple of young blokes are getting out. Plainclothes. Aye, but they're polis all right. One of them is ringing the doorbell.'

That was the signal. Leon and K crossed the garden at a run. Standing on the flagstones of a patio was a white picnic table. Hardly breaking step they grabbed it and between them rushed it to the high wooden fence. Leaping onto the table they were over the fence in a couple of seconds.

They ran to the back of the house and crouched below a window. K listened on his radio. 'The two guys have gone in,' he heard Boyle softly announce. 'The front door is still open. I can't see too well, but it looks like they're all in the hallway, having a wee chat.' K nodded at Leon who carefully raised his head and peered through the window. The kitchen was empty, the door leading to the rest of the house slightly ajar.

K shot a quick glance at the back door. Too solid. It had a yale and a mortice lock. He tried the handle, just in case. It was locked.

The window wasn't so solid. Wiring for the alarm system ran along the edge of its interior. It had a simple catch. K nodded to Leon. They pulled a couple of heavy crowbars out of the toolbag and started carefully prising up the window on either side of the catch. They made as little noise as possible.

The wood around the catch splintered on their third attempt. It was a soft, splitting sound, scarcely audible on the other side of the windowpane.

They glanced at each other. Had the coppers heard it above the sound of their own voices? From somewhere inside the house came a loud peal of laughter. K held the window open for Leon who scrambled carefully into the kitchen. K stayed where he was, crouching below the wall and flicking on his radio. 'What's happening?' he whispered urgently.

'Wait.' Half a minute later Boyle's voice came through again. 'Two other blokes are standing on the doorstep. They must be the guys from the earlier shift. They're getting ready to leave.'

That was the signal. K switched off the radio and pocketed it. He passed the toolbag through the window to Leon who pulled out a couple of sawn-off shotguns. K climbed quickly through the window. Inside the kitchen Leon handed him a sawn-off. They pulled on their ski-masks.

There were voices from somewhere in the house. They were coming closer. Leon crouched behind a tall fridge; K stood behind the door. Beneath the black nylon and wool of his ski-mask he could feel himself starting to sweat.

Two men, well-built and in their mid-twenties, walked into the kitchen. They were laughing. K waited until the second man was in the middle of the room before crashing the door shut with his elbow. He levelled the sawn-off at chest height. The men spun around. The laughter on their faces paralysed. Their eyes blossomed in shock.

'Don't do anything,' K snarled quietly, 'stand still and you'll stay alive.'

One of the plainclothes policemen remained frozen. The other made a slight move sideways. Leon, coming up from behind the fridge, clubbed him savagely with the stock of the sawn-off. The man went down. The other man shot his hands into the air. 'Don't,' he yelped loudly.

'On your knees,' K ordered.

'Why, what are you going to do?'

'Do it.'

Leon shoved him down onto his knees. He took out a pair of handcuffs and manacled the man's hands behind his back. The man on the floor was moaning quietly. Blood was seeping from his ear onto the kitchen's white lino tiles. Leon pulled the stunned man's hands behind his back and hand-cuffed him.

K bent down and relieved the men of the holstered Smith and Wessons beneath their jackets, depositing them in the toolbag, before taking their two-way radios and throwing them into a bowl of washing up water in the sink. Leon took out a roll of masking tape and began taping the men's mouths.

K moved out of the kitchen and down the hallway to the front door. He checked the alarm control, set on the wall nearby. The alarm was still turned off. He opened the door. Boyle was standing beside the van in the driveway next door. K signalled and Boyle was on the doorstep in seconds.

'Where's Lionel?' he asked as K shut the door behind him.

'Where do you think he'll be at this time in the morning?' K replied quietly. 'He'll be in bed. Find him and do it. Don't make a production of it. Just do it. And make sure it's done right. Hurry up. I want to get out of here.'

Lionel had been having bad dreams. Nightmares. Since he had said yes to Dunaff, ever since he had grassed up Clapham Fats, the same awful spectre had been coming back to haunt him, night after night. It was Boyle. The mad Scotsman had him trapped somewhere, he didn't know where, and was holding the bayonet under his chin. Holding it on the same spot he'd held it in the Paki flat in Brockley – just above the Adam's apple.

Christ, it was so real he could feel it. The cold shaft of steel pressing into his throat, tearing into his epiglottis, ripping up towards his brain. The mad bastard was leering at him with his black, broken teeth, his mad, urine-coloured eyes gleaming with blood lust. Jesus, it was so real he could smell the madman's breath.

A door crashed somewhere in the house and he drifted up a little out of sleep. Had he had it again? The nightmare? He wasn't sure, his mind was too tired to know. He was still half asleep. Dozily he moved his head and half opened his bleary eyes. But it *was* only a nightmare. It wasn't real. This was real. Lying in a warm bed in a room in a safehouse in Woking. With two armed coppers downstairs. He was safe. Boyle was a bad dream. Nothing more. He relaxed . . . let himself drift off.

Jesus, it was back again. Even *more* real. Boyle was there, his mad face with a fresh set of red, jagged scars so close Lionel could smell the fetid breath, could feel the prick of his bayonet, could hazily make out the mad eyes. He could feel the weight of Boyle's body on top of him, on top of the bedclothes. Boyle was straddling his chest. This was new. He hadn't felt this before.

He tried to move but he couldn't. Boyle's weight wouldn't let him. His arms were under the bedcovers. Oh, dear God, what a nightmare. It was so real. He was even dreaming that his eyes were open. He could see where he was, where Boyle had him trapped. It was in his safe room, in his safehouse in Woking. The bayonet was pressing under his chin. He could feel the steel of the bayonet. He could see the familiar room.

Sweet Jesus, it isn't a dream. Christ, it's real. Oh no. Dear God, don't let it be real. Oh no. Oh no.

Boyle was leaning forward. The point of the bayonet was gradually piercing Lionel's throat. Lionel threshed and jerked below the bedclothes, trying to shake Boyle off. It was impossible.

'Thought you could get away from me, did ye, ye bastard?' Boyle hissed. 'Well, you thought wrong. I'm here to show you what happens to black bastards who squeal to the law. *This* is what happens.'

Lionel screamed. 'Noooooo.'

Boyle grasped the hilt of the bayonet with both hands and shoved.

The scream turned to an obscene gurgle.

K heard the scream from the hallway and glanced up as Leon joined him from the kitchen carrying the toolbag. They pulled off their ski-masks and K deposited his sawn-off in the bag. 'Those two secured in there?' he asked.

Leon nodded. 'Yeah.'

Boyle came down the stairs. His gloves were smeared in blood. He was wiping the blade of the bayonet on a pillowcase.

'Done?' asked K.

'Definitely.'

They exited the house and walked smartly to the van parked next door. It was six minutes past eight.

Rattling in the van northeast on the Esher bypass, K said, 'When we get back, you take this heap of shit somewhere and burn it out. Okay.' They nodded. 'But before that we've got another job.'

'Yeah, what?' Leon asked.

'When the filth finds that Lionel's been topped, they'll interview his girlfriend. They'll want to know how someone found out where he was hidden. So, on second thoughts, maybe we ought to ice her. We don't want her telling the law that we paid her a visit. Do we?'

'No, we don't.' Something in Boyle's voice made the other two glance at him.

His face was leering in anticipation.

Chapter Twenty-Three

Once more she slept with the benefit of Temazepam. It occurred to her, as she was drifting into sleep, that she was taking it more regularly now than when she had lived in London.

She woke early, made coffee and thought about her conversation with Don Pennington. Last night she had been exhausted; too tired to take on board the significance of what he had told her. Now, in the grey light of what looked to be a rainy day, she thought about it.

She was not, she concluded, all that surprised. Pennington's investigations into the set-up behind Lassiter's Canadian company fitted perfectly with the startling realization that had come to her so suddenly on the flight home.

What was surprising – what had shocked and dismayed her last night, and depressed and troubled her now – was that Richard Jamieson was involved. There could be no doubt, she thought. He *had* to be. As a director of Drumanon he *might*, just might, have been unaware of what was happening, but as a director of Lassiter Enterprises Inc he *must* know . . . he had to be involved in it up to his neck.

And she was going sailing with him this weekend.

She stared out of the kitchen window. Perhaps the trip might be rained off; maybe storms were forecast in the

Channel? She moved into the lounge and turned on one of the breakfast shows. The forecast for the south coast was for heavy showers, clearing in late afternoon to make way for a perfect weekend.

God, in the shape of the weather, was not going to let her off the hook that easily. Damn. She would have to make up her own mind: take the responsibility for the decision herself.

She thought of Francine and smiled. Francine would undoubtedly advise her to go. She could hear her now: Chérie, a good-looking man . . . a weekend of screwing on a fabulous luxury yacht . . . it doesn't happen to a girl every day of her life. So go, enjoy yourself. So what if he's been a naughty boy? That's someone else's problem.

But that was Francine's way. She wasn't sure that she could do that; divorce her social life so completely from her work. And anyway, she thought, weren't there some professional ethics here? She suspected Jamieson of some sort of corporate misfeasance. Could she then go sailing with him? She smiled. She doubted whether her professional institute would have any precise ruling on the matter. But she knew who would. Her father. And she knew what he would say. And John Shephard.

What the hell was it to do with Shephard? Just thinking about him got her annoyed. She ought to go sailing with Richard just to spite him. 'Bloody hell.' She swore loudly at the walls of the empty flat. It was just typical of her luck with men that, having found one she fancied, she was now finding that he was mixed up in . . . well, she didn't want to think about that.

But she didn't *know* he was mixed up in anything. And Francine would have said that, as long as she didn't know *for sure*, then why not go ahead and have a good time? Turn a blind eye.

She grinned, thinking of Francine. Then it occurred to her. Of course. That was it; that's what she would do. Francine had told her what to do at lunch yesterday. Eleanor allowed herself a weak smile. She could go sailing with Richard with a clear conscience. Well . . . almost clear.

She left for the office a few minutes later, piling onto the back seat of the car the Drumanon files she had been working on at home.

The rain was coming down steadily, the wipers swishing monotonously across the screen as she headed out of Bournemouth. So early in the morning the roads were fairly clear and she made the office in fifteen minutes. Putting up her umbrella, she made a dash from the car park to the office door, taking with her what files she could carry.

The offices were empty. She powered up the PC on her desk and watched the screen come to life. For a few seconds she thought about the words, then, as the sentences inside her head marshalled themselves into order, she began. It took less than two A4 pages to summarize what she knew. She printed out the pages, read them twice, sealed them in an envelope marked for Philip's attention and walked down the corridor to his office. She placed the envelope in the centre of his desk.

Now, she thought as she left his office, it was up to Philip to decide on the next move, to take some of the responsibility. He would probably need the weekend to think about it; sort it out in his own mind before deciding what to do next. Which meant that she could go sailing with Richard. The shit wouldn't be hitting the fan until the weekend was over. After that, well, who knows. It wouldn't be her responsibility. At least, not entirely.

She could hear movement in the main office downstairs. She went to take a look. It was Alice, taking off her raincoat before starting on the first and most important task of the day: replenishing the Cona. Eleanor helped by filling the glass jug with water. They talked as they waited for the coffee to percolate. Alice, born and bred on the Dorset coast, was an expert on local weather lore. She confirmed the Met Office forecast. It would rain heavily all day but by early evening Brownsea Island would be emerging out of the rain to become clearly visible across the wide harbour. That, she declared with absolute conviction, would herald the end of the rain and a gloriously warm weekend.

Eleanor was pleased. Having made up her mind to spend the weekend on Jamieson's yacht – probably the only weekend she was ever likely to have on it – she wanted it to be as extravagantly enjoyable as possible.

She and Alice chatted over coffee as the practice came to life. They heard Stephen clonking up the stairs, followed a few minutes later by Lindsey's lighter step. Some of the admin staff and a couple of articled clerks arrived, shaking off their raincoats and complaining about the weather. Eleanor drained her mug, told Alice she would see her later and returned to her office. Two days away from it and her desk was piled with work; as Philip was in the habit of reminding her, there were more clients than Drumanon to take care of.

She got the call just after ten. Philip's voice was strained. 'Eleanor, for God's sake come and see me.'

She was shocked to see how awful he looked. His face was ashen and his hands were visibly shaking. He reminded her of the way he had looked at David's funeral; ill.

'For Christ's sake, Eleanor, what is all this?' His voice was thick and throaty, as if his larynx was seizing up.

She seated herself in the chair opposite his desk; the one she had sat in at her interview. She made an apologetic face.

'I'm sorry, Philip. I know it must come as a shock but, as I've said in there,' she nodded at the report lying on the desk in front of him, 'right now, there is no way I could give Drumanon an unqualified audit report.'

'Why not?' He seemed angry, perplexed, bewildered. It was a stupid question; she had told him why not in the report. Still, she realized that the whole messy business must have come as an enormous jolt to him. He was obviously upset.

'Basically because I don't believe that there's any underlying substance to Drumanon's transactions with Campanalla or Van Dameer. Or for that matter with Lubbenau, although they are outside the scope of my audit.'

'What are you saying? That forty million pounds' worth of business doesn't exist?'

'Right.'

'But what proof have you of this?'

'Come on, Philip, I don't need proof. I have doubts, based on what I've said in that report. That's sufficient. Those doubts lead me to question many of the transactions which have been presented to me in Drumanon's accounts.'

'But Drumanon has been a client of this practice for years,' he pleaded. 'Dan Lassiter is a personal friend.'

'I understand that, Philip, and I sympathize, but unless Drumanon can produce every despatch note from Campanalla, every goods-received note from Van Dameer, every item of shipping documentation – the way-bills, the sailing dates, the names of the vessels, the shipping agents – as well as every receipted transaction from the salesmen, then I'll have to qualify their audit.'

'All these damn doubts of yours seem to revolve around this visit you made to Campanalla's showroom.' Philip's voice was sharp, spiteful, almost as if it was all her fault.

'No, that's not entirely true. And, anyway, *is* it Campanalla's showroom? Or is it Lubbenau's? Or is it still being run by Van Dameer? Who knows? But what I *do* know, what I saw quite plainly when I was there, is that there is no way that forty million pounds' worth of business is being generated out of that place.'

'How can you be so sure?'

She shrugged. 'It's in my report, Philip. It's all there.'

He frowned and stared at the document on his desk. He appeared to have difficulty in focusing on it. He seemed in shock. He looked up. 'And after going to London you decided to go on to Amsterdam and Geneva?'

'Some ex-colleagues from my previous firm agreed to help me. They inspected the local business directories and registers. They found no trace of any companies called Van Dameer or Lubbenau. When I arrived, we went to the premises.' She shook her head. 'They don't exist, Philip.'

'But they *must* exist. There are transactions, invoices, payment schedules, files. Drumanon does business with these people. Money is being made.'

'They're shadow corporations. Puppets. Dan Lassiter has been pulling Van Dameer's strings for years. I suspect he's doing the same with Lubbenau. In fact, for all intents and purposes, Lubbenau *is* Van Dameer.'

'I don't believe it. I simply don't believe Dan would do something like that. You must have more than just these notes to back up what you say.'

'I have. I know that Dan forged a letter from Van Dameer cancelling the distribution contract. He told me Van Dameer had turned greedy, that the company wanted to up its ante, increase its margin. Dan said he'd been trying to negotiate a new agreement with them for a year, that the file was full of correspondence.' She paused. 'It's all balls, Philip. I've seen the file. There's nothing in it except blank Van Dameer letterheads and instructions from Dan, telling Van Dameer the exact words to use in its faxes confirming receipt of goods from Spain. Schmidt, the man who ran Van Dameer and now Lubbenau,' she paused again, 'the man who *is* Van Dameer and Lubbenau, doesn't have very good English.'

'You've met him?'

'In Geneva.' Eleanor thought for a moment, then decided not to mention that she'd met Schmidt in the company of Richard Jamieson.

'But what Dan Lassiter keeps in his files doesn't warrant what you've said here.' Passmore tapped the papers on his desk. 'I mean, it doesn't make sense. If Van Dameer didn't exist, why would Dan switch the contract to Lubbenau? A company which, according to you, also doesn't exist. Why replace one non-existent company with another? It doesn't make sense.'

'You know, Philip, that question always bothered me. It also bothered me why Drumanon didn't undertake the distribution of the kitchens and conservatories itself. I mean, I could never understand why Lassiter was prepared to pass all that lucrative business over to somebody else. Why he was happy to see Van Dameer make a profit instead of his own company. I know Dan put me off with an explanation at dinner that evening, and like a fool I accepted it. But I wasn't happy. I'd calculated that Drumanon could have increased its profits by nearly five million if it hadn't been using Van Dameer.'

'But that's Dan's decision,' Passmore grunted. 'That's the way he wants to play it.'

'I know, Philip. But it didn't make sense. It just isn't commercial. And then to *change* the contract – that was even worse. To go from a company he knew to one he didn't. I used to think about that all the time, everywhere. In my sleep, even in my health club. But it always eluded me. Why did Dan change from Van Dameer to Lubbenau? Why did it seem to me to be such a wrong move? Why didn't it make sense? And then it came to me last night, on the plane, coming back from Switzerland.'

'What came to you?' Passmore's grey face was lined with anxiety. He was frowning.

'Value Added Tax.'

'What?'

'VAT.'

'VAT? What do you mean VAT? What are you talking about?' His voice was strained. Eleanor could detect a touch of hysteria.

'It's simple. Because Van Dameer doesn't exist, it doesn't have a Dutch VAT number. A few months ago the European Community passed a law stating that all supplies of goods to other EC countries must have VAT charged on them – *except where the company to whom the goods are sold can provide its own VAT number*. Van Dameer couldn't provide its own VAT number. And as Customs and Excise are linking their computer system to the corresponding computer banks in Europe, sooner or later either the British Customs and Excise or the Dutch tax authorities would have picked it up. They'd have found that Van Dameer wasn't a big international trading company; that in fact there wasn't a Van Dameer. As soon as that law came into force Lassiter *had* to move the so-called distribution operation outside the EC. And as the Swiss are outside the scope of these new VAT requirements, he gave the operation a new name and moved it to Geneva. That way, there would be no chance of Customs and Excise or any EC tax authorities checking up on what was actually going on.'

'So it was switching the distribution contract to Lubbenau that made you suspect something was wrong,' Passmore croaked.

'That's right. And the funny thing is, I only learnt about the switch by accident. I found out about it from some papers in a file I'd picked up. I'd never have known otherwise. But once I knew, it bothered me. I couldn't see any benefit in moving the distribution *outside* the EC. Doing that meant missing all the advantages of the Union. Now, knowing what I know, it makes perfect sense.'

Passmore appeared crushed. His fleshy face seemed to have collapsed. He was hunched in his chair. 'But there's more than forty million pounds' worth of business being done out there,' he pleaded. 'The distributors *must* exist. There are salesmen in every region of the country – all over Europe – selling Campanalla products.'

Eleanor shook her head. 'There's one self-employed sales-man in London who sells a few thousands pounds' worth of Campanalla kitchens and conservatories a year. I expect he has an agreement with a few mates up and down the country who work for him when it suits them. On a commission-only basis. They probably market the air-conditioning systems as well. Basically, Philip, the sale of Campanalla products in this country is a one-man-and-a-dog operation. I expect it's the same in the rest of Europe.'

She paused, gazing sympathetically at the shattered man across the desk. 'A couple of days ago,' she went on, 'I did some quick calculations from the schedule of payments into Drumanon's bank account – that part of the sales revenues paid in by this non-existent regional sales force. I worked out that the average value of an order was £16,000. That means they have to be taking 2,500 orders a year to make forty million.' She shook her head slowly. 'It's not happening,

Philip. You have to face it. The whole set-up is an illusion.'

'So where's the money coming from? We know how much is going into Drumanon's account. How is it getting there? Why?'

It was bloody obvious. But she could see he didn't want to accept it.

She appraised him. She had not spelled it out in her report – she was too cautious for that – but she knew that anybody with half a mind, anybody with any commercial training, could figure out what it was all about. Philip had read her report, had listened to what she had told him. He *must* be able to see it, she thought. He just couldn't bring himself to accept it.

Her voice was low, insistent. 'Drumanon is laundering money, Philip. The whole distribution network has been set up to launder hot money. On an enormous scale. Dan Lassiter is a money launderer.'

He stared at her across the desk like a sick dog. After a few moments he croaked, 'For Christ's sake, Eleanor, do you realize what you're saying? Dan Lassiter is my friend. You're accusing him of being a criminal. You're accusing Drumanon of being involved in a very serious offence.'

'Yes I know, Philip,' she said gently, 'and I'm sorry. I know you're close to Dan and it must come as a shock.'

'But the point is you have no proof. No real proof. I mean, most of what you've told me, most of what's in this report, is conjecture.'

'I wouldn't say that, Philip. Dan Lassiter has lied about the ultimate ownership of the company. That in itself is an offence. Drumanon is owned by a Panamanian shell company with a corporation in the Dutch Antilles. That's a fact, it's not conjecture. And you know as well as I do that that kind of set up is very suspicious.'

He glowered at her and grunted but said nothing.

'But, as I said before, I don't need proof. I'm not a policeman, nor a judge. I'm just an auditor – a watchdog. What I've got are doubts; doubts about Drumanon's commercial transactions which are sufficient to prevent me giving the company an unqualified audit report. The fact that I suspect something else, that I think the company is involved in money laundering, well, that's what I'm reporting to you. But it's not up to me to prove it. I'm merely telling you what I suspect, based on the evidence and my own intuition. It's up to someone else to prove it.'

'Yes, well, there could be some other explanation,' he replied gruffly. He was blowing in the wind. He knew it, Eleanor knew it. Dan Lassiter was Philip Passmore's friend; together they were part of the old boy network. Philip was loath to accept that Lassiter might be a crook.

'I trust you haven't been discussing this with anybody else, Eleanor,' he went on. 'I mean, if you're wrong, and I think you are, Drumanon could sue us. They could put Hagerty Clark out of business.'

She shook her head. 'No. I've not talked about it with anybody. You're the first person I've raised it with. I haven't mentioned anything to Dan Lassiter or Richard Jamieson.'

He nodded. He appeared to be getting a grip on himself. 'I'm going to need some time to think about all this. It's a hell of a shock and I've no idea which is the best course of action to take. I probably ought to talk to a lawyer.' He ran his fingers through his hair. 'I just don't know what to do.'

Eleanor gave him another sympathetic look. 'I understand how you must feel, Philip, and I am really sorry. I hate to be the one to bring you the bad news. But Hagerty Clark has to protect itself and there are enough doubts about Drumanon to warrant us asking them for a lot more explanation.'

'Yes, well, I think the best thing is for me to talk to our solicitor. Maybe he can put me in touch with a lawyer who knows about these things. Then I'll think about it over the weekend. We can talk again on Monday morning.'

She gave him a smile and stood up. 'Yes, I think that's best. Try not to worry too much about it, Philip. I'm here and I'll give you all the help and support I can.'

He nodded vacantly as she made for the door. She left him slumped in his chair.

Back in her office there was a stack of phone messages. One was from a Mr Malin asking her to call back. It went into the non-urgent pile.

The rest of the morning was busy. She had no time for lunch, though during a brief lull in the prolonged and heavy showers she got one of the admin clerks to go out for sandwiches.

Shortly after lunchtime she left her office to retrieve a file from Steven. Philip was standing at the top of the stairs. He was wearing his raincoat. His face was as haggard as it had been earlier. He saw her and gave a little start. His mind was obviously somewhere else. 'I'm going out. To talk about that business we discussed this morning.' His voice, even though there was no one else around, was low and subdued. 'It will probably take the rest of the afternoon.'

She nodded. 'Okay. I hope it goes reasonably well. I'll see you Monday morning. Try not to worry.' She smiled encouragingly.

He grunted, giving her a distracted, wide-eyed look, and hurried down the stairs. She watched him go, thinking how badly he seemed to be taking it. Poor Philip, he was obviously much more sensitive than his restrained, English middle-class demeanour made apparent. David's death, Lassiter's transgressions, he took them all to heart.

Back in her office the girl on the switchboard told her that Mr Malin had called again. She grimaced. The guy never gave up. She supposed she would have to talk to him sometime but, with luck, it would be after her weekend on the yacht. She glanced out of the window. The rain was streaming down. There was no sign of any break in the weather and of the promised glorious weekend. She hoped the Met Office and Alice weren't giving her the business. After the week she'd had, she could do with a luxury cruise to the Channel Islands. A couple of days of sun and sea and . . .

'Do you have the Drumanon fixed asset file?' Lindsey was standing in the doorway of the office.

'What?' Eleanor jerked herself out of her reverie.

'Drumanon's fixed asset file?'

She searched among the files in the office for a while before she remembered. 'It's in my car. On the back seat.'

They glanced out of the window simultaneously. The rain was sheeting down. The phone on the desk bleeped. It was a client. Eleanor told the girl on the switchboard to put him on hold.

'Look, here are my keys.' She picked them off the desk. 'You go and get the file. Just press the button on the remote control.'

Lindsey made a face. 'I'll get wet,' she whined.

'Come on, Lindsey,' Eleanor said encouragingly. 'You'll only be out there a minute. Take my raincoat. And the umbrella.'

She turned her attention to the phone and told the girl on the switchboard to put the client through. 'Hello, Jack, good afternoon,' she said heartily. 'Yes, it is a wet one . . .'

She listened to the client as she watched Lindsey pulling on the raincoat. It was a Burberry and heavy; it would keep her dry enough for the few seconds she was out there. It was light cream – not really Lindsey's colour, she thought, though at least it was the right size. Lindsey grabbed the umbrella and disappeared.

The client was on the line for ten minutes. As soon as she put the phone down it warbled again. It was another client. For God's sake, she thought, it's Friday afternoon. What's the matter with these people? It was a time when the phone was usually quiet; when clients didn't bother her, when she could get some work done. Then she realized. The rain. None of them were out playing golf or sailing. They had all been forced to stay in their offices and work. So . . . they were bothering her.

This call took even longer and she needed to concentrate and make copious notes. At last the call came to an end and she put the phone down. She sighed, and searched her desk for the schedules she'd been working on before the phones had gone mad.

Gradually she became aware of the strange sounds coming from downstairs. Lindsey had left the office door ajar. She cocked her head to one side and listened. They didn't sound like the normal noises of the office – the footsteps, the sharp bursts of laughter, the phones. She could hear a couple of deep voices; slow and ponderous. She didn't recognize them. There were other voices too. They were high and edgy. She wondered . . . was that someone crying?

She stood up slowly, edged round her desk and moved to the office door. Yes, it *was* somebody crying. She walked along the short corridor to the top of the stairs.

Below, standing in the small reception area, were two policemen. They were wearing bright yellow waterproof vests over their uniforms. Eleanor noticed the rainwater glistening on the shiny plastic. The girls from the admin office were crowding around them. A couple of them were crying.

Eleanor hurried down the stairs. Steven was standing close to the front door. He was in his shirtsleeves and soaking wet, his hair plastered over his face, his shirt and trousers sodden. He was shaking violently. Alice was holding him, her short, strong, sunburned arms gripping him tightly.

'For God's sake,' Eleanor cried, 'what's wrong?'

Steven looked up. His eyes had sunk into two dark holes in a face which was pinched and the colour of ashes. 'It's Lindsey.' His teeth were chattering, he could barely speak. 'She's been hit by a car.'

Eleanor felt as if her heart had stopped. She thought she was going to faint. All the sounds in the small lobby seemed to disappear, rolling away from her down a long, long tunnel. She was on her own. The world had forsaken her.

Alice held Steven with one arm and put a hand on Eleanor's wrist. She gripped it tightly. 'Are you all right, dear?'

Reality came back with the warmth of Alice's touch and the compassion in her voice. Thank God for Alice. Round, motherly Alice; so capable, so strong. Eleanor squeezed the hand squeezing her. 'I'm fine, fine.' She looked at Steven. 'What happened? When?'

'A few minutes ago,' Steven croaked, 'outside.' Alice let go of Eleanor's wrist and went back to holding Steven. 'She must have gone to get a file from her car. She was crossing the road.' He paused. 'They didn't even stop,' he croaked.

'Oh God,' Eleanor cried. 'It's my fault. She was getting the file from *my* car. I asked her to go. I must help her.'

Steven shook his head. 'No, no. There's nothing you can do. The ambulance is with her now. They sent me back inside.'

'But I must. This is all my fault.' She made to push past him. From behind her came a deep, commanding voice.

'Excuse me, miss. You work here?'

She turned. It was one of the policemen. 'Yes.'

'There's nothing you can do out there, miss. You'll only be in the way.' She glared at him. He was right, of course. But she wanted to *do* something. 'Did I hear you say that the young lady who's been knocked down was running an errand for you?'

'Yes. It's all my fault.'

The policeman gave her a sympathetic look. 'It's not your fault, miss. You mustn't think like that. You didn't knock her down. A couple of tearaways did that. But we'll find them all right. Somebody got the car number.'

'Is she badly hurt?'

'It's hard to tell, miss. The car was going very fast.'

'But is she alive?'

'Yes, she's alive. They'll be taking her to the hospital soon.'

As he said it they heard the wail of the ambulance siren start up. Someone opened the front door. The rain had slackened. The small crowded lobby fell silent and they watched. For an instant, they glimpsed a flashing blue light as the white, yellow-striped vehicle hurtled past, throwing up a spray of water.

'Jesus, Lindsey,' Steven wailed.

'Where're they taking her?' Eleanor asked the policeman quietly.

'To Poole hospital I expect. I'm afraid I'll have to take a statement from you, miss. Just a short one. And from this young man.'

Eleanor waited while Steven gave his statement. It didn't take long. A woman had come rushing in, yelling at the girl on the switchboard to call an ambulance. She'd seen the car hit Lindsey and drive off. She'd taken the number. Steven had been in the downstairs office at the time and had gone rushing out to help. He'd stayed with Lindsey, holding her hand and doing what he could for her until the ambulance had arrived. He hadn't noticed the rain. Eleanor could see the front of his sodden shirt was spotted in blood.

As Eleanor was about to give her statement, one of the admin clerks whispered that Philip was on the phone. Eleanor asked Alice to take the call and to tell him what had happened.

She told the policeman how Lindsey had come to be in the street at the time. The other policeman handed her the file Lindsey had gone to retrieve from her car. It had been lying in the road. The brown manilla folder was saturated and crumbling, the sheets inside it soaked beyond saving. Eleanor stared at it. It didn't seem important. Not any more. She wondered if it was for this that Lindsey was likely to die.

The policeman finished taking her statement. After he and his colleague had left, Eleanor told Alice to close up the office and send everyone home. It was close to four thirty. 'We'll get no more done today,' she said. 'Everybody's too upset. It's not worth hanging on.'

'What are you going to do?'

'I'm going to the hospital. Has anybody phoned Lindsey's parents?'

'I'll do that,' Alice said. 'I know them.'

'Thank you.' She said it with relief. Thank God for Alice.

Back in her office, Eleanor made an attempt to clear her desk. The nightline was ringing but she ignored it. She wasn't capable of talking to clients now. She looked out of the window. Alice's predictions were coming true. The rain had stopped and shafts of sunlight were spreading over the harbour. Over to her right, a vivid rainbow was vaulting the Purbeck Hills. It seemed totally inappropriate.

She gave up on clearing her desk. She closed her attaché case, went downstairs and wandered into the administration office. It looked much bigger empty. Lying across one of the desks was a coat. A cream-coloured raincoat. It took her a moment to realize it was hers. It was soaked through and streaked with dirt from the road. She picked it up and felt inside the pockets. She found her keyring. The remote control appeared intact. She put the coat back on the desk then saw, smeared across its back and shoulders like a shoulder scarf, a deep red stain. Eleanor looked at her hands. They were sticky and smeared with blood.

She slumped onto the nearest chair and burst into noisy tears. The sound of her howling echoed around the empty office.

When she had finished, when her chest was empty and wrung out, when her throat ached and she could cry no more, she stood up, washed her hands and went in search of one of the office's black binbags into which she stuffed her raincoat. She was glad to get out of the office.

She arrived at the hospital. Alice was there, waiting in a corridor with Lindsey's parents. 'How is she?' she asked.

Alice motioned her to one side. 'She's in intensive care,' she said in a low monotone. 'Her heart stopped once, but they revived her. It's touch and go.'

'Oh God.' Eleanor leaned against the wall. 'Poor Lindsey.'

The policeman who had taken her statement walked past. 'Have you caught them yet?' she asked.

He shook his head. 'The car was reported stolen earlier today in London. It could have been a couple of drunks. The woman who saw it said they definitely weren't kids. We'll find them, don't worry.' He nodded sympathetically at Lindsey's parents and walked on.

After a couple of hours Alice went home. Eleanor stayed. It had become her vigil. She felt so responsible. Finally, after another couple of hours with no news, Lindsey's mother approached her. 'Look, it's very kind of you, but there's no need to stay. There's nothing you can do, nothing any of us can do. And you look very tired.'

'But I feel so guilty.'

Lindsey's mother shook her head. 'You shouldn't. It wasn't your fault. We know that. Lindsey was in the wrong place at the wrong time. If you'd gone to get that file it would have been you. It might have been any of us. Please don't feel responsible. Why don't you go home and get some rest? You look worn out.'

'What about you?'

She shrugged. 'We'll stay some more. We have to.'

She drove home slowly. She noticed that the sun, absent for most of the day, had decided to dazzle before it died. It was low in her rearview mirror and intensely bright. The forecasts had proved reliable. The storm clouds had gone and the roads into Bournemouth were drying out. She pressed the button to open her window. She needed air. The breeze was warm.

She drove onto the gravel drive and parked in her usual spot, close to the side wall of the old house. She got out, gathered up her things and locked the car.

From nowhere a large hand grabbed her shoulder and spun her around.

The hand belonged to a big, swarthy man with dark hair. He looked Greek or Italian.

'Bitch,' he snarled. 'Fucking bitch. You won't get out of it this time.' For some curious reason she noticed he had a strong London accent. Then he slapped her across the face. Hard.

She staggered back against the car. He made to hit her again. She came off the car and brought the binbag up to fend him off. As a weapon, the raincoat inside the plastic bag was useless but it diverted the force of the man's blow. He swore loudly and grabbed the bag from her hand. She swung her attaché case at his head. It caught him a glancing blow on his ear. 'Shit,' he yelped. He moved to one side, out of range of the swinging case. A man was standing behind him.

There were two of them.

The second man was small and skinny, like a weasel. He wore a dingy grey anorak and crumpled dirty trousers. Eleanor noticed his eyes. An animal's eyes. Yellowish. A mad animal's eyes.

She swung her case at the big man again. He ducked inside the arc and punched her. His fist, like a hammer, caught her on the shoulder. The case flew from her hand. The little man stepping forward, kicked it over the gravel, out of the way. His boots were big and black; like weapons.

She lashed out with her foot, aiming for the big man's crotch. Her breath was rasping in her throat. The man stooped and parried her kick with his forearm. Now he was inside her defences.

His hand shot out and he grabbed her by the throat, slamming her back against the car. 'You bitch. Hit me would you? That's the last bit of fucking trouble you're gonna give anybody.'

His fist hit her high on the side of her head. The pain was instantaneous. Lights exploded inside her brain and the world turned misty. From somewhere, miles away, she heard the big man's urgent voice. 'Stick her, Donnie. Do it now.'

In a blurry, detached fashion she watched the little man move towards her. He was grinning. She saw broken, black teeth.

He was pulling at something up his left sleeve. It came away in his hand. It was long and had a dull sheen which glittered in the rays of the dying sun. In her befuddled state it took her a moment to realize what it was. Then she knew.

At that instant she knew she was going to die.

Chapter Twenty-Four

Fear cleared the mist in her head.

The little man brought the bayonet up to her face, its honed point a hair's breadth from her left eyeball. She closed her eyes and stayed absolutely still.

She heard him snigger. 'Ye dinna think shutting your eyes will save youse, d'ye? I can dig out your eye just as easy with it shut.'

She couldn't understand him. His accent was too broad. But she knew exactly what he was threatening. He rested the blade on her cheekbone, its point pricking at the corner of her closed eyelid. Despite the grip around her throat, she whimpered.

'Get on with it, for Christ's sake,' the other man snarled. 'We've got her this time. Now stick her.'

'Nah, you heard what K said. If we can, make her talk. Seeing as she's still in one piece, she can talk. You're gonna talk aren't you, whore?' He was addressing her. Eleanor knew his face was close to hers. She could smell him. 'Tell us what you've been saying. Who your foreign friends are.' He pressed the point of the bayonet a little harder against her eyelid.

She was rigid with terror, her arms at her sides as stiff as concrete posts. Her nails were boring into the flesh of her palms.

'Not here, you maniac,' the other man growled. 'If you're gonna get her to talk, if you're gonna slice her, do it inside.'

There was a pause. It seemed to last a millennium. Then the cold, pricking point moved from her eye. She was too frightened to open her eyes wide. Fearfully, she squinted at the men.

The swarthy man gripping her throat was watching her carefully. The other one had moved off a few steps. She opened her eyes wider and watched him sheathe the bayonet inside his left sleeve. He picked up her shoulderbag and upturned it, dumping its contents onto the gravel. The keys weren't there. She knew that. She had dropped them when the big man had spun her around.

Despite the pressure on her windpipe she breathed as deeply as she could. She had to fight her fear. If the man gripping her neck shifted his attention, even for a moment . . . could she?

'The keys are no fucking here.' The little ferret-like man was moving her things around on the gravel with the toe of his boot. Something glinted at its cap, just above the welt.

'They'll be by the car, for Christ's sake.' The big man didn't take his eyes off her. With just one hand he was strangling her, his grip slowing the flow of blood to her brain. Soon she would go under. After that there would be no more chances. If only . . .

Vroooooooom.

It was the most welcome noise in the world. The sound of a flat six.

The Porsche was in a hurry. It turned in between the stone gateposts and fishtailed slightly on the gravel. The little man looked up, the big man looked away.

Now.

She brought her left hand up and over his outstretched

arm, curling the hand as far around his wrist as she could. With both hands she twisted his wrist outwards. The man yelped. His grip on her neck broke, his fingers ripping cruelly at her windpipe as they were torn away. With her two hands twisting his wrist, she pivoted on the ball of her left foot and lashed out with her right. She didn't know where on his body her crashing foot connected but it was soft and the man screamed. She twisted the wrist even further outwards then shot both her arms out straight. The man went over on his back.

Now she was running.

The little man was moving across to intercept her, his hand scrabbling at his left sleeve.

Jamieson in the Porsche had realized what was happening. He drove the car directly at the man. The man saw it at the last moment and tried to leap out of the way. The low wing of the car caught him a glancing blow, sending him spinning over onto the gravel. The car's wheels locked and the Porsche ploughed to a halt in a cloud of dust. Jamieson was out in a flash. 'What the hell's happening here?' he yelled.

Eleanor looked behind her. The big man was climbing slowly to his feet. He looked in pain. The little one was scrambling up off the gravel. He seemed unhurt. Jamieson went for him, aiming a blow which caught him on the side of the head. The man staggered slightly then ducked and weaved inside Jamieson's guard.

She tried to scream, but the recent squeezing of her throat allowed only an ugly croak. 'Look out. He's got a knife.'

Jamieson jumped backwards. The crouching man aimed a low kick at him, his boot catching Jamieson on the outside of his calf. Jamieson went down with a bellow of pain.

Eleanor glanced behind. The big man was coming up fast. In front, Jamieson was rolling on the gravel clutching his leg as the little man circled, readying to kick him again.

What now? If she ran she abandoned Jamieson. If she stayed then—

Vroooom, vrooooooom, vroooooooooom.

They chicaned past the gates and around the big lime tree as if they were at Monza.

One – two – three. Engines roaring, tyres churning, quadraphonic in-car entertainment systems blasting at full power. An ear-splitting cacophony of sound. Suddenly *that* was the most welcome noise in the world. The cars slewed to a stop and what seemed like scores of young people tumbled out of them. The couple downstairs were throwing another party.

The little man shot a swift look at the noisy convoy and started running towards her. Eleanor dodged out of his way as he pelted past. The big man had already turned and was running, both of them heading towards the open ground and the line of trees at the back of the house.

The young men and women from the cars stared silently at the scene: the scattered belongings from her shoulderbag, her attaché case scuffed and battered on the gravel, Jamieson slowly getting to his feet. She crossed to him. He was having difficulty. Blood was dripping onto his shoe. She helped him up.

'What happened?' demanded one of the young men.

'Muggers,' Eleanor croaked briefly.

'Do you want the police?' asked a girl.

'I'll call them. I live upstairs. It's okay. Really. Thanks.'

The group shuffled away, glancing backwards as Eleanor helped Jamieson across the drive to her car and leaned him against it. She picked up her case and the things from her bag and retrieved her keys. The group filed into the downstairs flat as she supported the hobbling Jamieson to her front door. She helped him inside and double-locked the door behind her. She was surprised at herself. Her heart wasn't calm, but her head was still in control.

'Muggers?' his voice was querulous as she helped him up the stairs. 'What the hell were they after?'

'Never mind that now.' Her throat ached: it hurt to talk. She sat him down in the lounge. The light was fading from the room and she turned on a couple of lights. Blood from Jamieson's leg plopped monotonously onto the polished wood floor. She rolled up his trouser leg. 'That's bad. You'll need stitches.' She looked up at him. 'How could he do this to you?' she asked hoarsely.

He bent forward examining the wound. 'Some sort of blade in his boot. It's not what you'd expect from a mugger.'

'It must hurt.'

'It does.'

She went into the bathroom and found a bottle of antiseptic and a roll of bandages. She grabbed a clean face flannel from the towel cupboard. Back in the lounge she squatted at his feet and bathed the wound. Jamieson screwed up his face but said nothing. She used the flannel as a dressing and bound it tightly over the deep wound with the bandage. 'That's the best I can do.'

'That's good. Thanks.'

'You'll need to go to the hospital and get it stitched.'

'Shit. What a hell of a start to a sailing weekend. Assaulted by a couple of muggers.' He looked at her quizzically. That was not what he thought they were. She could tell.

Sailing. She had forgotten about that. What with Lindsey and the attack . . . 'I must get something for my throat,' she said to him.

She went to the drinks cabinet and poured a couple of large measures of malt. She noticed her hands were shaking, yet, miraculously, she still felt capable; in control. It was almost as if the assault had happened to somebody else. She handed Jamieson his glass and picked up her own. The chunky, cut-glass tumbler was heavy and comforting in her hand. She took a large gulp of whisky and held it at the back of her throat, swirling the liquid around, letting it deaden the ache.

The benefit was psychological. The harm was on the outside, the muscles of her throat ached with a dull throbbing pain that travelled up into her ears and head. Still, she thought, the whisky helped. Helped her think.

'They weren't muggers, Richard,' she croaked quietly. 'They weren't interested in my money. They wanted me. They meant to kill me. After I'd told them what I know.'

'What do you mean, "told them what you know"?'

She wasn't listening. She had suddenly realized their situation. 'Oh, my God. They may come back. We have to call the police.' She banged her glass onto a coffee table and made towards the phone.

For a wounded man Jamieson was quick. He lurched to his feet and hobbled hurriedly across the room. He reached the phone first and slapped his hand down decisively on the handset. 'What do you mean? *What* do you know?'

'Richard, what the hell are you doing? We have to call the police. Jesus Christ, those men are killers – maniacs. They could come back.'

'Forget the police.' His voice was loud, sharp, edged with fear. 'I want to know what those men wanted. What are you supposed to know?'

'Richard, for Christ's sake get off the phone.' She tried to prise his hand away. He kept it jammed firmly on the receiver as he fended her off with his arm. He was staggering slightly, his face grey with the pain of his wound. And with something else. Panic.

She gave up. She could have got him away from the phone easily, especially in his present condition, but there seemed something pathetic about them scrabbling over it. Jamieson was like a child clutching onto a toy, refusing to give it up. Scared to let go.

She stepped away from the phone and stared at him. 'You're involved, aren't you,' she croaked softly. It wasn't a question. 'I figured you might be. I mean, as a director of Lassiter's company, reporting to God knows who in the Dutch Antilles, you just *had* to be involved.'

'How do you know about that?'

'The same way I know about Lubbenau and Van Dameer. I checked.'

'So you weren't over there seeing your little friend.' His voice was bitter, accusing. 'I thought it was too much of a coincidence.' His voice rose. 'What have you done, you bloody bitch?'

It was as if he had slapped her. Her head went back and she stared at him. His face, like his words, had turned ugly: his eyes staring malevolently, his mouth a thin, venomous slit, the skin around it stretched in tension and pain.

'I think you had better go,' she said quietly. 'That cut needs attention.' She moved to the coffee table and retrieved her whisky.

'What, and let you call the police?'

'The police already know about you, Richard. And about Dan. They've been watching Drumanon for weeks. Even if it was for the wrong reason.' She let out a short laugh, like a bark. She stopped. It hurt her throat. 'They even asked me to help them. Keep an eye on the company. They think Drumanon is smuggling drugs. Not money. They haven't caught on yet that you're just a pathetic, bent accountant; a miserable money launderer. They think you're narcotics traffickers, that you're mixed up in murder, that—'

She stopped. Up to that instant she had never actually believed it; never really taken John Shephard seriously.

Jamieson and Lassiter – whatever they were, they weren't murderers; they weren't capable of killing people. But only minutes previously she had met two men who very definitely were. They had been about to kill her. And they were mixed up with what was going on at Drumanon.

What had the man said? She had scarcely been able to decipher his thick accent. Something about telling them what she knew. Telling them who her foreign friends were. *Foreign* friends.

'Christ, it was you who set those men on me. You told them I'd been to Europe – that I had a friend who was helping me check up on Lubbenau. You bastard,' she screeched.

He shook his head emphatically. 'No. No, I didn't. I didn't know what you were doing. I've never seen those men before. If I'd set them on you, why should I try fighting them off?'

'Don't lie to me, Richard. If you didn't set them on me it must have been Dan Lassiter. You told him about me.'

'For Christ's sake, I've only just got back from Switzerland. I was going to tell Dan I'd seen you in Geneva but I couldn't contact him.'

She'd heard enough. Jamieson was a lying shit. 'Richard, get away from the phone.' Her voice was low, commanding.

'And let you call the police? To hell with that – *aaahh.*'

She brought the heavy whisky tumbler crashing down onto the hand covering the phone. Jamieson yelled in pain as his hand leapt off the handset. She kicked him on the knee of his injured leg. He went over with a crash.

For a moment she had a twinge of guilt. Kicking him on his wounded leg. It was a pretty shitty thing to do.

He sat up. He was clearly in pain. 'Eleanor, for Christ's sake,' he pleaded, 'don't call the police.'

'To hell with you, Richard. You set those men onto me.'

'I'm telling you I didn't.' He made to get up.

'Stay where you are,' she ordered. 'If you get up I'll kick you again. Where it hurts.' He eased himself back to the floor and stared at her. The flat was silent. Below they could hear party noises: the heavy thump of the bass, the raised happy voices. Outside, darkness was falling fast.

Jamieson groaned despondently. Eleanor watched him. Sitting on the floor clutching his bruised hand and in pain from his leg, he seemed to be collapsing slowly. As if something inside him was crumpling.

'Eleanor, at least give me a chance to get out.' His voice was flat, pleading. 'It's not only the police who'll be after me. Those two guys, they'll be coming after me too.'

'What? Don't be silly. They're your friends, Richard.' Her voice brimmed with acid.

'They're not friends of mine. They work for whoever's behind all this. The Profit. I've just attacked one of them. Helped you against them. They'll think I've changed sides. The Profit's going to tell them to come after *me*.'

She considered him through narrowed eyes. 'Tough shit,' she said and picked up the phone.

'Eleanor,' he wailed, 'you don't know these people. They'll kill me. You don't know what you're involved with here. What they're like.'

'You're the one involved with them, Richard, not me. I was involved with you. Remember?'

'That was Dan's idea.'

The handset of the phone stopped in mid-movement, halfway to her ear. 'What?' she screeched. 'What do you mean, Dan's idea?'

'He said I should . . .' he searched for the word, ' . . . seduce you. You know, get involved. Go to bed with you. So I could keep an eye on what you were doing on the audit. Take your mind off it. Divert you.'

'You mean you were fucking me to order?'

'No, not really. I liked you.'

'Thanks very much.'

'Your coming in on the audit was a big mistake. We didn't want you. We wanted some junior who didn't know what they were doing. But you honed in on it, leapt in and took over after . . .' he looked away and his voice went quiet '. . . after David Rudge died. And once you were involved it would have seemed too suspicious not to let you carry on. It would have made Drumanon look conspicuous, like we'd got something to hide. We didn't know you'd go checking around for Christ's sake . . . checking on Van Dameer and Lubbenau. We didn't even think you'd get to know about Lubbenau. But as a precaution, Dan said I should take you to bed. Keep an eye on what you were doing. Get your mind off your work.'

'You bastard. So all that coy, reticent shit at the beginning was just an act. Like taking me onto your bloody yacht. And I suppose this weekend's sailing was also meant to take my mind off my work. Just another diversion, something to keep me amused, to—' she frowned. 'Or was it to get rid of me? Throw me over the side in the middle of the Channel?'

'For Christ's sake, Eleanor. I'm not like that.'

Her laugh was bitter and cynical. 'Sure you're like that. I told a policeman once that you and Lassiter were not the kind of people who would smuggle drugs. Not criminals. But you are.'

'No I'm not. I don't like violence. I hate it.'

'Of course you do. That's why you get other people to do your dirty work.'

He watched her put the phone to her ear. 'For God's sake, Eleanor, give me a break. At least give me a few hours' start.'

'And allow your two friends time to come back here and finish the job? Do you think I'm bloody stupid?' Her voice was climbing higher. 'Forget it, Richard. You're wasting your time.' She stopped. Her throat felt as if it was on fire. 'Anyway,' her tone was calmer, 'I've already reported everything I know.'

He frowned. 'Who to?'

'Philip Passmore of course. Who else? I wrote him a report. This morning. And later I sat in his office and filled him in on all the details. Everything I've found out about Drumanon. He's already talked to a solicitor.'

Jamieson stared at her wide-eyed. Slowly his body began to shake. She thought he had started to cry. With a shock she realized he was laughing.

'You told Philip?' He only just managed to get the words out. He was becoming hysterical.

She frowned at him, wondering what was so bloody funny. 'Yes, of course. Hagerty Clark are Drumanon's auditors. I needed to tell Philip.'

'Jesus Christ, Eleanor.' Slowly, painfully, he climbed to his feet and stood balancing with the foot of his injured leg angled awkwardly on the floor. 'For a bright woman you really are very dumb.'

'What the hell do you mean by that?'

'Christ, don't you realize? Haven't you figured out who's

in charge of the whole operation?'

'What do you mean?' She was confused.

'Passmore is the boss. Philip Passmore controls everything that happens at Drumanon. He runs the business. He's in charge of moving the money.'

Jamieson staggered to the door and looked back. 'You told Passmore everything you knew this morning. Those guys turned up this evening. Who do you think called them in? Don't be stupid, Eleanor. It was Philip. It was Passmore who arranged David Rudge's accident. And now it's Passmore who wants you dead.'

Chapter Twenty-Five

It was then she got the shakes.

She heard Jamieson clump down the stairs and fiddle at the locks of the front door. Trembling, she followed him down and double-locked it after him. Shuddering behind the door, she heard the Porsche start up and drive away.

She began to cry; an endless series of wracking, quaking sobs. Having cried so much over Lindsey, she wouldn't have believed it possible to cry so hard over herself.

A few words of her mother's came to her: something about the best way to forget your own troubles was to help somebody else with theirs. Taking care of Jamieson had postponed her anguish. Now he was gone the trauma was upon her. The terror and pain of the attack and the horror of what Jamieson had told her, howled around her head like avenging furies. She was pulverized by fear: panic twanged her nervous system like a bowstring. She felt as if she was shaking to pieces.

She crawled back up the staircase on her hands and knees, bawling like a child.

She tottered to the phone and managed to punch 999. Through chattering teeth she reported the attack. Afterwards, she searched for her address book and found the card Shephard had given her. It took three attempts to jab out the numbers. He wasn't there. 'It's Eleanor Lambert,' she stuttered to the man who answered, 'tell him I've been attacked. Tell him he was right.'

She curled up on the sofa in a foetal position and let the tears stream and the shakes take her.

How long she stayed there she didn't know. Suddenly the doorbell was ringing and there was a banging at the door. She got up slowly. She ached all over. She shuffled to the window. Night had fallen. A police car, its blue light silently sweeping across the dark trunk of the lime tree, stood at an angle in the drive. She managed to get down the stairs.

A policeman and policewoman were standing on the step. She had to stop herself falling into their arms. They helped her back upstairs and into the lounge. The doorbell rang again and the policeman went to answer. It was John Shephard. He strode into the lounge, his dark, serious face crumpled by concern. She stood up. This time she didn't try to stop herself. She fell into his arms.

He helped the policeman take her statement about the assault whilst the policewoman made a cup of tea. It was loaded with sugar but Shephard made her drink it. Afterwards he made some calls on her phone. By then she had stopped crying and the shakes were down to a manageable level. He told her he was getting her out of the flat. A couple of policemen would stay there for the night, in case the two men came back. The policewoman helped her pack her overnight case. Everything seemed like a dream. He helped her down to his car.

'Where are we going?' she asked as they drove off.

'My place. It's nowhere near as nice as yours, but it's safe.' He kept glancing in his mirror.

'What's wrong?' she asked fearfully.

'We've got a tail. I'm just checking.'

'A tail?' Her voice was panicky.

'It's okay. Four of my blokes are in the car behind. Just in case we're being followed.'

He lived somewhere near Ringwood, in a one-bedroom flat.

Eleanor, who had slowly grown calmer, was gratified to see he wasn't a slob; the place was clean and tidy and well furnished, though it seemed empty and unlived in.

He gave her an embarrassed smile. 'It's rented. I'm not here very much, I'm afraid.' He turned on a gas fire in the living room, sat her in an easy chair and made her a mug of tea. It, too, was sweet. Along with the sugar he'd laced it with a slug of Irish whiskey.

'Drink it,' he ordered softly as he sat down opposite. 'You've had a helluva shock. You need to boost up your blood sugar.'

She sipped the tea and after a while told him what had happened: Lindsey's accident, the attack at her flat, Jamieson's confession.

He listened quietly, saying nothing until she had finished. 'You say Lindsey was wearing your coat?'

'Yes.'

'And she got something out of your car.'

She nodded.

'I think it's obvious her accident was meant for you.'

'The thought had not escaped me,' she said bleakly. 'Philip Passmore phoned the office whilst we were talking to the police. He must have told those men that they'd got the wrong person.'

'Yeah. So they went to the flat and waited for you.'

'But supposing Lindsey dies?' Eleanor's voice quavered. 'It'll be my fault.'

'No it won't. It's not your fault. Anyway, she isn't dead yet, so try to take it easy.'

She made an effort to calm herself. She studied him over the rim of the mug. His eyes were tender and concerned. He was quiet for a while, then said, 'You said I was right.'

'What?'

'When you called and spoke to the duty man. You said I was right. What did you mean?'

'I meant you were wrong.'

He chuckled. 'I see.'

'No. I meant you were right *and* wrong. About Drumanon. You were wrong about the drugs. Drumanon isn't smuggling narcotics.'

'You know that for sure?'

'Yes.'

'Then what the blood—' he stopped. 'What the hell are they doing?'

'They're laundering money. About forty million pounds a year. And my senior partner, my boss, is the man behind it all. The bastard.'

The living room was filled with silence. 'Laundering money,' he repeated. He looked doubtful. 'You're absolutely sure about that?'

'Yes.'

'How? How can you be sure?'

She told him about Jamieson and what he had said in the flat. He listened intently, his face absorbed and serious.

'I should have seen it straight away,' she went on. 'I think working down here has softened my brain. When I think about it, it's bloody obvious. But you see, what I've done throughout the whole of this affair is ignore the *commercial* aspects, the business considerations. I accepted it when Dan Lassiter told me he was happy to let Van

Dameer make a profit that *he* could have been making. I accepted all the bullshit he gave me about moving the distribution from Van Dameer to Lubbenau, even though it was outside the Economic Community. It took me for ever to see it was the new VAT regulations inside Europe that had *forced* him to change.'

She shook her head in disgust at her blindness. 'It was only when I went to Campanalla's showroom that I even *began* to catch on.' She stopped again and gave him a wan smile. 'I bet you haven't seen any drug dealers anywhere near the place, have you?'

'No.'

'That's because it's a legitimate business. There's a nasty, self-employed salesman there, who really is selling kitchens and conservatories. I'm sure he doesn't know anything about narcotics or money laundering, although,' she paused, 'I've got an idea his boss does. The point is, it's small; it's a rinky-dink business. I had a chance to look inside the warehouse. They've got maybe £30,000 worth of stock in there. Yet Van Dameer, and now Lubbenau, is supposed to be turning over forty million. I worked it out. Forty million means fifty orders for kitchens or conservatories a *week*.' She shook her head. 'That place will be lucky if it's selling two a month.'

'So it's a phantom business?'

She shrugged. 'Not exactly phantom, more a front for the *real* business. Somebody from Van Dameer, Schmidt probably, came across and set the thing up with Richard Jamieson. I guess that they went to see the banks in London, Birmingham, Manchester and all the other big cities where there are narcotics franchises and told them about the distribution agreement they'd entered into for Campanalla's products. They opened accounts in Drumanon's name with the banks, ostensibly to enable Van Dameer's supposed agents to deposit monies directly into their account. The banks would have checked up on Drumanon, found it was a legitimate business which had been around for a long time, and would have been happy to get involved.'

She took a sip of tea. Her throat was aching. 'Shortly after that the banks would have started getting cash and cheques, supposedly from people who had bought kitchens and conservatories. You'd be surprised how many people buy expensive items like that with cash. The money was deposited in Drumanon's account from where most of it was transmitted to Campanalla's bank in Spain, supposedly in settlement of what it owed Campanalla. From there,' she shrugged, 'who knows? Hong Kong, the Cayman Islands?'

'And you're telling me that this Bournemouth company is laundering forty million of Britain's narcotics profits? That it was set up specifically to handle money from the dealers' franchise areas?' Shephard sounded incredulous.

'Why not? You thought it was smuggling narcotics. Drumanon is perfect. Ideal. Nobody's ever going to think of a company selling conservatories and kitchens and such as a money launderer. The authorities suspect fringe banks and insurance companies, not provincial trading companies. Drumanon only needed two things. One, some legitimate business to act as a cover – a few million turnover in Italian ceramics, Dutch furniture and so on, and . . .' Her voice tailed off.

'And what?'

'And an auditor who knew what was going on.' She stared at him. 'The point of setting up the Van Dameer contract was so that it wouldn't be possible to reconcile the money coming into Drumanon's accounts with what had supposedly been despatched by Campanalla. But it would still be too dangerous for

Drumanon to try to slip what they were doing past a *legitimate* auditor. The company wouldn't get away with it; anybody who knew their job would eventually become suspicious, have too many questions. The auditor *had* to know what was going on.' She let out a hollow laugh. It hurt her throat. 'It's so bloody obvious. But I didn't see it. Instead, what did I do? I reported the whole thing, all my suspicions, to Philip Passmore.'

Shephard noticed she had finished her tea. He stood up and moved to a small collection of bottles on a sideboard. 'But David Rudge was doing the audit. Are you saying he was bent?' He poured her a large whisky.

She took it gratefully. 'No. Passmore gave David the job because he thought David was too dumb to figure out what was going on. Anyway, David had to report to Passmore.' She took a sip of the whisky. 'I killed David,' she said quietly.

'What do you mean?'

'I'm responsible for David's death. I was always telling him about the auditor's duty of care. About checking everything. About taking nothing for granted. David took it to heart. He started looking into things at Drumanon – the ownership of the company, the contract with Van Dameer. Of course, he didn't know about Lubbenau. He wasn't supposed to. Nor was I. I remembered this evening how I found out about Lubbenau. It was from a file I took off Philip's desk. David even started checking out Van Dameer's marketing. It was way beyond his brief, but he thought I would approve.' She stopped. Her eyes filled with tears. 'His father told me that David looked up to me, that he wanted to be as good an accountant as me.' She rummaged in her bag for a Kleenex.

Shephard watched her sympathetically as she blew her nose and fought back the tears. 'You didn't kill him,

Eleanor. You didn't know about Drumanon. None of us knew.'

She wasn't listening. 'So David went up to the showroom in south London and said who he was and the salesman told his boss and . . . and the next day David was dead. And Philip seemed so upset at the funeral,' she wailed. 'What a hypocritical bastard.'

She shook her head. 'Christ, what a mistake, David wanting to be like me. He was *better* at the job than me. He figured something was wrong almost from the start. I didn't. And I've done nothing in this business that David hadn't already started. All I could do was be irritable with him . . . tell him to take his questions to Philip Passmore. Imagine that. It was like telling him to jump into a snake pit.'

Shephard said nothing. He watched her silently, knowing she needed to talk, to get it all out.

'After David died, I took over the audit. Philip was off, supposed to be ill. He was probably gloating over David's death. I marched in and took over. I remember now that neither Philip nor Richard Jamieson were very keen on me taking the audit on.' She laughed again, a painful, croaking sound. 'I assumed they were being chauvinist, that they wanted to protect their precious audit, that it was something they didn't want a female taking over. Christ, how wrong could I be.' She took a long swallow of the whisky and held up the glass. 'Is there any more of this?'

He stood up. 'Sure.' When he returned with her drink he said, 'Look, you'll have to excuse me for a minute, I've got a couple of calls to make. Jamieson may be right; the two guys who attacked you could go after him. If we find him, we may find them. Help yourself to the whisky.' He was gone about ten minutes. When she'd finished her drink she did as he suggested and helped herself to more. He returned and sat down with a look of satisfaction. 'We're watching his yacht and his flat. As soon as he surfaces, we'll take him.'

'I was supposed to go sailing with him this weekend.' Eleanor saw Shephard frown, as if she had said something to wound him. 'Imagine that. Sailing with that bastard.' She screwed up her face. 'Didn't you say you'd been following him?'

'Yes, but only when he was on his boat. He was making regular trips across the Channel. To the French ports. And to Jersey. We thought he was bringing drugs over. But we never saw anything. We searched the yacht a couple of times, when he wasn't around. Nothing. Now we know why.'

'Did he make a trip last weekend?'

Shephard nodded. 'Yeah, to Jersey.'

'With some woman, I suppose.'

'No. His crew was a couple of guys. They were almost certainly taking cash out of the country. We didn't think of that. No one thought to check out what he was *taking off* the boat. Only what he was taking on. Last weekend he offloaded six binbags of rubbish at the yacht marina. Six bags? For three blokes and a day's sailing? We should have sussed it. The bags were collected by a guy we thought was the local refuse collector.'

'Jersey. That's where we were going this weekend.'

'He was using you as a cover.'

'The bastard.'

He looked at her quizzically. 'You know, for someone who doesn't approve of bad language, you use an awful lot of it.'

She felt her face colouring. 'Well, I've got a bloody good reason. Jamieson wasn't taking *me* to Jersey, he was taking sackfuls of cash.'

Shephard nodded seriously. 'I'm afraid that's true. It was dirty money, Eleanor. Drug money. A few days ago the

Hampshire police found the body of a young woman. The Met reckon she was a money courier for one of the London Profits. The word is that a lot of cash has been moved down here ready to be shipped to France. The girl probably brought it down from London.'

Eleanor shuddered. 'These people. They kill each other for no reason.'

'I told you. They're worse than animals.'

She gave him a hard stare. 'I know. I've met a couple.' She frowned. 'And this girl, this courier, would she have given the money to Richard Jamieson?'

'No. She wouldn't have been permitted to meet him. She would have passed it to somebody who'd have given it to Jamieson. In the drugs world, the important people, the people at the top, protect themselves. There's always someone in between. The intermediary would have passed the money to Jamieson who would have smuggled it onto his yacht. That's where we reckon our man, Adams, was thrown overboard. From Jamieson's yacht.'

'Richard told me he hated violence.'

'He wouldn't have done it. It could have been those two that attacked you.'

'Maybe Adams found some money on the yacht. Maybe that's why they killed him.'

'No. Jamieson wouldn't leave the money unattended on the yacht. It would be more than his life was worth. It's difficult to know what Adams *did* see. We know now why he hadn't seen any sign of drugs. So what could he have possibly seen? It must have been something to do with the money laundering.'

Eleanor frowned, recalling the incident when she had bumped into Adams in the empty corridor. It had frightened her at the time. Now it seemed like nothing. 'Maybe he saw something in Dan Lassiter's office the night I ran into him,' she suggested. 'Or in Richard Jamieson's. I checked their offices afterwards and I couldn't see what he might have discovered. When I told Lassiter about it, he said . . .' She stopped. 'Oh my God,' she wailed.

Shephard was startled. 'What?'

'I killed him.' She put her hands up to her face, trying to block out the sudden understanding. 'I killed him.'

'What? What are you talking about?'

'I killed Adams. I killed David and I killed your policeman too.' She was keening, as if she were in deep grief.

'What do you mean, you killed him?'

'I told Dan Lassiter at that dinner party that I'd bumped into a man in the corridor. Adams. They were all there, Jamieson, Passmore. Jesus Christ. I told them and they had him killed. It was my fault. I killed him.'

Suddenly he was across the floor and holding her. His arms around her were strong and comforting. She buried her face in the front of his jacket and, for the third time that day, she wept.

After a while Shephard said, 'Come on, you've had enough. It's been a terrible day. You need to get some sleep.' He led her into the bedroom and brought her case in. 'Try to sleep,' he told her. 'In the morning stay in bed as long as you want. I'll be away early but there'll be a policewoman here.' He turned towards the door.

'No, wait,' she pleaded. 'Where are you going to sleep?'

'The couch in the living room. It's comfortable enough.'

'Couldn't you stay? Here? I mean, with me?'

He stared at her. He looked bewildered.

She knew she must look awful. Her face felt puffy from all the crying and her makeup had long gone. She guessed she looked a complete wreck. It didn't matter. 'Couldn't you stay and hold me? I mean, you're not on duty or anything, are you?'

'No. I'm not on duty,' he said quietly, 'not in my own home.' He was perplexed.

'I don't want sex or anything,' she went on. 'Not right now, not at the moment. Maybe one day. Soon. When I've got over all this. But couldn't you just stay and hold me? I'm frightened. I know I'm pathetic but . . .'

He reached out and touched her cheek. 'It's okay.'

She changed in the bathroom. The mirror confirmed her fears. She looked terrible. Her hands were trembling and she struggled to take her clothes off. She put on an outsize T-shirt and a fresh pair of panties. He was already in bed. Almost as soon as she crept in beside him she began once more to shake violently. He held her tightly. 'It's all right, it's all over now. You're safe.'

His body against hers was solid and strong. He smelled good, a kind of natural, wholesome, male smell. Gradually it began to dawn on her that it *was* all over. That she was safe. Finally, she slept.

She awoke with a start. It was light and Shephard was gone. The digital alarm on the bedside table said seven fifteen. She got up and padded through to the lounge. Shephard was immersed in a conversation on the phone, speaking in a low voice. He was wearing a pair of boxer shorts. Eleanor noticed he had a good body. He saw her and the look on his serious face changed to a smile.

He finished the call and put the phone down. 'I hope I didn't wake you.'

'No.'

'I've called the hospital. Lindsey is out of intensive care. She's off the danger list.'

Some of the weight lifted off her. 'Thank God.'

He went to make coffee whilst she dressed. She showered, brushed her teeth and found the change of clothes she had thrown into her case the night before. It was the outfit she had intended to wear on her sailing trip with Jamieson; a pair of snug-fitting French blue trousers, a Breton top and canvas shoes.

Shephard had dressed and was percolating coffee. The flat was filled with the aroma. She sat at the kitchen table and gratefully took the mug he offered. She refused breakfast but he insisted she have a slice of toast. For all his attentions, Shephard seemed pre-occupied. 'What's wrong?' she asked.

He shot her a surprised glance. She was good at assessing his mood. 'The Hampshire police have found Richard Jamieson. Early this morning. His car had been forced off the road, somewhere in the New Forest.' He paused.

'Well, go on. What is it? Tell me.'

'He'd been stabbed to death.'

She knew she should have felt something. Sorrow, pity, perhaps even elation. She felt nothing. It was frightening . . . frightening to discover that, overnight, her heart had become an iceberg of indifference. 'Oh.'

'It was probably the two that attacked you. Maybe they killed him because they believed he'd changed sides. Because he'd helped you. The question is, did Jamieson call Passmore and Lassiter before he was murdered? Did he warn them about you? Whatever, I'm putting a couple of teams together to go and see them. We'll be bringing them in for questioning. About the money laundering and about the guys who attacked you. I'm on my way to Passmore's place in a few minutes.'

'Let me go with you.' Her voice was urgent, imploring.

'I can't do that,' he smiled, 'it's against regulations.'

'But you're not going to make a drug arrest, are you? I

mean, it's not dangerous.' She was excited. 'You're going to question them about money laundering. If they see me with you, if they know I'm on your side, they may talk. Before a lawyer gets to them.'

He chuckled, captivated by her eagerness. 'You've been watching too many cop shows on television.'

'But I could be useful. Let me come.'

He stared at her. 'All right,' he said finally. 'I guess I can justify it.'

'Great.' She gave him a big grin and he laughed.

He drove the Granada. Though it was barely past eight the sun was already warm in a cloudless sky. The promised glorious weather had arrived.

Passmore lived in a village outside Wimbourne Minster. Eleanor, remembering the way from the couple of times she had been to the house, gave Shephard directions. Somewhere along the route they were joined by a small convoy of cars, a couple of police vehicles and a Carlton with three burly men inside. Eleanor thought it an excessive use of manpower for one arrest.

Passmore's was a large house on the outskirts of the village with a barn off to one side and a paddock at the back where his daughters kept their horses. The cars swept into the drive and the police piled out. 'Stay here,' Shephard ordered.

Uniformed officers were moving around the back of the house as she watched Shephard lead a small posse of detectives and uniformed police to the front door. A woman, Passmore's wife, answered their loud knocking and the men went inside.

Eleanor got out of the car and stood in the sunshine, watching the house. She thought about David; about the day, a beautiful Saturday just like today, she had sailed down the river with him. Now, waiting for Passmore to emerge in defeat she did feel something. An exulting sense of vengeance . . . of wild justice. In the warm sun she shivered with the cold delight of spite.

The front door crashed open and John Shephard burst out of the house, his face paralysed in shock. A bunch of his men surged out behind him. The group walked quickly – half ran – towards the barn. Mrs Passmore stood watching at the doorway her hands up to her grey, ghastly face. Shephard and the others disappeared through the big open doors of the barn.

Something compelled Eleanor to follow. She hurried after them across the broad sunny yard. The contrast inside the gloomy barn half blinded her. Blinking rapidly she noticed the group in a far corner. Slowly, apprehensively, she moved towards them.

John Shephard was crouching over something. The rest of the men were looking on. It appeared, as she got closer, to be some sort of bundle. She joined the group. No one noticed her, their attention exclusively centred upon the thing lying on the floor.

It wasn't a bundle. Close up, she could see it was Philip Passmore. She could tell it was Philip from the clothes and from the shape and size of the body. She ought to have been able to tell who it was from the face which lay with one cheek pressed to the barn floor. But she couldn't. Not from the face.

Most of its forehead was missing.

Chapter Twenty-Six

She stared inanely at the bundle of nothing that had been Philip Passmore.

She had never known Philip mute and unmoving; never seen him when he wasn't talking; when he wasn't standing or sitting or walking about the offices. She wanted him to move. It was an alien state, him lying there, silent and inert, with his cheek pressed into the dirt and straw of the barn floor.

Stupidly, part of her expected him to get up. Even without half his head.

Shephard glanced up from the body and saw her. 'For God's sake, get her out of here,' he ordered. His words broke the spell holding the small knot of policemen. One of the uniformed men took her arm. 'Come on, miss, this is no place for you. You shouldn't be here.' She looked back once. Shephard had gone back to examining the body.

She blinked in the bright daylight outside the barn. The policeman accompanied her into the house; into a large, high-ceilinged, deep-carpeted lounge, strewn with big chintzy sofas. Mrs Passmore was standing by the bay windows, clasping her two daughters. A couple of policewomen were there. Eleanor crossed the room to the forlorn trio. 'I'm sorry,' she said simply.

Clutching the sobbing teenagers, Mrs Passmore nodded an

acknowledgement. Her face was streaked with tears. Eleanor slumped into a chair. A policewoman offered her a cup of tea. Outside, men were coming and going as more official vehicles arrived. It was going to be a long wait.

She wished now she had not been so eager to come with Shephard. All her feelings of vengeance, her desire for wild justice on Passmore, had evaporated the moment she'd seen his pitiable condition. Looking at the body she'd felt almost nothing. It was as if her emotions were anaesthetized.

Later, some people arrived. Eleanor guessed they were relatives. They took the daughters away, leaving Mrs Passmore to stare at events outside the windows. After a while she came over to Eleanor. Her ripe plumpness had crumpled. She was depleted, exhausted by emotion, emptied by tears.

'He was mixed up in something, wasn't he?' She spoke as if to herself. Her once loud voice was hollow. Eleanor held her with a steady look but said nothing.

'I knew it. I suppose I'd known it for years.' She shook her head. 'I never asked. Didn't dare enquire. Whatever it was, it got us all this. Got the girls a good education. I suppose that's all finished now.' Her voice trailed away.

'I knew something was wrong when David Rudge died. Philip was so upset. He was ill. He acted as if it was his fault . . . as if he was responsible. He wasn't the same after that. He seemed . . .' she searched for the word, '. . . scared. Something was frightening him.'

Eleanor stood up. 'What? What frightened him, Mrs Passmore?' she asked quietly.

'It was something to do with you.' The woman looked at Eleanor for the first time. Her puffy eyes were vaguely hostile but she was too washed out for real bitterness. 'Philip was worried about you . . . about something you were doing.

476

He said once that you were much brighter than you'd appeared at your interview. Yesterday he came home in a terrible state. Went straight into the study and made a long phone call. That's what he did before David . . .' Her voice trailed off. 'It was something to do with you. I know it was.'

She glanced out of the window. 'Then the men came. This morning.' Her voice was little more than a hoarse whisper. 'They'd come for him. It was early. We hadn't even had breakfast. Two of them. Horrible men. They dragged him off. Literally. Dragged him away in front of our eyes. The girls were there. Oh God it was awful. Afterwards, I went to see . . . I made the girls stay here and went to the barn. I didn't know what to do. Oh God.' She began to cry.

The door opened and John Shephard walked into the room accompanied by a number of policemen. Among them Eleanor recognized the big figure of Detective Chief Inspector Winchcombe. She moved away as Winchcombe approached Mrs Passmore. He gave Eleanor a non-committal nod.

Shephard motioned her to one side. 'This is a murder investigation now,' he said quietly. 'Winchcombe's in charge. There's nothing left for me or my blokes to do. We're leaving.'

She nodded as she watched Winchcombe sit Mrs Passmore down on one of the chintzy sofas and begin questioning her. She turned to Shephard. 'Do you think the men who killed Philip are the same ones who attacked me?' she asked in a low voice.

'From the descriptions, almost certainly. We've had some help from my contact at the Met. The Scotsman is called Donnie Boyle. The other one is Leon Mouandros. They're minders for one of the big Profits. They protect the money men, mutilate people who don't do as they're told, that kind of thing. They're both killers . . . with the added attraction that Boyle is certified insane. We're pretty sure they're under orders to kill everyone connected with the money laundering.'

She gave him a frightened look. 'Don't worry,' he went on, 'I'll be staying close to you.'

He made a move to leave the room. Eleanor fell into step beside him. 'But who's giving them these orders?'

'The Profit. We reckon he's maybe the one who has the narcotics franchise that runs all the way from here to south London. Our problem is, we're never going to know who he is.'

They reached the front door of the house and Shephard surveyed the busy scene of men and vehicles around the barn. 'This is turning into a bloody full-scale operation. We've got a couple of homicidal maniacs out there, touring the countryside with knives and guns, executing people.'

'Executing?'

'Sure. This was an execution. The organization's classic, time-honoured method of punishment for those who screw up and know too much. Two bullets in the back of the head. No one gets to resign from that business, Eleanor. Not even the accountants.' He gave her a sardonic smile. 'Yours is getting to be a dangerous profession.'

She pouted. 'Only for those mixed up with this kind of thing. With criminals.' They began walking slowly towards the Granada.

'There are lots of them, Eleanor,' Shephard replied. 'Plenty of bent accountants, lawyers and bankers out there to help the bad guys. So long as they're paid enough.'

They reached the car. He turned to her. 'And for every one of them, there are a hundred who have an *idea* that something's going on . . . guess they could be part of a scam . . . suspect they might be helping to launder dirty money. But they're happy not to ask too many questions. So long as the big fees keep rolling in. Plenty of people in the professions turn a blind eye, Eleanor.'

She recalled her feelings about Jamieson and the sailing trip and felt herself colouring. She changed the subject. 'What about Lassiter? Have your men picked him up?'

'No. They radioed in. His wife said he went out early. She's not saying where. Maybe she doesn't know. My blokes are hanging on at the house. He may come back. It's beginning to look like Jamieson didn't get a chance to call him. It's obvious he didn't call Passmore. Maybe Lassiter thinks that the hit on you was successful.' He climbed into the driving seat and she got in beside him. He was staring distantly out of the windscreen.

'What's wrong?'

He didn't look at her. 'There's something about this business that doesn't add up. Jamieson told you that Passmore was the boss, that he was in charge of the money laundering operation. Right?' She nodded. 'Yet Passmore got blown away. Which means he *wasn't* the boss. Someone else is at the top. Maybe Lassiter.'

'What? Are you suggesting that Jamieson was reporting to Passmore who was reporting to Lassiter? That can't be right. It's too convoluted. No one has a structure like that.'

Shephard laughed. 'This isn't a normal business. In the narcotics business everything is done to *hide* the chain of command. Safeguard the people at the top, protect the identity of the Profit.' He started the car.

'What I don't understand is, why do they call whoever's in charge the Prophet?'

He looked at her and laughed. 'No, not prophet. Profit.

It's rhyming slang. Profit and loss. Boss. Gettit?' The car moved off slowly.

'Oh.' Suddenly a picture leapt into her head. Another sunny Saturday morning. With David Rudge. And Dan Lassiter. 'Wait,' she yelled.

He hit the brakes.

'I know where Dan Lassiter may be.'

'What? Where?'

'Wareham. I met him there once. I was with David. Dan said he often went to Wareham *on a Saturday*.'

'*Wareham*? Why the hell should he want to go there?'

'I don't know. But I've suddenly got this feeling. That's where he's gone.'

'You've got a *feeling*?' They sat silently, staring at each other. Then, slowly, Shephard's serious, slightly irritable frown was replaced by a grin. 'What the hell,' he said lightly. 'Why not? What else have I got to do? Only hours of paperwork. Never underestimate instinct, eh?'

He got out of the car. In line behind them were the Carlton with the three big plainclothes policemen and a couple of police cars. Shephard went to the Carlton and spoke briefly to one of the men before indicating to the drivers of the other cars to follow.

He walked back to the Granada. As he opened the door his lightweight cotton jacket flapped open. For a second Eleanor glimpsed something tan and compact strapped beneath his left armpit. A holstered gun.

She gave a start. He climbed into the car. 'Okay?' he smiled at her.

She looked at him, wide-eyed. 'What's that under your jacket?'

He glanced at her sharply. 'I'm sorry. You're not supposed to see that. It's called a Glock.'

'It's a gun.'

'Yes.'

'I didn't know you carried guns.'

'Sometimes we have to.' He turned in his seat and looked at her. 'I'm sorry. Believe me, I don't like it any more than you do.'

It was mid-morning. The sun was bright and the roads were busy. It was a while before Shephard broke the silence. 'I'm beginning to forget what brought me down to this part of the world.'

'Narcotics smuggling?'

He nodded. 'We had solid information that hundreds of kilos of cocaine were being brought in, regularly, somewhere on the coast. Yet, after months down here I'm still no closer to finding where it's coming in. Or who's behind it. Instead, what we've discovered – correction, what *you've* discovered – is one of the biggest money laundering operations ever exposed.'

'Well, at least you've discovered something.'

'Sure. But I'm starting to wonder if the two are connected . . . whether whoever's running the one is running the other. I have to admit it's unusual; the organization rarely runs the two operations together. Usually the people handling the drugs are completely separate from the people handling the money. But I don't think that's how it is here. I think it's possible that the Profit who sent those two guys after you, the one running the franchise from here to London, is the one who manages the money laundering. I think that could be Lassiter. If we nail him it'll be a major coup.'

'So long as you get to him before those two men,' she said darkly. They drove over North Bridge and into Wareham.

Shephard smiled and shook his head. 'He's the Profit.

They won't be after him. They work for him.'

She frowned. If they worked for him, she reflected, then . . .

Shephard interrupted her train of thought. 'If he's in Wareham, where will he be?'

'What?'

'When you saw Lassiter, where was he?'

'At the quay.'

'Right. We won't make it too obvious.' They drove into the car park at St John's Hill. She saw it immediately. 'There's his car,' she cried.

The convoy pulled over. The policemen piled out of the cars and Shephard issued a series of swift instructions. He turned to Eleanor. 'You wait here,' he told her.

'No way. You said you'd stay close to me. You staying close to me means me staying close to you. I'm coming with you.'

A troubled look passed over his face. 'All right, but you must keep well back. I don't think there'll be trouble. People like Lassiter usually come easily, but . . .' His face clouded over. He was tense. Eleanor could sense it.

The uniformed policemen had disappeared down the narrow, cobbled close which led to the far side of the quay. Shephard and the others turned into South Street and towards the river. They moved at a rapid pace and Eleanor had to trot to keep up with them. They turned left into the broad entrance to the quay.

The pub was open and a number of people were sitting drinking at the tables outside. The quay was dotted with parked cars and with tourists enjoying the sunshine and the quayside's quaint, Georgian ambience. Many of them were watching a plump couple in their late fifties unloading wicker backets from a small Lysander moored at the quayside.

Eleanor saw Lassiter almost immediately. He was dressed in a casual shirt and slacks and sitting on a bench at the far side of the quay. He was holding a newspaper, though he seemed more interested in the activities of the couple. 'There he is,' she said excitedly.

'Tell me where,' Shephard ordered calmly, 'but don't point.'

'On the bench.'

Shephard gave a hidden signal to a couple of the men who had entered the quay from the other side.

He turned to Eleanor. His face was determined. 'My blokes and I will make the arrest. We'll take him quietly if we can. You stay here until we've got him secured. Understand?'

'Yes.'

Shephard and his men sauntered slowly across the quay. Eleanor followed for a short distance then stopped. Any closer and Lassiter might see her. She turned to her right, to face the river, keeping a group of tourists between herself and Lassiter. She noticed a kid, a girl, in jeans and a bright yellow T-shirt, peering fearfully over the edge of the quay. Sunshine was glittering on the green water.

From the corner of her eye she saw three men come onto the quay from South Street. One of them, a clean-cut man in his mid-twenties with cropped blond hair, was dressed in the latest casual fashion. Even at that distance Eleanor could see his clothes were expensive. Neither of the men with him were anywhere near as well dressed. In fact the ferret-faced little man with him looked more like a—

Oh dear God. It was *him*.

For a moment her heart stopped.

It was the other man, the big, swarthy one who saw her. He said something to the others who shot a look in her direction. The three of them started rapidly towards her.

Eleanor tried to scream. The muscles in her vocal cords had gone into spasm. All she could produce was a small squeak. They were almost on her. She tried again. This time her larynx didn't let her down. The sound burst out of her. 'John,' she screamed. 'It's them. John.'

Shephard and the men with him spun around, their faces angry and confused. Lassiter looked up from the bench. The little man, Boyle, made a grab for her. She dodged out of his way. Suddenly the other two saw the uniformed policemen on the far side of the quay. They tugged at something inside their jackets. Jesus Christ. Guns.

Someone screamed, then someone else. Boyle grabbed at her again. She dodged him, moving nearer to the edge of the quay. Next time he would have her. Or she'd go into the river.

The well-dressed one yelled, 'Get out of the way.' The weasel-faced Scotsman crabbed swiftly sideways, *away* from her. She didn't understand. She switched her gaze to the man who'd shouted. His arm was raised. In his hand was a gun. Aimed at her. He was less than twelve feet away.

'Oh no,' she wailed.

Crack.

The sharp, solitary sound came from somewhere to her right. The man pointing the gun crashed onto his back as if he had been hit by a train. She glanced in the direction of the noise. John Shephard, crouched and with his arms out-stretched, was holding a gun.

The quayside erupted. Everywhere people were crouching, running, screaming. The swarthy man opened fire on Shephard and the police. He had some kind of small machine gun. The weapon fired three shots at a burst. Mesmerized, Eleanor watched the spent rounds ejecting in a high arc from the gun's breech. She watched too long. Boyle made a rush and grabbed her arm. His grip was like a steel clamp. 'Hud still,' he hissed.

'Donnie, we're in a fucking jam,' the big man, Mouandros, yelled above the noise. He loosed off another burst. His voice was filled with panic. 'We gotta get out.'

The quayside was a maelstrom. A policeman was stretched out on its tarmacadam surface. The others had ducked behind the parked cars. Eleanor noticed Lassiter. He was making a hunched run along the edge of the quay. Towards them.

'The boat,' shouted Boyle. He hustled Eleanor forward. She tried to resist. 'If you dinna move I'll gie ye a kicking,' he snarled. She understood nothing except the last word. She looked at his boots and moved.

Lassiter arrived, white-faced and out of breath. 'What the fuck are you doing?' he screamed at the men. 'You've ruined everything. What are you doing here?'

The men seemed to know him. 'The boat,' repeated Mouandros.

They made a rush for the Lysander moored at the edge. The couple who had been unloading the baskets had taken cover in the little yacht's cockpit, below the stone wall of the quay.

Boyle, holding Eleanor with one hand, pulled a handgun from his belt and pointed it at the couple crouching below. 'Get out of the fucking boat,' he screamed. They scrambled out.

The woman was petrified but the man appeared agitated. Like Lassiter. 'You can't take the boat,' he squawked. 'You don't understand. This is important.' He picked up a wicker basket.

'Get out of the way,' the Scotsman snarled.

'You don't realize—' the man began.

Boyle put his gun to the man's forehead and pulled the trigger.

'Donnie, no,' yelled Mouandros.

The explosion blew part of the man's head away. His body flew backwards over the quayside and splashed into the river. His wife screamed as the basket fell to the quayside and cracked open. What looked like flour spilled out from a black bag inside.

'Christ, Donnie,' Mouandros shouted, 'we need them. We need someone to sail the boat.'

'She'll do.' Boyle shoved the heavy woman off the quayside. She fell awkwardly into the Lysander's cockpit.

'But we don't need this one.' Boyle jabbed the barrel of the gun hard into Eleanor's temple. Eleanor shut her eyes and waited.

'*Nooooo*.' A loud, fearful bellow echoed across the quay. She opened her eyes. John Shephard was coming for her; coming in a low crouching run, his arms outstretched holding the handgun.

'Don't,' she screamed.

Mouandros fired. Shephard, out in the middle of the quayside fifty or sixty feet away, was totally exposed. Something hit him with enormous force. It spun him over onto his back and his gun flew from his hand. Eleanor watched his body twitch. Then he lay still.

'John,' she wailed.

'We need her, Donnie,' Mouandros yelled. 'As a hostage.' He fired another burst at the policemen peering around the parked cars.

Boyle pushed Eleanor off the quayside and she fell into the boat. Dan Lassiter jumped down beside her and grabbed her arm. She didn't care. She slumped onto a cockpit locker with

Lassiter beside her and stared sightlessly over the river.

Boyle leapt into the boat. A few seconds later Mouandros followed. He was clutching a child by the arm. It was the girl in the bright yellow T-shirt. The kid was no more than eleven or twelve, skinny and scared to death. Her eyes were wide in fright and she was shaking as if she had had a seizure. Mouandros pushed her down onto a locker.

'What do we want her for?' snarled Boyle.

'We need another hostage. She's it.'

Boyle glared at the child with murder in his yellow demented eyes.

Mouandros looked around. 'For Christ's sake, get this thing moving.'

A policeman peered cautiously over the side of the quay. Boyle grabbed the quaking girl and put his gun to her head. 'Anybody comes close and I'll blow her brains out,' he shouted. 'Stay away.'

The policeman's head disappeared.

'Start the bloody thing,' Mouandros barked at the woman. She looked at him, dull-eyed and mute. She didn't move.

'I know how,' Eleanor said quietly. She got the outboard started on the third pull.

'You'll need to cast off,' the woman mumbled.

Boyle jumped up onto the side deck and scrambled his way forward. He pulled the bayonet from his left sleeve and sliced through the bow line. Coming back he did the same to the stern line. He jumped back into the crowded cockpit. 'No problem.' He grinned.

Eleanor gave him a stony look. 'It will be if we have to tie up to anything else,' she said flatly.

The grin left his face. 'You're a mouthy bitch,' he hissed. 'When the time comes I'm gonna enjoy killing you.'

She stared at him and felt nothing. She didn't care any

487

more. All she could think of was John Shephard, fallen and motionless on Wareham quay.

'Where we gonna go, Leon?' Boyle's voice was anxious.

'To the harbour. At Poole. Take us there,' Mouandros ordered Eleanor.

'We'll have to turn it round in the river,' Eleanor said.

'Do it. Just bloody do it.'

The middle-aged woman had come out of her daze. She moved to the stern and took over the tiller. Expertly she manoeuvred the small yacht away from the quayside, turning the bow downstream. From the middle of the river they could see the quay. More uniformed police had arrived and the crowds were being hurried away.

Eleanor stood up, trying to glimpse Shephard's body. Boyle pushed her back. 'Sit down, bitch.'

She clattered down next to Lassiter slumped lifelessly on the locker. Perspiration sheened his face. For a man accustomed to command, he had lost any vestige of authority. Without a suit, a big desk, and the power of the company behind him, he seemed piteously ordinary.

'This is your fault,' she spat at him. 'All of it. This kid's terrified out of her wits. That woman's husband has been shot in front of her eyes. You're as guilty as these two.'

He looked at her as if she were talking a foreign language. 'The old guy was bringing the coke in,' he mumbled. 'I don't know why they shot him. They weren't supposed to. None of this was supposed to happen. It's nothing to do with me. I look after moving the money. That's all I do.'

'So what were you doing on the quay?'

'I'm supposed to come to Wareham whenever there's a shipment. To watch her,' he nodded at the woman on the tiller, 'and her husband unload it. Make sure there are no hitches. I don't know what these two maniacs are doing here.

They were meant to be going after . . .' He glanced at her guiltily and looked away.

The chugging outboard had propelled them beyond Wareham and into the open countryside. Eleanor remembered the route from the time she had sailed down the Frome with David. The river was busy. Many of the boats moored at its banks had people aboard and all types of craft were cruising upriver towards Wareham. Eleanor noticed that no boats were following them down. She guessed the police would be getting other craft off the river.

'Can't this bloody thing go any faster?' Mouandros snarled at the woman on the tiller.

'Four knots is as fast as it will go,' she mumbled.

'Jesus,' Boyle wailed, 'how are we going to get away doing four knots? I could walk faster. The polis will be waiting for us, Leon.'

'I know. I know. You don't have to tell me, for Christ's sake.'

Eleanor watched the two men from her seat on the locker. Panic was setting in, like gangrene. She gazed across the flat river meadows. In the distance, a police Range Rover was tracking them. Boyle caught her eye and followed her gaze. 'Stay away, you bastards,' he yelled. 'Stay away.' They were too distant to hear him.

Eleanor moved across the cockpit, away from Lassiter, and sat next to the shivering girl. She put her arms around her thin body. 'What's your name?' she asked.

'Carol,' the kid whispered.

'It's all right, Carol. It's going to be fine. Don't worry. The police are over there. We'll be okay soon.'

The woman holding the tiller heard her. 'It's not going to be fine,' she whined. 'They'll kill us. All of us.'

Eleanor turned and glared at her. 'Shut up, for God's

sake. Can't you see she's frightened enough already. She's only a child.'

'Being a kid won't save her. They're murderers. They killed my husband.'

'You should never have had anything to do with them,' Eleanor whispered viciously. 'You must have known what you were getting into. The kind of people you were working for.'

Tears were streaming down the woman's face. 'But we didn't know this could happen. All we had to do was pick up the stuff. It was regular work . . . good money. I didn't know that there were people like them in the business.'

Eleanor recalled the time in her flat when John Shephard had told her what kind of people inhabited the world of narcotics. She hadn't believed it either.

The outboard motor coughed, spluttered, cleared itself, then coughed again. 'What the hell's wrong with it?' Mouandros yelped.

The woman at the tiller stared at him. 'Weeds,' she muttered.

'What?'

'Weeds from the river are choking up the water inlet,' Eleanor told him quietly.

'Shit. What are we supposed to do about it?'

'Lean over the stern and unclog it.'

The engine stuttered loudly once more then cut out completely. For a moment there was silence.

Eleanor, holding Carol's thin shivering body, stared at the sunlight dappling the water. She listened to the lapping of the river and the sounds of the birds. The momentary feeling of peace and serenity was bizarre.

Across the fields, on the other side of the river, two more police Range Rovers had appeared.

'For Christ's sake, get out of the bloody way.' Boyle clasped the woman at the tiller and pulled her viciously to one side. He grabbed Lassiter. 'You do it. Clear the bleeding weeds out.'

Lassiter protested. 'What the hell. I don't know what to do.'

Boyle's boot cracked into Lassiter's shin. Lassiter screamed and fell back heavily onto a locker, rocking the small vessel. He clutched his injured leg and screamed louder. Blood trickled down onto his canvas shoe. 'Do it,' Boyle hissed, 'or I'll kick ye again.' He shoved the sobbing, hobbling Lassiter to the stern.

Lassiter leaned over the transom, his arms deep in the water, his ample rump high in the air, and began to pull the clogging weeds away from the inlet. Boyle turned from him and with Mouandros watched the police vehicles sitting on the skyline beyond the river banks.

The Lysander had lost leeway and was bobbing around in the water. Eleanor noticed that for the past few minutes no other craft had met them coming the other way. The police had cleared the river. They were out there on their own.

Lassiter leaned further into the water, his backside rising higher into the air. He was badly balanced. Eleanor, clasping Carol and sitting on a locker close to him, watched. How easy it would be, she thought. She edged along the seat, closer towards the stern.

Whooooosh . . . thaaacker, thaaacker, thaacker . . .

The helicopter came in low from downstream, churning the waters and rocking the small Lysander. Startled, everyone except Lassiter looked up. Boyle and Mouandros struggled to keep their feet.

Now.

Eleanor shot out her leg and crashed her foot into Lassiter's backside. He plunged over the stern and hit the water with a loud splash.

Boyle spun around. 'You bitch.' His hand went to his left sleeve and the sunlight glinted on the bayonet. Carol screeched.

'Donnie, leave it,' Mouandros shouted. 'Those bastards are watching us with binoculars. We need her. In one piece.'

Lassiter had surfaced. He was splashing around a few yards from the stern of the stationary boat. 'Help me,' he gasped. 'Help me get back.'

Boyle moved to the Lysander's stern and stared at Lassiter flapping around like a seal a few feet from the boat.

'Okay, so we need her,' he repeated as he sheathed the bayonet, 'but we don't need him.' He pulled the handgun from the belt of his trousers, and fired five rounds into Lassiter's body. The gun clicked empty.

Lassiter screamed once and went under. The water around him turned dark. The woman close to the stern scarcely seemed to notice. Carol whimpered as Eleanor wrapped her arms tightly around her and pressed her head into her breasts.

Boyle put the gun back in his waistband and stepped past Eleanor. He looked down at her. 'You're next.' He grinned. The scars down his cheeks were red and livid. She noticed his rotting teeth.

Mouandros grabbed her, hauling her up and away from Carol. 'Get that bloody motor started,' he ordered. 'If it don't start, you'll go over the side and get the same.'

It took five pulls on the lanyard to get it going.

Eleanor stayed at the tiller, keeping the boat in the middle of the river and watching out for clumps of floating weed. She glanced back once at the spot where Lassiter had gone down. There was no sign of him. She looked away. Boyle had killed him without compunction. She guessed that's what he and Mouandros had always intended . . . why they had been on Wareham quay.

Whatever else he'd been, Lassiter was not the Profit. Eleanor had never thought that he was.

The helicopter flew over twice more, low enough for them to see the pilot's face peering down. Gradually the river was beginning to broaden. They were the only craft on it.

Carol was crying, her little body racked by uncontrollable sobs.

'Can't you shut her up?' Mouandros demanded.

'She's frightened, for God's sake,' Eleanor said. 'What do you expect?' She did her best to comfort the child with her free arm. 'We're going to be okay, Carol,' she whispered. 'We'll be safe soon.'

They passed Swineham Point and chugged slowly out into Wareham Channel. Ahead, opening up to view, were the broad waters of the harbour.

'What will happen to us?' the child wailed quietly. 'I'm scared of the water. I can't swim. Supposing they throw us into the sea?'

'They won't,' Eleanor whispered. 'But I'll get something.'

She motioned to the woman to take over the tiller. 'Where do you keep the life-jackets?' she asked.

The woman nodded her head at the cabin. Eleanor moved forward to the companionway leading down to the small saloon.

'Where the hell do you think you're going?' asked Mouandros.

'The child's crying because she's frightened. She can't swim. I'm getting her a life-jacket.'

Eleanor climbed down the few steps into the saloon and

opened a locker. Inside were a number of bright orange life-vests. She pulled out two and reached for the third. Her hand touched something. It was round and solid. She edged her fingers along its surface. It was some sort of tube. She lifted a life-jacket to take a look. It was a signal flare. The kind David had shown her.

She thought quickly. If the men abandoned them in the small Lysander . . . if they were thrown overboard . . . the flare could save their lives.

Straightening up, she struggled into a life-vest. Afterwards she picked up two other vests and, holding them close to her body, slipped the rocket flare out of the locker and underneath her vest.

She climbed the companionway and emerged into the cockpit. Boyle and Mouandros scarcely gave her a look. She edged past them and gave the woman a vest before helping Carol on with hers. It was difficult, holding the heavy rocket flare beneath her vest.

They had been on the river more than an hour and had reached the mouth of Wareham Channel. On their port bow, about a mile away, were two vessels bobbing at anchor a few hundred yards in front of the ferry terminal.

Eleanor didn't need her spectacles to see the words 'Harbour Master' painted in large letters on their sides, nor the blue uniforms of the police on their decks. Slowly the two vessels began making for them. 'Steer away from them,' ordered Mouandros. The woman put the tiller over and the bow eased to starboard.

They chugged out into the harbour. Eleanor noticed that almost nothing was moving. Not even the sailboarders at Sandbanks. The Harbour Commission had shut the place down. Even the weekend sailors had stopped what they were doing. Everybody was waiting for them. It was as if the vast harbour was holding its breath.

The harbour master's vessels drew closer until they were within loud-hailer distance. The voice across the water was clear and distinct. Eleanor recognized the tones of Detective Chief Inspector Winchcombe. 'You in the boat. Give yourselves up. You haven't a chance. There's nowhere to go. Do not harm your hostages.'

Mouandros raised the Uzi and fired a burst at the distant vessel. 'So long as I got this, the bastards will stay away,' he snarled. Despite the defiance, Eleanor noticed his tone was hollow.

'Yeah, but what the hell are we going to do?' Boyle whined. 'Where are we going to go?'

'Jamieson had a yacht moored here,' Mouandros said. 'We'll take it. Sail it out to sea somewhere.'

'Who's going to sail it?'

'How do I know? You got any better bloody suggestions?'

Eleanor watched them from her seat. They were losing control, turning on each other. Which made them even more dangerous. Mouandros looked at her. 'Which is Jamieson's boat?'

Eleanor pointed it out. It was at the end of a line of yachts moored to buoys about half a mile from the shore. The woman steered towards it. The rolling waters in the middle of the harbour were making Carol more jittery by the minute. Eleanor, protecting the rocket flare, held her as closely as she could.

The harbour master's vessel stayed about two hundred yards distant across the water. Winchcombe's voice came to them over the loud hailer. 'You in the boat. We have armed policemen aboard. And on shore. They are covering you. You must give yourselves up with the hostages unharmed.'

Boyle and Mouandros glanced at each other. Mouandros

shook his head. 'They won't try a shot from the boats,' he said, 'they're unstable. They might miss and hit one of them.' He jerked his head at Eleanor and the others. 'Shore's too far unless they've got a real expert. It's almost out of range.'

Boyle was reloading his handgun. 'Well, she's not out of range,' he spat. He grabbed Eleanor by the arm, yanked her to her feet and standing close to her, pressed the muzzle of the gun against her temple. Even in the middle of the harbour she could smell the rank odour of his body. She wondered if he could smell her fear.

She wasn't sure how long she stood in the bobbing boat with the gun against her head before Boyle threw her back onto her seat. 'I guess they got the message,' he sneered.

They came astern of Jamieson's yacht. The woman at the tiller cut the engine. Carol was crying loudly. She seemed even more frightened of the sea than of Boyle and Mouandros. The mooring ropes that Boyle had cut were too short to secure the Lysander to the yacht.

'You'll have to hold on while we get aboard,' Eleanor told Boyle.

He gave her an evil look. His voice was filled with hate. 'If ye dinna stop that kid crying, I'll stop her.'

Eleanor helped the wailing, reluctant child climb the short transom ladder leading to the stern deck. Carol's struggling and the rocking of the vessels made it difficult. Pressing one arm close to her body to hold the parachute flare under her life-vest, she helped Carol with the other. She slipped and almost fell back into the Lysander.

'What the hell's the matter with you?' snapped Boyle.

Carol's cries grew louder as they crossed the yacht's afterdeck and dropped into its spacious cockpit. Even so, Eleanor let her go.

She turned her back, slipped the parachute tube from beneath her vest and pulled off the caps at both ends. The trigger sprung free. She took a deep breath and pulled out the safety pin before slipping the tube back under her vest.

Clasping Carol she pulled her gingerly to her body as she remembered David's warning.

Christ, it was dangerous. If she slipped, even if she merely knocked against something, the flare would go off – straight into her face. She tried not to think about it.

The portly woman came stumbling across the afterdeck, followed immediately by Boyle and Mouandros. They looked around.

'How the hell do we get this bloody thing started?' Mouandros snarled.

'Eleanor shrugged. 'I've no idea. You'll have to get into the cabin.'

The doors to the companionway were locked. Boyle kicked at them viciously with the heel of his boot.

'We'll break them open,' said Mouandros.

'But if we can't start the thing, how the hell are we gonna sail out of here?' Boyle yelped.

Carol began screaming.

'What the hell's wrong with her?' Mouandros was forced to shout above the noise.

'She's terrified of the water,' Eleanor pulled the child closer to her.

'Shut her up. Shut her up, or by Christ I'll shut her up.' Boyle was yelling. Eleanor stared into his frenzied, yellow-flecked eyes. He was over the edge.

Carol's hysterical screams echoed across the harbour.

'Jesus, shut her up. Shut her up,' bellowed Boyle.

Eleanor tried placating her but the screams grew shriller. From across the water came the sound of Winchcombe on the loud hailer. None of them could hear him above the sound of the screams.

'I'll shut her up,' Boyle yelled crazily. 'I'll shut her *and* keep those bastards away.' He grabbed at the screaming child, yanking her away from Eleanor who felt the parachute flare slipping from beneath her life-jacket. She clutched at herself and saved the flare – but lost the child.

Boyle dragged Carol up onto the afterdeck and threw her across it. The child's body crashed against the guardrail. Boyle ripped the bayonet from his sleeve. 'I'll stick her. That'll shut her up,' he screamed.

'Donnie no,' Mouandros bellowed from the cockpit. 'Don't kill her.'

Carol, with her hands up to her face, was screaming incessantly. Boyle, the bayonet close to his body, moved across the deck towards her.

Eleanor pulled the parachute flare from beneath her life-jacket. 'Get away from her, you bastard,' she yelled.

Boyle stopped halfway across the desk and turned to look down at her. 'You're next, bitch,' he screeched. He saw the tube pointing at him. 'What the fuck is that?'

Eleanor crashed the trigger with the heel of her hand.

Whoooosh. The rocket erupted from the tube. It hit Boyle somewhere in the chest. The impact threw him backwards as far as the stern rail. He looked down. The rocket had partially penetrated his body. It was sticking out from his chest. He screamed. It was then the phosphorous flare exploded.

Whooooof.

Boyle's face and upper body were suddenly consumed in a sheet of white fire. Carol stopped screaming and like everyone else stared aghast at the hideous, flickering sight of Boyle's face melting in white, phosphorus fire. From somewhere beneath the crackling sound of burning came a long, hideous scream. For a moment longer Boyle's body remained upright, flaring like an enormous roman candle. Then it tipped backwards and from beneath the stern came a splash and a dying hiss.

There was a moment of hushed silence in the yacht's cockpit. Then Mouandros came to life. 'You bitch, you bitch,' he yelled. He jabbed the barrel of the Uzi into Eleanor's body.

Eleanor looked down, scarcely feeling the cruel press of the metal below her heart. There was no escape now. This was finally it. It didn't really seem to matter. She was too tired to care.

Mouandros' head exploded in a blast of blood and bone.

The force of the Remington Magnum bullet sent the big man's body crashing out of the cockpit and over the coaming, as the crack of a high-powered rifle echoed across the harbour.

For a moment Eleanor choked at the sight of blood pumping across the balsawood decking, before she scrambled up onto the afterdeck and grabbed Carol. She pulled the silent, stunned child's body into her own and turned her head away.

On the harbour master's vessels and on the quayside, sergeants from the special operations unit were screaming at their men, demanding to know who had fired without permission.

No one owned up.

James Hagerty began quickly but carefully dismantling the L96A1 sniper rifle and scope and placing the parts in his golf bag. It had been a good shot. As a hunter he appreciated the difficulties of a clean head shot at over eight hundred yards. Still, Philip Passmore's office had afforded him the best possible vantage point from which to fire.

From the moment the Lysander had turned down river he had calculated that Boyle and Mouandros would come to the harbour and that they would head for Jamieson's yacht. He had needed to move fast, though it had been easy enough to drive to his apartment in Westcliffe, pick up the rifle and return to the office. The slow speed of the Lysander had been on his side.

He had followed the débâcle on the quayside from his windowseat in the pub, the place from which he always watched a shipment coming in. He had watched the shootings and hostage-taking and had known it to mean the end of everything; the end of the business he had managed for more than fifteen years.

He had met the men from Miami in the late seventies. They had told him that he was exactly the kind of guy they were looking for: a sharp businessman with no criminal record; the right man to begin organizing their franchise business in Britain and to set up their money laundering operation. It had been simple enough to set the wheels in motion; to arrange the death of his partner, Edwin Clark, and recruit Philip Passmore.

Passmore had found Drumanon, and Lassiter had come across from Canada to take it over. Passmore had set up the scheme with Campanalla. Passmore had been his protection, his cut-out. No one, not even Lassiter, had known that he was the man behind Passmore, the man behind everything . . . the one pulling the strings.

But Passmore had been weak. Hagerty had always known that and, like any good businessman with key personnel, had made allowances for it. He hadn't needed Passmore to be tough, it wasn't a necessary qualification for his job, unlike K and those like him whose job had been to set up the Profits in

their franchise areas. But he hadn't realized how weak Passmore was until David Rudge's death. Passmore had been ill, had almost started falling to pieces . . . had allowed the woman to get into the Drumanon audit. That had been a mistake.

Still, he thought as he finished packing away the rifle, Lambert had done some of his work for him. She'd killed the Scotsman. After that he'd had to choose. Kill Mouandros or the woman? He'd chosen Mouandros. Mouandros could identify him as the Profit. All the woman could do was guess.

She may have guessed already, he thought. She was smart. He'd always known she was bright, guessed it from the start.

Passmore hadn't seen it and had persuaded him that Lambert would be the perfect cover for the practice, that she could handle the legitimate business. He knew now he should have said no, that they should never have recruited her. *That* had been the mistake.

Afterwards, well, he should have insisted that Passmore keep her away from Drumanon. Or had her killed.

But it was too late for self-recrimination. He was a pragmatist, a businessman, a sportsman. He'd always known it might end like this. He had made plans.

He glanced out of the window and stared grimly at the harbour. The men in Miami never forgave failure. When they heard what had happened they would put a price on his life. A contract. They would never stop wanting him dead. For the rest of his days there would be somebody looking to kill him. The hunter was about to become the hunted. It would be a new experience.

Hagerty shouldered the golf bag and walked rapidly down the stairs. He locked the office door behind him, placed the golf bag in his Range Rover and drove away.

One of the harbour master's vessels came alongside the

yacht and a couple of men leapt down onto its deck. Clutching Carol, Eleanor watched in a stupefied daze as they made the two vessels fast. Now that it was all over she felt herself once more beginning to shake. She glanced at the other vessel and narrowed her eyes. Standing at the bow was a familiar figure. It had an arm in a sling, but there was no mistaking that funny, serious, worried face. John Shephard.

Suddenly she was surrounded by men wrapping her in blankets. Someone gently prised open her grip on Carol and helped her up a ladder onto the harbour master's vessel. Shephard was waiting for her. She threw her arms around him and he winced. He held her close with his good arm.

'I thought you were dead,' she said.

He smiled his quiet, serious smile. 'A bullet nicked my shoulder but I cracked my head going over.'

'Bloody hell.' She glared at him. 'I've been sick to my stomach believing you were dead and all you've got is a scratch and few bloody bruises.'

'I see your language hasn't improved,' he said.

She smiled faintly. To have allowed herself to laugh might have set off the hysteria bubbling below the surface. 'I was hoping that I might stop swearing when I came here,' she said.

'I'd hoped I might stop shooting people,' he replied sombrely.

She glanced at his troubled face. 'I'm glad you did, all the same,' she said softly. She was silent for a moment. 'The man on the quay. Is he dead?'

He didn't look at her. 'Yes.'

'I don't know what to say,' she said. 'I'm sorry you had to do it, but I'm not sorry it was done.'

He gazed at her for a moment. 'You're right,' he said finally, 'it had to be done.'

She turned and stared out over the ship's rail at the harbour. The place was coming to life. A few small, white-sailed yachts were catching the breeze and scudding across the water. In the distance, a blue-hulled Nauticat 521 was making for the harbour entrance at Southhaven Point. She took a long, deep breath and tossed her head, encouraging the breeze to tug at her hair.

'I came here to enjoy all this,' she said quietly. 'To find some peace and sanity. To get away from what I thought was the nightmare of my life in London.' She resisted the urge to let out a cynical laugh. She couldn't trust herself to laugh.

'So what will you do now?' he asked.

'I don't know. I have the feeling I'm out of a job. I'm pretty sure that Hagerty Clark has had it.' She shrugged. 'Start again, I guess.'

'Where?'

'Somewhere a long way away. I can't stay here. Not now. I guess it was a mistake to come. Perhaps this is what I get for running away.'

'I don't know.' His voice was soft as he watched the breeze gently tossing her hair. 'Maybe some good will come out of it, Eleanor.'

She turned and gazed into his deep, serious eyes. After a moment, she said softly, 'Yeah, maybe.'

She turned back and for the rest of the trip watched the sunlight shimmering on the surface of the dancing green water.

A selection of bestsellers from Headline

HARD EVIDENCE	John T Lescroart	£5.99	☐
TWICE BURNED	Kit Craig	£5.99	☐
CAULDRON	Larry Bond	£5.99	☐
BLACK WOLF	Philip Caveney	£5.99	☐
ILL WIND	Gary Gottesfeld	£5.99	☐
THE BOMB SHIP	Peter Tonkin	£5.99	☐
SKINNER'S RULES	Quintin Jardine	£4.99	☐
COLD CALL	Dianne Pugh	£4.99	☐
TELL ME NO SECRETS	Joy Fielding	£4.99	☐
GRIEVOUS SIN	Faye Kellerman	£4.99	☐
TORSO	John Peyton Cooke	£4.99	☐
THE WINTER OF THE WOLF	R A MacAvoy	£4.50	☐

All Headline books are available at your local bookshop or newsagent, or can be ordered direct from the publisher. Just tick the titles you want and fill in the form below. Prices and availability subject to change without notice.

Headline Book Publishing, Cash Sales Department, Bookpoint, 39 Milton Park, Abingdon, OXON, OX14 4TD, UK. If you have a credit card you may order by telephone – 01235 400400.

Please enclose a cheque or postal order made payable to Bookpoint Ltd to the value of the cover price and allow the following for postage and packing:

UK & BFPO: £1.00 for the first book, 50p for the second book and 30p for each additional book ordered up to a maximum charge of £3.00.
OVERSEAS & EIRE: £2.00 for the first book, £1.00 for the second book and 50p for each additional book.

Name ....

Address ....

....

....

If you would prefer to pay by credit card, please complete:
Please debit my Visa/Access/Diner's Card/American Express (delete as applicable) card no:

Signature .... Expiry Date..............